THIS CRIMSON DEBT

COMMUNITY OF BLOOD, BOOK ONE

ROSE SINISTER

Iron and Salt Press

IRON AND SALT PRESS, LLC

In memory of

Victoria, and Daniel, and Anne

You made me, you shaped me,
you gave me the world.
Then each of you passed too soon.
I wish I could show you this book.
Our problem is, we think we have time.

Chapter One

Last Rites

They call the week between Christmas and New Year's Eve the "Dead Week," when existence is confusion, no one knows what day it is, and obituaries spike. I don't think anyone makes it out entirely unscathed. We all enter the New Year a little worse for wear, buffeted by chaos and disoriented under the weight and expectations of the looming unknown.

My first Christmas all on my own had been rough, but I'd survived, and I tried to tell myself the New Year would to be better. And next year...next year I might even put up lights, and a tree. But there hadn't seemed to be a point to either, this year. My sole concession to the holidays had been an overpriced fir-scented candle I'd bought on a last minute whim, but the familiar scent was hardly the comfort I'd hoped it would be. The three tiny flames sputtering in a pool of molten evergreen wax seemed sympathetic to my plight. I was struggling to burn brightly, myself.

As I curled up by the radiator on December 30th, some combination of experience and precognition kept my attention neatly divided between the mindless TV chatter and my iPhone, and when the desperate text messages started buzzing, I think I was relieved for the interruption from my own thoughts. I didn't even have to look at the screen to know what I'd be doing for the rest of the night.

Becca's flight had been delayed three times due to nasty weather across the Rockies, and even though the Blue Line ran 24/7, she had three suitcases with her (she pleaded, by way of explanation), and she'd have to lug it all six blocks from the closest stop to her apartment, all alone in the ice and snow after midnight, if she couldn't get a ride.

Cabs exist, I wanted to tell her, as I extinguished the candle and locked up my apartment, but I could never refuse Becca Moreno when she said she needed me, and that was the simple truth of it. Honestly, driving forty minutes from my place in the suburbs to pick her up from O'Hare and deposit her home safe in the Loop was among the least arduous rescue missions I'd performed on her behalf over the years. I only shivered a little bit in the frigid interior of my car as I chose an appropriate playlist on my iPhone and waited for the windows to defrost, before heading off into the late December night toward the airport, and the return of my favorite prodigal chaos monster.

Three suitcases, I marveled. *And probably not a single folded item of clothing in any of them.*

I pulled up to the passenger pickup curb just as Becca struggled out of baggage claim with all three aforementioned pieces of luggage in tow, my timing impeccable as always. The smallest suitcase was unfamiliar to me, shiny and new and still sporting a price tag, so I assumed she'd had to buy yet another roller bag to haul away all the Christmas presents her family had showered her with, and that was a good sign for me, fingers crossed. Becca's grandmother had exquisite taste in expensive cashmere sweaters and imported Italian leather goods that Becca would never wear...but I did. We once estimated some 30% of my winter wardrobe over the years had come from Becca's unworn castoffs.

"Is that a Stanford hoodie?" I asked, squinting my eyes at the suspicious cardinal red shade of the sweatshirt Becca sported as she climbed into the passenger seat.

Her sheepish expression betrayed her. "One of Nonna's sorority sisters insisted I take it. Said that it might help open doors for me when it came to finding a job or a husband."

I rolled my eyes so far into the back of my head I thought my optic nerve might snap. "Becca, we went to Loyola. It's a perfectly good school."

"Yeah, but you should feel how warm this thing is..." her voice trailed off as she flipped the hem inside out to show off the plush material. It definitely looked luxurious, in that very Californian "oh, this old thing?" kind of way.

"How was your flight?"

"Rough? There was a lot of turbulence coming over the mountains, and Nonno could only get me on standby for business class on the return flight, so, of course, all the seats were full, because of the holidays."

"Oh, poor you, flying economy."

"Yeah, well, I'm sure he'll make a furious call to AmEx about it in the morning."

"I pity whoever has to take his call."

"Me, too."

We both laughed. I'd only met Becca's family once, on a spring break trip to her grandparent's winery our senior year at university. Her grandfather had been rude to me the entire time. Months later, Becca confessed that he thought we were dating. I'd thought Californians were supposed to be progressive and all, but Becca laughed and said I didn't know shit about California conservatives.

Becca filled me in on her recent adventures while I drove, and I tried not to indulge the pang of envy that threatened to obscure my ability to be happy for my friend. A week spent in Napa wine country and San Francisco during the Christmas holidays seemed absolutely magical, but Becca made evenings at the San Francisco Opera Association, and multi-course meals at Michelin-starred restaurants, sound bland and unfulfilling.

"I swear, if Dad and Parker tried to introduce me to one more insufferable, Tesla-driving, Bay Area finance bro, I was going to murder both of them in their sleep with an empty magnum bottle. Nonna acted like it was the scandal of the century that I'm almost twenty-five and still unmarried. I wonder if she even knows what century it is." Becca scoffed, picking up my iPhone and taking over the playlist like she always did. Her taste in music was usually better than mine anyway, so I let her. "What did you do for Christmas?"

I hesitated. "Well...I went to midnight mass on Christmas Eve at St. John Cantius over in River West. I've wanted to do that for a long time, so that was nice..." I was supposed to go with my coworker Ruby and her family, but they'd cancelled at the last minute, and...that was fine. Really.

"Thought you would have driven to Toledo like you normally do."

"It's fine."

"Your dad still dating the accountant?"

"I don't want to talk about my dad and his latest fuckbuddy, okay?"

"Harsh. She could be nice?"

"I don't want to know." It still felt like only yesterday since Mom died, and all of my dad's girlfriends were a betrayal of her memory. Thinking about it made me grumpier than I wanted to be.

I'd *been* grumpier than I wanted to be, in recent weeks. I'm not entirely sure why—maybe it was the realization that the last vestiges of my childhood were finally gone. I'd graduated college and spent an obligatory year in a shitty apartment in a trendy neighborhood with the best (if messiest) roommate in the world. Now we'd gone our separate ways, me out in the suburbs in my spacious but bland one-bedroom and Becca in her tiny upscale studio. I had a grown-up job, a 401(k), and a health insurance plan. Thoroughly adult. As grown-up as could be. I'd even floundered through my first real big girl breakup, and I was getting on fine without Dylan, honestly.

So what was stopping Dad from thinking that he'd earned a brief respite from his parenting duties for once, and taking a damn vacation? It wasn't like he hadn't earned one. Realistically, I knew he was still relatively young, and I'm not saying that I wouldn't have wanted to take a vacation somewhere sunny and warm for Christmas, if I'd gotten the opportunity. If anyone had invited me. But no one seemed to want me these days, and that...that was fine.

I didn't realize how maudlin my thoughts had turned until Becca playfully poked my upper arm at a red light.

"Cheese fries?" That was Becca's solution for most matters of emotional distress, and I had to agree with her instincts.

I insisted on dropping Becca off with her luggage in front of her apartment building before we wandered off in pursuit of cheesy comfort, however. Becca could get too easily distracted. It was my job, as her sensible best friend, to keep her on track. The doorman stepped up to help Becca corral her luggage, and I promised to drive round the block until she got her stuff upstairs—I'd have offered to help, but her luxury building didn't have ample guest parking, and street parking in downtown Chicago was a nightmare at any time or day.

Still, it was nice to take in the holiday lights from the cozy heated interior of my car, and instead of circling the block per my original plan, I drove across the Chicago River and back, a small smile of satisfaction creeping across my face in spite of my mood. The moon overhead was golden and nearing full, partially obscured by thin high clouds that teased snow. *That would be a lovely way to start the new year.* I tried to focus on the positive.

Leafless trees and evergreens lining the downtown streets were festooned with endless strands of twinkling lights, and I reflected that, while California at Christmastime did seem magical, Chicago had its own holiday magic, too. And I loved downtown, with its historic skyscrapers full of Art Deco details, the clattering L overhead, and the illuminated marquees of theaters and department stores, with the zeal of a thoroughly converted transplant. Moving to the big city for college was a dream come true, and staying afterward, finding work that paid my bills and kept a roof over my head, that was living the dream.

Even if I was forced by necessity to live the dream out in the suburbs, for now. Not all of us had millionaire grandparents willing to foot the bill for our high-end studio apartments. Once again, I tried to curb my envy, a pang of deeply instilled Catholic educational guilt reminding me that envy was one of the seven deadly sins...*blah blah blah*.

Maybe resentment and envy were becoming more of a problem than I'd realized. I knew that meant I should probably make time for confession, but...I didn't want to. Not yet. I was clinging to my melancholy like something necessary, like water, like air. I knew, theoretically, that these feelings plaguing my life were nothing more than the result of my own dissatisfaction, my own personal winter of discontent...but the knowledge didn't fix anything. It itched, somewhere just out of reach for my mind to scratch.

I wasn't jealous of my friend, exactly. But I did often wish that I had the same ease and opportunities in life as she did.

Becca was waiting for me on the sidewalk by the time I got back to her building, not quite shivering yet, but she scurried into the car with an inelegant scramble that reminded me of a raccoon diving for cover. She'd swapped out her Stanford hoodie for a long black velvet and brocade winter coat with a superfluous number of buckles across the front, and a black faux fur hat that made her look like the gothic heroine of a tragic Russian novel, but she needed to take the coat to a tailor to have the sleeves altered to fit her—they covered her hands almost to her fingertips, and I knew Becca well enough to know that she wouldn't roll up the sleeves and risk distorting the trim and velvet at the cuffs.

"Windy Grill?" I suggested, already plotting course for a favorite twenty-four-hour diner where we'd sopped up many a hangover, but Becca wanted to try a different late-night establishment that I had never been to, over by Millennium Park.

"You're not going to try to stick a dildo on The Bean again, are you?" I'd thought I was going to have to bail Becca out of jail over that stunt last summer. She'd said it was part of a political protest, but I never understood exactly what she was protesting.

"No! I wasn't even thinking about that! I just wanted to see if *he* was going to be out."

"He?"

She flashed a devilish grin, but refused to say another word until we were seated inside the dim interior of a place that looked far too fancy for cheese fries. I wasn't typically a fan of any place lit up with so many Edison bulbs. That usually meant "out of Grace's price range," but Becca promised to foot the bill and reimburse me for gas money.

"Spill," I demanded the moment we were seated.

Becca held up a finger to shush me as she scanned the room. I couldn't tell whether or not she was disappointed by the absence of her mystery man among the other patrons, but once she was certain he wasn't there, she leaned forward, excitement flushing her cheeks, and whispered, "He's an enigma."

"Who?"

"Picture it: He's tall and lean and, like, chiseled. Dark hair, deep, soulful eyes—he looks like a Tim Burton character, only *hotter*."

"Is that even possible?" I deadpanned, raising my eyebrows. "This a real person or someone your imagination conjured into existence?"

"I know, I know—I can imagine quite a bit." She grinned. "But he's absolutely real. I first ran into him—"

"What about Katja?" Hadn't we just been talking about her? Back in...well, I guess that had been September.

Becca looked instantly uncomfortable. "Katja, it turns out, had a boyfriend all along. She wasn't even the interested party. He just thought she'd have a better chance of luring me into their bisexual unicorn-hunting bullshit. How many times has this happened? I'm over it." She drummed her fingers on the tabletop and looked out the window at something I couldn't see, eyes glazed over and unfocused.

"I'm sorry."

"Eh. Whatever," Becca snapped back quickly. "So I started running into this guy around Halloween—"

"Since Halloween, and this is the first time I'm hearing anything about him? What's up with that?" Another pang of guilt. I hadn't been a very good friend of late.

"Oh, hush. I didn't even know his name then. We just kind of, like, ran into each other. He was dressed as a *vampire*." Becca giggled. "Full-on eighteenth-century costume. And there were, like, girls all over him. But it was almost magic—our eyes met across a crowded room, and he walked over to me and said hello, and then—well, I don't really remember the rest. Actually, I got really wasted that night."

"You did." I nodded, forcing a small smile so Becca wouldn't think I was lecturing her. "I had put you in a cab and stay up all night watching you to make sure you were still breathing. We're not in college anymore."

"Mistakes were made," Becca agreed.

"I assume you've seen him again since then?"

"Yes! We keep running into each other all over. I've seen him at Whole Foods, and goth Target over on State Street, and he was there when we went to see the holiday lights at the Botanic Gardens in early December, too, but you were in the bathroom when I ran into him, I think. *And* he even bumped into me when Carlos and Miguel and I went ice skating just before I left for California. It's like he's watching me or something."

"And this isn't a massive red flag, how?"

"It's not like that! He's super hot! I think he's a local, and it's just a crazy coincidence. One of these days I'm going to get his name and his phone number. It's destiny. I just know it."

"Maybe he's a serial killer. Have you thought about that?"

"Oh, please. Why would a serial killer dress up as a vampire for Halloween? Isn't that a little too on the nose? Besides, I've just got a good feeling about him. He makes me feel all kinds of cozy inside."

"You don't even know him. That fireplace is called 'projection,' and you're setting yourself up to get burned." I couldn't help myself—Becca was sometimes too trusting, and I was forever worried that she, of all my girlfriends, was going to end up trusting the wrong person in the wrong way, eventually. The thought of it filled my stomach with ice.

"Don't be cynical. Just because you and Dylan didn't work out—"

"Ugh. Why do you have to bring him up?" I tried not to think about Dylan at all. *He was supposed to spend Christmas with me and my family this year.*

"Because you're still hung up on him, and you have been since August."

I pressed my fingertips against my closed eyelids until I saw splotches, hating the fact that Becca always knew how to look right through me, when she wanted to. "Well, maybe your handsome mystery man has a brother—"

"If he does, and his brother's as tall as he is, he won't be your type."

"Oh? How tall are we talking?"

"He's like, six-four..." Becca winked at me over a plate of overpriced cheese-slathered truffle fries, and I made a gagging sound.

"Becca! You are five feet tall! That man will break you!"

"That's the entire idea. And I'm five one."

"You're a half-inch taller than me at most. At *most,* you pervert."

"If he's anywhere near as well-endowed as the dildo I stuck on The Bean..."

"I don't need to hear this." I covered my face completely with my hands as my cheeks turned blushed and heated, my shoulders quaking with laughter.

Becca giggled, which made me laugh even harder, and the next minute were howling, sides splitting, gasping for air. "Holy Mary, Mother of God, pray for us sinners, now and at the hour of our deaths, amen," she wheezed, making the sign of the cross.

"I missed you," I told her once we'd both caught our breath.

"I was only gone for ten days."

"I always miss you when you go back to California."

When we returned to the car, there was a parking ticket on my windshield.

⸺◆◇◆⸺

Becca didn't have to work on New Year's Eve, because Becca didn't exactly have a job, unless you counted occasional freelance illustration gigs, but I was gainfully employed. I should have thought to bring my work clothes with me when I picked her up at the airport. It's not like I hadn't spent the night at her apartment before, if we stayed out too late. Hell, we wore the same sizes. I probably could have borrowed something to wear to the office for the day. It would have been a little more black than usual, but I doubt anyone would have noticed.

Fuck, I could have called out sick. Should have, even.

But mature, responsible Grace Kelly "someone's gotta pay the bills" Cordero wasn't the type to call into the office with a suspicious 'cold' on the eve of a major holiday, just because I'd stayed up past my bedtime the night before. If my parents hadn't raised me better than that, religious guilt was the deciding factor.

I'd made the decision to be out too late the previous night, and I would pay the damn consequences. My 5:00 AM alarm was hell.

Darkness. Wake up. Coffee. Shower. More coffee. Get dressed. Style hair. Make-up. Pack for New Year's Eve at Becca's.

I trudged to the closest Green Line stop in the pre-dawn gloom, bundled up in my parka and grumbling at the accumulation of ice on the sidewalk that had materialized overnight when snow did not. But when the rising sun finally did make an appearance as the train car approached downtown, Chicago glowed, glass and stone reflecting wan winter luminescence that took my breath away, no matter how many times I saw it.

Despite the cold, for one perfect fragment of an instant, the entire world was warm and bright and honeyed, golden light pooling against the cerulean shadows of the skyscrapers. And then the train's path took it between taller structures that blocked the early rays of sunshine completely. I descended the L platform in dim half-light, and walked through office doors that sunlight wouldn't touch for months. The day went by in a blur. I had a brief meeting with my supervisor about the deadline for a grant proposal I was working on, but I was ahead of schedule again, and the meeting could have been an e-mail. I needed a few more data points from engineering, but when I reached out to the department head after lunch, most of the team had already left for the day, so I spent the rest of the afternoon mindlessly browsing Pinterest, trying to decide how I was going to style my hair and makeup that night. When I finally left the building again after 5:00 PM, the sun had already disappeared below the horizon.

I picked up gyros and Greek salad from our favorite takeaway place, then hoofed it the twelve blocks to Becca's apartment so fast, the cold air burned my lungs like fire. She provided the vodka and pastel aluminum cans of fruit-scented sparkling water over dinner as we made our plans—because God forbid Becca drink wine if it wasn't white Zinfandel from a box in the fridge at my apartment. You'd never guess she grew up surrounded by world-class vineyards as far as the eye could see.

Temperatures had dipped well below freezing, even before taking windchill into account, when we finally went out into the night, but we were already a few cocktails in at that point. It was easy to fool ourselves into the dangerous presumption that, with enough alcohol and fleece-lined tights, we could manage a couple of hours bar hopping around the Loop until midnight as long as we kept moving. As though wearing long coats over our cocktail dresses was enough to ward off the frostbite we were tempting for the sake of youth and beauty. Becca wasn't even wearing a parka—she'd insisted on donning the same black velvet and brocade number with all the buckles she'd sported the night before. The damn thing didn't even have a quilted lining. I watched her carefully for signs of hypothermia, even as I ignored my own shivering.

Fortunately, many of the open businesses we walked past had outdoor heaters cranked up along the sidewalks, and with so much foot traffic, there wasn't a lot of ice on the pavement, which made our inappropriate choice of footwear marginally less precarious.

We stumbled and giggled alongside locals and tourists, hopping in and out of trendy bars and gastropubs long enough to warm up before heading back out into the night. Becca paid for exactly zero drinks—she was friends with too many bartenders. I think I got one cocktail on the house, but that's because Becca simply passed me one of her freebies, before being handed another. That was usually how it went when we went out, Becca getting all the attention and me, just a few steps behind, making sure that all that attention didn't get her into trouble.

Becca could be too trusting, I kept telling her. But believing in and seeing the best in people has always gotten her what she's wanted, so there's that.

Everywhere we went, her eyes scanned the crowd.

"No mystery man yet?"

"Not a sign of him. I was so certain I'd see him out tonight—I felt it in my *blood*, Grace."

"That's not macabre at all. Well, maybe your blood lied to you."

"Blood never lies. Don't you pay attention to the CSI shows? Blood never lies," she repeated ominously before choking on the water I'd insisted she drink in between bar stops, as another fit of giggles left her hanging onto a lamppost for support.

I forget what stop we were at. I'd lost count—had we already stopped at four bars, or were we en route to the fourth? I think the cold was the only thing keeping us from being inappropriately tipsy for being in public. Becca's cheeks were flushed and rosy, and ice crystals collected on her lashes just like a Man Ray photograph I saw on display once in a traveling exhibit at the Art Institute, and when she laughed, I thought the whole world was suddenly a thousand times more beautiful than it had been the moment before. Becca always looked lovely, but winter was her season, her high contrast features luminous against the darkness of the winter night and the glow of all the holiday lights.

I looked away for just a moment, my attention caught by the tempting aroma of a sidewalk hotdog vendor, perhaps, or the particular cut and drape of a tailored wool overcoat on a passerby (both things equally as likely to catch my eye before *it* happened), and when I spun around to catch up with Becca, I found her deep in animated conversation with a tall man who looked vaguely familiar...

Like a Tim Burton character brought to life, only hotter, indeed.

Beyond the fact that he fit Becca's description to a T, the only other things I noticed about him was his height—good God, he was easily a foot taller than either of us and then some—and how much like Becca he was, with his seasonally inappropriate choice of attire. That should have been a red flag, but Chicago always has its share of guys who show off by wearing T-shirts and shorts the moment it gets above forty. It still should have been too chilly to justify his lack of a jacket, but his fitted short-sleeve button-down shirt was nicely tailored, and I could appreciate his decision to show it off. The fabric had just enough stretch in it to fit nicely over his well-muscled arms and chest without being exactly tight, and I've always been able to appreciate a well-dressed man.

I was also a little bit drunk, and getting very cold despite my parka and fleece tights, so when Becca pulled me over to join their conversation and introduce us, announcing with bouncing-on-tiptoes excitement that we'd been invited to a private party at some penthouse nearby, I wasn't as skeptical as I should have been. He seemed friendly enough. Becca vouched for him. The world was spinning, all glittering nighttime magic and champagne-bubble anticipation, and Becca was effervescently giddy, next to her crush.

I pushed aside a pang of—not quite jealousy, but I couldn't pin down and identify the strange emotion that writhed in my chest— and acquiesced, glancing down at my phone. It was a little after 11:00 PM, not long until fireworks. With a sigh, I resigned myself to crashing at Becca's place alone after midnight, and I was thankful that I kept a spare copy of her keys on my key ring (a necessity, given how many times Becca lost her own keys or locked herself out of her own apartment).

The last thing I remembered with any clarity was walking through a semi-private entrance to a marble lobby inside one of those soaring residential buildings near Lakeshore Drive, alongside Becca and her new object of infatuation. He swiped a magnetized key card, and we entered the warm glow of a private brass-and-mirror elevator that would carry all three of us up to the penthouse. I smiled at Becca across the car on the ride up. I remember being, not exactly happy, but relieved to be getting out of the cold. And excited for the opportunity to see inside one of the beautiful skyscrapers Chicago was so well known for, and looking forward to ringing in the New Year with what I anticipated to be an exceptional view of the fireworks display on Lake Michigan.

I don't remember the fireworks, though. And for a long time, I couldn't remember anything else about that night, either.

CHAPTER TWO

ALONE IN THE DARK

THERE WAS DARKNESS. AND cold. And pain. I remember the dull, heavy ache of my limbs curled up around me, and the soothing coolness of the hard surface I was resting on. There was something dense and soft enveloping me—someone had covered me head to toe with plush, expensive bath towels—and I began to make sense of my surroundings. Awareness washed over me in waves of cramping and nausea that quickly demanded that I move from the bathtub I'd awoken inside of over to the toilet, and I was sick everywhere at once.

Somewhere between the gurgled retching and voiding of my bowels in an unfamiliar washroom, a part of my mind remembered horror stories of people who woke up in bathtubs full of ice with their kidneys stolen, and my hands reached to the small of my back to ensure there were no deep gashes where the organs ought to have been.

For several awful minutes—perhaps the better part of an hour—that was the only comfort I could derive from my situation as I vomited on the marble floor and kept my butt planted on the toilet seat, shaking and trembling in the cold sweat of the worst hangover I had ever experienced. That part, I decided, wasn't fair—I hadn't turned twenty-five yet, and I'd been counting on a good several months before my body arbitrarily stopped metabolizing alcohol. It was a rite of passage all my friends who had already arrived at their quarter-century milestone assured me was inevitable.

The worst part was, I couldn't remember getting *that* drunk the night before—had I been? I couldn't remember much at all of the night before, which was more concerning.

Becca. Where was Becca? Even in my groggy, disoriented state of mind, her absence stood out like a warning. It wasn't like her to abandon me in strange places, even if there was someone hot involved. We looked out for each other first. That was the promise we always made.

The mass exodus of everything I'd eaten in the past forty-eight hours finally subsided after what seemed like an eternity, leaving behind a gnawing hollow in my gut that wasn't exactly hunger—even the thought of food was enough to bring on another wave of dry heaves—but a creeping desire for *something* that seemed to branch out across my body, a craving I could feel down to my fingertips. I tried to relax, to pull myself together. Maybe some girls in my age group frequently found themselves getting blackout drunk and waking up in strange places, but this whole situation was out of character for me.

It was usually my job to play the stick in the mud mom friend, making sure that the girls in my circle didn't go off with strangers or get stuff put in their drinks. Hyper-vigilant, remember your phone, fill up your gas tank when it reaches a quarter empty, put on a jacket or you'll freeze to death, and don't forget to drink water. Yes, I do have ibuprofen in my purse. And breath mints. And safety pins. And tampons. Do you need me to call you a cab? Let me know when you get home safe. *Remember to use a condom, for Christ's sake!* The Pope might not approve of condoms, but the Pope never had to worry about getting knocked up.

I did not make a habit of passing out drunkenly in rich strangers' bathtubs.

I took a few uncertain deep breaths, and balked, startled by the realization that I might not have been breathing before I did—but that wasn't possible, of course. *Of course.* I was just completely out of sorts, I tried to assure myself. I'd had too much to drink. Maybe someone had slipped something in my drink. All things considered, waking up in a stranger's bathtub was bad, but at least I was fully clothed, and someone had had the decency to tuck me in under some towels. I didn't think been molested. Then again, I'd rushed to the toilet so quickly, would I have even noticed if my undergarments had been askew? That was a terrifying thought. I wondered if Becca had been the one to cover me up, and then I wondered again where Becca was—I wondered where *everyone* was.

I pulled my phone out of my bra to check the time, but my eyes had only a fraction of a moment to register the blinding light of the screen informing me that it was a little after 4:30 before the battery died. Four in the morning would explain why no one had tried to come in to use the washroom I'd been hogging.

I pressed my fingertips to my temples and tried to massage away the driving pain in my skull. There was a tightness in my sinuses, and my mouth hurt as though I'd taken a blow to the face. Had someone hit me? I couldn't remember. I couldn't remember...

I wouldn't have been able to comprehend what was wrong with me in that moment. I hadn't even noticed that my heart had stopped beating yet.

I was, however, mortified of the mess I'd made on the floor, the pungency of my puddled puke an overwhelming assault on my sense of smell. The background radiation of my normal anxiety around tidiness and social gaffs was reaching dangerous levels, and I hastily repurposed the bath towels that had been covering me in the tub to sop up the bile and spit and the flecks of blood as best I could. Then I tried to clean myself up, rinsing the vomit out of the strands of my long brown hair that had gotten caught in the crossfire and washing my hands. I rinsed out my mouth with the tap water, but it tasted horrible. For such an obviously expensive washroom, you'd think better-tasting water would have come out of the tap. I was thirsty, but I didn't dare swallow any water. My lips felt more cracked and dry after rinsing than they had when I first woke up.

It was right around the moment I leaned into the mirror over the sink to check that I hadn't knocked any teeth loose that I realized the washroom lights had been off the entire time, and I stopped in my tracks, inspecting the white-on-white pristine luxury that surrounded me.

There was an arrangement of white orchids in a low stone vessel filled with moss and damp-smelling potting soil on the wide modern sink, and an identical low white vessel on the opposite side of the countertop held a thoughtful assortment of sundries, the kind a considerate wealthy person would leave out for guests to use at a party; individual bottles of mouthwash and hair ties and hair pins and...I could count each rolled-up hand towel on display in the basket below the sink. I could see the perfect white grout lines in between the perfect Carrara marble tiles on the floor and on the walls, every detail perfectly clear in total darkness.

Flipping on the light switch felt like getting smacked in the head, and I instinctively flinched, covering my face with my hands and squeezing my eyes shut for several seconds until my vision adjusted, and then I gazed more carefully at my face in the mirror. There were no bruises blossoming black and purple across the front of my mouth where I felt the most sore, but my lipstick was smudged, as though I'd pressed my lips against other lips a little too enthusiastically. But I couldn't remember any epic make-out sessions the night before—or any time recently in the nearly four months prior, to be honest. Not since Dylan dumped me for the chance to screw around with lots of hot European women when his opportunity for remote work finally materialized, and he'd flown off to Portugal in September.

"It's nothing personal," he'd said on our last date, at the Field Museum, looking up at the ancient bones of Sue the T-Rex. "I care about you a lot, but opportunities like this come along once in a lifetime, and I'm too young to settle down with just one person for the rest of my life."

"Who said I wanted to settle on you, anyway, *Dylan*." I sneered his name to my reflection, but there was something off-putting about my face in the mirror, and I turned away, helping myself to one of the hair elastics in the ceramic dish and tying back my hair in a low ponytail as sleek as I could manage. At least I didn't look like a complete mess. The rest of my expertly applied makeup was still in good condition—three cheers for eyeshadow primer and waterproof mascara. I blotted away the remnants of my lipstick on a piece of tissue and sprayed the bathroom with an expensive bottle of air freshener I found under the sink as well.

I couldn't do anything about the towels, but I made a mental note to promise the hostess I'd replace them, and tried not to calculate how many hours of overtime I'd have to work to make that happen. Those towels were not cheap.

My primary concern was getting home—no easy task when I didn't have my parka, with my ID and cash and keys and everything necessary securely zipped away in a hidden pocket in the lining. I pressed my ear against the washroom door before exiting, just to make sure that the coast was clear, and while I didn't hear any sounds of an ongoing party, once I strained my ears to listen, I discovered that I could hear the entire mechanism of the skyscraper, as though it were a living, breathing thing—the electric buzz of lightbulbs, the swooshing of the elevator down the hall, all manner of pumps and generators and HVAC systems humming along, perfectly maintained...I was halfway convinced I could hear a baby crying in a different apartment several floors below.

At this point, my concern that I'd been slipped some sort of terrifying party drug was the only rational explanation I could hold on to, and I didn't appreciate the side effects. It was all very distracting. Everything was very distracting. Everything was Too Much. I took off my shoes so my heels wouldn't make a racket clacking over the marble floors that continued throughout the penthouse, and finally exited the shelter of the washroom, tiptoeing around as I tried to get my bearings.

The layout was impressive in the extreme—I don't think I'd ever been in a nicer home. The main living area, as far as I could see, consisted of a two-story open floor plan accentuated by massive chandeliers, and an incredible curved staircase with chrome and glass railings leading up to the second floor. Much like the washroom, the decor was dominated by white stone, white furnishings, and a tastefully minimalist aesthetic, but the effect was marred by the clutter and debris still left over from the party. It looked as though everyone had simply walked out en masse hours ago. There were plastic champagne flutes and streamers and party hats strewn about, and cocktail-saturated paper napkins stuck to the floor. No one was around, and for the first time since waking up, real, quaking fear began to grip me.

"Hello...?" I called out in a whisper that wasn't very quiet. Almost on cue, automatic blackout roller shades that covered floor-to-ceiling windows began to rise, revealing multi-million dollar views of the lake, dark water dotted with pancake ice stretched out as far as the eye could see. The sky outside was inky black and clear, devoid of overhead clouds for once, and even with all the light pollution, it was still impressive how many more stars appeared visible from this vantage. I moved closer to the windows without thinking about it, distracted by the sky above me, entranced, in fact, by all the stars—so many more than I'd ever seen before in my life.

And then another round of bewildering sensory overload pummeled me again; a punch to the solar plexus that ought to have taken my breath away. In horrifying, synchronized apprehension, I realized several things all at once:

It wasn't just after 4:30 AM. There were too many cars and buses and people down below. The city was awake and had been for hours. People were just getting off of work. I could hear snippets of music being played on car radios down below me—hundreds of feet below me. I could recognize individual parts of songs as the cars drove past if I listened carefully.

If it was only a little after 4:30 *PM*, then I had been in the washroom more than sixteen hours. No wonder I'd been so sick and felt so ill. No wonder my limbs ached and trembled.

But no, this...whatever this was, it was more than being sick, more than a hang-over or the weird after-effects of an unknown substance. I was hearing things I shouldn't have been hearing, seeing things in the dark I ought not to have been able to see.

And I wasn't breathing. I was certain of it this time. If I didn't specifically think about it, my lungs were still and motionless in my chest, no automatic rhythm of the rise and fall I'd spent my whole life experiencing without really noticing it. My heart...

I drew in a large, shaking breath with focused, deliberate intention and let it out slowly. I was pressed so close to the plate glass windows that my lips were a fraction of an inch away from the cool glass, and even though the windows were double-glazed, I knew it was below freezing outside. But my breath left no telltale fog behind on the glass.

And my heart was *definitely* not beating. For all the noise and swirling chaos buffeting me, no frantic pounding hammered in my chest. The drumbeat of my pulse should have been filling my ears, drowning out the world in the roar of my blood. Instead, I'd been turned inside out, overwhelmed by external stimuli, unable to anchor myself to anything familiar inside my own body.

I didn't even realize that I wasn't alone anymore, until a voice behind me spoke.

"...Grace...? What are you doing here?

Chapter Three

WELCOME TO THE COMMUNITY

THE WOMAN STANDING IN the middle of the room was a stranger to me, even if she did know my name—but that was a small detail I wouldn't worry about until later.

She was perhaps a few inches taller than me, still petite but not tiny, and her short, cropped blonde hair was ruffled from sleep. She wore a tailored, masculine black velvet dressing gown with quilted satin cuffs, and simple black velvet slippers. Everything about her was a study in contrasts, and she existed in sharp relief to the white and chrome surroundings. Her pale coloring was stark against the expensive-looking robe draped softly over her body, and her choppy haircut looked self-inflicted, even though everything else about her—her attire and the way she wore it; her perfect, understated manicure—screamed not just money, but old money. Quiet luxury. She was young-looking, maybe my age, but held herself with confidence I'd envied in women with twice as many years of lived experience.

And she was packing heat under her dressing gown. Maybe that explained the confidence. I could just discern the outline of a large handgun in its holster under the velvet and involuntarily flinched. Chicago being Chicago, I had no doubt at all that she would use it if she felt the need to do so.

These thoughts and observations flashed through my mind in less than a fraction of a second.

"I was here for the party," I stammered, trying to match the face of the woman to some half-remembered recollection. I'd seen those porcelain blue eyes before. I was certain of it, even if I didn't know her name.

"The party was last night. Everyone left before sunrise. Who let you in? Is this a prank, or a threat…?" Her hand moved almost imperceptibly closer toward the gun underneath her robe, and I took a step backward, making full body contact with the window behind me. I wondered how thick the glass was, and how long it would take me to plummet to the sidewalk if she shot me and I flew out of the shattered window like some implausible stunt from an action movie.

I shook my head. "I don't know what happened, but I just woke up in your bathtub. Maybe I had too much to drink? I'm sorry, I didn't mean to overstay my welcome, I just woke up. Someone covered me with bath towels. I'm sorry…" I apologized a second time, but I didn't mention that I'd also thrown up all over those towels. I could confess my sins later. Right then, it felt absolutely crucial that I convince the woman with the gun, the woman who seemed to know my name when I did not know hers, that I had been hidden, not hiding. "I think my friend must have left without me. We were invited up here, though. A tall man in a blue shirt with short sleeves. He said we could come up. He found me and Becca in a bar nearby…"

I realized I was babbling. Maybe I was even incoherent.

She peered at me, squinting her eyes for what might have been a heartbeat, but I had no way of measuring, and then she closed the space between us with a speed that seemed unnatural—she didn't sprint across the floor, though she might as well have. She simply walked, quickly, and she was suddenly standing right in front of me, her cool hands on my cheek, her face flooded with concern.

"No…" she whispered

"I—"

"And you're certain you've been here all day? Since last night?"

"Yes—yes, ma'am," I said, more for the benefit of the concealed handgun than anything else. I had no desire to add getting shot to my growing list of problems. I was still shaking, and I turned away to avoid making eye contact with her. Eye contact was hard under the best of circumstances.

Her exhale was sharp, and then she swore, so forcefully I would have stepped back even further if I hadn't been flattened against the window, and she grabbed my face firmly with one hand and stuck her fingers in my mouth with the other, feeling along my gum line where my teeth were the most sore, pressing hard so that I cried out in pain, and she swore again, "Fuck."

A simple statement. To my horror, I felt *movement* above my eyeteeth, and my tongue prodded the space where something sharp and needle-like was beginning to protrude. I think that was the moment I started to know, or part of me did. I threw my hands over my mouth and felt like I should be hyperventilating, but it was hard to have a panic attack when my body had decided it no longer needed to breathe, and I'd lost all presence of mind to remember how to work my lungs on my own.

"No. No, no..." I ran out of air to make any more sounds, but my lips still moved, desperately trying to form words that wouldn't come from the parched leather that was my throat and mouth. A growing chasm in my awareness bisected the space between what my mind couldn't grasp, and what my body was already fighting.

The floor started falling up when my knees gave out. Cool hands caught my forward lurching, her arms around my waist strong and certain as she guided me away from the window and over to a white leather sofa set back far enough to afford a more dramatic view. I barely registered the scenery as she helped me sit down, and I drew my arms around my shoulders, rocking back and forth, trying to process overwhelming sensations, trying to ward off an impending meltdown.

Focus, Grace.

But there was something sharp coming out of my mouth, dammit, and it hurt, everything hurt, my teeth hurt, and my throat burned, and my legs were numb, and my belly ached with a hunger that burned like fire...

She sat opposite me on the sofa, the expression on her face an equal mixture of pity and annoyance, holding perfectly still for several quiet moments before she asked, "Do you remember who did this to you?" Her voice cut through the racing thoughts in my head like a surgical scalpel—so sharp it felt almost soft until my mind latched onto what she was referring to, what "this" was, this...impossible thing. Impossible.

I shook my head, my brain like a dial tone, the sum total of all my thoughts coalescing into a dull, singular noise in my head. At that second, I could barely remember my own name.

She stood and walked away, instructing me to stay where I was until she came back. I couldn't have moved to follow had I tried, but my ears listened to every footfall she made as she disappeared out of sight, to the sounds of drawers opening, and glassware clinking. When she returned, she was carrying two sturdy coffee mugs, a pair of scissors, and a clear plastic bag plump with dark red fluid, which my eyes locked onto. Blood. I knew there was blood in the bag, and something dark and terrible flared in my belly.

I wanted it.

I was going to be sick.

"Grace." Again, her soft but forceful voice caught my immediate attention, and I had no choice but to look up at her and meet her gaze. She had the most commanding presence I had ever known, and an accent that I was in no position to try to place. "I need you to sit still. Don't move. I will bring it over to you. If you try to stand up, you will knock things over, do you understand?"

I nodded, but the moment the scissors cut into the bag of blood, the smell hit my nose and then the rest of my body, obliterating thought. The whole world zoomed out—the strange woman who knew my name, the stark white penthouse decor, the bag of...blood. The blood pulled me back, my peripheral vision full of stars turned red. Inside my mouth, my teeth continued to lengthen and change, and I barely felt the pain anymore. My eyes watered from the overwhelming need for it. Somehow, I sat there on that damn white sofa and waited patiently. I don't know how I managed.

She divided the blood between both mugs and brought the first one to my lips, supporting the vessel as I grasped at it like a toddler grabs a sippy cup, and the blood poured over my cracked lips and tongue, sliding down my throat, cold and thick and slippery, the taste of old copper pennies and iron nails in my mouth. I was swallowing desperate droughts of electric battery acid, and it was everything I wanted, and I knew, *I knew* what had happened to me, even if I didn't understand the details. This was nothing like the movies. I shuddered violently when the mug was empty and experimentally licked my lips and gums and brand new fangs of the bloody film clinging to my skin and teeth.

Even as the blood gurgled and settled in my stomach, the awful metallic taste soured in my mouth, inviting another wave of nausea. My shaking hands made their way to cover my lips by instinct. I didn't want to vomit anymore.

"Take it easy," the vampire—the *other* vampire— soothed. "The first time can be rough. Your body still isn't used to it. It's easier if you sit still for a few minutes, and you'll be fine, I promise."

She lifted her own mug next as I slowly shook my head and watched her, watching as the blood seemed to physically soften her. She leaned back against the sofa in repose, eyes closed, an almost slack-jawed smile on her parted lips, her fangs barely visible, but there. Underneath that velvet dressing gown, I could see the nipples on her small breasts were firm and erect, and I wondered why I was staring at her chest, but my eyes had been following the lines of her throat as she swallowed the blood, and I wondered if that's what I looked like when I...?

Jesus, Mary, and Joseph. What kind of party had I been to last night? None of this could possibly be real.

"Where's Becca?" I demanded. My hostess sat up again and looked at me.

"Your friend went home when the party was over. I promise you. This situation with you...this doesn't happen. Not at my events. I've never had a guest die at any of my parties. And no one's ever been turned before, either."

Turned. I didn't like that word.

The woman held out her hand to take the empty mug away from me and briefly changed the subject as she walked back to wherever she'd retrieved the blood from. "It's a blessing, really, that you took as long to come around as you did. Sometimes it happens in minutes," her voice called out from the other room. "If you'd come back while the house was still full of guests, God only knows what would have happened.

"Anyway," she returned, "normally, I heat mine up first, but you didn't look like you could have waited another minute, poor thing. I know how it is. That first night is hard for all of us." She almost sounded sad, and she sat down next to me at an angle, leaning forward and meeting my horrified, shell-shocked gaze.

"Us?" Nothing felt real. I exhaled the remnants of air in my lungs, drew in a fresh breath, and released again, slowly, as the woman said the word I already knew, but didn't want to.

"Vampires. Community members. Us. Surely I can spare you the long-winded introductory lecture?"

I scoffed, the words coming out all in a rush. "I don't believe in vampires."

She reached out her hand to touch my face again, wiping away a small trickle of red stuff that had escaped the corner of my mouth, and silently held my gaze as she licked the blood off her fingertip. "'The greatest trick the devil ever pulled was convincing man he didn't exist,'" She shrugged. "No one believes in vampires anymore. And here you are."

There was a lump in my throat and tears burning at the corners of my eyes, but I willed them both to go away. This wasn't the time or place to cry. I could do that later, at home, in my own bed. I had work in the morning.

"For what it's worth," she continued, "It's not…normal to bring someone over quickly, in one night, like you were. It does happen, but it's rare. You've survived something that very few people ever do, and I can't imagine how you must be feeling right now." She sighed and ran a hand through her choppy cropped blond hair.

"How do we fix this?" I needed to know, my voice a whisper drained of hope. There had to be an answer. A mistake had been made somehow. She'd said so herself. This wasn't normal.

She seemed offended by the question. "There isn't anything to fix, sweetheart. You survived, but you died first. We're dead. That's what we are. I can't fix that."

Her hand rested lightly on the top of my thigh in an oddly intimate gesture. I still didn't know her name, had too many other pressing concerns to even think to ask. "I'm sure—you're going to be all right—" she insisted.

But nothing was all right. I wanted to scream, and I was drowning in the infinite implications of what she was telling me, battered by waves of crimson in a sea of blood inside my mind, and I didn't, I couldn't—

"I don't want this," I gasped. "Please. I didn't ask for this. I'm not—"

"You are." Her voice was firm, pulling me back to a world I was desperate to escape. "One of us now. Welcome to the Community, Grace Cordero. I honestly do wish the circumstances were different. There's a reason we normally take a week to turn someone, and why we don't do it without consent."

No. Please. Anything but this. "Why would anybody want to kill me?"

She shrugged. The gesture was almost offensive. "I don't know. But we will find them, and we will hold them accountable. Until then..." she seemed to be trying to figure out what to do next. I could almost see the gears spinning.

I had a million other thoughts and questions—including, *'you said you usually heated it up first, what does that taste like, can I have some more, and can I try it warm, please?'* But I was dumbstruck, so I continued to sit on the sofa in silence. I wanted more blood, and I wanted to not want it. My tongue explored the place where the fangs had been, but they'd receded back into my gum line. My mouth still felt sore, like the memory of getting braces, but it wasn't as bad as it had been before—before I'd tasted the blood.

One by one, more lights throughout the penthouse started to turn on automatically as we sat there, and I welcomed the all-too-brief momentary respite, allowing myself to be mesmerized by the way the light dazzled around the shimmering crystal of the chandeliers, reflecting off the polished marble floors and sleek white leather and chrome furnishings throughout. There was a baby grand piano on the far side of the grand main room of the penthouse, also white, and I wondered if it was in tune or just for show. My nana used to teach piano lessons out of her converted garage when I was little, and I'd taken lessons until I was almost seventeen years old. I hadn't practiced in years, but I found myself fighting a sudden urge to walk over to the baby grand and start playing something sad and melancholy. I stopped myself. I had standards, and I refused to start off as a tragic stereotype.

Just beyond the piano, near the foyer entrance, a massive seasonal floral arrangement sat atop a round, formal table, all white winter flowers and glitter-encrusted bare stems styled to look like snow set against dark holly leaves and red berries. The high-contrast coloring of the bouquet reminded me of Becca. My hostess had insisted Becca was home safe. I wanted to believe her. The alternative was unthinkable.

Like my darkening thoughts, the debris left over from the party the night before marred the crisp white perfection of my surroundings, and I absentmindedly started corralling all the trash within arm's reach. I always hated clutter, and emotionally, I was entirely out of my depth—straightening things up always helped calm my nerves, whatever the circumstances.

Even after becoming a vampire.

Especially *after becoming a vampire.*

"I should probably help you clean up, at least," I offered, feeling much better after the blood I had just consumed stopped sloshing, and started to settle and circulate a bit. I stood up and started looking for a place to dump the items I'd collected, but the blonde vampire shook her head.

"Leave it. I've got cleaners coming over in about an hour, and you're a much bigger problem right now."

"Me?" I asked, almost laughably innocent. I still thought I was going to be able to go home to my own bed and sleep off this nightmare.

"I had half a dozen different Community members up here last night, and a few hundred mortal guests in and out as well. If word gets out in the Community that someone killed one of those mortals, to say nothing of turning them like you were, this could go...very badly. For me. I can't let anyone find out what happened. Not right now." She walked away, back toward the place where she had gotten the blood from earlier, and I followed, arms still full of clutter, still looking for a trash can, still holding on to the one thing I could control. We walked into a kitchen that could have come straight off the showroom floor, and she continued to talk, pointing out a hidden trash can under the center island as she did, looking relieved when my arms were finally free.

"...And since you don't remember who bit you and left you like this, I have no way to know who to start shouting at. And I can't just let you wander off into the night." She pursed her lips, her blue eyes thoughtful, and she brought another bag of blood out from a different hidden compartment somewhere in the modern space—it was the kind of kitchen where all the appliances are built into cabinets and cleverly tucked away, so you couldn't even see where the refrigerator or microwave was. I watched my hostess pour boiling water out of an electric kettle into a large bowl and drop the sealed bag of blood into the hot water.

"Honestly, I'm probably fine to go home. I just need cab fare. I can pay you back." I added the last part a little more weakly than I meant to.

"Do you want to kill people?" the blonde woman asked so sharply that I was taken aback. It honestly hadn't occurred to me—that *other* part of being a vampire—yet.

"Because you will." She sighed when she saw my panicked face, and her voice returned to its usual softness. The edge was still there, but you'd never know it until she cut you. "I'm sorry this happened to you, Grace, you seem like a nice girl, but I have too many responsibilities right now to deal with a fledgling, the cleaners are coming soon, you absolutely cannot be around them, and I have work to do."

As she spoke, her eyes darted towards a collection of blueprints not-quite strewn across the surface of the kitchen island, laid out as though they'd been the subject of conversation at some point the evening before, and for the first time, my eyes registered the architect's renderings of a towering modern skyscraper. Something finally clicked.

"You're Calliope Jones." The recognition came all at once. I recognized her face—her dark blue eyes, really—from the myriad of posters and advertisements I'd seen all over the Loop for as long as I'd lived in Chicago. Calliope Jones, CEO of the Calliope Jones Group, powerful commercial real estate developer and hedge fund manager, practically a local celebrity. Becca had been briefly obsessed with her in our sophomore year—the local gossip blogs called Jones "The Chicago Vampire" because of her stern but perpetually ageless appearance, and the fact that she was never seen outside during the daytime, and...*holy shit*. "You look much younger and prettier without all the makeup. I didn't recognize you—"

"The point of the makeup isn't to look young and pretty. The point is to make me look serious about cementing billion-dollar deals," Calliope cut me off with almost palpable impatience, clicking her manicured nails on the marble countertops.

"I thought you had to be close to fifty, at least. Your posters have been up for years..." I marveled, still reeling over the fact that Calliope Jones knew my name. Calliope Jones, in person, looked nothing like the severe, well-kept older woman who appeared in all her advertisements. I thought about the carefully curated public image I was familiar with from billboards and transit advertisements that had always struck me as off-putting and artificial.

The illusion was shattered by the reality of in-person Calliope. Her ice blonde hair was so light it was nearly colorless, and her youthful, wrinkle-free complexion was pale and perfect without all the heavy contouring makeup she usually used for her photos. If we'd met the night before and she'd been presenting as the Calliope Jones most of Chicago knew, no wonder it had taken me so long to recognize her.

I gasped. "How old are you?" In the movies, vampires never aged. I knew that much.

Something catlike about her body language reminded me of the feral strays we took in at the shelter I used to volunteer at as a teenager. She twitched, shifted her weight, narrowed her eyes. She seemed annoyed by my question, as annoyed as she was by my presence, and the inconvenience I was causing her. "That's rude, you know." With a voice like that, I didn't think Calliope Jones needed makeup to make billion-dollar deals. I'd be lying if I said I wasn't impressed by her. "I was twenty-three years old when I chose this life," Calliope said, slowly, emphasizing the word *chose,* "and I've been a vampire for one hundred and ninety-five years."

"I'm twenty-four." I slumped forward against the kitchen island, propping my face up between my hands, and looked past the pile of blueprints, across the kitchen island, and out the windows at the urban skyline and the dark waters of the lake beyond. I tried not to stare at the bag of blood gently warming in the hot water.

Calliope furrowed her perfectly smooth brow, and I tried to imagine a future where I'd never get wrinkles there, either. I wasn't vain enough to see that as an advantage when so much else had been taken away.

Someone had killed me. Why were we being so calm about that detail? The more I tried to remember what had happened the night before I woke up in Calliope's washroom, the more blurred and confusing things got. *Someone drank my blood and killed me!* I wanted to scream, but my lungs were out of air again.

Calliope filled a plain stainless steel thermal tumbler with the warm blood—I nearly doubled over when she cut the second package open—and handed it to me, lid sealed. "I need to get dressed and make some phone calls," she finally said, leading me to a plush media room on the first floor, and handing me a remote. "You can watch TV or charge your phone, but for the love of God, do not make any phone calls or log on to social media until we figure out what to do next, please. And don't spill. The rug in here will cost a fortune to have cleaned."

She seemed very much at her wit's end when it came to me. She turned and left the small private theater without another word, and then I was alone again, abandoned in the dark.

...The day my mom died, the school counselor called me out of AP biology and stood in the hallway like a halfway deflated party balloon, and told me to grab my stuff, that I wouldn't be coming back that day. I was a straight-A student, but I still worried that I might be in trouble—maybe someone had said something about the party with the boys and the alcohol the weekend before, but my cousin Victoria was older than me and had already graduated. None of her friends from college knew any of my friends from Sacred Heart.

It didn't even occur to me that Mom might have died—that was impossible. Of course she was sick, I knew that, but she'd beaten cancer before, and we had a plan, a whole big binder and spreadsheets I'd printed out for her after visiting with the oncologist. Aggressive treatment, he'd said. I'd held Mom's hands as they shook inside the doctor's office, my naive heart full of perfect faith. Treatment meant that there was something they could do. Mom was only thirty-five.

Twenty pairs of eyes followed me as I grabbed my books and neatly put my notes away, and then I saw the tears in my counselor's eyes, and I knew, *I knew*, and everything just...shut down. Mrs. Jacobsen handed me a rosary; a nice one with cloisonné beads like you found at Catholic gift shops, and we walked toward the school office in the kind of silence that isn't real silence—all around you, the world keeps on going, people are talking, maybe even talking to you, but you don't hear what they're saying, it's like they aren't even there.

I hate that feeling.

Dad told me in front of Principal Lee that Mom had had a stroke that morning. The cancer had gotten into her brain quicker than anyone had realized, and she was gone. He was crying, Mrs. Jacobsen was crying, and Principal Lee wrapped his arms around me in a giant hug that squeezed the air out of me, but I just stood there, numb, my mind racing through all the implications of the impossible thing they were telling me, that my mom was dead, I wouldn't be able to see her after school for coffee and cannoli like we always did on Fridays, that she wouldn't be there to take pictures for the Spring formal or help me with last minute SAT flashcards, she wouldn't...see me graduate or go to college or get married or...

Dad cried more in the cab ride back home, where all the aunts and cousins and Nana were already gathering, and I sat next to him on that stupid false spring day in April, looking out the window at the bulbs poking up through the leftover snow on residential lawns, and I was nothing, just numb.

Finding out I was a vampire now rendered me just as paralyzed as I had been then. Part of me felt like I should be weeping and distraught, but wailing and gnashing my teeth was never my style. I knew the tears would come later, and when they did, I wouldn't be able to stop or hold back, so I just sat there, in the darkened media room Calliope Jones—*the* Calliope Jones—had led me to, with a tumbler of human blood in my lap, frightened by how much I wanted it, terrified of the way my body had reacted so viscerally to that first, chilled mug.

I was a vampire. I was dead, or undead, or...whatever. It was as surreal as I knew it to be true. My gums itched, and my heart was a hollow void in my chest, an unnatural stillness I could almost choke on. The back of my throat craved iron and salt, and my hands began to tremble again as my fingertips traced the outline of the lip atop the container of blood that I hadn't had the courage to open yet.

I was a vampire, and I was...thirsty. I hated it already.

I cracked open the lid and took a careful sip as it all came flooding over me again, and I did almost choke at the smell of the blood that instantly overwhelmed me. I fell out of the chair to my knees in a profane imitation of prayer as the fucking fangs slid out of my itching gums again with a wet, sucking sound that made me gag, but the shift was not as painful as it had been the first time.

Don't spill, don't spill, don't spill...I clutched at the tumbler and drank resentfully, shuddering in repulsion and betrayal as I realized that already, my body was adjusting, or maybe I was adjusting to my body, and I wasn't sure which frightened me more. But the blood was electric fire in my mouth, soothing the tension in my shoulders, the knots in my neck, the pounding in my head. It didn't taste good, but it didn't need to. I needed the blood to fill my empty veins and calm the tremors in my fingertips, to take away the pain of everything that had happened, wrapping me in a scarlet cocoon of protection.

The comfort didn't last long.

I pulled myself to my feet and sat back down, rocking back and forth, trying to remember everything I knew about vampires from books and movies. Not that I'd read or seen many. Vampire stories had always been more Becca's thing, and I—I needed to find Becca. Whatever had happened to me, I couldn't let it happen to her, too. Panic thundered in my chest, heartbeat or no. I had to protect Becca from this.

I didn't want this life, whatever it was. I wanted to go home. I wanted my heart to start beating again.

I didn't want to cry.

Think, Grace. Think. All I had in my possession was my cell phone. I wondered, briefly, if the pepper spray that lived in the pocket of my missing parka would have helped me when I'd needed it, but I didn't think that would have stopped whoever attacked me. Pepper spray wasn't much of a deterrent if someone really wanted you dead, the self-defense articles always said.

Someone had wanted me to die last night.

Upstairs, though at least one closed door and down what I assumed was a rather long hallway, I could hear Calliope's voice, rising higher and higher in a one-sided conversation, "*...because you're the only one in the Community I trust who wasn't at the party last night, Harold, and I need her to be with someone trustworthy who isn't also a suspect until I figure this out...I don't care if this isn't a great time for you, it's an absolutely horrible time for me, and I'm doing the best I can!...How do you think she feels?...Harold, dammit, you owe me this after Macau...Yes, I am bringing up the past, don't weasel out of it...Do me this solid, and I'll consider the debt canceled...Now who's the one bringing up the past?...Just get here, Harold, and soon.*"

CHAPTER FOUR

HAROLD

WITHOUT A HEARTBEAT TO mark the seconds ticking by, I had no way to gauge how much time passed in the darkened room Calliope had ushered me into. I might have been left alone for an hour or more, but eventually, a sound in the foyer indicated the arrival of the elevator, and a knock at the penthouse doors a moment later brought the scurrying sounds of Calliope rushing downstairs to welcome her visitor.

"It's good to see you."

"Spare me." I heard the voice of a man, almost imperceptibly low, respond to Calliope's perfunctory greeting.

She kept her voice hushed as well. I strained my ears to listen to their murmuring accusations and defensive replies. "Well, it's been what, five years since the last time?"

The man let out a resigned sigh. "I suppose so. Didn't mean for it tae be that long. You picked a hell of a time for a bloody complication on this scale, you know."

The feigned confusion in Calliope's voice was so obvious, I could imagine it writ across her face like vulgar graffiti. "Darling, that awful thing? It was so long ago. Surely—"

"You know, Cal. *You know.* It's only been thirty years, this winter. You were there."

She backpedaled. "I *am* sorry about the timing. I wouldn't have called you if there was anyone else."

"...What the hell am I supposed to do with her, anyway...?"

Their voices continued, not quite bickering, all the way to the media room. Hearing them talk together, I almost thought her accent sounded like a Masterpiece Theater character, but it came and went. Calliope flipped on the overhead lights, and I let out an involuntary yelp as the darkness disappeared and the high-pitched electric whine of the lightbulbs filled my ears.

I squeezed shut my eyes shut and counted to ten. When I looked around again, my vision adjusted quickly, and the background noise of the building slowly receded to the peripherals of my observation—I still noticed it, but only when I wanted to notice it.

"Don't get too comfortable sitting in the dark, sweetheart," Calliope chided. "It's a bad habit to start when you're new." She was wearing a wig now, natural-looking and precisely coiffed, her makeup applied with a heavy hand and—I observed—some kind of treatment around the eyes that made the skin there appear crepey and wrinkled. If I really focused, I imagined I could catch a faint whiff of Elmer's school glue. That was a creative trick, for sure. She'd changed clothes, too, swapping the black dressing gown for an expensive-looking knitwear pantsuit, probably Italian, and a stylish pair of eyeglasses perched low on her nose. She looked every inch the Calliope Jones I knew from ads on the L, and nothing at all like the androgynous young woman who had been holding a coffee mug full of blood up to my lips earlier in the evening. I couldn't take my eyes off of her. I wanted to study every trick she knew. *I used to think I was good at makeup...*

A man walked in behind her, his feet making hardly any sound at all on the marble floor, his movements careful and deliberate. He had a look about him like a man who didn't want to break anything. Unlike Calliope, the fine lines around his squinty eyes looked authentic, like he'd spent too much time outdoors without sunscreen or sunglasses. He didn't look exactly old, but it was impossible to tell his age, one way or another. He could have been twenty-five and worn out when he was turned. He could have been a well-preserved forty. He could have been anything in between. His nose had been broken at least once, and there was a faint remainder of what might have once been a deep scar on his chin.

He didn't look cruel or violent, I decided, but I also didn't think he'd had a soft life before he became a vampire.

He was anything but handsome by my standards—his brown wavy hair was in need of a haircut, he could use a shave, and his sideburns were almost comically anachronistic. He wore a pullover knit sweater in shades of green and brown, and brown wool pants in a high-waisted, cuffed style that hipsters went wild over at thrift stores. Something about the ease with which he was dressed told me that he'd probably been wearing those clothes since they were new. I wouldn't have given him a second glance if I'd saw him walking down the street. Compared to Calliope's hyper-distinctive styling, he looked nothing more than ordinary.

I wondered how dangerous he was.

"This one?" he asked Calliope, but he was staring right at me.

"I don't keep a random assortment of fledglings up here, obviously." She crossed her arms and rolled her eyes at him. I wondered how long they'd known each other. It had to have been at least thirty years.

He sat down and looked at me intently for several uncomfortable seconds, his greenish-gray eyes scanning all over my body, looking for clues, and I would have blushed if I could have, feeling very naked in my vintage black cocktail dress. I'd imagined myself looking very much like Audrey Hepburn when Becca and I were getting ready the night before, but under the weight of his unblinking gaze, I now felt like a small child playing dress-up, only masquerading at sophistication. Like I'd done something horribly wrong and was now in unspeakable trouble.

"Harold—don't scare the girl." Calliope turned her chiding tone to the man in question now. The same one she'd been speaking to on the phone. When was the last time that name had been popular?

"Hello," he said to me at last. "I'm...Harold Laing. And you must be Grace?"

"Cordero," I offered. "Grace Kelly Cordero, no relation to the princess."

Calliope made a sound that might have been second cousins to a laugh, putting me somewhat more at ease, but Harold didn't react at all.

"You were human last night." It was a statement. He didn't take his eyes off me.

I nodded, shifting my weight awkwardly.

"...you hadn't been drinking anyone's blood before that?"

"No offense, but that sounds really gross." I was keenly aware of the empty tumbler that had once been full of someone's blood sitting in my lap, but he didn't have to give me that skeptical raised eyebrow look. Again, I felt like I ought to have been blushing, and was somehow certain blushing was permanently out of my future experiences.

He turned his attention to Calliope again. "You're more connected tae the Community than I am. You're sure you've never seen her before?"

"Harold, she's brand new. I've turned more than enough fledglings to know what the first night is like. Her fangs hadn't even come in the first time I touched her. You can *feel* the newness on her." Calliope sideswiped Harold's question about seeing me before, but she'd recognized me by name immediately upon finding me in her home, even from behind, and I didn't think that was from some alleged brief introduction the previous night when she was busy hosting her party.

"May I?" Harold held out his hand before touching me, unlike Calliope had, and he didn't immediately stick his fingers in my mouth, either. He paused until I nodded, as though awaiting an invitation, before lightly pressing the back of his hand to my cheeks and forehead, like a concerned parent checking to see if their child had a fever. His touch was cool and rougher than Calliope's perfectly manicured fingers. He seemed like someone who worked with his hands a lot, and I wondered if he was a craftsman. Maybe a woodworker. He looked like a woodworker. After a moment, he sighed and spoke again to Calliope. "You're right. She's someone's fledgling. You think someone in the Community got carried away at the party and tried tae cover their tracks? Midnight kiss that turned into a snack?"

I didn't like the sound of his theory.

"Your guess is as good as mine, but that's the best I've got, too. Somebody lost control, tried to turn her when they thought they'd killed her, and when that didn't seem to work, they left the body in my bathtub for me to find. Except, of course, the body didn't remain a body, and here we are." Calliope sighed.

"You're lucky it took her so long tae come around. If she'd been like—well, you know, your party might have gotten a little more exciting."

"Christ, Harold, you think I'm not aware of that? When I think of how many mortals were in and out of that bathroom for hours until the party was over, just inches away from a new fledgling…"

"What would have happened?" I whispered. I didn't like it when people talked over me as though I wasn't there.

"You could have hurt someone, badly." Calliope answered.

At the same moment Harold said, "You would have killed people." Harold's response was much more matter-of-fact.

I bit the inside of my lip to keep it from quivering until I tasted my own blood, summoning a reappearance of the fangs, and I dropped my head low, broken and ashamed. "I think I killed your bath towels when I woke up," I confessed to Calliope without looking at her face. "I'll pay to have them replaced, somehow. I'm sorry."

It took Calliope a second to catch my meaning, and then she just laughed again, a short laugh, but genuine and not mean-spirited. "The towels can stay dead, then. It's no trouble to replace them, don't worry about it. I'm glad you had the luxury of modern amenities...most of us made do with far less our first night. I'd much rather deal with ruined bath towels than a dead body. One is easier to dispose of than the other." The casual way she talked about disposing of a dead body horrified me. Would that be me some night? Making jokes about the *inconvenience* of people dying?

It was a relief to know that she didn't expect me to replace her damaged property, at least. And even more of a relief that I hadn't...that no one had...*fuck.*

"Do you remember—?" Harold asked me the question, but Calliope cut him off with a wave of her hand.

"She doesn't remember anything, do you, sweetheart?" She directed the last part at me, and I shook my head because she was right.

"I don't remember anything after getting into the elevator with Becca and...that guy. Maybe handing over my parka when we arrived, but..."

Calliope snapped her fingers. "Yes, your coat. The blue puffy thing? I think I found it on the coat check rack. I'll show you both out." She spun on her heels, leaving Harold and me to scramble to our feet. I didn't exactly chase after her, but I followed close behind, Harold keeping up the rear, exiting the room as silently as he'd entered it.

"Where am I going?" I gasped, still trying to work out how to have enough air in my lungs to speak, now that I wasn't breathing automatically anymore. "I need to get home. My apartment is in—"

"Harold is going to take over your education," Calliope informed me, the set of her jaw and the tone of her voice making it clear that this was already decided. "I have...a lot going on, and I can't devote time to a fledgling vampire right now. Harold will shelter you and show you what you need to know until you can manage on your own." She handed me my impractical stilettos that I must have dropped by the window when she first found me, and I knelt down to fasten the straps and buckles.

Everything was happening very fast again, and I struggled to keep up. "I'm fine, really," I insisted, even though I was anything but fine. "I'm sure I can figure things out on my own. Just give me my coat, I can find an ATM and get cab fare back to my own apartment. I'm a quick learner. I can do...I don't know, vampire correspondence school or something. I'll check in every night. I'll do everything you say to do, and I promise I...I promise I won't kill anybody!"

In the foyer by the elevators, Calliope handed Harold my parka and a thick envelope. "She doesn't seem as dangerous as some of the other new fledglings I've met, and that's what has me worried. Keep her out of the sun, show her how to hunt properly, and help her set up her finances. I can have my secretary handle that part if you prefer."

"I am not going off into the night with some random guy I just met—" I interrupted, but they both ignored me. I stood up and reached out for my parka, only wobbling slightly in my heels. Calliope and Harold were still taller than me, but not by much.

"Don't let her reach out to her family just yet. We've got time to figure out how to handle that..."

"Calliope, I know how tae raise fledglings." Harold slipped my parka over my shoulders, and I started to panic. I needed to find a way to escape them.

A ding in the foyer announced the arrival of an elevator car, but it wasn't from the elaborate brass door at the end of the small hallway. Hidden behind a discrete panel I hadn't even noticed before, the service elevator opened, and the after-party cleaning staff fanning out, hauling their buckets and carts of trash bags and cleaning supplies behind them. But it wasn't the scent of bleach and all-purpose industrial cleaner that attracted my attention.

Something snapped in my mind, like too many rubber bands wrapped around a watermelon in a viral internet video, an explosion of crimson overwhelming my capacity for rational thought. There was blood in their veins. I could smell it instantly, burning up inside them, hot and thick and *alive* inside their arteries. Somewhere deep inside my chest, a growling, animalistic thing took over, all base hunger and want and need, and I lurched forward, grabbing out instinctively for—

Harold caught me in his surprisingly strong arms and turned my body toward his, pulling my face into his chest. It was harder to smell the blood inside the cleaning crew when I was pressed tight against the itchy wool of his pullover. The sweater was definitely vintage, I decided. He smelled like leather and motor oil and sawdust, like the faint metallic ghost of old blood long since visibly washed clean. He smelled like soap and wool and...I felt my body relax and my fangs retract, and I was shaking, trembling again with fear and hunger.

I would have killed people if he hadn't stopped me. I wouldn't have been able to stop myself.

"Well. I suppose I should be relieved that she is a normal fledgling, after all." Calliope's heels clicked down the hall.

Far away, it seemed, I could hear her laughter, guiding the crew into the penthouse and giving instructions in perfect Spanish. I imagined she was explaining away my horrific behavior. *"Oh, just a hungover party guest, you know how it is..."*

After a moment, Harold released his grip on my body but kept his hands on my shoulders and gave me another inscrutable *look*. "I really do think you should come with me," he said solemnly. "At least for the first few nights."

There was no way I could argue with him after that.

I don't remember the long elevator ride down to the ground floor. Harold pulled me close to him again as we walked across the lobby, and I held my breath when we strode past the doorman. A dark-gray BMW sedan was waiting by the valet when we exited the double glass doors of the building, and Harold insisted on opening the passenger side door for me and making sure I got settled, rather than the valet.

His older car was clean and perfectly maintained, but boxy, and several decades out of style, like something from the 1980's. I buckled up out of habit, but Harold left his seatbelt undone. Unlike in modern cars, this one made no annoying dings if the driver's seatbelt remained unbuckled, and he navigated the downtown traffic with a practiced ease that I envied.

I'd stopped commuting to work in the downtown Loop in my own car after a series of nerve-wracking fender-benders inspired me to take advantage of my employer's transit pass benefit, but I guessed it was probably easy to keep your cool behind the wheel if you'd been driving since the dawn of the automobile and didn't need to worry about getting whiplash if a distracted driver rear-ended you. I asked him how old he was.

"About two hundred or so." He'd barely said a few dozen words in total to me so far.

"And in all that time…" I took a deep breath. "You've never killed anyone?"

"No." His response was brief, even curt. Then, "No, I've killed hundreds of people. More than I can count. Some of that wasn't my fault, exactly." He paused. "…and some of it was." His voice was sad.

I sucked in a long, shaky breath, exhaled slowly, and moved my hand toward the BMW's passenger door handle. I was riding in a car with a serial killer, my cell phone was dead because I'd forgotten to charge it when I'd had a chance, my friends and family were probably worried sick about me, and I'd just committed several felonies by drinking blood. At least, I assumed it was illegal to drink blood. So even if I did jump out of the car at the next stoplight, and ran to find the police, what was I going to tell them? That I'd gone to a party and someone had put something in my drink, that now I could see sounds and hear colors, and that a self-confessed serial killer and a famous billionaire mogul were trying to convince me that I was a vampire?

I remembered Calliope's warning to "keep her out of the sun" and wondered what would happen if I couldn't find shelter at sunrise fast enough? Some deep-seated part of me already knew the answer wasn't good. My eyes met Harold's as we turned to glance at each other at the same time, and I immediately twisted to look away. The

"Are you still hungry?" he asked, as he pulled up to a red light. Without waiting for my response, he reached into his trouser pocket and handed over a battered, dented metal flask. It might have been silver-plated at one time, but the plating had all worn off at least half a century ago. The engraved design on the surface was hard to make out. Some kind of owl, maybe. I eyeballed at the flask skeptically. It looked like something that would be sold at a flea market with the words "warning, for display only." It was probably lined with lead or asbestos.

"This looks like it will give me tetanus," I said aloud, without quite meaning to.

Harold sighed. "If you don't want tae kill people, you're going to have tae keep yourself from getting hungry. A hungry vampire is a dangerous vampire. You don't have tae kill, if you don't want ta. I promise. But you have tae feed…"

I nodded, tears welling up in my eyes again. The lump in my throat was back, too, and a quiver to my lower lip that I couldn't stop this time. I didn't want to cry in front of Harold. I brushed a tear away with the back of my hand and opened the flask. The blood inside smelled older than the blood Calliope had given me, but I drank it, hating the way my body betrayed me as the blood danced over my tongue. I hated that it made me feel *good*. I hated myself for wanting more.

And then the tears came, finally, and I couldn't hold them back any more than I could stop myself from lunging at the cleaning crew—at innocent people. I choked back sobs and wrapped my arms around my knees as I pulled my legs up onto the car seat, tears rolling down my cheeks and throat, wetting the neckline of my dress. I cried because I was frightened and ashamed and disgusted with myself, because I felt violated and broken, and my life had been stolen from me. I cried because I was embarrassed to be crying in front of a man who was two hundred years old—probably too old to care about existential dread from a silly girl a tenth his age.

And I cried, thinking about my mother, and about heaven, and hell. I didn't think vampires went to heaven, and I was never going to see my mom ever again.

Harold let me cry and kept driving for some distance I lost track of. Eventually, I realized the car had stopped, and that we had pulled into an ordinary suburban garage…somewhere. I had no idea where I was or how to get my bearings, and I berated myself for not at least trying to pay attention on the drive. I looked around the garage at the tools and equipment and mountains of cardboard boxes, and it reminded me of the chaotic clutter of my parent's home—the endless stacks of outdated electronic devices, crates of European-royalty-themed collectibles, the suitcases full of Dad's concert T-shirts that he bought at every show and never wore. What was the point in holding on to so much...stuff?

Calliope's home had given me hope that vampires were more sensible about such things, but I got the distinct impression that Harold was about to dash those hopes, and the thought of living with a hoarder was almost worse than the thought of living with—of being—a vampire. I sniffled and dabbed my eyes with the palms of my hands, and flecks of blood and mascara stained my skin when I took my hands away from my swollen face. It wasn't fair that being a vampire meant I couldn't blush but could still ugly cry. Everything was a nightmare.

I looked over at Harold, who hadn't moved since turning off the car. He sat quietly in the driver's seat, letting me finish processing my trauma or whatever. I appreciated that he hadn't tried to comfort me. I didn't want to be comforted. I wanted to go back in time to the night before and convince Becca that we were better off spending New Year's Eve at her place, binging medical dramas and dancing around to music we listened to in college.

"I'm sorry..." I whispered, my voice still hoarse from crying.

He turned to look at me, and his eyes were kind; the soft green-gray color reminded me of paintings of ocean waves. "What are you sorry for?" he asked, and I didn't have an answer. He reached over and pulled a handkerchief—the fabric kind—out of the glove compartment and handed it to me. There was a small drop of dried blood on one of the corners, but I ignored it and dabbed at my eyes. So much for waterproof mascara, after all.

"What someone did tae you...it isn't right," he continued. "It's not how things are done. The Community won't stand for it. But even so, even if they did, I'd still want to kill the sonofabitch who did this tae you. You didn't deserve...this. I guess crying is an all right response."

I liked how matter-of-fact he was, and I shrugged, almost smiling in spite of myself. But another thought occurred to me. "What if I just stayed outside all night long and waited for the sun to come up? That would probably take care of the problem, and I wouldn't have to worry about killing anyone." Once again, I remembered Calliope saying, "*keep her out of the sun,*" and the blackout shades on her windows, and I'd seen the movies.

I wasn't prepared for his reaction; his gurgled cry of "No!" was so much more forceful than I would have imagined coming from him, I flinched. He flexed his knuckles a few times, struggling to reign in his own emotions. "You don't want that, I promise." There was a crack in his voice. "Let me get you settled, and then...we'll talk."

NO SUN

HE HAD TO INVITE me into his house. That was a thing. The garage seemed to be a liminal space, with a kind of implied invitation, since he'd driven me into the garage in his car. But when we got out and approached the entrance to the mud room, I stopped, uncomfortably rooted in place, until he opened the door first and formally invited me inside. Some invisible weight on my shoulders lifted, like a lead X-ray blanket being pulled away, and I staggered forward in my stupid, impractical shoes, to cross the threshold.

The mud room led to the kitchen. I didn't want to take off my parka and feel naked and exposed in front of him again, the way I'd felt when he'd looked at me in my little black dress at Calliope's place, so I left it on and followed him through the rest of the house. All the appliances in the kitchen were decades old, basic beige, and aside from the usual sink, stove, and refrigerator in their normal places, there was nothing else to indicate that the kitchen was ever used for cooking. Every surface, from the countertops to the kitchen island to a small wooden table that had also been crammed into the space, was covered with automotive tools, and an entire car engine rested on top of the table.

"Run out of room in the garage?" I raised an eyebrow. There were several blood-stained, mismatched drinking glasses resting around the kitchen sink, and I gagged a little. Everything smelled like engine grease and dust and old, dried blood.

"A lot of the stuff in the garage came with the house," he admitted. "I've only been here about ten years. I'll get around tae clearing out the former owner's stuff eventually."

Only ten years. The mind boggles. "Did you kill them?" I tried to ask casually. He looked offended.

"Jesus, Grace—no, I didn't kill them. The Pendletons were a very nice elderly couple with grown grandchildren, and I made them a cash offer on the house with all the furnishings. I'm not a—"

He was going to say, "I'm not a monster," I'm pretty sure, but he'd also just admitted to killing hundreds of people not even an hour earlier. I appreciated that he stopped himself. I gave him a look of my own. We're all victims to the lies we tell ourselves, from time to time.

Harold sighed, and finished the house tour. He was definitely more than a crafts-man—judging from the variety of tools and supplies inside his home, he was a veritable jack of all trades. All the other rooms I saw were just as messy and cluttered as the kitchen was, but he wasn't technically a hoarder. It looked like he remembered to take the trash out every other month or so.

I tried not to roll my eyes at another small pile of bloodied glassware collected on a small table in the hallway. Harold's housekeeping skills were about on par with my dad's, once mom was gone. A flat-screen TV in the front room was coated with a layer of dust so thick, I wondered if he ever turned it on. The formal dining room on the main floor was completely taken over by woodworking tools. I recognized most of the newer electric drills and table saws from the summer Dad and his brothers built a tree fort in my backyard, but there were other hand tools organized on pegboards on the walls that I could only guess the function of. The faint smell of sawdust and solvents lingered in the air, though the floors were neatly swept. At least Harold was diligent about preventing fire hazards.

In a room that was probably designed to be a library, there were few books on the built-in shelves lining the walls, but in their place were a wide assortment of crafting tools and supplies. Leatherworking stamps, a soldering iron set up on a table underneath a light-up magnifying glass, even a decades-old Kenmore sewing machine in the corner beside a basket filled with dirty wool socks and yarn. *Did Harold actually spend the time darning his socks?*

I stifled a near-hysterical giggle at the thought of spending an immortal lifetime on such an antiquated, mundane task.

Upstairs, in a guest bedroom across the landing from his own quarters, we established where I was going to sleep during the day for the foreseeable future, and I was quietly relieved to see an ordinary full-sized canopy bed with thick draperies surrounding the mattress in the space I would be occupying. I'd been dreading the possibility of needing to sleep in a fucking coffin the entire time Harold led me from room to room. I'm not sure I could have handled the indignity, or the claustrophobia.

"Coffins aren't really a thing anymore." He shrugged, as if he could read the unspoken fear across my face. "Between the blackout curtains and the canopy, you should be fine, but be careful in the morning—this side of the house faces east."

I shuddered, remembering his outburst when I had threatened to stay outside til the sun rose.

"Garlic?" I asked. *Since we were talking about coffins...*

He shrugged. "It's got a smell. But a lot of things do. It won't kill you. It smells better than a rotting corpse. I think that's where the superstition came from, anyway."

Thank goodness for small blessings. However frayed and damaged my psyche was already, I'm not sure my Italian-American ass could have survived any world where garlic was a deadly weapon.

"You have guests often?" The bedroom seemed set up for a vampire, what with the canopy bed and blackout curtains, but I hadn't seen any evidence anyone else lived in the house with Harold, despite how large it was.

"Not often. Sometimes my friend Avie crashes here on her way through town. It's been a few years, though."

"Friend?" I raised my eyebrow, and he laughed a little.

"Avie plays the flats."

I gave him a blank look.

"She's just a friend. She's not interested in men. It works out for her. There are a lot more women than men in the Community."

"Aw, you have a lesbian bestie..."

"Sure." He thrust his hands into his pockets and leaned back against the door frame.

"Any Mrs. Laing…?" I hadn't noticed a wedding band, but what did I know about the way vampire relationships worked in the…Community. That was the word Harold and Calliope kept using, right?

"No."

"Girlfriends?"

"No, Grace."

"…boyfriends?"

"I live alone."

"Just us then, huh?" I sat down on the bed and ran my fingers over the homemade patchwork quilt, examining the craftsmanship, the colorful scraps of old clothing, and I wondered if Harold made it. *Too colorful.* Between his gray car and drab attire, I thought I was getting a feel for the type of person Harold Laing was. He wasn't showy, for one thing.

He shook his head vigorously, and took a full step out of the bedroom doorway. "You don't need tae worry about that. I promise. I'm not going tae touch you."

"No, I didn't mean to imply—" I cut myself off, horrified by the awkward turn the conversation had taken. He thought I was coming on to him. I wanted to dissolve into mist and never rematerialize. "I'm sorry I asked."

"Well. Um. There's something you should probably see, in the basement." He cleared his throat after a moment. "Shall we?"

On the one hand, heading down to the basement of a confessed serial killer seemed incredibly foolish. On the other hand, I was a vampire after all, and what was Harold going to do—kill me? We were both already dead. I reluctantly stood up to follow him.

He flipped on the lightbulb illuminating the pitch black stairwell into the basement as we descended, and I remembered Calliope's chiding warning about not making a habit of sitting alone in the dark. It seemed like the only thing Harold and Calliope had in common was an abundance of unnecessary lights in their homes. It was a waste of money and electricity if you asked me. Why go through all that trouble if you could see perfectly well in the darkness?

In the corner of the unfinished basement, where in any sensible house an assortment of off-season items ought to have been neatly stored in weatherproof plastic bins, Harold had built an honest-to-God blacksmith's forge. I'd seen one before at the Ohio Renaissance Faire with my parents; between the ages of eight and fourteen when I was really into feminist fantasy novels, we went every year. Before my sophomore year of high school, all I'd ever wanted was a sword of my very own, but Santa Claus had never come through on that particular wish. I probably could have convinced Dad to buy me one if Mom hadn't been so against it; I think she was disappointed I thought the jousting knights were more interesting than the royal court.

I was pretty sure that putting a smithy in your basement was against a number of building codes in the state of Illinois, and probably voided Harold's homeowner's insurance, too, but I held back my snark, too impressed by the smartly organized tools laid out on a low work table, the collection of swords and knives on display in various stages of completion. They tended toward utilitarian—Bowie knives and short swords and rapiers and others whose names I didn't know. None of the blades had a lot of ornamentation, but solid construction and clean lines, and whatever I was expecting to find in Harold's basement, this wasn't it. I reached out to touch a pair of matched long and short Roman swords and let out a low whistle.

"Did you make all of these yourself?" I asked, feeling like an idiot the moment the words were out of my mouth. Harold nodded.

"I was apprenticed tae a master blade smith in Spain before I was turned. Crazy old man, but...absolutely brilliant. Always lamenting that pistols were ruining the ancient arts. I come back around tae blacksmithing every few decades or so—it's good tae keep up the skills, I suppose." His eyes met mine across the table, and they were very green in the yellow light of the overhead bulbs. "That one's Roman," he confirmed. "It's not perfect, I'm still working on getting the proportions right, but it's hard tae get into museums when they're only open in the daytime. Calliope threw a charity event at the Field Museum a few years back when there was a traveling exhibit of Roman artifacts on display, but that was the only time I was able tae see one in person."

"That's...amazing." I didn't want him to know how impressed I was, but I didn't know what to say next. My tongue wet my lower lip expectantly, something almost like arousal coiling in my center. For the barest fraction of a split second, I was thrilled by the swords and knives in Harold's basement; I almost asked if he would teach me how to—for just a moment, I thought about how excited my dad would be to meet my new friend. *He would love all this.*

Then the reality of my situation came crashing back down around me, my excitement curdling into something darker, and nastier. Harold wasn't my friend. And my dad needed to stay as far away from me as possible because I might—I could possibly—*fuck.*

I reached out a hand to steady myself as my knees wobbled slightly. I was still wearing the same stupid stiletto heels I'd worn when I died, and I promised myself, the moment I got a chance to replace them with more practical footwear, I was never going to wear those shoes again. Or the damn dress I'd died in. Harold probably thought I looked like an idiot.

He pulled a larger broadsword off the wall and unsheathed it from a meticulously tooled leather scabbard, which he'd probably made himself, as well, given what I'd seen upstairs. The flash of the steel glinting under the cone of the overhead lightbulb caught my attention and distracted me from thoughts about my sartorial predicament.

"Sunlight is a very painful death for us. Please don't think about it, ever," he said, his solemn eyes following the lines of the blade the same way they'd traced the outline of my body earlier.

Not out of hunger, I thought, *but respect for something deadly.*

"We'll sort out what happened tae you, find your maker, and bring him tae justice. You can't abandon fledglings. It puts us all in danger. Just hang on until we can do that much, at least." He held the sword out to me, and I took it in my hands, feeling the heft of it, the scalpel edge of the steel. His voice remained low, and deathly serious. "If you still don't want this life, after we've taken care of your maker, I'll take your head off myself, and you won't feel a thing, I promise. No sun?"

"No sun," I breathed, and felt my stomach turn to ice, as cold as Harold's eyes. There was something desperate and damaged there, and I didn't want to know what it was.

Chapter Six

UNDEAD LIFE HACKS

Despite Calliope's warnings, I huddled in the shadows of my temporary bedroom for a long time after that, my head swimming with dark thoughts, until the slow, inevitable rise of the sun below the eastern horizon heralded an end to my first night among the undead. I prayed that there would not be many more to follow, but I wasn't certain God was answering my prayers just then.

What was the correct saint to ask for intercession when one finds themselves transformed into a monster through no fault of their own...?

But I wasn't sure I could lay claim to blamelessness, technically speaking. I'd gotten dressed up and drunk and walked right into a vampire party on my own two feet, hadn't I? I'd never been exactly innocent.

I imagined placing my head down on a block, my hair falling over my face in a dark curtain that teased the promise of imminent oblivion, the back of my neck vulnerable and exposed. I closed my eyes, and the details in my mind's eye became more vivid; the metallic vibration of the sword being unsheathed, the briefest kiss of pain at the momentary sharp blow, and then—

Nothing, I hoped. Surely God wouldn't send me to hell if I'd already lived it on earth. Whatever relief I'd felt after Harold showed me the swords in his basement forge and promised to eventually behead me was short-lived. Heaven was beyond my reach, and purgatory didn't seem very accessible, either. But if I could avoid killing or hurting anyone as long as I remained a vampire; if I could somehow find a way to stop the one who had done this to me from hurting anyone else ever again, wouldn't that be enough to earn my soul's complete destruction? No bliss of paradise, but no torment of damnation, either?

Redemptive suffering had always seemed like cruelty to me before. Mrs. Jacobsen had counseled me to pray the rosary about it. But now I thought I understood the kindness behind the cruelty. Perhaps I had been chosen for this, that in existing for a while as a vampire I could prevent the suffering of others, and thereby invoke a measure of divine grace.

And surely, a just and merciful God would not...*could not...*

I shuddered, wiping away more useless tears. There weren't enough tears in the world to undo what had been done to me.

As the moment of sunrise grew closer, revulsion and dread drowned out my morbid imagination. I could *feel* the ball of fire rising, higher and higher, approaching the horizon. Soon the light would start to creep across the yard, sunshine like yellow acid crawling up the walls of the house toward my bedroom. The realization pitted my stomach, and sent shudders down my spine. I knew the shades over the windows were secured to the walls with staples, knew that there would be no daylight leaking into this room. Nevertheless, I spent the entire day with my head and all my limbs completely tucked in under the thick homemade quilt on a bed that wasn't mine, opaque brocade canopy curtains pulled close. I didn't need them for warmth but I was terrified, for the first time in my life, of letting even a diffused ray of light brush against my unprotected skin.

No sleep of the dead descended upon me at sunrise, however much I would have welcomed it. In the books that Becca read back in college, vampires fell into automatic slumber when the sun came up, practically corpses. Not me. I didn't sleep well. I tossed and turned until nearly noon, and woke up again at sundown, a little after 4:30.

I'd been so out of sorts the first night, it hadn't occurred to me that I could go back to my apartment to get clean clothes and other belongings, but when I woke up in my cocktail dress for the second night in a row, acquiring a change of attire became a matter of priority...right after getting more blood.

"Sleep well?" He was already in the kitchen when I staggered downstairs, still teetering in my stiletto shoes—there was no way in hell I was going to walk barefoot through Harold's house.

I stared at the space between his furrowed brows until he looked down. If I didn't know better, I'd have thought he was embarrassed.

"I need to go back to my apartment and get my stuff." The words croaked out of my mouth. Blood. I needed more, so much...more. It was hard to think about anything else. I felt my fangs pressed against my lips, filling my mouth, a dull ache radiating down my neck. *Blood, blood, blood...*

And clean clothes.

"You're probably better dropping off the face of the earth, honestly..." he pressed a cup into my shaking hands. It took the edge off.

"No." I shook my head. That didn't feel right. 'Responsible' wasn't the word, but I struggled to find a better one. Besides, what was I going to wear before I acquired new clothes, if I didn't go back to my apartment first? The thought of borrowing a pair of antique wool trousers and a sweater from Harold wasn't appealing. Becca was the only person I felt comfortable sharing clothes with, and that was because—well, it was Becca. We wore the same size, so I never had to worry about anything fitting in a weird or distracting way. "I need to get my own stuff from my own apartment, I need to charge my phone, and I need to tell people that I'm...I dunno. That they shouldn't worry about me."

"Worry about yourself right now."

I glared at him.

❖

When I threatened to walk out of the house in the cold to call a cab from the first gas station I could find, and he realized I was serious, Harold agreed to drive me to my old apartment. "Remember what happened with the cleaning crew last night," he told me. What made me think that I was going to be able to handle an entire cab ride to a different part of the city without losing control and eating the driver?

I had to admit that he had a point, but I didn't like the strategy he insisted on employing for our trek back into my apartment building, either. "I'm not sticking cotton balls up my nose." I glared at him and tried not to retch.

"Do you want tae go back for your stuff or not?" He crossed his arms over his chest, implacable, and I finally had to close my eyes and acquiesce. I could even admit that his trick sounded clever. Gross, but clever.

I made one last attempt to reason with him. "Harold, I'm just going to grab my stuff. There's no need to—"

"And what if you run into a neighbor? Do you want a repeat of what happened last night?" Harold sighed and raised an eyebrow at me, then opened a small, dark bottle filled with pungent-smelling liquid. As soon as he cracked the seal, the stench of a candy cane factory overwhelmed the small enclosed interior of his BMW, and I gagged. Harold saturated two small pieces of cotton ball with the peppermint extract and shoved one up each nostril, then handed the supplies over to me to do the same.

I looked at the stinking bottle—something that had been a kitchen staple around the holidays growing up, but which was as noxious to me now as the idea of drinking blood would have been to me then—and the puffs of cotton in my hands, then over the vampire sitting next to me, and then out the car window at the looming brick structure of my apartment complex, and remembered how I had lunged, uncontrollably, at the workers who had come to clean up the aftermath of Calliope's party—the growl that had come up from my chest when I smelled the blood inside their veins had been completely inhuman, and terrifying. I sighed a Harold-worthy sigh and did as I was told.

The peppermint-extract-on-cotton-balls trick was effective, even if I resented its necessity. It might have been a bit more irritating if I had still needed to breathe, but since my lungs and my heart only seemed to work intermittently now and entirely on their own schedules—an intake of breath here or there to speak, a thump or two of my heart if I felt something particularly emotionally stirring—it wasn't exactly a burden.

But the second Harold and I passed the main entrance into the lobby, three neighbors I only halfway recognized came tumbling out of the elevator, already drunk and on their way out into the cold Friday night to party some more, and I was very glad for Harold's vampire life hack.

"Do you even need this yourself, or are you just playing along for my sake?" I asked in the elevator, pointing at his nose.

"Not always. If I'm hungry."

"You're not hungry now, though, are you?"

"Nope. Are you?"

I shook my head. Harold had also insisted I drink quite a bit of blood before we went out. I'd tried to warm the bag of blood he'd given me up under the hot tap water, since Harold didn't have an electric kettle like Calliope did, but I noticed that Harold took his blood cold, right out of the fridge, and I asked him why.

"Human blood is hot," he said. "If I get used tae drinking it chilled, or even stale, then I won't be as likely tae see people as food every time I step foot outside the house."

I turned off the hot water tap. Cold blood wasn't that bad, I decided.

I continued shaking all over as the elevator climbed toward my apartment on the fifth floor. No, I wasn't hungry. I wasn't entirely sure what I was feeling, but I was confident, at least, that I wasn't hungry.

We stepped out into the hallway from the elevator and took a left toward my apartment, just down the corridor. Mercifully, the coast was clear—no neighbors bustling about in the narrow, enclosed hall. But the moment I put my keys in my apartment door, it swung open, already unlocked. The inside of the apartment was dark and cold and chill—the lights were off, as well as the heater, exactly as I'd left them, but I knew that I'd secured my door before leaving the last time.

Harold and I exchanged nervous glances.

"Did you leave your door unlocked when you left?" he asked, hopefully.

"No," I whispered in return, uncertain why I was whispering. "I would never do that."

Harold cleared his throat uncomfortably and shifted his weight. "Well, I'd offer tae go on in ahead of you and make sure it's safe, but you have tae invite me in first."

"Fine. I invite you in."

"You've got tae be inside the apartment for the invitation tae be valid. I'm sorry, that's just how it works." To his credit, he looked ready to fight, his whole body tensed, and his hands already balled up into fists.

I slipped inside the apartment and gestured for Harold to come in after me. "Quickly. I invite you. Someone's been in here. I can feel it. I don't know how I know, but I do."

Harold wasted no time following inside and shut the door behind him with a touch so light, I barely heard the latch click. "Let me just scoot…" He stepped around and in front of me without touching, even in the cramped entrance by the door, before efficiently scanning the one-bedroom floor plan. I said a silent prayer of thanks that I'd picked my dirty underwear up off the bathroom tiles before I'd left to go to Becca's place on New Year's Eve.

But everything was immaculate and empty, just as I had left it. Except for the note, written in lipstick, in big, bold letters across the TV screen:

GRACE. CALL ME. THIS ISN'T FUNNY. BECCA.

"That was my Chanel…" I mourned, examining the stump of what was left of my once-favorite lipstick. It had been an expensive indulgence that resulted in a few days of eating ramen, but I'd thought it was worth it at the time. "Becca must be pissed."

"Are you certain your friend is the only person who has been in your apartment?" Harold asked, still on alert. I looked around my apartment and *felt* for something, a sense that anyone else might have been poking around, then pulled the peppermint-saturated cotton out of my nostrils and inhaled deeply a few times. The first inhale, I could only smell peppermint, but after that, everything smelled fine, normal, like home. My scented candles, my houseplants, the smell of my favorite cleaning supplies, and on top of that, the faint whiff of Becca's signature Tom Ford perfume.

"No one has been in here since Becca. I'm certain," I insisted, and we exhaled at the same time. "Look," I continued. "I'm going to take a shower and clean myself off—I've still got what's left of New Year's Eve's mascara on, and it's really starting to bug me. I'll be quick, I promise but, uh, make yourself at home. I'm sorry I don't have anything in the fridge you'd like, but help yourself to the TV, let me just—" I grabbed a nearby bottle of cleaning solution and a microfiber rag to erase the evidence of Becca's lipstick vandalism.

"I can wait." Harold sat down on my sofa with stiff formality that made me think, for an awful moment, of all those nineteenth century photographs of dead people, dressed up to appear as though they were still alive. It was creepy and inhuman. He nodded at me, but that only served to make his posture even more jarring. Corpses weren't supposed to nod their heads.

"Okay, well, um, just shout if you need anything, I guess…" I stood awkwardly in the front room for what would have been half a heartbeat before running into the sanctuary of my bedroom and, without thinking about it, locking the bedroom door behind me. I stripped off my dress and tights and stepped into the scalding hot water of the shower, scrubbing away the dirt and grime of New Year's Eve, along with whatever was left of my humanity.

Under the steam of the hot water, I felt warm again, and could almost convince myself that I wasn't…

Dead.

But I was one of two corpses in the apartment, after all, so I turned off the water and stood dripping in the unheated bathroom. The steam turned to frost on the bathroom mirror, obscuring my reflection, but I didn't feel cold. Eventually, the heat rising off my skin began to dissipate as well, the borrowed warmth only a memory.

It didn't take long to pull my suitcase out from underneath the bed and pack up my winter clothes and shoes, my laptop, phone charger, and other essentials. My bedroom was neat and organized, as tidy as the rest of my apartment, with everything in its comforting, familiar place.

I reached into my jewelry box, and slipped Mom's Cartier tank watch around my wrist—the one Mom had wanted for as long as I could remember, because the late Princess Diana had owned a Cartier wristwatch. The secondhand model Dad scored at an estate sale just before their fifteenth wedding anniversary became Mom's most treasured possession; I'd wanted to bury her with it. Dad had insisted that I hold on to it, instead. I usually kept the watch locked up safe in my jewelry box, but it felt right to wear it now.

I was very careful not to touch the cloisonné rosary Mrs. Jacobsen gave me when Mom died, or the St. Joan of Arc medal Nana gave me at my Confirmation, both of which also lived in the jewelry box. I didn't *think* either religious symbol would burn me if they brushed up against my skin, but I didn't want to touch them, either, and I shuddered, brief nausea rising up inside me again. I placed my hand on the cool glass top of my thrift store dresser and waited for the churning sensation to pass. My stomach stopped sloshing, but the self-loathing lingered.

I never imagined being damned would feel like this.

Once I felt marginally better, I stepped into a comfy pair of dark-rinse denim skinny jeans, a thick cashmere turtleneck, and (finally) a pair of sensible low-heeled booties in place of the high heels I'd been wearing since before I died. I *almost* kicked the damn heels under the bed and left them there out of spite, but, being a creature of habit, I set them back on the shoe rack in my closet with a sharp final glare. Those shoes were definitely not leaving the apartment with me.

I blow-dried my hair most of the way and then, examining my face in the mirror at last, tried to find any semblance of the person I once had been. My face was pale and bloodless, but whatever else becoming a vampire had done to me, it had worked wonders for my complexion. My skin was perfectly smooth, without a blemish, or acne scar, or broken capillary to be seen. Even my eyelashes and eyebrows appeared to be darker, fuller, and more lush.

Maybe there were benefits, but I still didn't like the off-putting *otherness* of the creature staring back at me from the other side of the glass, so I turned away and finished my preparations to leave—perhaps for good. Rent for January was already paid, and I had a small amount in savings that could cover February's rent, but hopefully, I wouldn't have a head attached to my body anymore by March, fingers crossed.

I grabbed my favorite scarf and gloves on the way out, pulling my suitcase behind me as I left the bedroom and rejoined Harold.

"Anything exciting happen?" I asked, half-sarcastic. Harold was sitting exactly as he had been when I left him, the TV still black, but the accent lamp beside the sofa was on, as well as the kitchen light. I felt a little bit ashamed for having locked the bedroom door behind me. I wasn't sure what I'd expected him to do—certainly not attempt to join me in the shower. I was surprised to find myself thinking about that even now. That seemed decidedly un-Harold-like behavior.

"Your kitchen sink was dripping," he informed me.

"Yeah, the superintendent was supposed to fix that after the holidays."

"I took care of it."

"Oh. Thank you." I wasn't sure what else to say. I was fairly certain I wouldn't be coming back to this apartment.

We found my car where I'd parked it on the street, iced over and buried under six inches of snow, and Harold helped me shovel it out of the nasty brown winter crud that entombed it. I noticed that my fingertips didn't get numb as we worked in tandem with the ice scrapers, and found myself counting another blessing of my new condition, in spite of myself. I finally got the car door open and started warming up the engine when the fuel gauge caught my attention.

"I'm going to have to stop for gas," I pointed at the needle. The tank was well under a quarter full—shame on me for not following my own advice.

"You still have the peppermint?"

I rolled my eyes and raised my chin at him, so he could see up my nose. I'd re-inserted the cotton buds after the shower, worried we might run into more neighbors as we exited the apartment building. We hadn't, but if I was going to be stopping for gas on the way back to Harold's place, there was no sense in digging them out again. Better safe than sorry about a bloodbath at the Shell station.

"Here." Harold reached into his pants pocket and pulled out the envelope Calliope had handed him back in the foyer the night before. "Use what you need, and we'll figure out the rest later." Inside the envelope was several thousand dollars, cash, in mixed bills—mostly twenties and hundreds—and an American Express Platinum Business card with the name of an LLC I didn't recognize. I let out a low whistle.

"Does she just keep these things stashed in a drawer somewhere?" I asked. Harold looked thoughtful for a moment, then nodded.

"Probably so."

I wondered what it must be like to have that much money. Harold's house was nice enough—it probably cost about a million dollars, given the neighborhood, and he'd said he'd made a cash offer on it a decade ago (*though you wouldn't be able to tell it was a million-dollar house from the inside)* but Calliope was on a whole other level. I wondered if all vampires were loaded one way or another.

"Drive straight back," Harold instructed, double-checking that I had the correct address programmed into my GPS. "And call me if you get lost." My phone was finally charging in the cup holder next to the driver's seat and began to go wild with notifications.

Back in my own car, wearing comfortable clothes again, listening to a favorite playlist of familiar comfort songs, I started to unwind, tension and anxiety dissipating into their normal background radiation levels, and I almost felt normal again, for the first time in two nights. If it wasn't for the fact that I couldn't feel my heart beating, or that I hadn't had to turn the car's heater on very high, beyond defrosting the windows, or that I had bits of cotton saturated with peppermint extract up my nose to keep me from getting violent whenever I might smell people, well...if it hadn't been for any of those things, I could almost pretend that everything that had happened since New Year's Eve was all a bad dream.

But this was no bad dream. I ran my tongue against my gum line and pressed against the sore spots where my fangs appeared every time I...*fed* (and I winced, thinking the word). I definitely was a vampire. There was no getting over that. I'd felt the...magic, or whatever it was, when I'd invited Harold into my apartment, just as I'd felt the lifting of the invisible barrier that allowed me to enter his home. And I had *felt* Becca's presence in my apartment, too, before I'd even smelled her. To be fair, maybe I would have been able to smell a recent visit from Becca inside my apartment anyway, because the perfume that Becca wore was seriously strong—but everything else was undeniable.

I'd died, and I'd come back, somehow, as this...thing, that was only supposed to exist in movies. My body knew the truth that my mind was still desperately trying to claw its way out. The cognitive dissonance was enough to drive anyone mad. I wondered what happened to other fledglings like me, the mistakes, abandoned newborn vampires who didn't get discovered by...ethical monsters, like Harold and Calliope. I vaguely remembered weird stories that occasionally broke the news about people who suddenly went on violent killing sprees before being taken down by the cops in a hail of bullets, and you always heard the newscasters say that drugs were to blame. I wondered how many of those people had been just like me, confused and disoriented and lost to some inhuman nature they didn't know how to control?

A tear trickled out of the corner of my eye, and I sniffled, delivering a full-on assault of peppermint as I tried to inhale through my nose, which made my eyes water even more, and I swerved slightly on the expressway, nearly sideswiping another car, whose driver laid on the horn and sped away from my Accord quickly. Without fully meaning to, I screamed at the other driver at the top of my lungs, animalistic and unhinged, and felt...better.

I pulled over at the next exit to get gas. The filling station was across the street from a large shopping center, flanked by a number of high-end department stores, and I got an idea that was only slightly inspired by the envelope full of Calliope's cash burning a hole in my pocket. It wasn't even 8:30 on a Friday night, and the shopping center was almost certainly still keeping holiday hours...I pulled my Honda out of the gas station and into the parking lot across the street, taking in a few sniffs through my nose to test the peppermint oil.

Yup, still gag-inducing.

Well, I thought, *this is either going to go over well, or I'm going to end up another weird story on the nightly news.* Inside my chest, my mostly still heart fluttered once or twice for good measure. If you had pointed out to me that I'd already started to think of the possibility that I might slaughter Friday night shoppers as little more than "weird," I would have been horrified, but at the moment, all I was thinking about was the possibility of getting clean sheets and a new duvet for my bed at Harold's house. I didn't need the ostentatious luxury of Calliope's penthouse, but I also wanted *some* creature comforts.

Fortunately, the mall wasn't terribly crowded for a Friday night. Maybe it was the weather. It was easy to give people a wide berth, and, for the most part, they seemed to avoid me, as well. Which was good. I didn't want to look anyone in the eyes and have to deal with unbidden thoughts about what they might taste like. My phone buzzed with a number I didn't recognize as I entered the central atrium, and I ignored the call, remembering Calliope and Harold's warnings about not reaching out to people until there was a plan.

I tried to imagine how the conversation with my dad would go:

"*Oh, hi, Dad. Sorry to interrupt your vacation with your new girlfriend. I just wanted to let you know not to worry about me, I'm fine, but apparently I'm a vampire now, so I won't be coming home for any more holidays, and it's probably a good idea if we never see each other again, but I still love you, okay, bye!*"

...honestly, Dad had been so distracted by his recent girlfriend (the third since Mom) I doubted he would really process anything I said. He'd just say something like, "Sounds fun, kiddo, be safe, don't do anything too stupid out there in the big city!"

Becca was going to be an entirely different matter, but that was something I would consider later, once I'd gotten my stuff back to Harold's house and fully charged my phone. I'd actually been shocked to discover that Harold used a cell phone at all, being two hundred years old and everything—but of course, he was an Android user and kept no charging cords for my iPhone at his house. Why couldn't phone companies be sensible and all use the same chargers?

It didn't take long inside the shops to find what I was looking for. Bedding was on post-holiday clearance, and I splurged a bit on nicer quality items than I might otherwise have chosen for myself, especially since it was Calliope's money. If she hadn't been worried about me replacing her expensive towels, she almost certainly wouldn't begrudge me brushed flannel sheets and a nice down comforter. I also grabbed a few scented candles to take away the musty smell in my temporary room. Before I left the housewares department, my eyes wandered over to a display of "Gifts for Him," and I had another thought.

Hip flasks were popular gifts around the holidays, weren't they? And there were always more than a few left over after the Christmas rush. A substantial polished pewter flask, with a good stainless steel interior lining, and smooth, clean lines that were at once modern and timeless, seemed perfect. I held the flask in my hands and decided it had good heft, too—it wasn't flimsy and mass-produced like some of the other flasks I had seen before. It felt *right*, I decided, satisfied with my purchase. I had it gift-wrapped and, on my way out, decided to pick up a decadently large-sized bottle of Becca's favorite perfume from the fragrance counter as well—it came with a free gift tote that was actually quite nice.

It was probably going to take a lot more than a $300 bottle of perfume and a faux crocodile leather tote bag to smooth things over with Becca, but at least I felt like I had some leverage now. I eyed the Chanel makeup display across the way from the fragrance counter but decided against replacing my ruined lipstick just yet. I'd let Becca replace that one. Fair was fair.

All in all, I figured, I probably spent less than an hour inside the mall. I was only shaking a little bit when I got back to the car. I hadn't lunged at any shoppers. I hadn't caused a bloodbath. But...I'd had thoughts about it. A tightly wound knot in my stomach told me it would be a good idea to avoid other people as much as possible for the time being. When I checked my phone again, I had three more missed calls from the unknown number but no new voicemails or texts, so I ignored the notifications and continued onward to Harold's house

⬤

CHAPTER SEVEN

NOT ALL GOOD DAYS ARE GOOD FOR EVERYONE

HAROLD LIVED IN WINNETKA, on a narrow, winding avenue set aglow with an abundance of old-fashioned street lamps. Many of the traditional-style homes in the neighborhood still had their holiday lights up, and even though I told myself not to do it, I found my eyes wandering to the windows where Christmas trees remained visible on full display. I didn't recall seeing any Christmas tree set up at Harold's house, and I wondered if he'd had a bad holiday, too—or if Christmas and other celebrations were something vampires didn't do.

It was hard to keep from feeling self conscious as I navigated the quiet, tree-lined streets. Winnetka was an affluent part of town. It wasn't far from Rogers Park, where Becca and I had gone to school, but aside from our annual visit to the Botanic Garden's holiday light display in nearby Glencoe, I hadn't been out to this part of the North Shore much in recent years, except to occasionally rescue Becca from Tinder dates gone sour.

As I passed driveway after driveway sporting shiny new Lexuses and Cadillac SUVs, my sense of discomfort grew. I was as outclassed in Harold's neck of the woods as I had been in Calliope's, and my Honda, no matter how well I struggled to maintain it, was out of place. My extended family might, on the whole, be upper-middle-class, but my mom had been a real estate agent, and Dad was a commercial HVAC repair technician. The only reason I didn't have student loan debt was because of Mom's life insurance money.

Harold's house, a sizable colonial-revival building with stone a facade and symmetrical wings on either side of a center hall, was one of the last homes on his street, set away from the neighbors by snow-covered lawns and a low brick retaining wall.

An elegant assortment of trees surrounded the house—a tall leafless ash and a pair of equally bare dogwoods flanked the center walkway, and I knew they would be beautiful in the springtime, on soft bright mornings I would never see. A few dense, well-kept holly shrubs with dark waxy leaves poked out of the snow underneath the downstairs windows, and around the back a low line of cypress shrubs defined the property line.

Gas lamps with flickering blue flames provided a warm glow to the exterior gray stone, reflecting off the snow like something out of a calendar painting, and the house looked perfectly ordinary from the outside, almost inviting, even.

But I thought the neighbors would probably wrinkle up their noses if they saw how cluttered and unkept the interior was. I wondered if the village had any provisions in its charter or bylaws preventing vampires from residing in the neighborhood, and decided to pester Harold about it.

I found him pacing outside by the garage when I pulled up; the number of footprints in the snow indicated he had been pacing for some time. He had his phone pressed to his ear as my car approached the driveway, and my own phone buzzed with the unrecognized number again.

I groaned. Of course his number was unrecognized. My phone had been dead when I gave him my number, and once my phone was charging, I'd been too distracted by my need to put gas in my car to remember I hadn't added him to my contacts.

"Hi. I'm back," I answered the call on the second ring, making eye contact with him through the windshield. "I'm fine, I—"

"Get in the garage," he snapped, disconnecting. I pulled in next to his car in a spot cleared to accommodate a second vehicle.

He didn't even wait for me to get all the way out of my car before he started shouting. "Ya promised tae come right home! Where were ya?"

I faltered a step back into the front seat, and Harold pressed his fingertips to his temples, as if willing himself to calm down.

He took a deep, almost shaky breath, paused, and continued, much more measured, "Why didn't you answer your phone? I thought you were charging it?"

"I didn't know it was you!" I confessed. "I didn't get your number before we left the apartment, your calls came up as unrecognized. And I didn't want to answer any unrecognized numbers because of what you and Calliope said about keeping a low profile—why didn't you leave a text or voicemail?"

He seemed somewhat appeased, nodding as he accepted my answer, but his tone was still harsh when he replied, "I don't leave texts or voicemails. Ever." His greenish eyes flashed with barely controlled emotions I couldn't decipher before I looked away. "In the future, make sure your phone recognizes my calls, and next time, answer it. What took you so long? I thought you just needed tae get gas. I was—" he paused again, as though he were trying an assortment of different words on for size, before settling on, "I was worried."

He sounded very sincere.

"I stopped at the mall," I admitted. "There was one right across the street from the gas station, and I needed to pick up a few things." It didn't seem to be the right moment to tell him one of the items I picked up had been for him, a kind of "thank you" gift, so I stopped there.

"Grace...you canna—" he looked like I would have given him an aneurism, if it had been possible.

I shook off his concern, maybe more for my sake than his. "I was fine, I promise," I lied. I had not been 'fine,' exactly...but he didn't need to know every thought I had. "I kept my nose stopped up with peppermint, and I just got what I needed. I was fine. No one died, and I didn't lose control. I'm good. You don't need to worry."

"It's not just you I'm worried about, you know." He helped me with my suitcase and brought it into the house for me while I wrangled the shopping bags. I didn't need to be invited into the house a second time.

"It's you, and it's anyone you might hurt, of course, but there's also the Community I'm concerned about, and Calliope, and me, frankly." He continued his lecture as we struggled our way past the clutter in the kitchen. "We all have ta work together if we're going tae live among mortals and stay under wraps. What you did endangers all of us, and if anything had happened, Cal and I would both be on the line. The Community could hold us accountable for your lack of control until we track down your maker. We've assumed that responsibility. I've assumed that responsibility. For you. Please don't run off on your own." He stopped, seeing the guilty expression on my face.

"I'm sorry," I whispered, genuinely meaning it.

The mattress on the bed in my room yielded a puff of dust as my suitcase settled into the ancient coils when Harold set it down, and he wrinkled his nose. "I suppose you're going to need new furniture in here, too. Were you comfortable last night, at least?"

"It was a lot more comfortable than the bathtub...?" My response felt unconvincing. I was looking forward to washing the new sheets and making up the bed with fresh linens in a few hours, but I had no long-term plans for the space, and didn't want to make any. He'd said I would only be staying with him for a few nights...right? "Honestly, it's fine. I don't know how long I'll be here, and I don't want you to go through the trouble. You already did so much last night."

After promising to eventually behead me the night before, Harold cleared out at least a decade's worth of clutter from the bedroom across the hall from his, relocating the boxes and piles of items to other piles in other rooms throughout the house. I'd counted no fewer than three vacuum cleaners, and a strange assortment of half-disassembled small electronic devices. What a centuries-old vampire needed with a toaster oven or a blender was beyond me, but he'd been tinkering with them at some point. Finding out vampires were real had been weird enough, but Harold made everything somehow weirder, with his sock-darning, blender-deconstructing, sword-smithing ways. Bela Lugosi would never.

At least the bedroom was cleaner now.

Once he set down the last of my stuff, Harold retreated just outside the bedroom doorway and stood there. I knew it wasn't an invitation thing, because I hadn't felt it. He was just giving me space. He got points for giving me space. I told him I really did need to call work, and my dad, and Becca, at least, or else Becca was going to find a way to get the National Guard looking for me. "I'll tell them I'm sick with the flu or something until we figure out the rest of the story."

Harold made a gesture that wasn't quite a shrug, and threw up his hands to convey, "Do what you think is right, but please don't fuck things up," and left me alone.

I took in a deep breath I didn't need, and looked down at my phone. It was still lit up with a flurry of missed calls and messages, mostly from Becca, but at least one call was from work. Most of my coworkers had opted for a four-day weekend, since New Year's Day had been on a Thursday, but I'd volunteered to come into the office on Friday to finish up the grant proposal, and HR wanted to know where I was, and if everything was okay. I called the after-hours Human Resources line first, and left a voicemail, claiming a once-in-a-lifetime opportunity for travel had come up over the holiday, and I'd decided to leave immediately. I regretted not putting in my two-week notice, but hoped they could find a suitable candidate to replace me shortly.

With so many people looking for work right now, I thought, *my successor should thank me.* The paperwork was almost finished, anyway. They'd be able to find someone to send it off in time, as long as engineering provided the updated data I'd requested on New Year's Eve.

Dad was on a date with his newest girlfriend when I returned his call, and was thoroughly distracted. I could hear a woman's voice in the background, over the din of what sounded like a busy restaurant, and I assumed that was Crystal, or whatever this one's name was. They'd just gotten back from their holiday trip to Cancun, so I don't know what they needed another date night for. Anyway, Dad seemed relieved that Becca's dire calls to him proved to be over-exaggerated.

"I know she's your best friend, honey, but she can be a little dramatic, don't you think? Anyway, feel better. The flu sucks! Next year, get your shot, kiddo. You young kids aren't immortal, after all!"

(Thanks, dad)

I hung up before the woman's voice could finish calling out "Get well soon!"

I texted Becca before I called.

Grace: hey. I just got your messages. I've got the flu. I thought I was hungover at first, but it turns out I'm pretty sick. Sorry I didn't call sooner. Hope you had a good new year? :)

The smiley-face emoji was somewhat out of character, and I cringed the moment I hit "send." Sure enough, within seconds, my phone rang.

"Who are you, and what have you done to Grace?" Becca sounded like she'd been rehearsing that line.

"Honestly, Becca; It's me. It's Grace. I'm fine. I mean, I'm not fine, I've definitely caught the flu, I'm sick, but I'm fine, I'm absolutely not dead, everything's okay." I coughed a little, but knowing Becca, I was unconvincing. It was just good to hear her voice and know that she was safe.

Becca was thoroughly unconvinced. "You haven't answered your phone for two days. I've been worried to death. I tried to go to the cops, Grace, but they laughed at me."

"Wait, what—you tried to go to the police? Why?" I envisioned a SWAT team storming into Calliope's penthouse, guns pointing everywhere as they looked for me, and cringed. I thought I'd only been joking when I said Becca was going to send in the troops.

"Because you disappeared after midnight, and I couldn't find you, and I wasn't sure if you'd run off with some guy or something." Becca began, and I braced myself for the flurry I knew was coming. "And then everyone was getting kicked out of the apartment, and I kept saying, 'I can't find my friend, she came up here with me, but I can't find her,' so then some woman I didn't know said you must have taken a cab home, and no one could remember seeing you, and then I took a cab over to your apartment yesterday—do you know how expensive that was? But the L was running on a holiday schedule. And I had to take a cab back because you weren't at you apartment. You haven't even been home, because the black dress you wore to the party wasn't hanging up in your bathroom where you always hang your clothes that need to be dry cleaned, and I know you didn't take your clothes to the dry-cleaners because they were closed yesterday because it was New Year's Day, so where the hell are you, *anyway*?"

I had underestimated how many crime dramas Becca binged. "Well, now your fingerprints are all over my apartment, so you'll be the number one suspect in my disappearance," I reminded her, but the intended joke fell flat.

"Seriously, Grace, where the fuck are you?" Becca's tone turned exasperated.

"I told you, I'm sick. I'm staying with…a friend. A new friend, I don't think you've met them, anyway. They're taking care of me while I get better because I didn't want to get you sick, too." *Trust me, Becca, you don't want what I've got.*

Becca was silent on the other end of the line, but in my mind's eye I could easily picture the expressions passing over Becca's face, the fear and concern transforming into anger before she even spoke again.

"You know what, Grace? Whatever. If you want to ditch me at a party and run off with some hot guy we just met, who am I to judge? But don't fucking lie to me, okay? I know something's up. I'm just sorry I embarrassed myself trying to be a good friend and look for you. Apparently, the police were right to laugh, so that's on me. Call me when you're 'feeling better,' or whatever, okay? Thanks for letting me know you're alive." Becca hung up before I could say anything else, and once again, I felt like I'd been punched.

Downstairs, I found Harold in the kitchen, working on the engine block again, and covered up to the elbows with grease. He'd changed out of his usual wool pants and pullover sweater into a well-worn pair of Levis and a stained black T-shirt, showing off surprisingly well-developed arm muscles, and I raised my eyebrows without meaning to. Clearly, his story about blacksmithing in Spain had truth to it.

"Is this what you do all night, normally?" I crossed my arms and leaned back against the kitchen sink. The blood-stained glassware that had been there the night before clinked behind me, so I turned around, located the dish soap, and started washing the dishes—not for Harold's sake, but for mine. I was going to go crazy with those dishes piling up. Besides, the blood would attract flies, wouldn't it?

"*Better tae wear oot as roost oot,*" he responded, without looking up right away.

"I'm sorry?" I rubbed my ear and tried to reconstruct the incomprehensible sounds into a cohesive sentence. Maybe my vampire hearing was going haywire.

Harold briefly glanced up at me, registered my confusion, and shrugged. "It's good tae have something to occupy your time," he clarified, enunciating much more carefully. "Otherwise, you get very…ope—" he dropped a ratchet, and bent down under the table to retrieve it, hitting his head on the way back up and swearing briefly in a language I didn't recognize "—bored."

"So much for vampires being creatures of preternatural grace and beauty." I scoffed, setting the cups on an ancient drying rack and wiping down the sink.

"What, you don't think I'm beautiful?" Harold joked, running his greasy hand through his hair and flashing me what might have been a charming smile without the fangs. My stomach lurched, and I froze on the spot, horrified at the cavalier display of his monstrosity, and he quickly self-corrected. "That wasn't necessary," he apologized. "You've got enough going on without thinking I'm hitting on you."

"Well, thanks for letting me know you don't think I'm worth hitting on."

"That's not what I said, Grace..."

"Hey, no, it's fine. I see how it is. You're two hundred and fifty, I'm twenty-four, the age gap is really inappropriate—"

"I'm not two hundred and fifty!" Harold had to pause to do some math. "I'm...two hundred and twenty this year."

I rolled my eyes. "My apologies. I know you senior citizens get sensitive about your age."

Harold stopped what he was working on and gave me his full attention. "Do you need something? Do you have questions? Are you thirsty? Do you need tae...talk?" He wiped down his palms on the legs of his Levis and looked uneasy.

"I called my dad," I told him. "He was out with his new girlfriend. He didn't seem too worried about me. I guess Becca called and told him I was missing or something, but I just said I had the flu and I'd call him later in the week."

Harold seemed satisfied by that outcome.

"He also wanted me to remember that I'm not immortal, and I needed to get my flu shot next year...!" I snapped my fingers in an "aw, shucks," gesture.

"Flu shot..." it took him a moment to register what I meant. "Do you really have tae get vaccinated for influenza every year?"

"Yeah, I mean, you're supposed to...I guess the disease changes every year. It's not like chicken pox or something...didn't you ever get any vaccines?" I tried to remember the history of vaccination from my health sciences module at school but drew a blank.

"Smallpox," Harold answered without missing a beat. "I still have the scar. See?" He rolled up his T-shirt sleeve to reveal a small round indentation on the pale skin of his very muscular shoulder that even the changes of his turning couldn't completely erase. He seemed proud of it.

I was impressed. "I never got that one. I think they eradicated smallpox before I was born."

"That was a very good day."

"What, the day I was born?"

"Um, no, I meant the day they eradicated smallpox. I'm sure the day you were born was a very good day too, of course—"

"I was born on the anniversary of the death of Princess Grace Kelly of Monaco."

"Well...not all good days are good for everyone, I suppose." Another person would have made those words sound glib, but when Harold said it, it felt sincere.

"Sure. Maybe some people had the happiest night of their lives on New Year's. I bet there were some people getting engaged, getting their first kiss, babies being born, all sorts of wonderful things were happening. It just also happened to be the night I died."

"Again, I'm very sorry this happened to you." Harold leaned forward slightly, as though he was going to try to hug me, but I side-stepped away. A very real part of me wanted the comfort of feeling those arms wrapped around me again, the way Harold had held me close in the foyer of the penthouse, but I definitely did not want him coming close to my favorite cashmere sweater with those grease-covered hands.

We stood awkwardly in the middle of the kitchen together before I said, "Anyway, I just wanted to come down here and find out where your washing machine was."

He rolled his eyes but pointed the way.

⚬

CHAPTER EIGHT

AN UNEXPECTED GUEST

I PESTERED HAROLD WITH the inane questions first, following him around the house at all hours of the night.

"What about flying? Do vampires fly? Am I going to have to worry about floating away?"

"You can't fly. You're a vampire, Grace, not a bird." Harold looked up from darning his damn socks and shook his head. "You watch too many movies."

"Animals."

"What about them?"

"Can I talk to them now? Is that a thing?"

"Don't let me stop you. I think the neighbors have some sort of big yellow dog they let outside on nights the weather's nicer." When Harold wasn't darning his socks or working on his engine rebuild in the kitchen (why did he have an entire spare engine, anyway?), he oiled his woodworking tools, scouring away small spots of rust with steel wool. He never seemed to sit still; his hands were always busy with some project, some chore. He mended small holes in a sweater with a crochet hook. He sharpened the blade of his disturbingly large pocketknife on a whetstone.

"But it's not like, a mystical connection or anything like that?"

"What, you think you're Dr. Doolittle now?"

(*It might have been almost worth it if I'd been able to talk to animals*, I thought. *Almost. Maybe.*)

I shadowed him around like a lost puppy, my questions flippant, silly. I wasn't really worried about floating up towards the ceiling and out of an upstairs window or figuring out how to transform into mist.

We both knew, I think, what I was actually avoiding, those first few nights. The elephant in the room. What the hell had happened to me, and why, and what was going to happen now—these questions were too terrifying to contemplate.

Better to stick with interrogations about order chiroptera.

"*No*, Grace. You canna turn into a bat."

If I could, I would have flown away.

A week after I died, a significant winter storm moved over the region, dumping several inches of snowfall during the day while we slept. Well into the evening, thick flurries continued to swoop and tumble and coalesce into shapeless mounds that obscured the recognizable world outside the house, rendering the roads all but impassible.

I felt a kinship with every buried thing shrouded in frost; affinity with every iced-over branch burdened to the point of breaking. The weather forecasters promised that the snowfall would turn to sleet and freezing rain by dawn, and I wondered if melted snow remembered what it once had been.

Mostly, I tried to figure out what I was going to do with the boxes full of stuff that cluttered up his space. If Harold could find endless ways to keep busy each night, I could, too. After several evenings spent wandering from room to room whenever I wasn't badgering him with urgent questions about things that only seemed to work in fiction, I finally started to get a feel for what items he tended to store in which places, and what function he used each room for.

Tonight, Harold hovered, as I sorted through boxes of unnecessary kitchen gadgets and household ephemera.

"You really haven't gone through any of this since you moved in. This coupon expired in 2003." I waved a faded slip of paper at him and examined it closely. "Not that I think you're the target demographic for...store-brand denture cleaner." I shook my head. "I don't need to see your teeth, thank you. I know what your fangs look like."

I felt, more than I saw, the silly grin disappear from his face as grabbed the expired coupon out of my hand and crumpled it up. "You really don't have tae do all this. I know it's a bit of a clashmelt mess, but it's not so bad so long as the boxes are piled up in one spot. You spread everything out and you're making it worse."

Every overhead light and accent lamp in the front room of Harold's house—which he insisted on referring to as "the parlor"—was aglow and buzzing, illuminating a space which, on the surface, was even more chaotic than the condition it had been in when I'd arrived a week before.

"Trust the process. You should see what Mom's collection of Bradford Exchange stuff looked like before—" I stopped. The memory of helping Mom organize her Princess Diana memorabilia the year I turned ten was mine. I didn't want to share it with somebody who never knew her, would never know what her laugher sounded like and what kind of hugs she gave, or the way her eyes lit up when she saw the way I rearranged her glass collectibles cases and dusted everything off.

"It's just like a museum, Gracie. You know, there are people who do this kind of thing for a living. You could be a museum curator someday. How'd you like that?"

I used to like museums. I used to like a lot of things.

"The cardboard attracts bugs and is a fire hazard. And everyone deserves a calm space to live in. So I'm doing this for me, not for you. Anyway, Harold, some of this stuff looks like it belongs in a museum..." I moved a small stack of cardboard boxes off of a sheet-draped piece of furniture to reveal a worn and threadbare mustard yellow mid-century sofa, coughing as dust from the disturbed sheet filled the room, more from habit than any irritation to my lungs.

When I stepped back to admire the sofa, I backed into the boxes, which tumbled over with a sad and broken clatter.

"Ope. Careful there," said Harold, holding out a hand to steady me if I needed it. I did not.

We both peered inside the dinged-up cardboard. Inside the first were two Tiffany-style lampshades in a green leaf design, now sadly crunched, broken, and bent out of shape. Not that the rest of the lamp parts were in any better condition. When I pulled the patinated brass bases out of the second box, the frayed and shredded cords caught the edge of my sweater sleeve, snagging a few threads. I flapped my hand rapidly to untangle myself and only made the snags worse.

"Well, shoot…" Harold mumbled. "Didn't even know those were there."

I grimaced at the destruction. They were pretty lamps, once; a matched pair would have looked lovely on either side of the sofa. I sighed and picked up the pieces to lug over to the "trash" pile, but Harold pulled them out of my hands and carried them off to the library where he kept the oddest assortment of tools.

"You can't hold on to everything…" I reminded him, thinking about the dusty flat-screen TV. Just as I'd suspected, it wasn't even plugged in. He'd found it on the side of the road on trash night, he confessed sheepishly, when he saw me looking around for an outlet for it. It didn't work, but he said he "just" needed to solder some new capacitors in place to bring it back to life, something that sounded almost as complicated as becoming a vampire—something I still didn't entirely understand myself.

Calliope had said it usually took a week. She and Harold both were adamant that what happened to me was wrong and unusual, but here I was, fangs and all, surrounded by decades of junk, trying to sort out someone's life, if I couldn't sort out my own.

I sighed again, this time louder, and got back to work.

"You doin' all right over there?" He called from the other room.

"Nothing is all right…" I muttered, more to myself than to him, but of course, he heard me. Outside, the wind from the snowstorm rattled the windows.

Harold came back and sat on the sofa, elbows on his knees, hands propping up his chin, and he looked at me with a solemn expression for several moments. In his vintage trousers and yet another one of signature pullover sweaters, he looked like a man entirely out of time, lounging on the midcentury furniture.

He could have walked straight out of a nineteen fifties sitcom, I decided, except for his hair. Even without the sideburns, his hair was too long for any style out of the fifties. I'd done the math when he'd told me how old he was, and looked up men's hairstyles of the eighteen tens on Google. Once I'd seen the proof in digital replicas of museum paintings and newspaper etchings of the era, I couldn't unsee the resemblance. He was straight out of a Regency romance novel, with the sartorial style of a black and white TV show dad. And he wasn't too bad to look at, for a dead guy. You could tell that he'd been strong and active in life; he was short and compact but wiry and well-muscled, like someone who would be a good dancer, or a gymnast. I found myself wondering about his broken nose, and the scar on his chin, and decided that he had the sort of face that a broken nose suited.

He wasn't preternaturally beautiful like some dark creature of the night from one of Becca's movies, but he was interesting-looking, and handsome in his own way, after all, which I thought was better. He had a look about him that was both kind and dangerous all at once, and I wondered what his story was, where he'd lived before he became a vampire, and why he'd ended up in Chicago, of all places. He certainly wasn't born in the city. But I kept those thoughts to myself. Harold was likable, even if he had killed people, as he claimed. Even though he had promised to behead me, once we found my maker. I didn't *want* to like him.

...but I caught myself glancing into his greenish eyes regardless.

He blinked first. "I think you know the most important thing right now, is that no one else finds out what we are. There are, um. Rules. I should probably tell you those."

"I'm listening."

"Well, I guess there are really only three. Don't tell mortals about us, that's more trouble than any of us want. So no blood cults, that's rule number two, but I don't think you'll need tae worry about that—" he started to smile again, looked like he thought better of it, and went back to being serious. "The third rule, of course, is never tae turn anyone without consent...I suppose you know why."

"Because it sucks and it's cruel and—"

"It's bad for Community morale, for one. No one wants members of the Community who don't want to be here. And it makes you a security risk. Not you, in particular. But...people turned without consent are more likely tae get mortals mixed up in things. And we don't want that, so—"

"So it's more about covering your own asses than the irreparable harm it actually causes the victims."

"I didn't say it like that, Grace."

I wanted to retort that it sure as hell sounded like that's what he meant, but instead I asked what happened to vampires who broke the "rules." He shrugged, said it depended on the situation; some things couldn't be helped. "I mean, you can't exactly follow rule one and rule three at the same time, right?"

I thought about that, wrinkling my nose. I couldn't imagine a way for someone to consent to becoming a vampire without knowing about vampires, either. "I don't even know how a person becomes a vampire." I reminded him, as I cleared off another sheet-covered piece of furniture and revealed a mustard-yellow armchair that matched the sofa. It looked comfortable, but when I sat down, a broken spring in the cushion poked my butt, causing me to jump up and squeal.

He laughed, and even I cracked a small smile. It probably would have been funnier if I'd been watching it happen to someone else. "You don't need tae know how tae turn someone," he said. "You won't be doing it anytime soon."

"Anytime ever." I corrected him. "You promised. We figure out who my maker is, and then I'm out. My life is already over. I died, after all, right? That's what Calliope said. And I don't have a heartbeat and I don't need to breathe and I haven't needed to use a toilet since—so, anyway…"

"Fledglings have tae die before they can resurrect. That's…that's how it works." He exhaled slowly, paused, and drew in a deep breath before he started talking again. I'd begun to notice he did this a lot when it seemed like he wanted to take his time before speaking. His eyes looked gray now, as he turned his face toward the shadows, away from the lamplight of the rest of parlor. Gray like death. "Sometimes we have tae help the process along. Break their neck or stab them I guess, or…whatever it takes. Draining a mortal completely is not as easy as the movies make it look. When I created my fledgling, we used morphine. But I don't think I'd do that again. She said it wasn't pleasant."

"When was this? Was it Calliope?"

"What? God no." Harold looked so taken aback, I thought he might fall over, and he laughed again, shaking his head. "Hell No. No, I didn't turn Calliope. She's as old as I am. We were turned around the same time."

I gave him my best skeptical expression as I pulled the sheet off of a second matching yellow armchair, checking the cushion extra carefully this time before I sat down. "She said she was a hundred and ninety-something. You said you were two hundred and twenty." I didn't think maker and fledgling quite explained Harold and Calliope's dynamic, but they obviously had a history, and I was curious.

He scratched his chin near his scar in a gesture that was almost jarringly human. "Well, it's been a hundred and ninety five years since I was turned, and I was twenty-five years old. Calliope was only a year or two younger than me when it happened. So I count my age from when I was born, and she starts from the night she was…re-born. I never realized the discrepancy before, but it makes sense for her."

"You look older than twenty-five." I'd thought he was closer to thirty, at least, you know, physically.

"Twenty-five year olds today are soft. When I was twenty-five—"

"Back in my day…" I croaked, gently teasing him.

"—by the time I was twenty-five, I'd been on fishing boats since I was seven, sheared sheep on my family's croft for almost ten years, learned the basics of black-smithing and tinsmithing from my Daa, joined the Royal Navy and apprenticed as a carpenter onboard ship, fought in a few naval skirmishes in the Napoleonic wars, survived being swept overboard and lost at sea for several days, *and* apprenticed a second time tae a master swordsmith in the south of Spain."

My jaw dropped. It was one thing to know that Harold was old, but it was another thing entirely to hear him talk about things I'd only read about in history books, or casually dropping a swashbuckling history that sounded like something out of a novel I would have read once. "Where did you grow up?" I asked. "You have an accent sometimes, but I can't really place it."

"West Burra…You know where the Shetland Islands are?" Harold stared up at the ceiling as he spoke, and his voice was far away.

I didn't want to admit that the only thing that came to mind when I heard "Shetland" was "ponies" like you saw at petting zoos, so I shook my head.

"All the way at the top of Scotland, in the North Sea. Remote. I was still a boy when I left."

"I don't know…You don't sound Scottish." I smirked at him playfully. "And you did say 'ope,' so…" I tried to stifle a giggle. Harold didn't seem like a typical vampire, but he was a very typical midwesterner. It was almost endearing.

He let out an exaggerated, long-suffering sigh. "I've been in America longer than you've been alive! Longer than any of your living relatives have been alive. I've had a lot of time tae practice my American accent—what do you want me tae do, call you 'lass' and talk like Scrooge McDuck?" And he did finish the sentence in a hilarious imitation of the cartoon character's accent, and I fought to suppress another giggle. Harold sat up, and leaned forward, closer to me, even though I was still seated a few feet away.

"We were more Norse than Scottish. My mam grew up speaking Norn; it's a dead language. Even I've forgotten most of what I once knew." He continued. "And my past isn't important. I promise you, I'm very boring. I didn't sail on the Titanic or fight in your Civil War or do anything you'd find interesting. Sheering sheep and fishing for herring isn't riveting stuff. I've never been anywhere anything truly historic happened, I never saw any of the major battles of the Napoleonic Wars. I've never crossed paths with history in any meaningful way. I've just been trying to survive, trying tae stay comfortable as possible, and ever since I've had the luxury, trying tae cause as little harm as possible along the way. It's not a bad life, but it's very..." he exhaled again, and shrugged. "...boring. Not that I'm bored, mind you."

"Boring, but not bored. Got it." None of his history sounded very boring to me, and I wanted to know more, but there was something else he'd said. Something I hadn't considered. "So where is she, then?"

"Who?"

"The woman you turned, where is she now?"

"Wherever she is," Harold answered, shaking his head, "...I hope she's happy." Another sigh. "She deserved tae be happy."

"My ex-boyfriend dumped me," I offered, feeling like I needed to confess some sorrow from my own past now in exchange. "Because he got an opportunity to work remotely overseas, and he didn't want to pass up the chance to sleep with as many hot European women as possible."

"Unsavory rake." Harold muttered, and I couldn't tell how serious he was being. He gathered up the sheets that had been keeping the dust off his furniture, and wadded them up into balls he kneaded in his hands as he continued. "You still don't remember anything about the party?"

I shook my head. "I keep trying, but the whole night is a blank. One minute I'm walking into an elevator with Becca and some rando in a tight shirt, the next minute I'm waking up dead in a bathtub with fangs and no heartbeat."

"The man you described..." Harold seemed lost in thought. "...when you first told me about the man who led you upstairs, for a moment, I thought perhaps James was back in town. But...Jimmy would never do that tae you. Never."

"Who's Jimmy?" I didn't recognize the name.

"James. James Medlock. Calliope's last fledgling. He was the lanky tall dark an' handsome type you described. We were friends, back in the late '70's, and in the '90's. The most recent '90's. He left her in...1999? That was a bad year for Calliope Jones. But, if James were back in Chicago, I would have known about it. He would have reached out, I think. I'm sure of it. And he wouldn't have been at Calliope's party."

"Bad blood?"

"Ha. You know, you can be very funny. She thinks I slept with him. He left her for another man. I didn't, mind you. Sleep with him. But I knew he was a friend of Dorothy's. Do they even say that anymore?"

"You mean gay?"

"He preferred men. Yeah."

"And you? Do you prefer...?" *Not that it was any of my business if Harold was gay, but....*

"I've had over two hundred years tae get around and find out that I prefer options."

"Fair enough." I chewed the inside of my lip, and tasted blood.

"Does that bother you?"

"It's the 21st century, Harold. In Catholic school they taught us, 'don't do drugs, don't have sex before marriage, and don't you be gay!' but I'm guilty of two out of those three things, and we were also taught 'judge not, lest you be judged,' so...Becca's bi, and I love her to death. I don't give a shit who you sleep with." *Because you made it pretty damn clear that you weren't going to be sleeping with me.* Not that I wanted to sleep with Harold, either, I reminded myself.

"So it's sex and drugs for you, huh?" The sly grin was teasing his lips again.

I avoided eye contact. "I mean, not habitually, but...sometimes I like to get out of my head for a bit. It can get pretty overwhelming in there."

"You don't say."

"Hey! Judge not!" I reached down and threw a wadded-up ball of packing paper at him. He didn't even try to duck. It bounced harmlessly off his head.

"You know what? You're pretty cool for a Catholic."

"Gee, thanks. You're all right for a grumpy old fart."

"*I'm* grumpy? Have you met yourself? Looked in the mirror recently?"

I glared at him until the smile slipped away from his face like a stone disappearing below the ripples on the surface of water. Mirrors and I had not been on friendly terms since I'd been turned. I could't exactly tell you what was so off-putting about my reflection, but I hated looking at myself in the mirror more than I had to, hated looking myself in the eyes; dead hazel eyes.

Sometimes I imagined that the monstrous mirror girl would crawl out of the glass and consume me. It was a frequent theme in my daytime bad dreams. Just three nights ago, that damned broken TV had been the source of an embarrassing meltdown I didn't want to think about. It's just—I'd seen my face dimly reflected in the dusty screen in the front room just after feeding, and the sight of my own mouth marred by fangs and dripping blood had sent me right into an emotional spiral that I couldn't climb out of. Harold found me unmoving just before dawn, and carried me up to bed when I was unresponsive. I'd spent most of the day awake and sobbing...I didn't even want to guess what he must have thought of me. I watched as his eyes flickered over to the TV, and back at me, and we both flinched.

"Grace?"

"I just don't like mirrors, OK?"

"I shouldn't have made a joke about it—"

"It's fine."

"Do you need—?"

"I'm *fine.*"

"*Thump*," went the dead organ in my chest, as if to remind me, "*I'm still here.*"

"Maybe I am grumpy." My stomach growled and I ignored it.

"Well." Harold stood up and surveyed the mess once more, "I'm going tae work on a few things of my own. You can be grumpy in here all you like. Do what you have ta do tae feel better." But when he left the room, he dragged the busted old TV off into the library as well, and didn't say another word.

It couldn't possibly have been easy for him to rearrange his life to take care of someone he'd only just met, but to his credit Harold never complained about my presence, or appeared to resent me in his space, for all the trouble I'd certainly caused him, and I appreciated that about him, more than I wanted to.

I was startled out of my thoughts some time later by an approaching sound that wasn't the wind howling around the eaves, or the tapping of tree branches against the windowpanes. It was a car—I was pretty certain, at least—although the engine wasn't running—I strained my ears to listen. Someone was pushing their car down the street, I decided, and even with the engine off, and the car squealed and clunked to a slow, grinding stop in front of Harold's house. No one in their right mind should have been out in this weather. The car's engine sputtered and attempted to turn over a few times once the car stopped moving, but continued making unhealthy automobile sounds, and finally, whoever had pushed the car down the street gave up.

He hadn't mentioned any visitors. And no one knew where I was staying—right? Fear turned my toes into roots that worked their way through the floorboards.

"Harold?" I called out when I remembered he was no longer in the room with me. "Harold!"

He stepped out of the library, a small light strapped to the front of his forehead casting strange shadows across all the piles of boxes surrounding me. He held his hands out at his sides, palms up, an unspoken "what?" on his lips. He looked annoyed that I'd called him away from his project. The wind picked up again, clattering icicles off the roof, and I wondered, for a split second, if I'd imagined things.

"There's a car outside." I tried not to feel foolish.

"Outside where?" He cocked his head to one side, listening intently. It was getting nastier outside, but he seemed to be listening for something beyond the storm.

"Outside your house, Harold. It just pulled up. I'm surprised you didn't hear the racket; even I know what a car that needs an oil change sounds like."

He looked like he was about to say something else when we both heard the car door slam, and the crunching sound of footfalls approaching across the snow. I ran over to one of the windows and pulled the blackout curtains aside just quickly enough to catch a glimpse of a tall thin shadow fall across the lawn before Harold grabbed me by the shoulder and pulled me back.

"What the hell are you doing?" His glare was louder than his whisper.

"Someone's out there. I think they're coming around the side."

"Did you see who it was?"

I shook my head. "Just a shadow. Harold—"

He held up a finger to shush me, and reached into a dark recessed corner near a nonfunctional grandfather clock, where he retrieved a large, nasty-looking sword. There was nothing elegant about this particular weapon; its purely utilitarian shape left no question as to its intended use—to bludgeon and slash and, at the very least, to maim.

Some people just keep a baseball bat by the bed, but no, not Harold Laing.

We were both perfectly still, and I concentrated to listen as the footsteps came round to the side entrance just as I'd predicted, arriving at the door right off the mud room that led to both the kitchen and the garage. Harold instructed me to stay put, but I followed a few paces behind him anyway. Maybe, if the intruder was trouble, I could throw a ratchet at them...or something.

He raised his sword and inched closer to the door, which rattled once, along with an almost perfunctory knock, before a key inserted in the lock and the doorknob turned and opened, blowing gusts of ice and sleet into the small room. He was about to swing, I think, but a muffled voice stopped him mid-action.

"Oy vey, careful with the sword, Old Man! What were you going to do, turn me into chopped liver there?" The side door slammed shut behind a tall, skinny individual, dressed in blue jeans and brown leather bomber-style jacket over a tucked-in red flannel shirt. A touseled mop of curly dark hair peeked out below a Cubs hat that looked much-loved. Her face was wrapped in a scarf.

"Damn it, kid—I might have. What the hell are you doing out in this weather? Dumbass bean pole, you could have blown away—" and he dropped the sword on the mudroom bench, wrapping his arms around the taller woman in an instantly reciprocated hug.

CHAPTER NINE

YOU CAN KILL THEM

"ARE YOU BACK IN town for good?" He asked, stepping away from his friend and ushering her into the kitchen. "And what's with the disguise, you hiding from someone, or are you trying tae be The Invisible Man?"

She unwrapped the scarf, letting it drape over her shoulders, and leaned casually against the sink, thumbs in the pockets of her jeans. The big belt buckle at her waist looked Navajo, all turquoise inlay and engraved scrollwork that resembled an owl.

I remembered Harold's flask, and wondered if owls were an inside joke between them that I didn't get, or if it was merely a coincidence.

"You know if I was on the lam I wouldn't lead anyone here. I got a sweet new gig down south." She started, her voice the kind of nasally New York accent that you heard in old movies. "No idea how long that'll last, but I figured I'd get away when I could and stash some stuff up here in one of my safe deposit boxes before I get too entrenched. Then the storm came up and I thought I'd better schlep on over to your place for some hospitality for a few days, if you'll have me."

"Always. *Imbu da fremd.*" He said, clasping her shoulder. "That's why I gave you the key."

"And thats why I was real surprised you'd come at me with the sword, I mean, sheesh. I hope everything's on the level with you. It's not Community problems, is it? You usually steer clear of that junk like the sensible person you are. Say, you're a real pal though. Who's the lady? And what is that ridiculous thing on your head? You look like a nineteenth century Appalachian miner."

"One out of three ain't bad." Harold said with a wry smile, as he unhooked the LED light from his forehead. I doubted nineteenth century Appalachian miners had LED headlamps, but the vivid mental image was nevertheless amusing.

"You're Avie." It was a guess, but it was a good guess. That was the only other vampire I'd heard Harold mention. Didn't need an invitation to enter, clearly a good friend...and definitely a lesbian. It fit.

She gave me a careful appraisal before cocking her head at Harold. "I didn't realize you'd have company."

"Not exactly company..."

"I'm Grace..." I cut Harold off and extended my hand, trying to be friendly. "I'm—"

"A brand new idiot, aren't you, doll?" She grabbed my hand with both of hers and held on to it longer than was necessary, even as I flinched and tried to pull away from her icy grip. Her expression changed as she peered at me, from affable to...something I didn't like.

"She's not yours." She turned to Harold, dropping my hand. "You setting up a way station for abandoned fledglings or something, Old Man?"

Harold scoffed. "Hardly. But, ah...you know, Community service—"

"Like you give a rat's ass about the Community."

His expression sobered into something resembling caution. "I'm repaying an old debt tae an old friend we both know you don't like. Let's leave it at that. But, uh, that does affect where you're going to have to crash, I'm afraid. Grace has taken over your bedroom, for the time being. But you can take mine. I can crash on the couch in the parlor with enough blankets..."

Avie shook her head vigorously, and the soft brown curls danced around her face like autumn leaves blowing in the wind. "You know I'm used to sleeping rough. Let me take the couch, an air mattress, a pile of blankets...keep me out of the sun and I'm not complaining." She turned her attention back to me. "You're cute, doll. How ya liking things so far?"

"Right...let's go figure out sleeping arrangements." Harold clapped his hands together before I could speak, picked up his sword from the mud room, and walked out of the kitchen. Avie pushed off against the sink and followed him.

"Don't shake hands with vampires you don't know, by the way." She mentioned casually as she strode past me. "You don't need to worry about not being polite or anything. Mortal rules of etiquette you're used to don't apply. Your maker should have told you that."

"Why not?" I asked, bypassing her assumptions about my marker. I had to take two steps for every one of hers; Avie was model tall and seemingly all legs.

"You don't want to give away information to folks who have no right to it." She said, as if it was the most obvious explanation in the world. "A lot of us learn to pick up on things. Touch can say a lot, is all I'm saying. You'll learn."

I decidedly *didn't* want to learn any weird vampire psychic tricks.

"What...did you learn from me?"

Avie shook her head and didn't look behind her; she was too busy navigating the minefield of boxes spread out across the parlor floor. "Nope. Not saying. Not getting involved in that mess. If Calliope Jones is part of it in any way, I don't wanna touch the situation with a ten foot pole. 'Old friend I don't like,' my ass."

"What's wrong with Calliope—?" but I didn't finish the question.

At the top of the landing, Harold halted and looked down the hallway, causing first Avie, and then me, to stop in our tracks on the stairs. "I suppose there's the room next tae yours...well, Grace's...I mean, it doesn't matter...but there's also some space in the attic, I think, if you want more privacy, or..." he shrugged.

"Old Man. I'm good. I wouldn't have stopped by at all if I'd known you had a guest. Put me someplace that's dark when it's bright out and I'll be happy to live another night."

"You wouldn't have gotten much further in your car without an oil change." I told her.

"Funny, you didn't strike me as the grease monkey type..." Avie looked at me sharply, but Harold's smile was almost approving. Just a small twitch at the corners of his mouth.

I shrugged. "My Uncle Gino owns a car lot. Certified pre-owned. He wouldn't let me go off to college without knowing how to maintain a vehicle."

"What about your cousin Vinny?"

"Ha ha. Very funny." I did, in fact, have a second cousin Vincent, but he hated being called Vinny—probably because of the movie. "At least you came to the right place. I think I know a guy who could probably help you out..." if Harold's kitchen and garage didn't have enough tools and parts to patch up Alvie's clunker, I'd be shocked.

He actually winked at me as I smiled at him, before he pivoted on his heels and continued down the hall. "Old Man, fix my car. Old Man, I need a place tae crash. Old Man, do you mind sharing your blood stash?" Harold's voice was a mocking singsong imitation of Avie's New York accent as he walked down the hall and playfully kicked open the door to the bedroom next to mine—the one where most of the overflow clutter from my room had ended up in.

"Well, now that you mention it, I was hoping you could spare a few CC's for a..." Avie peered into the over-full hall bedroom and punched his shoulder. "You're a slob. What would your mother say?"

"Hey! Most of this isn't mine!" He moved to return the punch, and she blocked his blow. In an instant they were facing each other like boxers in a ring, crouched and ready, but it was over fast. Avie was several inches taller than Harold and had better reach, but he was quick and certain and—he cheated. He feigned a swipe, got his arms around her waist, and wrestled Avie to the ground, where she landed with a dull thud that shook the dust up from the rug running down the hallway. I made a mental note to see if any of the vacuum cleaners I'd found actually worked.

"No fair! You changed sports on me! You can't switch from boxing to wrestling like that! It's unsportsmanlike!"

"Don't pick fights you can't win, kid. I've told you a hundred times..." he thrust out a hand to help her up.

I felt a bittersweet pang, watching Harold interact with his friend. I missed Becca with an ache that was almost overpowering. We hadn't spoken in five nights. I wasn't sure what there was to say. I couldn't bring myself to read her hurt and frantic texts.

Avie slipped off her bomber jacket and scarf and rolled up the sleeves of her flannel before she began attacking the piles with me. The Cubs hat stayed on, but she flipped it backwards while she worked, moving boxes and miscellaneous household items into neat, organized piles in the hallway. More stuff to throw away. Vampires don't need fondue sets. She was rummaging in a corner when I heard her swear under her breath, something that sounded vaguely Russian, before handing me a black plastic milk crate to set out in the hall, calling over her shoulder, "You're a sick fuck, Jack, you know that?"

I looked down at the contents of the crate in my hands. It held an empty and dented plastic milk jug, a funnel, a roll of black contractor's trash bags, duct tape and zip ties, a ski mask, box cutters, and a length of rope, plus a small bottle of bleach, and an unmarked glass jar of a white substance that looked like salt, which was the only item in the collection that didn't make a chilling kind of sense. It was all wiped clean, but still traced with the scent of old blood. I felt the room grow cold. "This is serial killer shit..." I whispered, not exactly meaning to say it out loud.

Harold snatched the crate out of my hands defensively. "Sometimes I have ta do serial killer shit."

Avie brushed off her palms on her jeans and poked her head out of the room. "Don't let him try to rationalize his murderous ways. He enjoys it." She winked at me.

I felt my eyes widen, and forced them closed. Deep breath in.

"Avital. Keep a lid on it, will ya kid? I'm up against a lot here."

Deep breath out. I opened my eyes.

I must have looked as horrified as I felt, because she glanced quickly from Harold, to me, and back at Harold, and her expression sobered. "Hey now, look, I didn't know nothing—"

Harold sighed and thrust the milk crate back into her hands. "Go ahead and put this in the car, will ya? You know the spot in the trunk?" He reached into his pants pockets and pulled out his car keys, and Avie responded with a brisk nod, disappearing down the stairs without another word. Moments later, the door from the kitchen into the mud room that led to the garage opened, then shut again. I realized that I'd been rooted in place again, and wriggled my toes, waiting for the room to stop spinning.

"I haven't done it in a while, Grace." He didn't seem apologetic, but why should he be? He knew what he was better than I did. "The kit is mostly a precaution. I don't even keep it in my car anymore, usually. I forgot I had it in there—"

"You don't need to justify yourself to me. You told me what you did, the first night." I felt my voice flatten to monotone. He'd told me he'd killed hundreds of people, after all. What had I expected? But I couldn't force myself to look up and meet his eyes.

He sighed. "Look, I'm sorry about—"

"What was in the jar?"

"I'm sorry?"

"The white stuff in the jar. What was that? Do you drug people when you do it, or...?"

"Oh. That." He cleared his throat. "It's a mixture of calcium citrate and phosphate mostly. Few other chemicals. I get it from a guy over on the Northwestern University campus. It's, uh...it keeps the blood from coagulating."

"Good to know." I found myself nodding, as if I was ever planning to put that information to use. I felt sick, even as my brain was filing the fact away under the tab, 'useful things.'

Harold continued. "It is a pretty swell trick, actually. Before that there really wasn't an easy way tae keep blood longer than a few hours sometimes, but..."

"Better living through chemistry?"

"Sounds about right." He reached out and put his hand on my shoulder. Aside from briefly pulling me away from the window earlier, he'd never touched me without asking before, and even though layers of clothing interfered, the weight of his cold hand on my body was searing. "I don't want tae scare you."

Inhale. "I'm not scared of you. It's everything else that terrifies me." *Exhale.*

"Well, look, don't let Avie get under your skin, okay? She's practically feral, but...she means well. She's good people."

"Even for a bloosucker?"

"Especially for a bloodsucker."

The downstairs door slammed, and Avie came bounding back up the stairs two at a time, creating a racket. "Say, it looks like you've got a whole mechanic's shop back there if you just clear out some of the old junk in the place. D'ya think maybe if the weather clears by tomorrow night, you could…?"

"Yeah, kid, we'll look over your car. How far you have tae go with it?"

She looked cagey. "I'd rather not say where, exactly. *Deep* South. I mean if I need to I can probably come up with the cash for a newer—"

"Let's see what we can do, first. I'm surprised you didn't take the plane."

"That old Cessna? The bird developed a bad habit of falling out of the sky last year. After the last crash, I was lucky to walk away, and there was no salvaging the twisted hunk of metal that remained. So I'm grounded, for the time being. Probably for the best. Aviation community is pretty small, couple of folks were starting to get suspicious about a pilot who only ever takes off and lands at night."

"Sounds like people read too many Stephen King novels." I pulled out one of the black garbage bags I'd reserved from the murder box and started filling it with trash.

"I know, right?" Avie grinned at me. "Some of those guys were starting to wonder whether or not vampires were real, or something."

I laughed, for the first time in several nights, and decided that Harold had okay taste in friends. Avie *felt* right, at least. Maybe I was picking up some weird vampire psychic tricks, after all.

After we cleared enough floor space for Avie to lay out a bedroll, Harold produced some extra pillows and blankets from a linen closet in the hall that I'd already had a chance to organize, and we headed back downstairs to the mess I'd been working on in the parlor before Avie's arrival.

"You don't think Marie had anything tae do with the plane, do you?" Harold asked, walking back into his library. Avie followed. I glanced inside the room at the project Harold had been working on when Avie showed up, but couldn't figure out what it was. He bent over the table with the soldering iron, fidgeting with some small pieces I couldn't distinguish through all the other tools and projects, LED lamp once again secured to his forehead. He must have shoved it in his pocket when he was still in the kitchen. How much stuff did he keep in there? And why did men's clothes always have pockets big enough to actually be useful? It wasn't fair.

"Hell if I know." Avie leaned forward on the table and handed him pieces of something as he worked. "On the one hand, it seems like her MO, but…the bitch would have said something by now, I'm sure of it. She doesn't like it if I ignore her for too long. You know how it is."

I left them alone and continued my organizational efforts with the piles of boxes in the corner of the parlor, but I eavesdropped shamelessly. Vampire hearing had its benefits.

"Sometimes I forget which one of you is the cat and which one is the mouse…"

"I think it depends who's telling the story."

"I don't think many folks in the Community care much for Marie DuChamps these nights. Even Calliope keeps her at arms length."

Avie scoffed. "Even Calliope keeps her at arms length…as if Calliope Jones kept up with any of her fledglings. She's notorious for cutting ties and responsibility. That's what she does, right? Destroys lives, pretends to be innocent, and walks away unscathed. God only knows how she manages to keep her hands looking so clean."

"You know, for someone who's never even met the woman, you seem tae keep close tabs on her."

"You're one of the only ones in the Community who doesn't. Maybe that's why you can still stomach her after all these years."

"Hey now—"

"I know, I know, I don't want to get into it again. I like you Old Man, I really do. You're more community minded than most of those motherfuckers on the rotational council. All that talk about mutual aid and you're one of the few who actually gives a damn and does the work. So I'm not coming after you over the vampires you've got irrational soft spots for. I respect your history. But I—"

"You don't like her. You don't have to like her. You can loathe her, even. Loathe her, loathe Marie…you've more than enough reason tae. I didn't like that DuChamps woman in 1906 when she was fresh, I didn't like her in 1920 when I ran into her in Kansas City, and the last time I saw her, in Cincinnati in '75, I still didn't like her. And I've never met anyone who did. That's what I was saying."

"I'm gonna catch up with her one of these nights. And when I do…pow. Pew pew."

"You'll be like the dog that actually catches the car its been chasing. Won't know what tae do with it."

"I'm gonna kill the bitch, is what I'm gonna do."

"So you keep saying…hey—careful with that."

"Ouch!"

"I warned you. It's hot. Get—get your hands off my stuff, will ya, Kid? Scram. I wanna finish this for Grace before sunrise."

"Softie."

"Out."

"Say, what's her story anyway? Why're you taking in other people's fledglings?"

"Shoo. Go ask her yourself."

"Fine, fine, I'll leave, I'll leave, I'm going I'm going—"

"Avie."

"Jack? Harold? Which one are you using these nights?"

"Harold is fine. Just—go easy on her, okay kid? She's having a rough time."

"Didn't we all…" Avie started walking towards the parlor.

So far, I'd met three vampires, not counting my maker who I didn't remember. Calliope Jones moved with deliberate precision, every gesture smooth and calculated. Harold—Jack? Had an organic silence to him. He walked without making a sound, moved through his world without touching things unless he meant to, always careful, even considerate. Avie, seemingly just to be contrary, stomped around like a bull in a china shop, heavy footfalls and swinging arms. There was strength and power in her long, lean limbs, but much like a teenage boy, she didn't seem to have—or care to practice—much control over her actions. It was hard to imagine her in the pilot's seat of an aircraft. She seemed—for lack of a better word—reckless.

I wasn't sure if I liked that about her or not.

She lumbered out of Harold's office and landed on the yellow mid-century sofa with an inelegant flop, sprawling out across the velvet, legs spread, arms stretched out over the back of the furniture, taking up as much space as possible. We watched each other warily for several minutes. I unboxed a collection of shattered ceramic platters in the shape of green leaves of cabbage and set the shards aside in the trash pile.

"You know what? I'm glad he's got someone around to help him clear up this mess. He was never gonna get around to it on his own." She seemed more approving of me than she'd been in the kitchen, holding on to my hand.

I shrugged. "People get overwhelmed. It's a lot of stuff."

"Not you? You don't get overwhelmed?"

I shook my head and laughed again, softly this time, afraid of becoming hysterical if I laughed too loud or too long. "I am absolutely overwhelmed. But not by..." I waved my hands around at the piles of clutter, "...things. Stuff doesn't overwhelm me. I see ways to organize it and I do. It calms me down. I'm actually glad to have a project. It keeps me from thinking about everything else."

"Life among the undead isn't all your maker cracked it up to be, huh?" Her posture didn't change, but some part of her bravado seemed to bottom out, just a little. I couldn't decide if she was offering sympathy or solidarity, though, and I didn't want her pity.

"I don't know my maker."

"Bullshit. Whose blood were you drinking for a week before you died?"

"I wasn't. I swear. I'm just a stupid girl who wanted to go to a fancy party with my friend. And I woke up the next night like this." I leaned against the armchair opposite the sofa and looked up at her from the floor, trying to figure out what she wanted. Maybe a friend of Harold's was a friend of mine, after all. But I couldn't be sure. I wasn't even entirely sure I could trust Harold.

Avie leaned forward slightly and peered at me. She wasn't certain about me, either. "You pulling my leg? That's really what happened?"

I rolled my eyes and shrugged as if to say, "Why would I lie?" I wasn't even certain on the specific mechanics of how I'd died and come back. I mean, someone had killed me, and I had to assume that drinking vampire blood was involved somehow, but my faulty memory made piecing everything together that much harder. I wasn't sure if I should say anything, at all...

"New Year's Eve. I don't remember much." *Exhale.* Focus. *Inhale.* "Harold thinks someone from the Community got carried away with me at Calliope's party and tried to cover their tracks. I didn't know I was going to a vampire party. I didn't..." I opened another box, this one full of fragile file folders and what appeared to be receipts and tax returns from the 1970's. I put the entire box into the trash pile. No one needed to hold on to that stuff. There was silence for a minute or two. I felt Avie watching me, but I didn't look at her. Harold trusted her with a key to his house. I guess that had to mean something, right?

"That's real fucked up." When she finally spoke again, she sounded angry.

"That's what I've been told. Glad I'm not the only one who thinks so."

"That's the most fucked up turning I've heard about in a long time. Shit. And of course it was at one of Calliope's parties...I guess there's a Community investigation, huh? What does the rotational council say?"

"I've never spoken to them. I...maybe I shouldn't have said anything. Calliope was worried she'd get in trouble if the Community found out about me, so she called Harold, and he brought me here, and—"

"Harold...." Avie growled his name loud enough for him to know she was talking to him, even if he was in the other room.

"I know. I know!" His voice called out from the library.

Avie shook her head. "That's not the way shit's supposed to work in the Community." She raised her voice again. "Who's on the rotational council for Chicagoland these nights, Harold?"

He didn't answer.

"Probably, what? Is Jennet still around? She was all right. Iqbal is okay, too" She turned to look at me again. "He's kind of a stick in the mud but he's fair, I've heard. He'll have your back."

"We're not getting the Community involved. Stay out of it."

"Come on Old Man, that's not fair to Grace here—or anyone else! If there's someone going around randomly turning pretty ladies at parties, that's Community business. They'd do the same thing if an itinerant vampire was getting into that kind of trouble on the road. Who even does that, turning people quickly? Don't most would-be fledglings die?"

"You said you weren't going tae touch Calliope Jone's business with a ten-foot pole. So don't. Drop it." Harold still didn't leave his library, and the two of them continued to shout at each other.

Finally, Avie stopped arguing and stood up, grabbing me by the elbow as she did and pulling me to my feet as well. Even though her skin wasn't touching mine, this time, I could almost feel the subtle threads of vibration that connected us—or maybe I was imagining things. Regardless, I gasped.

"Come on. I want to look for something upstairs in your room that I might have left behind last time I was here."

As soon as we were upstairs, she dragged me into the bedroom and closed the door behind us, leaning against it and blocking my exit. "Look here. I don't know what the fuck is going on. But there are some things you need to know that the old man is not going to tell you." She kept her voice lower than a whisper. I wouldn't have been able to hear her at all before I was turned, even though she stood three feet away from me.

"The Community is not your friend—" she stopped and all but visibly reconsidered something for a second, then went on. "Okay. Maybe he'd tell you that. He doesn't like them. He has his reasons for not liking the Community. But the Community has resources, connections, their own fucked up traditions and rules…and you have rights.

"When my maker turned me, I thought I was in love with her, Okay? Uncle Sam had just put the kibosh on the WASPs and I was pretty gutted. We all knew Jews had been disappearing all over Europe. I'd thought, if I joined the war effort, I could at least do *something*, you know? Anyway, that doesn't matter. Marie and I mostly knew each other from letters, I had no idea I was in love with a vampire. And if you'd told me before I found out on my own, I wouldn't have believed you. What, like that old Dracula movie? Come on. But she took advantage of my emotional state, you see? My desire to do something. And I thought I loved her. I trusted that bitch. She said we'd go to Europe and kill Nazis."

I nodded, wide-eyed, no idea what else I was supposed to say or do. I knew roughly when Harold and Calliope had been turned, even if I didn't know why or how. But I'd learned about the Women Airforce Service Pilots in high school. A student's grandmother had been a pilot with the short-lived World War II program; she'd come to the school to give a speech on Veteran's Day my freshman year. That made everything Avie was telling me much less fantastic than anything I could learn about

Harold and Calliope's histories. They were hundreds of years old, after all. But Avie, like me—both of us should still be alive.

I *felt* that.

Turning someone was supposed to be consensual, that's what Calliope and Harold had both said, but I thought Avie might have certain opinions on what constituted consent that was more involved than a simple yes or no.

"An actual blood-drinking Jew. How fucked up is that?" She threw her head back against the bedroom door and let out a dull, hollow laugh before she sank low to the ground, bony knees pulled tight against her chest. "She made me slit my own throat. That's how I died. The bitch made me cut open my own goddamned throat to bleed out in front of her and prove how much I loved her."

"Geeze Louise...*that's* fucked up." Morphine sounded an awful lot better than that. I was suddenly grateful I couldn't remember how I'd died. Maybe there were small mercies, after all.

"I'm telling you this for a reason, doll. So you know. You can kill them." She sniffled, and I didn't think she was faking solidarity anymore.

"Who?"

"Your maker. You can kill the one who turned you, if they do you wrong. That's an old, old Community rule. Maybe one of the oldest, I don't know. I don't know anyone who knows the so-called real history of vampires and the Community, but I know this. We aren't supposed to turn people without full consent. We're not supposed to turn people who don't understand what they're getting into, what they'll become. The Community itself won't always take action against shitty makers, but if you believe you've been done wrong by yours, you can take them out, if you can find and catch them. And no one will bat an eye...it happens every night.

"Think of it as a get out of jail free card." She lowered her head onto the top of her knees, and went very, very still.

I sat down across from her, hands in my lap. No touching. Even though I wanted, very much, to give her a hug.

"Look at me." She sniffled again, glancing up at me with bloodshot eyes. "I didn't mean to get all emotional on you like this. Don't know what came over me. But you seem nice, and you didn't deserve to get fucked over like that. So, I'm sorry you're in this position. I guess it just gets to me, all the bullshit injustice in the world, you know?"

I nodded. For the first time in a week, I felt a glimmer of hope. Even if I couldn't undo what had happened to me, if the Community didn't act, I still had options. There was something I could do. "Do you think...did your maker really try to sabotage your airplane?"

"Maybe. I don't know. It could have just been old fashioned mechanical error. I was lucky to walk away. A mortal wouldn't have. She's thrown me out of moving vehicles into oncoming traffic, set my homes on fire, shot me, stabbed me, staked me...tried to, at least. And I've done almost as bad to her. Last time, I almost got her head clean off. Next time she won't be so lucky."

Chapter Ten

DON'T CRY OVER SPILLED BLOOD

"Harold ran out to Menard's to pick up some motor oil and stuff, and he told me I should wait here for you so you wouldn't be alone when you woke up. Say, you don't look so great. Did you sleep all right? I didn't hear nothin' from you during the day, how long ago did you say it was you was turned? You still losing your fingernails and all that?"

I pulled my head out of the fridge and peered across the kitchen at the silhouetted outline of Avie, barely visible in the dim shadows near the mud room, as the light coming from the open refrigerator door nearly blinded me. I'd woken up with cracked lips and a loosened thumbnail that snagged on my clothes as I was getting dressed, providing another layer of sensory overload on top of my gnawing hunger, and all the other heightened senses I still couldn't always ignore.

"How long have you been sitting here waiting?" I asked, no small measure of irritation in my voice, only momentarily confused. I'd forgotten we had a houseguest, and it was creepy, finding her waiting for me in the dark. Harold always turned the lights on in the kitchen when he woke up. Now I wondered if he did it so he wouldn't startle me. Just because I could see well in the dark didn't mean I always thought to look around.

Avie shrugged as I pulled a bag of blood from the fridge. "Not long. I was in the garage until maybe ten minutes ago. Have you had a chance to check out the crap he's got stored in there? I never had a reason to poke around before. I found a set of lawn darts. Can you believe it? I thought those got outlawed in the seventies or something. He could rig up a whole *Home Alone* getup with all the stuff in this house. You ever see that movie, *Home Alone*? I think they actually filmed it around here. Cute movie. Gotta love the scrappy kids, yanno? Say, you need help with that? Here, lemme—"

But I'd already managed to pour myself breakfast without spilling—much. I wasn't sure whether or not I wanted to drink in front of Avie. I could already feel my fangs pressed against my lips, and my hands were beginning to tremble from the overpowering need for blood, but I also didn't want her to see me like—like that. Feeding was something I preferred to get over with quickly and furtively. Harold had already figured out that I didn't want an audience; for the most part he left me alone with my blood. But Avie stared pointedly at me with big brown eyes, almost like she was looking forward to watching me vamp out.

I didn't feel comfortable feeding in front of her, and I didn't feel comfortable turning my back on her. And my loose thumbnail was annoying. I wiggled it absent-mindedly against my forefinger as I stood there waiting for Avie to get the hint and leave me alone, until the nail came away completely and bounced off the kitchen floor, disappearing under the stove.

"Oy vey—that's a yes. Well, they grow back fast, you'll be all right, just gonna have a kind of screwy manicure for a bit, that's all. Say, you gonna drink that or not? You're looking kind of—"

She didn't have time to finish the sentence. My hands started trembling harder as soon as my thumbnail dropped off, and when I tried to grab the glass of blood with both hands, it just got worse, spilling blood over the rim of the glass. Avie reached out—maybe she was going to help me, I don't know—and I pulled away, and everything happened in slow motion all at once. I dropped the glass, we both reached out to grab it as it fell; she got to it a nanosecond before I did in the scuffle to keep the glass from hitting the kitchen floor. Blood splashed all over my face and dress. I reacted, Avie reacted, and what was left of the blood in the glass splattered everywhere when it struck the linoleum anyway, and shattered.

I staggered backwards, staring down at the shards of glass embedded in my bloodied hands. Maybe the cup had broken before it hit the floor, maybe I—I licked the blood off my hands and fingers without thinking, hungry, animalistic, and growling. I think I might have been about to crawl on my hands and knees and—Avie put her hand on my chest, right over my heart, and shooed me out of the kitchen. I vaguely remember her steering me over to the yellow couch in in parlor, and bringing me another cup of blood, promising to clean up the mess. All I could think or see or smell or hear was rust and salt.

And then Harold was sitting next to me with a pair of tweezers and his pocketknife, pulling bits of glass out of my hands, cutting open the wounds that had already healed over to make sure that all the pieces he could find were taken care of. Almost as quickly as he cut open my skin, it healed closed again. Aside from my missing thumbnail, my hands were perfect, unmarked. Not a lot of blood escaped from my injuries.

"You still with us, Grace?"

I nodded. Words—words still weren't something I could manage.

"I think you scared Avie. I don't think she's been around someone so new since she was a fledgling. She says she's sorry, for what it's worth, but I'm going tae keep her busy in the garage for a bit. Give you a chance tae get tidied up. Okay?"

Nod.

Harold's face had a pinched, concerned look that I didn't like. "I know I told you she can be a bit much, but I promise, she means well, she really does."

I got up to clean myself off without uttering a word. I wouldn't have been able to speak if I'd wanted to, my head still spinning in red. I *hated* when the hunger took over me like that. I was already thirsty again.

Harold said that most vampires only needed to drink blood every other night or so, but fledglings had to feed often, usually multiple times between sunset and sunrise. Something about how the body was still changing. Mine clearly was.

I'd noticed my eyelashes and eyebrow hairs right away, but in the nights that followed my...resurrection, I'd lost every single one of my fingernails and toenails, one by one. They'd grown back as I slept during the day, the same length as before, but made out of some stronger, more durable material. Starting about the third night after I died, my hair had fallen out in clumps, too—only to be replaced each following evening with strands that were somehow thicker, and shinier, devoid of split ends. My skin, seemingly perfect in the first two nights of being a vampire, had grown taut and red and shiny, then peeled off entirely over the course of a few nights, which was the grossest thing ever, but Harold had insisted that all of this was normal; it happened to all new fledglings. By now, most of the old dead human skin was gone, although a few itchy patches remained, here and there. My new flesh was still the same light olive complexion it had always been, but pallid, almost sallow. I'd always looked better with a tan, but like so many other parts of my life, that was no longer and option. Losing my last human thumbnail meant I'd been thoroughly reborn, my transformation bought and paid for by the quarts of blood I needed to sustain myself each night. I loathed it.

⬤

After I showered and changed clothes, I put my bloodied dress to soak in cold water, and crossed my fingers. The garment was dry-clean only; an expensive green designer wrap dress that I'd purchased on winter clearance sale my last semester of college as a sort of early graduation present to myself. Even on sale, it was the most expensive piece of clothing I'd ever bought for myself, but I'd justified the cost by telling myself it was a timeless silhouette that I could wear for the rest of my life, if I took care of it.

Now, a kind of strangled not-quite laugh caught in my throat, and I thought about Harold's ancient wool trousers and sweaters, and wondered if, someday, me and my hopefully-not-bloodstained wrap dress would be as strangely anachronistic as his style. I shook my head furiously to dislodge the thought. I wasn't going to be alive for centuries like Harold, or even decades like Avie. I was going to find my maker, and kill him, and Harold was going to cut off my head.

He'd promised.

He'd *promised*.

Dressed in an older pair of jeans and a long-sleeve fitted t-shirt, I walked through the mud room and into the garage, where Avie had done a fair job of clearing away enough clutter to make room for her own car—a beat-up old Civic that looked to be a few years older than my Accord. The plates were registered in Mississippi. Harold's car was pulled out into the driveway, and the garage door was wide open. The weather was still cold and windy and probably miserable if you were alive, but the streets had been cleared, and mounds of ugly grey-tinged slush accumulated near the curb.

I asked if I should move my car to create more space, but Harold just shook his head, and went back to lecturing Avie.

"I tell you what, kid, you're one lucky vampire. Your oil tank is almost empty and the whole serpentine belt was about tae blow."

"Told you." I interrupted with a self-satisfied nod. I picked up the oil tank plug and started wiping it off with a clean shop rag. I wasn't a car expert by any stretch, but I knew my way around most Hondas—thanks to Uncle Gino.

...I was 13 when my cousin Victoria got her driver's license and started picking me up from school on days when Mom had a lot of showings and couldn't get to Sacred Heart on time. By the time I graduated, I'd spent enough weekends and evenings after school hanging out at Uncle Gino and Aunt Francesca's house and car lot to have an adequate general knowledge of cars and car maintenance—among other things I learned under their roof. Victoria was already attending classes at the local community college by the time I turned 14, because she "got bored" and finished high school two years early.

I asked her once how she could get into so much trouble and still keep perfect grades. She shrugged, passed me a joint, and asked me if I wanted to do mushrooms with some boys from her college calculus class that weekend.

"It's not really trouble if it doesn't actually impact your life, Grace. You think my parents care if I get wasted on the weekends? I made the Dean's List last semester." She took another hit off the joint and slowly exhaled a steady stream of pungent smoke in the hazy air of the storage room above her family's three-car garage. Her older brothers had used it as a rec room when they still lived at home, and the fridge where they kept their pop and the fooseball table was still set up where they left things, but the rest of the space had been taken over by Victoria and her boy band posters. Baby of the family by almost 8 years, she mostly used the room to do drugs and read weird French literature. Recently, she'd started letting me do her hair and makeup when she was high.

Victoria made me feel cool and grown-up when all the other girls at school teased me.

"...I guess I could hang out with you and your friends, but it's new volunteer orientation at the shelter this weekend," I hesitated. "And it's kitten season, and Miss Dorris says there's a black siamese mix with blue eyes up for fostering. I was going to ask Mom and Dad if..."

"You need to be available round the clock to do kitten foster. They'll never say yes. Plus, what would your big brown dog think if you brought home kittens, huh? Do your volunteer work at the shelter and I'll pick you up. College boys are way more fun to hang out with than middle aged cat ladies, I promise you."

Victoria ended up getting a free ride to Princeton all the way through grad school, because she was no slouch. Now she worked as a consultant for an environmental nonprofit that did a bunch of lobbying—that's how I ended up finding out about my job as a grant writer for the startup. They made specialized software and testing equipment for environmental scientists. Some of it was a little bit over my head, but I never would have admitted that to my Ivy League educated cousin. She met her fiancé at school. I didn't know much about him, but his family had to be loaded—he and Victoria were going to get married in a castle in New Jersey soon. An honest-to-God castle. So she was obviously on to something with her personal philosophy on what constituted trouble, is all I'm saying.

It's a mindset I worked very hard to adopt later, when I went away to college and found lots of potential trouble everywhere. It's not really trouble if it doesn't affect your life.

Until it does. Because maybe I wouldn't have ended up a vampire if I hadn't been drinking on New Years Eve. I couldn't stop beating myself up over it.

"Look, I'm usually a lot better about maintenance, but you'll never believe the wear and tear your car gets in—where I've been at." Avie threw a ratchet up in the air and deftly caught it. She seemed very intent on avoiding eye contact with Harold when it came to discussing her recent misadventures. "Biggest potholes I've ever seen, and I've driven through Michigan and Ohio."

"Hey—"

"I think Grace is from Ohio." Harold said.

"I'm not really offended." I shrugged. Ohio was no place special. Certainly not Toledo. "Did you know there's like two dozen astronauts from Ohio? That says something about a state so bad people go to space to get away from it."

I never know with jokes. Sometimes the stuff I think's funny goes right over people's heads, and other times, I'll just say something, and it cracks people up. I thought Avie was going to keel over from wheezing, she laughed at my jab at my home state for so long, she ran out of air and just kept spasming. Finally, Harold slapped her on the back a few times, and she straightened up, wiping tears from her eyes.

"I like this one a lot, Jack. If you decide not to keep her, I will."

"You'd at least have someone around tae remind you tae change your oil."

"Old Man, I've been about as busy as I've ever been, and I wasn't given much time to come back up here and take care of business. I know I'm lucky."

"I wonder if you know just how." Harold didn't seem quite ready to let go of his lecture. "If you'd lost your serpentine belt out on the road before sunrise, you could have gotten stuck somewhere bad."

"That's why the only things I keep in my trunk are thick blankets, tinfoil, and black spray paint."

"What's the tinfoil and spray paint for?" After witnessing the contents of Harold's murder box, I was almost afraid to ask.

"You can use them to cover windows in abandoned buildings in a pinch, if you have to. Or you can sleep the day away in the trunk wrapped in blankets, if you think you're someplace safe enough that no one will try to break into your car."

"Risky, kid. Too risky."

"Says the man who used to jump trains. Say, didn't you tell me you once dynamited a mobster's car? And that was in, what, 1930-something. Which means you were older then than I am now."

"You're supposed tae heed my stories as warnings, not opportunities for oneupmanship."

"Now, that's real funny. Because I always thought you were showing off."

"Maybe. Just a little." Harold grinned at her. "But that's no excuse to be driving around in a car that could get you killed. I'd be devastated if anything happened ta you, kid." His voice softened, and I thought I saw Avie flinch, the shadow of some secret unspoken horror passing between them.

"Yeah, well, I ain't planning on checking out any time soon. Don't worry about me. I'll be fine." Her voice was gruff, and she leaned into the engine to tighten something. "Fuck me, I know I use to complain about the old knuckle-busting fan belts, but it is ridiculous how tiny they cram everything into these engines now. I can barely reach—and you know I'm good at working my fingers into some pretty tight spaces." She looked up and winked at me. If she was trying to get a rise out of me, I didn't give her the satisfaction. I'd been on the receiving end of Becca's double entendres for years, after all.

"How long have you two known each other?" I asked.

Avie and Harold exchanged glances.

"What is it now, fifteen years or something like that?"

"It was right around 9/11. I don't remember if it was before or after. It was a Sunday night, the Bears were playing, and you cockblocked my dinner at a south side bar."

"I did nothing of the sort. I was merely being friendly."

"Bull *shit*. Picture it, if you will: I've spent a good hour, hour and a half chatting up this little lady with big hoop earrings and a neck like a—"

"—swan?" I guessed.

Avie pointed finger guns in my direction and grinned like an idiot. "Naw, this girl was definitely more the Canada Goose type. I like 'em a little crazy, in a good way. The game's on, and everyone's paying attention to that, so I see my opportunity and suggest we go out to the smoking patio for some quiet, get to know each other better, yeah? Then we get out there and she says, 'Oh no, I left my drink at the bar.' And I'm like, 'I've got you sweetheart, I'll go get you another drink, I'll get you anything you want.' I come back outside just in time to catch this short, scruffy-looking, overconfident fellow slide up out of nowhere and light her cigarette with some kind of a fancy gold-plated Art Deco Zippo lighter, acting as suave as Alan Ladd. She takes a drag, he moves in like a—"

"I was not scruffy-looking! And the Zippo was a brass reproduction I got at Menard's, and *someone* never returned it when I accidentally left it behind in their car."

"Sure, Han Solo. You stole my meal ticket. Left me standing there with a Hennessy and soda in my hand and nothing to drink. It's those damn green eyes, I tell you, that's what it was."

"I made it up tae you—"

"Oh, right, here's the best part. This fellow here didn't even need to be out scouting the locals, he had a shady doc over at University Medical supplying him with hospital stuff! He was just out that night because he'd been 'feeling peckish'—in his own words, mind you. No respect for those of us who actually have to work for our supper."

"You told me you didn't like seeing people as food." I accused Harold, feeling nauseous.

Avie straightened up again and looked guilty. "Say, I didn't mean to ruin your sterling image with Gracie here Old Man. I'm sorry."

"It's not something I do often. I sort of stopped when I bought this place. You've got tae be more careful when you're settled. Avie just caught me at an in-between phase. I don't like seeing people like—like that. It messes with my head."

Avie sighed and slid under the car again to continue the oil change. I handed the part I'd been cleaning back to Harold, who reached down and handed it to her. They briefly whispered back and forth so low, I couldn't make out what they were saying, and Harold started picking up his tools and putting them back in his kit. This time, he didn't look at me.

I was about to head back into the house, when Avie's voice called out from under the car. "You ever learn about the Haymarket Affair?"

"I don't understand—?" But I knew about the Haymarket riots, vaguely, just from living in Chicago. There was a sign pointing 'Haymarket Martyrs Memorial' near the exit I usually took driving back to Oak Park.

"Go on. Ask. You wanna find out if the Old Man here is good people or not—"

"Aw, come on kid, that's not even—"

"May 4th, 1886." She crawled out from under the car, wiping her grease-covered hands on her jeans before I could hand her the shop rag, eyes bright. "I grew up hearing about that night from my folks, who knew about it all the way in Russia. Workers campaigning for an 8 hour workday, fighting back against corrupt cops, *someone* threw a bomb—"

"It was a hell of a night." Harold looked around at the clutter in the garage as if he were only just now seeing it for the first time. He seemed uncomfortable. "...And a lot of people got hanged afterward, and for a long time it didn't seem like any of the marching or songs did a damn lick o' good." He reached out a hand to Avie, and she grabbed it, pulling up to her feet again.

"But you were there. On the right side of history." She poked his chest. "And I'll tell you who wasn't—"

"Watch yourself."

"You *also* said you never crossed paths with history, Harold." But my accusation was softer, this time.

"Everyone crosses paths with history, Gracie." Avie finished the last of the adjustments and slammed the hood.

"Only my family calls me Gracie." Not even Becca was allowed to call me Gracie. I didn't exactly resent Avie for what happened earlier in the kitchen, but I also wasn't going to let her call me by the same name my Nana did. "My name is Grace. Miss Cordero, if you prefer."

Harold gave me a sharp look. I gave him one back. What?

Avie continued, thoroughly nonplussed. "All right, Miss Cordero. Jack's heart is in the right place, that's all I'm saying. Whether or not it beats. Yeah, he's a monster and he eats people. That's just the way it is sometimes. I don't always like it either, but once you get on the blood it's real hard...anyway. This man figured out he'd screwed me over in that bar that night, and what did he do? He helped me out. Gave me a place to stay for a few nights, and made sure I was topped up. What he's got, he shares.

"Which, you know, is what the Community is supposed to do. We're supposed to have each other's backs. But the night is hard, and you won't always find other vampires as willing to stick their neck out as this guy. He's got his head on straight. I'm pretty sure that's the best any of us can do, yeah?"

"...yeah. I guess."

Harold told me to go back inside. "I'm gonna finish up with the feral beanpole here."

Whatever they talked about after I left, Harold never told me.

Chapter Eleven

THE SWEETEST SERIAL KILLER EVER

AVIE HIT THE ROAD shortly after her car was up and running again. Harold insisted she could stay longer, of course she didn't have to head out so soon—but I think we were both relieved when she parted ways. I still wasn't entirely sure how I felt about her; in theory she was good-humored, and she passed along some very useful information for which I was grateful. Harold obviously had a soft spot for her. But I already knew Avie was the kind of person my anxiety could only ever handle in the smallest of doses.

Harold, for his part, muttered something under his breath when examining the contents of the fridge, and I was pretty certain he was worried about the blood. Between my monstrous fledgling appetite, and Avie's extra mouth to feed, the stash disappeared quickly—and the spill earlier in the evening didn't help matters.

My mind kept replaying the image of the full glass of blood falling to the floor; all that precious liquid gone to waste. I couldn't stop thinking about it.

"I'm glad I got to meet your friend." I told him, as we waved Avie out the door and watched as she drove away down the street. At least her car sounded better.

"That's a hoot, because she thought you were going tae try tae strangle her at least three separate times." He didn't seem upset, though. "I know, I told you, she's a lot. But..."

"She means a lot to you."

He turned to walk back inside. "Yes. Yes, she does...you know, she's the one who found this house. I believe Major Pendleton was a regular at one of her preferred dives, and they'd talk about the war sometimes, if they crossed paths when she was on the prowl. I don't think she ever fed from him; she probably pretended tae be her own granddaughter or something, just so she could talk planes. He and his wife were selling the house around the time I mentioned I might want to try getting settled again after...well, I'd been unsettled for a while. So it worked out. Last I heard, they had plans tae use the money tae cruise the world until they died, so...I hope they did."

"You are the sweetest serial killer I ever met."

He shrugged and didn't say anything else, but I thought he looked sad, like he did in the car the night he picked me up from Calliope's.

Calliope...

Suddenly, I had a thought. "Harold...who turned Marie DuChamps? The woman who turned Avie? It was Calliope Jones, wasn't it? That's why Avie doesn't like her."

"Avie has plenty of reasons to dislike Calliope. Not the least of them being a fundamentally different outlook on economics. Avie's about as red as you can get."

"Ah."

"And Calliope had some pretty sketchy investments in some German companies back in the 1930's."

"Ouch."

"But you're not wrong—that was a good catch. Marie is one of Calliope's. Turned her sometime after that big earthquake in San Francisco. I never liked her, for what it's worth."

"I heard you say that."

Harold looked around the parlor and gave everything a satisfied nod. "This looks real swell."

"Why didn't you like Marie? What's wrong with her?" I didn't want to let him get away with changing the subject.

"Marie DuChamps is a certifiable psychopath. I hope I never run into her again." He almost looked frightened when he said it.

I spent the next several hours finishing the parlor, rearranging furniture for optimal flow, and giving the room what Becca affectionately called, "the Graceover." I'd helped most of our friends set up their first apartments, in the life I used to have before. Maybe I should have been a professional organizer.

Maybe I should have been a lot of things. Breathing, for one.

But I'd discovered another good thing about being a vampire while rearranging the furniture. I wasn't exactly counting my blessings, but I never would have been able to move the sofa all on my own, or lug all the boxes of trash to the curb for garbage pickup without any help, when I was mortal. It didn't begin to make up for everything I'd lost—not even close.

But it made getting things done a lot more efficient. I liked efficient. Efficient felt safe.

And, I thought, Major and Mrs. Pendleton—wherever they were—would probably have smiled, to see their house looking so orderly again.

I was dabbing a small bloodstain on the sofa's upholstery with a watered down solution of dish soap when Harold called out from his library workshop,

"I have a surprise for you."

"I think I've had enough surprises for the month, Harold." I hated surprises. Especially recent ones. Particularly vampire surprises.

He ignored my suspicion. "Close your eyes."

"Harold..."

"Close. Your eyes." He insisted.

I heard him humming softly to himself as he entered the room, moved a few things around, and fumbled with what sounded like an extension cord. I didn't recognize the song he was humming. Finally he stood next to me, not exactly in my personal space, but close enough that I knew he was near. He made a small excited sound when he told me I could open my eyes again.

"You better not have rearranged all the furniture—oh." I felt a slow, small, delighted smile spread across my face as he flipped a switch on the extension cord, and the green-leaf stained glass lamps on either side of the sofa illuminated like the Tree of Life. "You fixed them…" I stepped over to get a closer look, admiring the neatly soldered repairs to the shades, the expertly re-wired cords. You could hardly even tell they'd been in such bad shape the night before. "Show off."

But I couldn't stop smiling. I looked over at Harold, his hands thrust deep in his pockets, an almost shy, boyish grin on his face made even more luminous in the soft glow of the lamps.

"Tis but a haand's turn. Like I said, I didn't even know these were in the pile o' stuff, but…I think they came out real nice."

Of course the moment had to be ruined, as the gnawing hunger ever growling in my gut gained momentum, building to a screaming crescendo that I couldn't continue to ignore. My veins felt like battery acid. I needed to quench the burning.

"I'm thirsty…" I whispered, shame rising in a pitch that almost equaled my horrible need.

"Tak at, git what you need from the icebox. You don't need ta ask me."

"You keep saying that, but I feel bad. I've gone through so much more than you. And Avie, and the spill…" I still kept revisiting the image of the spilled blood. So much waste. So much red, blood on my hands, blood on the…I shook the thoughts away like an Etch-a-Sketch, and walked to the kitchen.

By now there was only one bag of blood left in the brown cardboard box Harold kept in the crisper drawer, only one bag left out of the last supply he'd brought to the house only a few nights ago. I turned to look back to the front room at Harold, but he'd followed me into the kitchen.

"I don't want you tae feel badly, Grace." He gently took the bag of blood out of my hands, and opened it up with the pocketknife he always kept in his pants pocket. He poured most of the blood from the bag into my glass, and carefully transferred the remainder of the bag into his ancient dented hip flask. Watching his steady hands fold the plastic of the bag just so to create the perfect funnel was nerve-wracking; I imagined the blood spilling it all over the floor and and this time being unable to stop myself from falling to my knees and licking the the ancient linoleum clean of all crimson, but Harold never spilled a drop. He held out his flask to my glass, and we both drank.

Maybe I didn't mind having company when I fed, after all.

When the brief intensity of the blood high faded, Harold continued. "Being aware of your thirst is the first step tae having control over it. And having enough blood when you're new makes you less likely tae lose control when you're older."

I nodded, even though I wasn't sure about the getting older part. That, in fact, seemed out of the question. I hated feeling like I was already getting used to my new life. I wanted it over as soon as possible.

"I'll go out and get more blood first thing tomorrow evening as long as the roads are clear, okay?"

"Take me with you. I'm going to need to learn how to get supplies for myself eventually, right?" I had to get out of the house. Not having to breathe didn't take away my need for fresh air.

Harold shook his head. "Not yet. There are too many things that could go wrong. I can't risk you spilling anything in the car. I'll take you hunting when you're ready. Until then, it's a maker's job ta provide for their fledgling."

"But you're not my maker." I reminded him, as if either of us could have forgotten.

Harold was thoughtful and solemn again, as he often was. "I know," he said softly. "But for all intents and purposes, I might as well be. We choose our family, our kin, our...blood, in this life."

"There's no blood between us."

"And it's the damnedest thing, isn't it? Because sometimes it feels like, maybe, there should be."

I looked away. I didn't want to like Harold Laing so goddamn much.

◆○◆

He was gone when I woke up the next evening. In the kitchen I found a glass canning jar on the counter, filled with suspicious-looking blood that looked like it had been violently shaken. Tiny bubbles still frothed on the surface of the liquid, and I gagged when I took a small, tentative sip. It was blood, all right, but the texture was...gritty, somehow, and it tasted too strongly of iron. Still, I didn't think Harold was trying to poison me. I poked around in the fridge to be sure, and there wasn't any other blood left.

I wished he would leave me a text or a voicemail or a note sometime, but I guessed he'd gone off to get more supplies, and I could only imagine how long he'd be gone. The last time he was out for a pick up, it took him almost two hours. I didn't think I could wait that long for fresh stuff, so I choked down the blood in the jar as fast as I could, and decided that, even as a vampire, drinks served in Mason jars were rarely worth the hype.

I almost felt like vomiting, but at least I didn't have the shakes.

My phone rang with Becca's number, but I didn't pick it up. My fangs hadn't retracted yet, and I didn't want to lisp when I spoke to her. I let the phone ring til it went to voicemail, and noticed that I had actually missed a number of calls from her during the day, when I'd been asleep.

Becca: Why are you ignoring me?

She texted.

Grace: I'm not, I promise.

I texted back

Becca: I really need to talk to you. Please. So much is going on and I don't like what I'm hearing. Please pick up. Please?

I glanced around the kitchen trying to think of an excuse, when my eyes fell on a familiar-looking small dark bottle, and a few cotton balls, on the table Harold used as a makeshift engine block. And I got an idea.

Grace: Meet me at the Windy Grill in 40 minutes. We'll talk. I promise.

She replied a few moments later with a smiley face emoji.

Becca: :) can do

My parka was still in the mud room, and my key ring was still in the pocket. I darted upstairs for my purse and my wallet, ran a brush through my hair, and stuffed my nose full of peppermint torture on my way out the door.

"I've got this. I'm good. I can handle it." I tried to psych myself up on the drive, but in the back of my mind, a faraway wordless scream began to grow louder. I tried not to think about the cleaning crew that I'd lunged at. Or the holiday shoppers, whom I'd barely maintained my composure around. This was Becca, after all.

I could never hurt Becca. Ever.

Traffic on the expressway was worse than expected as I made my way downtown, and parking, as always, was a nightmare. I called Becca a few times to let her know that I was running late, but she didn't pick up. Finally, on my fourth trek round the block, while I was still looking for parking and trying to figure out what I was going to say, my phone rang from an unknown number, and I smiled, rolled my eyes, and immediately answered.

"Had to borrow a stranger's phone because you left yours behind in your apartment again, Bec?"

"Grace, where are you?" The cool, scalpel-edged voice on the other end of the line wasn't Becca's, but I recognized the owner immediately, and my smile evaporated into nothingness. A car behind me honked, and I realized that the light had turned green. I pressed on the gas and confessed. "I'm in my car."

"Yes, I can hear that. Where, exactly, are you?"

"...near the Loop."

"Grace."

To make the situation even more surreal, I passed a bus stop plastered with one of her advertisements, and Calliope Jones's stern eyes seemed to follow me as my car crawled along in the evening rush hour. "I'm not doing anything wrong." I protested, even though I'd been caught more or less red-handed doing exactly what I'd been told not to do. "Did Harold tell you to call me?"

"Why would Harold be looking for you, Grace? I only called to check in on you. Did I catch you at an inconvenient time?"

In that moment I decided that I hated Calliope Jones, too.

"Sweetheart, the last thing I want to do is pay out a lot of money to keep a story about fledgling vampire on a rampage in Downtown Chicago off the record."

"Well, there's not going to be a rampage."

"Because you're going to turn around and drive back to Harold's."

"I told Becca I would meet her. She says she needs to talk."

"Your Becca can work out her own issues like a big girl. I'm keeping an eye on her for you. She's going to be perfectly safe."

Funny how I didn't find that reassuring at all. "What have you done to Becca?" I raised my voice without meaning to.

"Calm down, Grace. You're obviously upset, and that's no way to be around people. Go home. No one's going to do anything to Becca. I promise. I'm just...keeping an eye on her. She was at my party too, if you recall."

As if I could forget. "Becca needs me. I'm going to make sure—"

"Do not. Get out. Of your car." Her commanding presence manifested just as clearly over the phone as it did in person, which was some kind of terrifying. "You've been a fledgling for a week, there's no way to guarantee the safety of anyone around you. The biggest danger to your friend Becca tonight is yourself, have no illusions about that. You should be grateful I called when I did. I honestly had no idea what you were planning." I could hear her fingernails tapping in the background, and I wanted to rip off her perfectly manicured acrylics, one by one. I wanted to—

Well, that was unexpectedly violent. I slumped down in my seat, suddenly struck by the infuriating realization that Calliope was right—I had no business being around people. Who was I kidding? Even with peppermint-filled nostrils, I was a danger to anyone I might encounter. And what if I snapped and hurt Becca? What if I—oh, God, what if—

"I'll turn around." I said, defeated.

"That's a good girl. I knew you were reasonable."

I wanted to ask Calliope if she'd ever called Marie DuChamps a "good girl," and how well that worked out for her, but I was, in fact, reasonable enough to know that would be a bad idea, so instead I thanked her for calling, assured her that I didn't need anything else at the moment—not materially, in any event—and disconnected as quickly as possible.

I got several more calls, all from Becca, on the drive home. I let all of them go to voicemail.

CHAPTER TWELVE

MEET YOUR MAKER

THE FIRST MONTH OF the year disappeared under banks of snow, my first month as a vampire, and I was equally buried, transformed into something I did not recognize or wish to be. Nights passed, and I did not return to my old apartment. Nor did I leave Harold's house again, and as far as I knew, we made no progress toward finding out anything about my maker.

Like any newborn, for the most part, I slept, and I fed, and I adjusted to the harsh sensations of the world I had been born into—the most overwhelming of which was my inescapable hunger.

To keep up with my all-consuming appetite, Harold relied on various suppliers—sometimes the blood he brought home was in hospital bags, sometimes canisters, and a few times, in quart-sized takeout soup containers (animal blood from a butcher, he apologized).

Staying under wraps meant not putting a strain on the local blood supply, and Chicago had a hard enough time keeping sufficient blood on hand for the mortals who needed it. If there was a lot of violence over the weekend, we drank animal blood the following week. It made my stomach cramp and tasted worse than the bagged stuff did, but it was still blood.

I couldn't survive on it all the time, though. The first hit of human blood again after a few nights of cattle or pig blood convinced me of that. I hated myself for my lack of moral fortitude—animal blood was surely less perditious than human—but my flesh was weak, and my body desired what it had been damned to desire.

For a while, I continued pestering Harold with questions, some more facetious than others, just to see his reactions; but once Avie left, he was frustratingly reticent to answer any inquiries of a personal nature. I felt like a pedestrian on a cold side-walk, peering into the windows of an interesting old house all lit up from within, when suddenly the curtains were drawn closed, and I was left shivering alone in the dark. I wondered what I'd done wrong.

Every night just before dawn, he cordially wished me a good sleep at the top of the stairs, and we retired to our separate bedrooms to survive the day alone. Every three to four nights, he left the house shortly after sunset, and returned a few hours later with more blood. As the weeks wore on, my voracious appetite subsided somewhat. I graduated from needing to feed four times a night to three, and then to just twice most nights, if I could help it. On that front at least, I was proud of my progress.

Otherwise, being a vampire, as far as I could tell, was a monotonous drag. Blood and sunrise were the only respites, and even those were brief distractions. The blood high always faded, and the sun continued to go down again, night after endless night.

I tried not lose myself. I made my bed each evening when I woke, and I continued to find organizational projects around the house to occupy my time. He really did have a set of lawn darts in the garage—it might have been fun to set up the targets in the backyard and play a few rounds of danger cornhole in the spring—but I wasn't planning to be around to see spring to come again. How long did it take to track down all the vampire guests at Calliope's party, after all?

Speaking of Calliope, I wanted to know what Harold's relationship with her was, and what was his relationship with the other vampires in the Community? Who turned him, and how did he end up in America all the way from Scotland or the south of Spain or where ever he said he was from? And why didn't he want to talk about his fledgling? Had she left him because he liked men? I imagined that could have been a sore spot. Maybe that's why he wanted to know if it bothered me?

These questions remained unanswered.

And then there was the whole family drama about Victoria's wedding at the end of January. I braced myself for it, as soon as I called to send my regrets—but there was no possible way for me to do her hair and makeup now that I was a vampire, and certainly no way to tell my deeply Catholic family about my newly acquainted nocturnal, blood drinking lifestyle—not without at least one of my aunts or uncles calling the priest for an exorcism. I'd much rather get beheaded.

So I told Victoria that I still had the flu. "Gracie. Please. You can't do this to me. There's literally no one else. *Madonna mia*, do not fuck me over like this." She hyperventilated on the other end of the line, and I sat paralyzed on the yellow velvet armchair in the parlor, incapable of finding any words that would make anything better. I'd been doing Victoria's makeup for formal events since I was fourteen, of course there wasn't anyone else. That was one wedding thing I promised she wouldn't have to stress over.

Aunt Francesca must have been sitting right next to Victoria when I called, because she immediately began shouting, "After all we did for you and your parents, huh? This is how you're gonna act? *Ma che coz'u fai!?* I told your father. I said, 'Christopher, don't you be letting that girl go off and live by herself all the way in Chicago, her mother just passed away, she needs to be with family, who knows what trouble she could get up to?' Oriana should be spinning in her grave, the way you're going on, you know that—?"

Aunt Francesca and Uncle Gino already had four kids of their own when my eighteen year old father knocked up his high school sweetheart their senior year, and like any nosey Italian American mother worth her salt, Aunt Francesca was deeply suspicious of a young woman experiencing flu-like symptoms for almost a month.

I'd barely finished trying to apologize to Victoria, who was still crying in an awful panic about having to find a last minute wedding makeup artist, when Dad's number started flashing up my phone screen.

"...you know, kiddo, I'm always going to love you no matter what. If there's any kind of trouble you're in, anything at all, we can handle it." Dad cleared his throat, which just made everything a thousand times more awkward. "We're family, Gracie. It doesn't matter what it is, you don't have to be scared to tell me—"

But I was scared. The whole world had become a terrifying nightmare landscape of blood and darkness overnight, and I was still drowning in the violence of what had been done to me. *I should have heeded Harold's advice and dropped off the face of the earth.* I was pretty sure that Dad thinking I was pregnant and trying to hide it was infinitely worse than letting him believe that I was dead.

Becca and I shared a couple of texts after I stood her up at the diner—I sent a funny meme about sloths that made me think of her, Becca sent back a hilariously blasphemous meme in return—but that perfunctory exchange was the extent of our interactions. The radio silence between us was disorienting and unnatural, worse in some ways than my fangs and bloodlust, but I couldn't even bring myself to listen to her voicemails. I deleted them after a few nights of staring down the notifications on my phone, not that that did much to ease my anxiety. I wasn't entirely sure, but I thought Becca might have started seeing someone. There was something cagey-yet-optimistic about her social media posts all of a sudden—something in her captions suggested she was happy about something (or someone), but not exactly willing to potentially jinx it. I knew I shouldn't be obsessing over her online presence. I just felt terribly left out and alone. Everyone's life was going on without me.

Becca: You going to be at the show tonight?

It was the first week of February, and after several days of heavy snow, the roads had finally cleared enough to allow Harold the opportunity to leave on overdue blood run. Our supplies had run dangerously low. I was all alone in the house early in the evening, mindlessly browsing the internet, when Becca's out of the blue text caught me by surprise.

I didn't know what she was talking about, so I responded,

Grace: No, I'm going to stay in. Have fun.

Becca: Grace, are you OK? I'm worried.

Grace: I'm fine

She didn't text me again.

Less than an hour later, a notification popped up on my laptop reminding me that a favorite local band that me and Becca had been obsessed with back in college was doing a reunion tour, and the first stop on that tour was at The Metro that night. *Right. That show.* I'd already paid for my ticket months ago.

I'd forgotten how excited Becca had been about the concert back in October when the band announced the tour, and another spiked pang of regret wrapped its thorns around me.

I was forgetting too much.

I reconsidered the concert.

Okay, so maybe it had been several years since my choppy dyed-black scene haircut and too much black eyeliner, and while I wasn't going to cut or dye my hair for a one-night show, I *did* have enough black items in my limited wardrobe to put together a suitable outfit, and I could always double-up on the black eyeliner. You barely needed a mirror for that if you were committed to being messy for the aesthetic. And, just the other night, when I was going through the attic, I'd even found a tattered old black cocktail hat with shredded netting that would make the *perfect* hair accessory.

I checked Mom's Cartier.

I had plenty of time to get ready and sneak off before Harold got back. There was one bag of blood left in the fridge, and while he'd kept the peppermint extract mysteriously hidden since the last time I went out, I had cotton balls in my toiletries and could probably get the same effect with some of the Tom Ford perfume I'd bought for Becca. I hadn't had a chance to send it to her yet—I wanted to figure out the best way to make my peace offering. I didn't think bringing it to the show was a good option, but...that stuff was certainly strong enough to block out the scent of any sweaty clubgoers, and she wouldn't mind if the bottle I gave her was only very slightly used. Would she? If I stayed in the back of the club and wore dark glasses, I wouldn't get in any kind of trouble at all.

I wasn't a brand-new fledgling anymore. I'd been a vampire for over a month. That had to account for something.

I smiled. It felt fun in a sneaky, rebellious sort of way to quickly throw together an outfit that would have made Grace from four years ago proud. And besides, I was taking precautions; how could Harold be mad at me if I just went out for a few hours on my own? Maybe I was new to being a vampire, but I was also a grown adult, and I didn't understand his penchant for a hermit-like existence. Calliope socialized all the time, and Avie clearly did, too—even if I was less approving of her motivations for hanging out at bars.

I brushed my teeth to remove the evidence of dinner, spritzed a cotton ball with a very generous splash of Black Orchid, and dashed out the door.

By the time I was backing my car out of Harold's garage, I was already singing along to a playlist of the band's greatest hits on my phone at the top of my lungs. For the first time in weeks, I felt—almost light. Almost alive. I turned up the volume.

It didn't take long to get to Clark Street this time, and I made good use of Calliope's generous allowance by paying for overpriced parking not far from the club. Inside the venue, I was glad I'd thought to bring the sunglasses; the strobing lights from the opening band on stage were painfully bright. I also decided the shades made me look cool as fuck, and the dark-tinted lenses hardly obscured my vision at all otherwise.

Even though I was—or had been—a vodka and soda girl, I bought a beer from the bar, just to have something to hold in my hand, and kept to the perimeter of the venue, people watching. I noticed a few familiar faces from my friends' group in the crowd, but it wasn't hard to avoid people. Maybe it was my cunning disguise. If someone I knew started walking toward me, I just thought, "go away," and they magically seemed to veer off. Whether or not that was a vampire power, I didn't know. Harold hadn't mentioned it, but then again, I hadn't asked. Given what he'd said already about flying and turning into mist or bats, mind control seemed right up there with manipulating the weather on the list of 'things vampires can't do, actually. Sorry for the inconvenience.'

The best part about going to a bar as a vampire, I decided, was not having to worry about what state the lady's room was going to be in as the night wore on and bladders got full. Another unexpected benefit. By the time the main act was ready to start, I was enjoying myself immensely. Even if the crowd and the crush of bodies, the noise, and the lights, were a little overwhelming. I pushed it all down, committed to having a good time.

At least I wasn't bored at home.

Despite Calliope's lecture that interrupted my last ill-fated rendezvous with Becca, I tried to assure myself that I had more self-control than she or Harold gave me credit for. My eyes darted about the crowd of concert-goers, scanning for any sign of my best friend, trying to correct the glaring error of her absence in my life as of late. I wasn't sure what I was going to say to her that would make things right between us without mentioning the V word, but I needed, at least, to see her.

But Becca wasn't surrounded by our usual circle of friends near the front of the stage, and she wasn't hanging out at the bar, either.

A hollow ping echoed in my chest—not exactly a heartbeat, but the ghost of one, perhaps. None of this was supposed to have happened. We were supposed to be friends forever. We should have been at the concert together.

I almost think I sensed her before I saw her, some way off to the side of the stage, holding hands with a man I almost thought I recognized...

My heart actually did thump for a beat or two, in time with the music, as I moved through the crowd possessed by a lithe fluidity of movement I'd never known before, despite my name. As I lowered my sunglasses to get a better look at the guy at Becca's side, something primal and wounded, deeper than a heartbeat, started rumbling in my chest.

He was exactly Becca's type; tall and well-muscled under his almost-too-tight shirt, and his hair was dark and full, the very image of a modern brooding gothic antihero. There was something about his face...

Like a Tim Burton character brought to life.

The blinding lights from the stage shot out into the crowd again, and when they did, Becca's date and I flinched in unison, instinctively turning away from the strobing brightness. The features of his face became clear, illuminated in an instant like flash of lightning, and the world lurched. My body was no longer my own.

I'm leaning against the wall in a hallway of a fancy penthouse apartment, sur-rounded by revelers I don't know, getting jostled by strangers who don't even see me in their drunken rush to the great room for the big countdown. I'm checking my text messages from Dad as the ball drops at midnight, when a different stranger is suddenly in front of me, interrupting my view, demanding a kiss for the New Year. He seems familiar—didn't we meet him downstairs?

*Confusion overwhelms my attraction—he's supposed to be with Becca, I'm pretty sure. Where is—I'm looking around for Becca as his cold hands rest on my shoulders, not sure what to do as his cool lips meet mine, but the initially welcome kiss goes wrong; his tongue tastes gross when he forces it into my mouth, the trace of something sour and metallic on his breath. I try to break away from the kiss as lips move further down my neck, his hands over my mouth and his body pressed against me, pinning me to the wall, and I can't move, and I can't scream, and oh, God, what is he **doing**—*

My hands reached instinctively for the side of my throat where I *knew* the man standing next to Becca had bitten me, and a sudden scream arose from the pent up whirlwind of rage inside me—loud and violent and incendiary. Becca's date locked eyes with me for the exact absence of a heartbeat before he spun off, running through the press of humanity that surrounded us.

I sprinted after him, knocking over club patrons as I elbowed my way through the throng. *I could taste the memory of his blood*, and it repulsed me.

"I'm going to kill you, asshole!" I shouted, hurling my beer at the vampire who'd attacked me. The contents of the still-full bottle rained onto the crowd as it sailed overhead, and exploded in a cascade of shards when it slammed into the skull of my assailant. The blow should have stopped an ordinary person. It barely slowed the vampire down.

Someone in the crowd shouted, "Stop her!" as arms and hands reached out to grab at me. The music on stage halted, replaced with the sound of unease spreading through the patrons. Somewhere in the crowd, Becca's voice called out my name, but I was too far gone. I pried groping fingers off of my arms and shoulders and heard at least one man scream in pain as bones snapped and cracked, but I continued chasing after the monster who turned me.

My maker.

He reached the doors first; I stretched out and grabbed him by the elbow as he tugged his arm forward, and the forward momentum propelled me past him, sprawling onto the sidewalk. I picked myself up much faster than I'd ever known I could and lost no time landing a solid punch to his jaw. Even though he was easily a foot taller than I was, he toppled and lost his footing.

"Holy shit, lady!" One of the bouncers shouted in amazement. "It's all right. Let us handle it."

Another chimed in, "Break it up, break it up!"

The vampire quickly recovered from my punch and returned with a blow of his own that sent me soaring backward again into Clark Street traffic. A car swerved, narrowly avoiding a direct hit, and laid on the horn as other drivers began to lean out of their car windows, shouting at the crowd now gathered around us.

"You're a monster!" I screamed at him, as a bouncer tried to grab me by the shoulders again, and I stomped on the bouncer's foot, hard. The burly man yelped and let go, and I launched myself at my maker again, throwing my arms around his neck in a chokehold, wrapping my legs around his waist.

He snarled and spun around, gasping vile invectives in my direction as he tried to dislodge me, but I held on tight until I felt the small bones in his throat give way and break. My moves were impressive, but futile—crushing his windpipe meant nothing when he didn't need to breathe. He slammed back into the brick exterior of the nightclub, smashing me between his body and the wall, and I let go, momentarily limp, slumped on the ground.

He kicked me when I was down, throwing off both of the bouncers at once. My ears were ringing, and I was vaguely aware of the blood dripping down my face from a cut I'd received when my head made contact with the bricks, but I pulled myself to my feet while he was distracted by the bouncers, cracked my neck, and steadied my stance for one more go at him, winding up to land another punch at his stupid undead pretty face, when a familiar shape in a dark green pullover sweater pushed me aside and made full body contact with my maker, landing a succession of solid, satisfying hits.

"Harold, what the fuck!?" I shouted.

"You left your Facebook open!" he returned without missing a beat. My maker was only able to get a few punches in here and there as Harold continued to make a bloody pulp of the taller man's head, and I thought I had a pretty good idea, in that moment, of exactly how he'd gotten his nose broken, centuries ago. As I'd seen with Avie, Harold did not play fair, and when the fight was as real as it was this time, his sheer brutality was terrifying and impressive.

"You're on Facebook?" I didn't mean to keep shouting, but the violence excited me, and I was just amazed to hear somebody over two hundred years old talking about social media.

"I am when I'm looking for you!" He shouted right back at me. "I would have been here sooner, but I wrote down the addreth wrong!" he lisped, and I gasped when I realized I could see the tips of his fangs, quickly realizing that mine were extended as well. I clasped my hands over my mouth, unsure how many in the crowd of observers noticed, but it began to occur to me just how bad the situation was.

My maker crawled backward like a crab on the sidewalk, trying to escape Harold's blows, as police sirens drew closer, and we all paused for a fraction of a perfectly coordinated second before my maker used the distraction to take off, accelerating down the street, zipping in and out of traffic until he was out of sight. Harold lost no time grabbing me by the arm and hauling me off in the opposite direction. After half a block, we were both running at top speed away from the venue, around a corner, and into the night. For a moment, I thought I saw a black four-door car following us, but it turned a corner quickly before I could even think to get a look at the driver, and I told myself that I was just being jumpy.

Not even the police were following us.

We rode back to Harold's place in his car.

"I can't leave mine in the lot. I didn't pay for twenty-four-hour parking!"

"Then let it get towed. Come on."

"You can't keep doing this, Grace." Harold gripped the steering wheel, his voice grave, the skin on his knuckles translucent white over the tendons where he wasn't bloodied. "It's not cool. It's not okay. That could have gone very badly back there. We could have—"

"I know, all right, I know!" I cut him off, nursing the sore spot where the vampire had punched me. It was already feeling better; my bruised and scraped-up tissue knitting itself back together at a terrible cost. Dark, violent hunger welled up in my belly, gnawing at my veins. Harold had a nasty cut across his nose, a split lip, and a black and swollen eye, but those injuries also faded as he sped along Lakeshore Drive, north toward his stupid colonial rich person's house. I sulked, looking out the window at the darkened skyline, as the city flashed by on one side, and the lake on the other.

"Grace."

"Harold."

Harold sighed. I sighed. We deliberately avoided making eye contact.

"That was him, though, wasn't it?" he asked slowly.

"Yeah…" I kept my gaze focused outside the window, trying not to remember all the details that had just come flooding back, overwhelmed by the violation of what he'd done to me. It was rape, whether or not he'd sexually assaulted me. He'd raped away my humanity, and that felt so much worse. My mind kept returning to the brush of his fangs on my neck, the moment before he bit me, the moment before he…without consciously meaning to, my own fangs extended and then retracted in my mouth. I was unclean, tainted.

Punching him had felt good, though. I wasn't going to apologize for that.

"Do you remember…?"

"I remember everything, okay, Harold? I remember all of it. I remember every dirty fucking thing he did to me."

"Do you remember his name, though?"

"…everything but that."

"Well. We know what he looks like now. We can tell Calliope, and she can put the word out tae the Community..."

"I thought you and Calliope weren't getting the Community involved. That's what you told Avie."

"Avie's all right, Grace, but she's the last person I want getting involved in this situation. She's got all of these...high-minded ideas about how things ought tae be, and sometimes it doesn't get through her skull that the world just doesn't work the way she thinks it should."

"So you *are* going to get the Community—the rotational council or whatever—involved?" I chewed the inside of my lip and tried to imagine what the rotational council looked like. Did they wear robes? Stand behind fancy podiums and bang out their decrees with a gavel?

Harold nodded. "You can't just turn people and abandon them. It's not right. We'll find him, where he's from, what he's doing in town. He's got tae answer for his actions tae someone. I've never seen him before but, but again...I don't get out much."

I was starting to suspect that Harold's lack of Community engagement was more of a hindrance than a help to my cause. I didn't want to resent him for it, but in that moment, I did.

We got home just as the sky started pelting freezing wind-blown rain. If I thought that Harold was over being angry at me, the idea dissipated when he jerked open the passenger side door and said, in a dangerous tone, "In the house. I need more blood."

I wondered, with a shudder, if he meant mine.

He threw open the refrigerator door, pulling out translucent hospital bags, cutting the first one open with his pocketknife and chugging it straight from the plastic. Some of the blood spilled out of the opening he'd made and over his hands, staining the cuffs of his green wool pullover sweater. I watched, wordlessly, as he leaned back against the fridge, and lowered himself into a seated position on the floor. For the first time, I realized how badly he was shaking.

I knelt down next to him, not knowing what to do. Guilt drowned out every other emotion.

"When I came home and found you gone, you have no idea how—" he stopped himself, shaking his head. "I didn't even feed first, even though I didn't last night or the night before, and I wanted ta make sure there was enough blood for you in the house before I left tonight, so I didn't feed early this evening, either. I saw your computer open and I...I figured you'd gone out. I barely remembered tae put the blood away and..." He lowered his head to his chest, breathing in and out slowly and deliberately, physically willing his dormant lungs to inhale, exhale, in, and out. His swollen black eye faded into memory. The broken nose, and the scar on his chin, remained.

He took another swig of blood, a small rivulet of crimson pooling out of the corner of his mouth. Unconsciously, I reached out to wipe the blood clean off his face, and licked my finger. He handed me the second bag of blood and the pocket knife. I pushed them back at him.

"I think you need it more than me. You left me a full bag when you left the house tonight." Another pause. "Would you like me to pour this into a cup for you? You're making quite a mess."

Harold nodded, downing another gulp from the bag, and tried to stand up. I held out my arm to steady him, then gently took the opened blood bag out of his hand, pouring the remaining liquid into a clean glass for him. He accepted my assistance with the resignation of a man who is tired, profoundly, down to his soul. I'd seen that look on my father's face more than once on the nights he'd forgotten to eat, amidst all the flurry of Mom's doctor appointments in her last days, and I looked away from Harold's face in shame, recognizing the huge responsibility he'd undertaken in adopting me as his fledgling. Whatever debt he owed Calliope, I couldn't be worth all this stress.

My gaze fell to the blood on Harold's hands; there was blood on the outside of the now empty blood bag, where Harold had gripped it, and blood on my hands, too, transferred there from the bag. Without meaning to or thinking about it, I licked the blood clean off of my own fingers, arousal rising up inside of me, and I grabbed Harold's hand, brought it to my mouth, tongue gently probing the cracks and calluses on his fingers that never fully went away when he was turned.

"Grace..."

I stopped myself with enormous difficulty, still holding Harold's hand up against my lips. Our eyes met, and I froze, completely at a loss for reconciling what I thought and what I felt and how my body was reacting. A breathless moan escaped my lips in spite of myself, and I moaned again when Harold gently probed his fingers past my lips, letting me suck the blood clean, my fangs almost caressing his fingers inside my mouth. I wanted to bite down, to taste more than—I wanted blood, Harold's blood, filling up my mouth and coating my tongue. I wanted—

I caught myself, took a step backward, and shook my head, a spiral of emotions tugging at my ability to process anything that was happening. "I don't know what came over me," I whispered. I lowered my eyes and couldn't bring myself to look up at his again. How was it possible for a person to go from so completely traumatized one minute to so...horny, the next, if that was even the right word? I wasn't sure it was sex I wanted, but I definitely wanted blood. I drew in a deep, shuddering breath of my own.

"I think I will have some of that second bag, after all, if you don't mind." I turned away from him, embarrassed.

"It's jus' tha bloodlust, Grace." Harold's voice seemed sharp and far away, like a crack of thunder in the distance. A warning. "It happens tae all of us from time tae time. It doesn't mean anythin'."

I wasn't sure if that was the explanation I wanted.

I finished off the rest of the blood while Harold went down to the basement. A few minutes later, I could hear him banging away in his downstairs forge. I went upstairs to plug in my phone and deal with the fallout from Becca, which I was very certain was not going to be pretty.

Chapter Thirteen

It's Not a Habit

I'D PUT MY CELL phone on silent earlier in the night when I arrived at the venue, and I'd forgotten all about it—until it started buzzing in my bra as I walked upstairs. The screen was cracked, and the case was chipped at the corner, but I could still make out Becca's lit-up name. To my credit, I only debated answering for half a second before I sighed and accepted the call.

"What the hell is wrong with you? Who was that guy?" She didn't even give me a chance to say hello. I could hear the sound of a cash register beeping in the background.

"Becca, I—"

"Is it drugs, Grace? Did you finally get in over your head with something? God, I was so worried about that the entire time you were with that shithead Dylan—"

"It's not—"

"You know, your dad called me after you bailed on your cousin's wedding, because he thought you might be *pregnant*, for God's sake, and I had to tell him that I haven't seen you in weeks. Weeks, Grace. This isn't like you. Please, just—tell me what's wrong. People care about you and want to help."

I grabbed the handrail on the staircase and froze. She had every right to be angry with me, and we both knew it. Her tone flashed back and forth between concern and rage, and I had no answers that would satisfy her. I doubted she'd believe the truth, even if I could tell her. "Where are you, Becca? I don't want to have this conversation if you're busy..."

"Oh? Do you want to say you're going to meet me somewhere only to leave me high and dry again?" She continued to rant, and I took the verbal barrage wordlessly, knowing that I deserved it, crushed under another enormous pile of guilt for standing her up. "No thanks. I'm at CVS getting first aid supplies for my boyfriend because *someone* decided to attack him out of nowhere tonight. That was some PCP shit, Grace. Is that what this is? Because I saw you with a beer bottle in your hand before you went off, so I guess you're not pregnant."

I made it to the bedroom and shut the door behind me, emotionally paralyzed. I had no idea what to say.

"Grace? Are you there? Hello?"

I tried to answer Becca, but the words wouldn't come. I moved my lips and tried to remember to breathe, but it wasn't a lack of air in my lungs that stopped me from speaking—once again, I felt like I'd forgotten how to talk entirely. On the other end of the line, Becca cursed in frustration and fumbled with her own phone. It sounded like she picked up some shopping bags, and a man's voice in the background called out, "be safe out there tonight, beautiful!" Eventually, the call disconnected, and I sat on my bed in silence, trying to figure out how to salvage things.

There had to be a way to fix this. There had to be.

Ten minutes later, my phone pinged with another notification, and I wasn't so certain that fixing things was an option anymore.

"Dear Grace," the Facebook messenger text began, and even through the cracks in the screen, I could still make out the words,

*"I don't even know what's going on with you recently. No one knows where you are or what you're doing, but I stopped in at your work the second week of January to bring you Starbucks because I hadn't seen you at lunch in so long, and they told me you'd quit right around New Years. Well, that was news to me. So much for having "the flu." It would have been fun to see you at the show, you know, I thought we'd been friends long enough we could stay friends through anything, and I know you've been really upset that your dad and his new girlfriend went off to Cancun leaving you alone for Christmas. Believe me, I *know* how hard it is when your dad starts to date again, and you*

could have talked to me, you know? You could have talked to me about anything.

*"But I think you're in a really dark place and I just don't know what to do about that. Just so we're clear, I know you hooked up with Gavin at the New Year's Eve party even though it was obvious I was into him, and I don't know if this is jealousy that we've put that behind us and started dating, or what. I would have told you I'd started seeing him, but you stood me up when I wanted to talk about it, and you never returned any of my calls. I *genuinely* did not expect you to act like a jealous psycho or something. And that guy that you're with really hurt Gavin badly. He probably needed to go to the hospital or something, you're just lucky that he didn't, and doesn't want to file a police report. I don't know what kind of substances you two are on, but if throwing away your job and your friendships is worth it for a good high and (hopefully) good dick, I guess that's the way it's going to be.*

I can deal with a lot, Grace, but I can't deal with whatever drugs you've been taking. It's like you're a different person all of a sudden, and I don't like the person you've become. So don't call me, don't text me, don't show up at my apartment wanting a Grey's Anatomy binge or whatever. I don't want the new Grace in my life right now, and I'm going to need a lot of time to reconsider our friendship. We're grown-ups now, and I have a life to live.

Love, Becca."

The "love" part was really over-the-top, I thought, wiping at my eyes and obsessively re-reading Becca's words, picking apart every sentence and spelling error. She thought I'd hooked up with him—is that what he told her? She'd probably written her message while riding in a cab. I could tell by her typos. And she'd just left a late-night drugstore. If I'd known which one, maybe I could triangulate on a map the approximate whereabouts of her "boyfriend's" apartment.

Gavin. What an exceptionally douchey name.

And, *of course,* it had been the guy who'd taken us up to the party.

You're an idiot, Grace. *Idiot.*

I picked up my phone and dialed Becca's number, thought better about it, and disconnected the call before Becca could pick up—if she would have even picked up the phone at all. What could I possibly tell Becca that wouldn't make matters any worse?

"Hey, I'm 99% sure that the guy you're dating is not only a vampire, he's the same guy who attacked me and left me for dead on New Year's Eve. How do I know? Oh, I'm just a vampire myself now, that's all, and it really sucks, to tell you the truth. Whatever Mr. Tall Dark and Terrible has been telling you, it's a lie, and you need to dump him and change the locks on your apartment door, because it's only a matter of time before he kills you, one way or another."

I knew Becca well enough to know that she wouldn't respond well to the "for your own good" argument. If anything, I'd only push her further away. I threw my phone across the room hard enough for the case to fly off, ricocheting when it hit the wall and landing in the shopping bags I brought from the department store a month ago. I'd already opened Becca's present to use some of the perfume earlier in the evening, but I'd forgotten about the flask I'd bought for Harold. Maybe this would be a good time to offer it up as a reconciliation gift, to thank him for stepping up again and...saving my ass.

— ◆ —

I could tell he was still in the basement when I got downstairs because of the loud banging that was audible even though the closed door from the kitchen. Whatever he was up to seemed to involve a lot of...pounding. Hammering! *Hammering*, I corrected myself, embarrassed at my own double entendre.

I slipped quietly down the basement steps, hoping I wasn't intruding on his private sanctuary or anything. It wasn't like I was walking into his bedroom, I reminded myself. I'd gone down to the basement with Harold the first night I'd arrived at his home, after all. It's where he promised to cut off my head once we found out who had turned me.

Well, now we had a face, and I had a name. I might as well ask him to decapitate me tonight, but it seemed almost vulgar to give someone a present and then ask them to keep their promise to kill you, and in any event, I'd decided I wanted to kill Gavin myself.

Once I figured out how.

Harold bent over an anvil near his workbench, manipulating a long piece of glowing red-hot iron. He hadn't turned on the overhead lights this time, but the dim glow of the forge provided enough light for me to see his face, screwed up in perfect focus as he repeatedly struck the metal with a large hammer and expert, well-honed precision.

But it was hard for me to focus on Harold's face as I approached the forge. He'd stripped off his sweater, and the black t-shirt he normally wore underneath, and stood in front of the flames naked to the waist.

I caught my breath. Sparks flew from the red-hot metal, and some of those sparks hit his exposed flesh, causing little sizzles where they made contact with his skin, creating tiny burns on his chest, forearms, and shoulders that healed almost as quickly as the injuries were created. I wondered if it hurt to get burned like that, and decided that it almost certainly did. That seemed to be the entire point.

I wondered what other kind of pain made the burns a welcome distraction.

I didn't mean to stare. It wasn't polite, and I certainly didn't want to think of Harold in that way, but after the bloodlust in the kitchen, I couldn't stop the intrusion of some unexpectedly daring thoughts about the man standing in front of me. Harold was shorter than most men—he was easily a whole head shorter than the vampire who had turned me—but I was a petite woman, and I thought that Harold was probably a very comfortable size for someone of my physique. I was by no means virginal or inexperienced, but I'd never found myself grappling with this degree of desire before.

He said it doesn't mean anything, I chided myself. Whatever feelings I might be developing for him, they weren't reciprocated. He'd said so himself, hadn't he? And anyway, it was probably a bad idea to enter a carnal relationship with someone you were hoping would keep their promise to cut your head off. I was pretty sure that asking someone to behead me counted as suicide, and that was a Big Bad Sin in my faith.

But so was pre-marital sex, and I'd done plenty of that before dying, too. And anyway, I'd been putting off going to confession. So I was going to hell, one way or the other...I was losing hope of getting out of that. Being a vampire was just delaying the inevitable. Maybe that meant I should take advantage of the opportunities I had, when I had them.

I cleared my throat when Harold paused to quench the iron he'd been working on into a bucket of water, but he kept his back turned, and his voice was stern when he said, "I'm busy, lass."

"I'm sorry, I—I bought you a present over a month ago, and I wanted to give it to you tonight, sort of a 'thank you' and 'I'm sorry' present rolled into one. You don't have to open it in front of me, that's fine. I'll just leave it right here and, um. Be on my way upstairs." It really was a good thing that vampires couldn't blush, I decided, because from what I'd seen before I tore my eyes away from Harold's body and forced myself to look elsewhere, at anything else at all, his backside was as pleasant-looking as the front of him. His jeans were dirty, but they fit...*really* well. I'd never noticed before.

I put the gift-wrapped department store bag on the wooden table next to three long knives and started to back out of the basement.

"You really didn't have tae..." Harold began, seeing the gift bag on the table where I had left it. But he set the iron he'd been working with aside and reached for his undershirt, briefly wiping the blackened bits off his skin before putting the shirt on again, inside out, and reached over to unwrap the present. A mixture of emotions crossed his green eyes as he took the flask out of its wrappings and held it in his hands, and I wasn't sure what to think. He didn't seem happy.

"It's a very nice flask…" he said, quietly, slowly, considering every word. "But I already have one, and I like it." He held the new pewter flask out for me to take. "You can use this one if you want tae. I'm sure it will last you many years."

I shook my head. "It's not really my style," I lied. "I bought it for you. If you don't like it, I think I can still take it back for store credit or something. It's not a big deal. I just thought that your old flask was a little worn, and maybe you hadn't gotten around to replacing it."

"I'm not going tae replace the one I have. It was given tae me…by someone very special. And I'm afraid I'm just too sentimental to be distracted by something shiny and new." He put the flask aside on his workbench, then turned away once more to resume his work.

"It was very thoughtful of you, of course," he continued, with his back turned to me. "But again, you didn't have tae."

Feeling like I was on a solid enough roll for making bad situations worse for one night, I gathered my reserves of dignity and went upstairs without saying another word. Behind me, Harold resumed his blacksmithing.

⸻◆⸻

"You know, in Portugal, they decriminalized all drugs."

"All of them?" I was so high, I couldn't stop giggling.

"All of them." The boy droned on, a bit self-important for my taste, making the case for all sorts of arguments I was already familiar with, and could explain a lot better, even when high.

I'd been doing pot and mushrooms since I was fourteen years old.

"Decriminalization is like a speeding ticket…" *blah blah blah*. I looked around for Becca, to make sure she was okay. I was high, but I wasn't stupid. My eyes scanned the cavernous warehouse space, searching for her. We were deep in the suburbs, but you couldn't tell. The underground nightclub had been set up well, with fabric panels draping the walls and strategic up lighting that gave the gritty space a lot more polish. Someone had even dragged in some potted palms, and they looked good. Made the place kinda classy.

Despite her small stature, Becca was never hard to spot in a crowd. She glowed like a beacon wrapped in black velvet, a force of nature on the dance floor, arms waving, spinning, moving to the DJ's mix. Becca's typical playlists were mostly dark and emo bands, but I'd seen her digital music collection—she was the kind of person who could appreciate any kind of music, as long as it made her feel something. I smiled. She seemed to be feeling good.

And that was good. I felt good. The night was good. Everything was good. I took a step away from the one-sided conversation with the boy who was a little too into the idea of Portugal. My mouth was dry, and I knew it was important to stay hydrated when you were on Molly.

"But, you know, it isn't trouble if it doesn't impact your life, right?"

I turned around sharply, instantly less irritated than I'd been moments before, and felt a sly, knowing smile spread across my face. I reached out a hand to touch his shirt. The fabric felt nice. He was nice. Everything was...nice.

"I've been saying that for years," I agreed with the boy, leaning in closer. He really was kind of cute. Not gorgeous, not like the kind of guy Becca could easily get, but I wasn't in the same league as Becca, and hot guys were seldom interesting, anyway. "I'm Grace," I said. "Grace Kelly Cordero. No relation to the princess."

"I'm Dylan. Pagliuso. No relation to, uh...anyone else named Dylan Pagliuso." He made me laugh, so I leaned in an kissed him.

I think I'd decided that I loved him before the club threw us all out at five AM, just as the sun was rising.

"I don't know what you see in him." Becca's tone changed after the first two weeks. She'd been supportive of me having fun with Dylan at the beginning, but the longer he stuck around, the more irritated she got. She leaned over her laptop in our tiny apartment, logged into Tumblr, reposting memes about SuperWhoLock and other fandoms I couldn't relate to. None of it held a candle to *Lord of the Rings*. "He's not that cute, he's not that interesting, all he does is work and do drugs."

"That's not true! We go out!"

"...to places where he can do drugs."

"Like pot and acid, Becca. Maybe Molly, *sometimes*. It's not like he has a problem, Becca. He's got a good job and his own apartment." Dylan was a software engineer.

"Yeah, in Oak Park." She scoffed.

"What's wrong with Oak Park?"

"I mean, it's a great place if you're planning to marry him, settle down, have a couple of kids you can pretend don't know what Mommy and Daddy do all the time to make them act so funny—"

"Becca. Just because your dad can't control his drinking doesn't mean that me and Dylan—It's not a problem if it doesn't affect your life!" I reminded her. Once upon a time, she'd told me she felt safe with me, knowing I could set boundaries, that I knew how to control my substances—I never let them control us. Now she rolled her eyes and turned away from me, closed off. Becca had stopped hanging out with me and Dylan after the incident with acid at the duck pond.

When our lease was up in Wicker Park, her grandfather wouldn't let her sign on for another year after our landlord tried to exorbitantly raise the rent without fixing any of the recurring mold problems. Becca's grandfather said if he was going to keep financing her stay in Chicago, she needed to be working on her career. Which, somehow, meant that she couldn't live with me? He paid for her studio apartment near the Loop. Becca's grandfather thought we were too gay for each other.

Which was just ridiculous. I had a boyfriend. He helped me find an apartment I could afford on my own out in Oak Park, close to him. His dad owned the building; I got a friends and family discount.

"I don't like this," Becca said, pursing her lips as I loaded the last of my belongings into Dylan's friend's pickup truck. "I don't think you're making the right decision, moving closer to him. You can do so much better than...than *him*. He doesn't actually care about you, Grace. You're just someone he likes to get high with."

I think we went almost two weeks without talking to each other that time, before I showed up at her new apartment with vodka and DVDs. So I had a boyfriend and had moved out to the suburbs. That didn't have to come between us. Nothing did.

She was right about him being a bad idea, though. When it comes down to brass tacks, Becca's usually been right about most things that really matter. I don't know how she does it. It's like she sees patterns no one else can understand.

Maybe, if I'd listened to her, things would have turned out differently.

Chapter Fourteen

Just Another Street Deal

I woke up the next evening to discover that my nights of aimlessly lurking my friends' social media pages were over—I'd been blocked by dozens of people in just under twenty-four hours. Confused, I logged out of my main account and tried one of my backups, relieved to find that the second account was more or less unscathed from the purge. I suspected that Becca was behind the Great Unfriending, but I also didn't expect her to remember the alt accounts we'd made back in college to shamelessly stalk (and discretely find information about) our various crushes.

It didn't take long to confirm the source of my sudden social media ostracizing. When Becca went on a rampage, she tended towards nuclear annihilation, furious fingers clacking away at her keyboard until she'd eviscerated the source of her ire—exes, classmates, and colleagues who crossed the line had all ended up in her crosshairs over the years, but I'd never imagined myself the target of one of her rants. We'd fought before, when I was still dating Dylan, but that was nothing like this. Even at her angriest, I'd never felt the full force of Becca's wrath directed at me—but then again, I'd never ghosted her for weeks and beat up her boyfriend before, either.

In a friends-only post, underneath a generic meme about how 'people will change over time, and some friends come and go, but real friends last forever,' Becca spelled out our limited encounters since New Year's Eve, how I'd lied to her and stood her up, even quit my job with no notice.

"Something hasn't been right, and I've had my suspicions," she wrote, giving a detailed play-by-play of what happened at the concert. *"It breaks my heart, and I am only saying this as a friend to anybody*

who can read this," her post continued, *"Grace Cordero and her new boyfriend beat up the man I've been seeing for the past three weeks really badly tonight, and I think everybody needs to know that Grace is unstable right now, and possibly dangerous. I have reason to believe she's on some kind of hard drugs, and you should avoid her, if you see her."*

The comments section was filled with concerned opinions from people I thought had been my friends as much as Becca's, giving voice to things they'd never dared to say to my face. How they'd never really trusted me, and I always seemed like I was hiding something, or how I tried too hard to be perfect, etc. Who the hell kept cleaning supplies in their *car*? Suggested Carlos, as though the fact that I liked to keep my environments neat and tidy was a damning indictment of my character. "Who knows what she's been keeping from everyone? It's always the quiet ones you realize were up to something."

The unfairness of it all was unfathomable. My life was dissolving between my fingertips like theme park cotton candy, and the harder I tried to hold on to who I once was, the more of a mess everything became.

"As for dat! What did you think would happen?" Harold was unnecessarily harsh when he found me crying over my open laptop. "I told you tae cut all ties and never look back. I wasn't wrong when I said that was the easiest way tae do it, but you didn't listen."

He could be so damn paternalistic, it made me want to scream.

"You can't keep me locked up in the house forever!" I shouted at him, weeks of frustration spilling out all at once.

"I am *trying* tad keep you from the stain on your soul you would suffer if you killed anyone!" he shouted back. "*I* almost lost control at the concert, and I—Anyway, it's different for me. I *like* this life, I like being a vampire, I like my house and my forge and my stuff, and I don't want tae have tae leave suddenly because of an incident we can't cover up."

"...even killing? Do you like that?"

"Dun ask me questions you dunna want answers tae," he muttered, and stalked out of the room toward his basement refuge, where he remained for the rest of the night.

⸻ ◆ ⸻

Hours after we'd gone to our respective bedrooms across the hall from each other at sunup, I awoke briefly during daylight hours and thought I heard him crying, calling out to someone who couldn't have been there. I imagined Harold thrashing in his sheets, damp with sweat, disheveled and...*no. Not like that.*

It was almost a comfort to know that Harold had nightmares sometimes, too, though.

He spent the next two nights barely acknowledging my existence, except to occasionally pop his head out of the basement or the kitchen or whatever other tool-cluttered room he hid away in all hours of the night. He never stayed longer than was necessary to check on me, to make sure I was in or near the house, and that I hadn't gone off on my own again. As if I could get very far without my car, which was certainly impounded at some lot that was probably only open during daylight hours. I remembered the parking ticket I'd found on my windshield outside the diner the night before I'd died, still unpaid.

I spent most of those two nights outside, perched for hours at a time on the low stone terrace at the back of the house, looking out at the frozen expanse of back lawn, and watched the blue moonlit shadows crawl through leafless trees, reflecting off the snow and ice-covered world. I wished I could somehow run away from all of this vampire bullshit, back to my old life and my old friends. I wanted to go home. I wanted to be human again.

It was the stupidest, most mundane things I missed the most—the smell of the coffeemaker waking me up too early in the morning, the comfort of recognizing myself in the mirror, the sun rising over the L tracks on my way in to work each day. I missed planning weekend outings with Becca, reminding her to charge her cell phone before we went out to the Greek Festival or art market, and shaking my head each time she inevitably forgot.

I didn't know what to do about Becca. Some kind of paralysis kept me from fully processing the fight, and her messages. I should have been focused on coming up with a plan to save her, but my mind wandered, attaching itself to other pain, like a lost kid at the grocery store reaching out to hold the hand of a stranger.

And I missed Dylan, too. Or maybe I just missed the idea of him, of being wanted. Watching the iridescent blue feathered tree swallows swooping in the pink-tinged sunset clouds over Lake Michigan together on long summer evenings, I'd felt loved and secure wrapped tight in his arms. We'd been making plans for the Christmas holidays just two weeks before he broke up with me, and I'd felt a quiet, satisfied thrill, imagining that we were building a future. Together.

Those coral summer skies were forever darkened now. What did the life we'd once imagined matter, anyway? Even if he hadn't broken things off in August, there was no chance at all for us now.

I closed my eyes and tried to remember Dylan's face, but my memory was hazy, like heat signatures rising off the sun-baked blacktop, and it was hard to recall specific details I'd once tried to memorize like flash cards. His hair had been blonde—or at least blond-ish, hadn't it? Lighter than Harold's. And his eyes were...some sort of warm hazel shade. Lighter than my own eyes, but nothing like the sea glass green-gray of Harold's eyes.

I felt so pathetic, mourning all my stupid crushed dreams, immured by my broken, unbeating heart. I imagined the organ decaying in my chest, riddled with soft dark spots like overripe fruit, bleeding the sickly-sweet ooze of rot. At the very least, I had an excellent track record of loving people who didn't care for me the way I cared for them. For people who left. Mom, Dylan...Becca. Clearly, the common denominator was me. I brushed away tears that froze solid on my cheeks as they fell. I should have been dying of exposure outside to the wind and cold, but I was already dead, so what harm could a sub-freezing wind chill do? My veins were antifreeze and stolen blood long since unpaired from the warmth of living things.

I never got cold anymore, as a vampire. Scarves and gloves and thermal undergarments lay forgotten at the back of the small dresser in my bedroom. I wrapped my arms around my shoulders, not to ward off the chill in the wind that rose up off the nearby lake, but to feel somehow held and less alone in the dark.

On the third night, Calliope Jones called my cell phone. I accepted the call immediately, the barest tremor in my fingertips as I brushed the battered touch screen. I hadn't spoken to Calliope since the night she'd caught me sneaking out to see Becca, and with the benefit of hindsight, I was glad that she'd convinced me to turn my car around. Becca might be irreparably furious with me, but at least she was still alive—for now. I hoped. I couldn't think about that. I wanted to resent Calliope, but she'd been right. And anyway, I was so lonely. My voice sounded far away and cracked when I whispered her name in greeting.

"Grace, sweetheart. Are you all right?" For a moment, I thought she sounded genuinely concerned.

"I don't know how to answer that."

"I heard you got into a street fight. I thought you were adjusting better than that."

"I've been better," I admitted, bitterness creeping across my tongue. I was not, in fact, adjusting well at all. "Who told you?"

"Word gets around. The Community is small. I should have reached out sooner. I've been so busy, and the nights get away from me…I didn't realize it had been over a month." Her clipped voice conveyed little but the absence of any apology she might have been trying to offer, and I doubted she actually cared about me, beyond what I meant for her reputation. I was just some random fledgling dumped at one of her parties.

"It's fine."

"I wouldn't have pictured you as the Rocky Balboa type. But I'm sure the intended recipient deserved it…?"

"I found my maker." I described Gavin, overlooking her dated attempt at a pop culture reference. "He's the one who brought me and Becca up to your party in the first place." I didn't tell her how stupid I felt for not realizing what ought to have been obvious sooner.

Calliope was quiet on the other end of the line for so long that I thought she might have hung up on me. "Are you sure…?" she asked, the whisper-quiet edge to her voice sharper than I'd heard from her before.

"I told Harold, too. He said he was going to say something to you." I wondered if Harold had told Calliope that he was going to be beheading me soon, as soon as Gavin was brought to whatever vampire Community justice awaited him. If she knew that part, her voice didn't betray any concern over it.

"Harold may have said something about it, but he was angry when he called, and I sometimes don't know what to think when it comes to him. Do you know where he is?"

I shrugged, even though I knew she couldn't see me. "Somewhere in the house, I guess. He's…"

"Off in his own world again?"

"Something like that."

"Let me talk to him."

"He hasn't been very talkative."

Calliope exhaled, terse and annoyed, and I could almost picture her pinching the bridge of her nose. She disconnected the call without saying goodbye, but sometime after, I heard Harold's voice, raised and quarrelsome, echoing from somewhere inside the house. I wondered how many times she'd called him in a row before he picked up.

He found me outside a few minutes later, a fine layer of ice crystals accumulating on my skin and clothes. "Are you trying tae sparkle?"

I rolled my eyes.

"I'll stick with glitter."

"Not in the house, please."

"Glitter is where you draw the line in your housekeeping?"

"Let's say I learned my lesson with Jimmy and Calliope back in the late '70's." He shrugged and gently brushed the ice out of my hair. "I. Uh. Thought I'd go make a pickup. One of my contacts at the Red Cross has some supplies for us, if you'd like tae get out of the house…? It's long past time I started showing you how that part works, at least."

"Calliope yelled at you, didn't she?"

"She made her point. Are you coming or not?"

I followed him to the garage, noting with a twinge the empty space where my blue Accord should have been. Harold held open the door of the BMW for me, and his lips stretched into an almost smile when I reached across the console to unlock the driver's side for him. Before riding in Harold's car, I'd forgotten how many modern innovations I'd taken for granted in most of the cars I'd been in.

We were silent for several minutes as he drove. I spoke up first. "We don't have to talk about what happened the other night."

"Good. Fine." He nodded and didn't say anything else.

"Just one thing—"

"Grace..."

I held up my hand to wave him off, and in the dim light of the car interior, the passing streetlights flashed glints off the polished metal links of mom's Cartier at my wrist. "This watch belonged to my mother," I told him, fidgeting with the clasp a bit, the way I often did. My own hands were slightly smaller than Mom's, and I knew I'd never grow into the vacant space she left behind. I didn't look at Harold, but I took a deep breath and continued.

"She died my junior year of high school. It was a stroke. She had cancer, and it got into her brain faster than anyone expected, and...I don't have many things that were precious to her, especially now."

I quickly looked over to see that Harold was nodding slowly, but his face was unreadable, and he didn't take his eyes off the road.

"So, if anyone I barely knew offered me a new watch to replace this one because they thought it was old and...worn out, or something, I'd be offended. I'd be hurt."

"You didn't know."

"Yeah, but I do now. I mean, I can guess, I little. Because your flask is like my Mom's watch, isn't it?"

He let out a low, shaky breath and was quiet for a pause. "Yeah." His voice was soft. "It's a bit like that. I'm sorry about your mam."

"I'm sorry about your..." I glanced at Harold out of the corner of my eye. His shoulders had gone stiff as he stared straight ahead. "...about your person," I finished.

"Thanks."

I didn't know what he was thanking me for.

"You don't have any other family? Any...brothers or sisters?" he asked, caution tinting his words, like he wasn't sure asking about my family was a good idea.

I wasn't sure it was, either. I felt a lump rising in my throat and choked it down. "No…" I whispered. "Just me. Mom had cancer before, when I was little. The treatments made her infertile, so I was all they had. And after Mom died, all Dad and I had was each other. I mean, I've got cousins and stuff but…it's not the same."

"And your father…he's seeing other people now?" He drove through bustling neighborhood streets lined with small brick single-family homes that grew increasingly worn down. Billboards along the road advertised personal injury lawyers and funeral homes.

"I really don't want to talk about my family, Harold. What about you? Any brothers or sisters?" I almost regretting bringing up Mom's watch. Talking about family was painful.

"Two older brothers," he said. Finally, a real smile. "And a baby sister. She was five when I last saw her."

"Did they know? About the…vampire thing?" I asked.

"God, no. They thought I'd died at sea years earlier."

"Oh." I was unprepared for his candor to return after weeks of little more than formal, perfunctory polite conversation, but it felt…good, to know he was opening up to me again.

"Da wouldn't have dealt with it well. He was very much a 'burn the witch and shun the nonbeliever' sort."

"Catholic?"

"Worse. Calvinist."

"Oh. Right. You said Scotland. Lot of Protestants up there when you were growing up?"

"We weren't friendly toward papists if that's what you're asking."

"Well, papists didn't like you either." I wasn't sure if I should be offended or not. "Why did you choose, then? To…become this—?" My voice cut off as the partially formed question hung heavy in the air between us. Why choose to become something his own father would have hated? Harold didn't seem like the emotionally masochistic sort.

"Not everyone has the best options tae choose from." Something shifted in his mannerisms. The interior of the car suddenly felt cold.

"So your choices were become a vampire, or...?" I didn't mean to press for any kind of emotional vulnerability; I just wanted to understand.

But still, he snapped. "Look, Grace, if you want me tae take off your head once all of this is figured out, you're going tae have ta accept that I don't want tae spend a lot of time telling you my life story or listening tae yours. I think that's fair."

I wanted to retort that he was the one who'd asked if I had siblings and brought up my father's dating habits, but I held my tongue and slinked down further into the passenger seat, making myself even smaller than I already was. I wanted to shrink into nothingness, beyond the ache I felt at the irreconcilable otherness that separated me from my family now, beyond the hunger that always nagged at the back of my mind, beyond the fear I felt for whatever might come next. If the Community didn't take action against the man who had left me like this, I was afraid of what I was going to have to do on my own.

I wanted to force all of these feelings down inside of me so far, I could pretend for a while that they didn't exist. And if some essential part of who I was and what I wanted was a casualty of that compression, I'd pay the price.

The truth is, another part of me wanted to explode into violence and rage and pain. I tamped down my emotions like gunpowder.

We pulled up to a darkened parking lot in a neighborhood I would have once called "sketchy," I realized with a tinge of shame. Most of the people milling about weren't white—not that I wasn't used to how multicultural Chicago was, I just sometimes remembered how overwhelmingly white Ohio had been. At least the suburbs where I grew up. Calliope probably would have called the block "primed for redevelopment" or something. There was a soul food restaurant across the street that was doing brisk late-night business, and a nightclub next door whose music I could hear clearly, even above all the other lively street sounds that surrounded us. It was late, and it was cold, but the street was filled with cars and honking horns, and the sidewalk in front of the music venue was thick with pedestrians. The band was good, and I nodded my head to the beat without realizing it, the drums and the guitar worming into my blood. I could feel the music in my fingertips. I hadn't realized that I'd been staring out the window.

"You like live music?" Harold asked, watching me.

I gave Harold a withering sidelong glance. The concert had only been a few nights ago.

"Right." He cleared his throat. "Well, maybe in a little while, when you can be trusted not tae start brawls and get the cops involved, we could check out some places. I used tae like music...and it's usually good hunting, if you—"

"Thanks, but no thanks." So much for not wanting to get to know me. With Harold, I never knew if he wanted to draw me close or push me away. No wonder he lived alone. He was a nightmare of standoffish comfort.

"It was just a suggestion."

"I don't want to hunt people." Except part of me did, and I hated it. I rubbed my finger along my gums, forcing the fangs to retract back in place. They hadn't slid down very far. "Speaking of the cops...Calliope said the Community knew about the fight. With my maker. Am I in trouble? Are you?"

Even if I didn't like Harold very much at the moment, I didn't want him to get in trouble on my behalf.

He turned to scan the area for his contact, then instructed me to crouch low in the back seat and try not to be seen by anyone before he continued. "The Community understands that things happen. You're young, and no one was seriously injured or killed. They probably didn't even need tae cover anything up. Fights at nightclubs happen between mortals all the time."

"So is the Community like...the mob or something?" I mean, for Chicago, given the city's history, that made sense.

He shook his head. "The Community...it's like this. All vampires are Community. But not all vampires are members of *The* Community."

"Clear as blood." I'd meant to say 'clear as mud' and was somewhat embarrassed by my slip-up, but the phrase worked either way.

"The Community considers itself a benevolent organization. If, by benevolent, you mean nosing in everyone's business and using people for their own ends. They're the vampires with resources, connections, and skills they've had a long time tae hone. But they aren't your friends. The help they give always comes at a cost. Don't get mixed up with them."

That sounded exactly like what Avie told me Harold would say. "Is Calliope a member of...*The* Community? The rotational council, or whatever?"

"She likes tae think she is." He scoffed. I'd never heard Harold sound so bitter. "But she's not on the rotational council. And she won't be, not for at least another hundred years. The rotational council is just a bunch of old dried up blood clots who've seen too many centuries go by and gotten bored, so they take turns arbitrating disputes and doling out aid tae anyone stupid or desperate enough tae reach out tae them. They get tae feel important, and younger vampires find out too late that the price of dealing with them might be more than they can afford."

"Personal experience?"

"Yeah. And no, I'm not going tae tell you about it. Now hush."

Lights flashed at the other end of the parking lot, and Harold got out of the car, silent as a ghost. I tried to get a good look at the interaction as it went down without becoming visible, and from what I could tell, it looked like any other drug deal. Harold's contact opened the trunk of his car. Harold confirmed that the goods were as specified, and they shook hands in that way that people who want to exchange money but don't want to look like they're exchanging money, always do. Just another ordinary street deal.

It was almost a letdown, that getting blood was as mundane as buying drugs or counterfeit watches. I already had experience being discrete and not getting caught.

I waited until Harold was back on the road again before I clambered out of the back seat and into the front.

"Al Capone was a werewolf, wasn't he?" The thought had occurred to me out of the blue as a bit of a joke, but the more I thought about it, the more I had to wonder.

I think Harold might have actually choked. "What the—where did this come from?"

I waved my hands as I laid out my thought process. "I mean, The Community, the mob, shady underhanded dealings in dark alleyways and parking lots, vampires...but Al Capone didn't seem like the vampire type. Was he a werewolf? Are they real, too? You know, ancient enemies and all that?"

"You're seriously asking me if...? I thought we were past the ridiculous questions game."

"I mean, maybe. Half-serious. Are werewolves real, though? Did you know Al Capone? I'm just asking…"

"You're nuts, you know that?" The corners of his eyes crinkled up a bit, and his lips moved in the twitches of a smile he was clearly trying to fight.

"On second thought, you probably wouldn't have gotten along well with Al Capone…I bet he was the mobster you threw a stick of dynamite at."

For some reason, that sent him over the edge, and he honest-to-God *cackled*. Like I said, I never really know when people are going to get my sense of humor or not. But it felt good to make Harold laugh. "All right, one: Werewolves do not exist. Not so far as I know. And I've never seen a ghost, or a fairy, or a…moth man or a…"

"Jersey devil or a chupacabra?"

"Na, none o' dat. Second…Al and I were not friends. I wasn't in Chicago in the '20's and '30's."

"You just called him Al so casually…"

"Ask Calliope about her speakeasies sometime. She had one in a basement underneath a shoe repair shop."

―――――◆○◆―――――

Chapter Fifteen

Queen of Icicles

A few nights later, Calliope drove my car over to Harold's house by herself. I had no idea how she'd gotten the vehicle out of impound without me being there, but when you were a billionaire with connections to the city's most wealthy and well-connected citizens, I supposed anything was possible.

Hell, maybe she owned the impound lot.

Harold welcomed Calliope inside through the front door, which felt like a shocking formality, even for him. I hadn't even entered the house through the front door yet; Avie had a key and still walked around the house to the side door.

Also shocking: Calliope had to have been invited inside at least once before. She crossed the threshold with no hesitation or pause, before Harold could finish saying hello.

"I'm glad to see you redecorated," She regarded the parlor I'd spent so much time reorganizing with something that bordered on approval, her gaze honing in on the vintage velvet sofa bathed in the green-shaded glow from stained glass lamps. "It's homey."

For a woman whose tastes ran toward white leather upholstery and gleaming chrome, her compliment seemed sincere. I'd bristled with suspicion when Harold informed me of her impending arrival, but as I watched her fingers lightly brush over the tidy repairs Harold had made to the lampshades, my tension began to evaporate. Calliope seemed on the verge of saying something, but held her tongue. Instead, she took a seat in my favorite armchair.

Given the choice between sharing the sofa with Harold or contending with the chair with the broken spring, I picked the latter. It was somewhat more comfortable once I'd piled the seat high with a dense collection of needlepoint pillows I'd found in the attic, but the buffer between my rear end and the pointy bit of the busted spring was precarious at best. I fought the urge to constantly fidget as Calliope continued to quietly scan the room, surveying the organized shelves of tools and knickknacks. Everything was still a bit more cluttered than I would have liked, more functional and utilitarian than sophisticated or cheerful, but it finally looked like a room people lived in, whether or not Harold and I were technically still people.

When Calliope finally spoke, it took me a moment to catch her meaning. "I don't think this is working out so well, is it?"

Harold seemed confused, as well. "How so?" he asked.

Calliope leaned forward and raised her eyebrows at Harold over the top of her ridiculously unnecessary eyeglasses, and I stifled a giggle that wouldn't have been appropriate, given the circumstances. They'd known each other for centuries, and still, Calliope didn't let down her obsessively maintained persona. I wondered if she did it to irritate him. "Grace is unhappy. I mean, the running off, the fights..."

Even though I knew that every nuance of every gesture she made was the result of meticulously honed practice, her performance was no less captivating. I sat on my hands to keep them from flapping. I'd yet to have a single interaction with Calliope Jones that didn't leave me unsettled.

She turned her attention to Harold. "And you're obviously miserable, or at least more miserable than usual. I should have known better than to expect you to drop everything and take on all the responsibilities of a fledgling, especially one who came about as a result of my..."

"Negligence?" He offered. Calliope's withering look could have killed houseplants.

"It was one fight. One. And I'm not any more or less unhappy than I would be anywhere else, under the same circumstances," I spoke up.

"Even if you were living with me?"

My lungs drew in a sharp involuntary breath, almost as though I still had a need for the air—it felt like all the oxygen had been sucked out of the room.

"I could take care of you. My spring season is going to be busy with my construction projects, but I could—I'd find the time to make sure you were comfortable, and adjusting well."

A week ago, I would have leaped at the opportunity to get out of Harold's house and get back downtown. I missed the skyline and bustle and all of it, and I needed to be closer to Becca. But now I wasn't so sure about Becca...

And then I remembered the way he had cackled at my questions about Al Capone, and the weary look that came over his face when he worried about me, the taste of blood on his skin, and the obnoxious old wool smell of his wardrobe. All the work I'd done, organizing and redecorating his house, would be undone in a short time, I guessed, if I were to suddenly leave. Not that it was my responsibility to clean up after Harold, he was a grown man after all, but he seemed to appreciate my efforts at making his house homier. And for all that Calliope's penthouse was grand and gleaming, it was also impersonal and harsh, designed less for comfort than to convey an image. I loathed having to admit that I was starting to like Harold's house.

But—warm blood, at Calliope's. The view across the lake...and the grand media room. I could watch the entire extended edition of *Lord of the Rings* in there, and it would be like having my own private movie theater. I could invite Becca over and explain everything to her, and she'd understand, and she'd break up with Gavin, and maybe, somehow, in spite of all the stupid vampire stuff, we could still be friends if she'd let me. I could find a way to make things work.

I imagined myself watching over Becca her whole life, sending wedding presents when she got married, being the strange, eccentric aunt to all her children, watching her grow up and grow old with well-earned silver threads in her hair (although Becca had long insisted that she was going to dye her hair blue the moment she went gray).

And then, someday, when Becca had lived years and years and decades longer than either of our moms had, when she got to be a Nonna herself, and a great Nonna, and then...would I leave flowers on her grave?

Thinking about Becca made me momentarily forget the plan for Harold to behead me. I choked. I didn't want Becca to see me like this and know what I had become. My vision went red, starting with pinpricks at the periphery that expanded to a glaze of crimson across my eyes, and I buried my face in my hands, softly shaking with sobs that I hadn't realized were sneaking up on me until it was too late to stop them.

I wasn't the only one caught off guard by my racing thoughts and emotions. Harold and Calliope called out to me in concerned unison, but when I pulled my hands away from my eyes, it was Harold's face that filled my vision.

"Do you hate it here so much?" He asked. He'd stepped over from the sofa and was kneeling close to me, almost, but not quite, reaching out. For a moment, I thought he was going to stroke my hair, and I bristled at the very invasiveness of the thought.

I shook my head, sniffled, and looked away from both of them, embarrassed. "My imagination ran away with me," I confessed. I didn't offer any details.

Calliope cleared her throat and offered to wait while I grabbed my things from upstairs.

"I'm fine here." I shrugged. "You don't have to go out of your way for me any more than you already have. I mean, unless Harold wants to get rid of me..."

Her businesslike demeanor turned to thinly veiled shock. "Well, I just thought—"

Harold cut her off. "Grace is fine here. She's good company. I don't mind, after all."

"I must have gotten the wrong impression." Ice crept into Calliope's gracious, pleasant expression as she squared her shoulders, and I felt a chill in spite of my cold blood.

"I need to drink." I stood up and excused myself from the mounting tension, in part to collect my thoughts, and because my obscene hunger finally got the better of me, and the tremble in my fingertips wasn't mere anxiety over Calliope's unexpected offer to take me back. She'd cast me off to Harold pretty definitively within an hour or so of finding me in her home. Why the sudden insistence that I was better off with her?

I stared at the contents of the fridge longer than I should have, wondering if I could justify taking the last bag of hospital blood for myself. The most recent batch Harold had brought back earlier in the evening was in take-out containers, and that usually meant animal blood. I fought back a grimace.

But it wasn't good manners to take the last of the good stuff for myself, either. I sighed and cracked open the plastic lid of the soup container, repressing a shudder at the unpleasant, almost gamey smell that flooded my senses and made my eyes water, but two minutes later, I was floating in a warm ruby sea regardless, on my knees on the kitchen floor. I hadn't even realized I was going down, and I hated the way it felt like losing myself, replacing some vital part of who I had been every time I drank.

I hated that I couldn't stop. Becca's fears and accusations about my substance use weren't far off.

The voices from the other room rose above my crimson-coated self-loathing. I tried not to eavesdrop on a conversation that wasn't meant for me, but then again, if Harold and Calliope had wanted to say things in private, they would have done so far away from the prying ears of another vampire—they were both old enough to know that, I justified.

"What's this all about? The truth, for once—" There was a hardened knife edge to Harold's voice, coarser than the scalpel tone Calliope so often took, but no less dangerous.

"I haven't the slightest idea what you're accusing me of. Perhaps you'd care to elaborate?"

"You show no interest in the broken girl you foisted onta me a month and a half ago, and now all of a sudden, you're calling her on the phone, showing up at my house, begging to take her back—"

Broken. I sometimes felt that way about myself, but it was even more uncomfortable knowing that Harold thought it, too.

"I. Do. Not. Beg, Harold. I'm offended at the very suggestion."

"I wonder if Vincente would agree with that statement."

Calliope gasped, as though Harold's blade was the first to draw blood. "Don't you dare. Don't you dare. He's dead and gone. Don't you—"

"Aye, that was a low blow from me. I take it back." Harold sighed. "I shouldn't be castin' up like so. But this sudden interest in Grace is strange. If you're bored and looking for a new pet..."

"...Iqbal expressed concern about you being the one to take over a fledgling's upbringing. Epiphanie, too, if you must know."

I'd heard one of those names before... *"Iqbal is okay, too—he's kind of a stick in the mud, but he's fair, I've heard. He'll have your back."* That's what Avie had said.

"So you got the council involved, after all?"

"I thought it was time. The situation is threatening to get out of hand."

"What the hell does that old fossil care, anyway?"

"Harold, *we're* old fossils."

"Not like him. He's got what, three hundred years on us? Tell me why I should care about his opinion."

"Well, he's Community, for one..."

"Fuck the Community."

"You're hardly young, Harold. And this 'fuck the Community' attitude of yours is old. You should be taking a more active role, concerning yourself with what goes on in the region. We all have obligations—"

"What do I have tae offer the Community that I haven't already sacrificed?"

"Her involvement was her own choice, love..."

"And how it ended? How much of *that* was her choice, too?" Harold's voice rose until he was almost yelling.

"...I shouldn't have brought up painful memories, either. I miss her, too." There was sadness in Calliope's voice, I thought. I wondered if they were talking about Harold's breakup with his fledgling, and if that was part of the reason he disliked the Community so much.

"What's past is past." He grumbled. The both of them were silent for several moments, and I steadied myself to my feet to return to the conversation when Calliope spoke a familiar name, and I felt my stomach bottom out again.

"...I've spoken to Gavin Richardson, of course," Calliope continued. "He's young, too young to be creating new fledglings, and he swears he never touched Grace. I think he was more interested in her friend, to be honest, but you know how fickle young romantic rivalries can be."

I froze in the doorway and glared at Calliope, furious. "I know what I remember," I insisted.

"Yes, and on the night I found you crawling out of my guest bathtub, you had no memory of the incident at all, sweetheart."

Calliope's use of the word "sweetheart" made me bristle like a pill-averse cat. Her term of endearment didn't feel very endearing at all, and Calliope's description of the night I resurrected as a vampire wasn't entirely accurate.

"Then again..." she went on, "Maybe our Grace doesn't need me, after all. It might be time to relocate altogether, give our girl a new identity somewhere else." She sounded almost optimistic, and if Calliope noticed how far my jaw dropped as I returned to the armchair I'd occupied previously, she didn't show it. She went on to offer all kinds of assistance—a new ID, passport, social security card. Anything I needed. Anything at all.

For a moment, the room went dark, a cold fury rising up from some visceral chemical reaction in my blood. Chicago was the place where I'd rebuilt my life after Mom died, where I'd met Becca and all our friends—even if they weren't my friends anymore. I'd fought hard to make a life for myself in the bustling concrete jungle of skyscrapers and elevated train platforms after graduating, and I had no desire to start over again elsewhere. I remembered what Harold had said about liking his life. I didn't like being a vampire, but I liked the city I called home, and I liked my identity.

"Grace. Kelly. Cordero. That's my name," I fully enunciated each syllable, my voice much more sullen than I intended. I looked to Harold as he nodded at Calliope. He seemed tense. But Harold had been tense every night since the night-club. Whenever he looked at me, even when he was laughing, he looked drawn and anxious, like a ship's line held taut. If the rope snapped, or the line lost tension...whatever might happen, he was clearly invested in preventing that outcome.

"Don't be stubborn, sweetheart. It's only a matter of time for each of us before we become liabilities to our own lives and have to start over. It's part of the price we all pay." Calliope reached into the pocket of her impeccably tailored winter white wool coat and handed my car keys over to me. "It's hard when you're a fledgling. You don't need to make it harder than it has to be, especially when you have people who want to help you make things easier. Think about it, is all I'm saying. I could have you set up in a nice house or apartment anywhere in the United States inside a month."

Harold cleared his throat. "I don't think it's a bad idea tae put some space between Grace and her old life...but I'm not entirely sure she's ready tae go out on her own. She needs more time."

"Surely you've been teaching her how to hunt?" The scalpel edge returned to Calliope's soft voice.

"Not exactly." I stared pointedly at Harold. If he was going to throw me under the bus, I'd drag him right down with me.

"Harold. We had an agreement." I couldn't quite identify the emotion in Calliope's voice since I was certain she wasn't actually concerned about me, but she shook her head slowly. Harold seemed on the verge of saying something, but she raised her manicured hand to cut him off before he could get a word out

"I'm not leaving the city," I interrupted, pounding my fists on the upholstered velvet of the armchair. "Not when 'Gavin Richardson' has been convincing Becca he's her new boyfriend. I'm going to make him pay for what he did to me. I'm going to kill him. And I swear to God, if he harms Becca in any way before I get my hands on him, I'm going to *hurt* him before I kill him—"

Calliope Jones was out of her seat before I could blink, before Harold had a chance to react. Her violent backhanded swing knocked me off of my pile of cushions I had just gotten comfortable sitting on, and out of the armchair entirely. The frame groaned under the force exerted on it and toppled over, antique wood splintering and tearing through the threadbare old velvet. Jagged, splintery points jutted up from the pile of rusted springs and horsehair stuffing.

"Careful!" Harold shouted at Calliope—or me, I couldn't be sure. One of the sharp points of wood from the armchair frame was aimed ominously close to the center of my back. I had a brief moment to recall what Avie had said about her maker trying to stake her, before Harold and Calliope began shouting at each other.

"Where is she getting these ideas? I trusted you to educate her correctly, at the very least!" Calliope was practically spitting, all composure temporarily abandoned. "But I guess I should have known better, given your track record."

"Watch what you say next *very* carefully." Harold growled.

"These selfish, unstable outbursts threaten us all, just like—"

"Enough!" Harold's voice bellowed so loud, it hurt my ears. "I'll na hear of this in my house. You dropped the ball on security at your own party. Take responsibility for that. I have taken responsibility for Grace, and tha's the final word. You forfeited your claim tae her, and you have no right ta criticize the way I handle my own affairs."

"You're a joke, Harold Laing. To the entire Community."

"Da mön is nane da waar for da dog barkin at her!" He shook his head the way a horse does when a fly is bothering it, and swallowed hard, but the rage was still there when he continued, much more carefully. "Rather be a laughingstock than a bootlicker. No, thank you. Get out." He spat the last words at her, and for an awful and serious moment, I was afraid that he and Calliope would come to blows.

Calliope pulled back and pulled herself together. "My driver is outside waiting," she announced, straightening her shoulders. "Do not make things difficult for yourselves. I am a wonderful friend and ally, and a terrible person to have as an enemy." She swept out of the room with a force like icicles falling off eaves and overhangs—pointed, sharp, and deadly.

Harold and I were both left slightly dumbstruck by her departure for several moments. Then he reached down and extended a hand to me.

"Are you all right?" His voice was sincere again, and I knew, however he defined our relationship privately, however mad I might make him, he cared, genuinely, about my well-being.

I nodded and accepted his hand. It was the first time we'd touched since the awkward moment in the kitchen the night of the concert disaster, and I didn't want to make things weird again, so I withdrew the moment I righted myself, surveying the ruined armchair behind me. "I was going to try to fix that cushion," I mourned.

"Well, it's only good for kindling now. Shall we have a bonfire?" Harold asked. "Anything else that's old in the house, we can add tae the blaze, and I'll have you order new furniture if you'd like tae finish redecorating."

"So I'm not going to leave the city?"

"Not unless you want tae, no. Calliope is used tae her money getting her what she wants, but she canna make you leave. And, if you want tae stay…" Harold picked up the remains of the armchair easily and began carrying it outside, despite its awkward heft and size. I followed him.

"If you want tae stay, I'd be happy ta have you around." Harold didn't turn around to look back at me when he spoke, and I didn't know what to say in return.

It's good to be with someone who cares about you, I thought. *Even if you care about each other in different ways.*

We burned both the armchairs and the sofa—they were threadbare, and the rotted wood frames were past salvaging, anyway—along with a few other boxes of assorted junk that I hadn't gotten around to dragging out to the curb yet, in the fire pit in Harold's backyard.

The mid-February sky was cold and clear of clouds, and I gazed upwards at the Milky Way, visible to me now in a way it never had been when I was alive. In spite of myself, I was still spellbound by how many more stars I could see in the night sky as a vampire, even with the smoke from the fire somewhat obscuring my vision. It was beautiful in a way I didn't want it to be. I didn't want to fall in love with the night any more than I wanted to fall in love with Harold.

Before us, the bonfire flared and crackled, red and yellow sparks rising up like jewels in the darkness, and in the heat of its flames, I was certain we both felt—briefly—warm again.

"What else did Avie tell you that I should know about?" he asked, not quite accusing, but worried, perhaps, about what I might know.

"Not much." I shrugged, staring directly into the blaze.

"Damn feral nomads..." he muttered under his breath.

"Is it true, though? I can kill him?"

"Officially, the Community won't come after you, no. But—"

"Could a gun do it? Or does it have to be a...stake, or fire, or a sword, or...?" I poked the charred remains of a cardboard box with a stick, and more sparks exploded into the night.

Harold took a cautious step back, his hand on my shoulder pulling me further from the blaze. "I suppose a gun could do it. If the bullet rounds were large enough, modern hollow points, maybe, depending on how many times you hit him and whether or not he has an escape route and access to a source of blood nearby. A well-aimed gunshot wound would definitely slow him down, though. If that's what you want to do. "

I asked if he'd ever shot a vampire.

"No." He looked up at the sky and was quiet for several beats. Like he was trying on words for size again. "...but I once knew three terrible vampire brothers who were put on a raft at sea at midday, and blown tae smithereens with dynamite." He smiled, as though he recounted the memory personally, which he couldn't have, obviously, if it happened in the middle of the day.

I was starting to wonder if he wasn't a little too fond of dynamite.

"Avie also said you had to drink someone's blood for a week to become a vampire."

Harold looked startled. "She did, huh?"

"Well, she didn't tell me, exactly. She asked, 'whose blood had you been drinking for a week before you died?' And you were right there in the other room when we were talking. But I told her I hadn't been drinking anyone's blood. And I told you that, too, the night we met at Calliope's. And what I'm trying to figure out, then, is what happened to me. Because everyone seems to think it's not normal. Like I'm some kind of...freak."

"You're not a freak. Just...unusual. A person usually has to drink our blood for about a week. Five nights, sometimes, maybe ten—but a week is the tradition, I suppose. That's the gist of it. The intended fledgling dies, and if all goes well, we have a new Community member. But some people, like—well, like you, get turned faster. It's rare, but it happens. Most people survive a fast turn. You're special."

I didn't feel special.

"I remember it now. What happened when he attacked me. I remember him biting me, and drinking my blood. I remember I got lightheaded, and it was hard to breathe, and my heart was beating faster and faster..." I rocked back and forth on my heels as the vivid details replayed in my memory, remembering the way the world had started to swirl and fold in on itself, how I'd been trapped and paralyzed, pinned against the wall.

"Hypovolemic shock, I think they call it. It's what happens when a body loses a lot of blood."

I nodded. I'd watched enough medical dramas with Becca to know what hypovolemic shock was. "But then, I remember—I think I remember; this is where it gets fuzzy—that he made me drink his blood, too." I looked over at Harold, and he nodded, knowingly. "He forced his arm over my mouth so I couldn't scream, and I remember tasting all that blood...but then everything went dark, and I woke up the next night."

"If we can drink enough blood tae kill a person in one sitting, and if they can drink enough blood tae trigger the turn before they die from blood loss, then, it can happen, sometimes. But I don't know how common that is."

"Not a lot of peer-reviewed scholarly research published on the process of turning someone into a vampire?" I picked up the stick I'd dropped when he'd protectively pulled me back, and began poking at the glowing coals of the bonfire again.

Harold made a face and shook his head. "God, no. I mean, I suppose I wouldn't be surprised if some mortals in science or government knew about us, but the Community doesn't want us found out. And there are so few of us, I don't know..."

"Hard to draw conclusions from a limited sample size?"

"You tell me, you're the scientist."

I scoffed. "Hardly. I was a communications major at Loyola. But I used to want to be a zoologist first. I took a lot of biology classes, kind of for fun. I could have completed a minor, but I wanted to graduate on time, with Becca."

"So, what did your biology classes teach you about all of this?"

Fuck. How to even answer that question? "All the science I've ever studied says we shouldn't exist, so...I guess I just want to understand the magic." I shrugged.

"Magic is more craft than science, I think..." Harold mused.

The last of the embers of the bonfire began to give out shortly before dawn, just as the first hint of impending daylight started to tinge the horizon violet gray instead of black. Harold and I covered the remains of the fire in the pit with armfuls of snow and damp leaves, and the glowing coals sputtered, hissed, and went dark.

Back up in my bedroom, after we wished each other a good sleep at the top of the stairs, I dragged my laptop under the covers and broke the absolutely unthinkable best friend rule: I logged into Becca's Facebook account without her knowledge or consent (Becca never changed her passwords), and started scrutinizing every single one of Becca's posts in the last month, looking for signs of, or information about, Gavin. I had to hand it to the vampire—he was very good at not leaving an online record. Becca might write gushing and romantic Facebook updates and Tumblr posts and Instagram captions about how happy she was, but her elusive vampire boyfriend was nowhere to be found on the internet.

Hunched over my MacBook, I began to falter under the weight of the rising sun in the sky on the other side of the blackout curtains, and from my huddled position under the duvet, I yawned, feeling my fangs pop, briefly, as I did. *That was never going to stop feeling weird*. But I continued to scroll through Becca's tagged images from the last six weeks, one after the other, paying special attention to the photographs taken after dark.

There. In an image dated 23 January, at 1:06 AM, just over three weeks after I died, a tagged image of Becca, taken by a friend and not approved to appear on her timeline, showed up. It was obvious to me why Becca hadn't approved the image. In it, she was standing stiffly, caught in a candid position in the middle of a conversation, her head angled downward to give her the appearance of a double chin. I had to marvel at the ability of any photograph capable of making my beautiful best friend appear unattractive, but Becca wasn't the most interesting part of the photograph.

Just beyond her, a tall man with dark hair, wearing a too-tight short sleeve shirt, was standing with his back to the camera. And next to him, almost completely obscured by shadows and other patrons in the nightclub, stood a familiar-looking blonde, pale-faced woman. She wasn't wearing a wig or the stuffy rich older lady wardrobe or the heavily contoured makeup of her public persona, but I would recognize her anywhere, now. I enlarged the photo as far as my computer's software allowed me to do and stared at the grainy, blurry image on the screen.

Right behind Becca, in the picture taken inside a posh downtown nightclub, Gavin Richardson and Calliope Jones were having a conversation.

CHAPTER SIXTEEN

SURVIVAL IS COMPLICATED

"Harold, she knows something!" I was triumphant the next night, thrusting my computer screen in his face the moment I found him in the kitchen. "She's obviously protecting him!"

He squinted at the grainy, blown-up image, and gave me a quizzical look. "I don't see what this proves?" His hands were busy setting out blood and glassware—the quart-sized takeout soup container on the kitchen counter made me sigh, my enthusiasm somewhat diminished when I remembered we were back on animal blood for a few nights. *Should have taken the good stuff when I had a chance.*

"It proves that she knows him well enough to hang out at clubs together, *and* it proves that they are both hanging out with Becca—don't you think that's suspicious? I don't think he's just some strange vampire who's new to town. You said, when I described him at first, you thought I was describing her last fledgling—James Medlock? Well, what if—?"

"What if what?" he narrowed his eyes at me in warning.

"What if she was trying to replace James? She... missed him, found someone who looked like him."

"Who even does that?" He shook his head, but, he didn't seem so sure.

I thought back on the type of guy Becca usually went for. They didn't all exactly look alike, exactly...but, she had a type. With men at least. I'd never figured out her type when it came to girls. "I'm just—"

Harold cut me off and handed me my breakfast, ignoring the face I made at the blood in my cup. "Look, it's not that I doubt you, but please remember that

Calliope is very rich, very well-connected, and beyond that, she is a vampire with nearly two centuries of experience under her belt."

As if I needed reminding...

"She is powerful in ways I probably don't even know about," he continued, "and that's saying something. Please, be careful."

"But what about the rotational council? Do you really think she's told them everything? Shouldn't we reach out to them ourselves—tell them what we know about Gavin, now that we know his name? Wouldn't the others want to know that she was protecting someone like him? What about Iqbal?" Calliope had mentioned another vampire, last night, but I couldn't recall their name at the moment.

"How do you know about Iqbal?" The empty glass in Harold's hand slipped from his fingers, shards flying across the kitchen floor.

I reluctantly set down the blood Harold had just handed to me, and went to the mud room to retrieve the broom. He hadn't moved when I returned, and he stared at me without blinking in that weird, inhuman way I hated. "Calliope mentioned him last night while you were talking and I was in the kitchen getting blood. And Avie. She said he was a stick in the mud, but fair—that he'd have my back." I looked down at the shattered glass on the floor, glad that it was empty when he dropped it.

"Be careful what you overhear." He said.

"I'm sorry, I didn't mean to eavesdrop... I couldn't help it."

Harold rolled his eyes and stepped out of the way as I swept up the broken glass. "I want you tae think good and hard about this notion you've got in your head about killing your maker. Especially if he's Calliope's fledgling. She tends tae pick the sort who are tough to kill, and dangerous. I don't want you tae end up like Avie, never aff o' da go, always putting herself in harm's way—for what? It's been decades dems tane forenst da tidder. Marie DuChamps is bad news, Grace."

"I don't know what 'tame forest titties' have to do with anything here. I'm not going after Marie DuChamps. I'm going after Gavin Richardson. For what he did to me. And to stop him, before he turns anyone else." I dumped the mess into the trash can and returned to my blood on the counter. A month ago, I wouldn't have been able to turn my back on it. I should have been proud of myself, but I was furious at Harold. He seemed equally exasperated with me, so that made two of us.

"The one. Against. The other." He clarified through clenched teeth, pulling his hands down the side of his face. "It's not against the rules to turn fledglings," he went on, in that typical matter of fact tone he often used. It wasn't comforting, this time. "There wouldn't *be* a Community if we didn't. And, even if he is Calliope's fledgling, the timeline doesn't add up. James left her in 1999. She can't have turned this man any earlier than that, and it takes decades before a vampire is ready tae turn fledglings of their own. Calliope was nearly one hundred when she turned her first. I was a hundred an' twenty."

"I know what I remember, Harold. I couldn't forget now if I tried. He drank my blood. He forced me to drink his. You said last night that's one way to turn someone."

"Whoever did turn you, did it in a rotten way, and that's not fair. We don't turn people without consent, and we don't abandon fledglings. But you're na cast by no more. I've claimed you, as true as my own. *If* you were still abandoned, or if you'd actually killed people in ways that attracted attention and were hard tae cover up...but you didn't. You're not his responsibility anymore, and you haven't been for a while. That's what community does—we look after each other. We choose our family. That means something."

"But I didn't have a choice." I deflated a bit, trying to piece together all the fragments of Community law I'd learned from Harold, and Calliope, and Avie. The three of them seemed to have completely different opinions about how things worked, or ought to work, and so far, no one had given me any straightforward information about anything. I gripped the countertop tightly as I drank, until the blood washed over me completely, and I stopped feeling lightheaded from the rush. Even animal blood could make me weak in the knees, and I didn't want to end up on the floor again.

I took note as Harold turned away from me until he'd cleaned the blood from his own teeth, and his fangs had retracted, before he continued, and I should have been grateful for his courtesy, but I was twitching with barely contained irritation. My left hand at my side wriggled of its own volition, and I scanned the kitchen, looking for something to to. Part of me wanted to throw my glass against the floor, too. I wanted to break things, or maybe set the world on fire. I settled on washing out my drinking glass. If I'd thought that turning my back on Harold would discourage him from going on, I was wrong.

"But if Gavin is Calliope's fledgling, *if*, Gavin is Calliope's fledgling, which you seem convinced of, then he's under her protection and responsibility, too," he continued. "And you saw how she was last night when you threatened him."

I nodded, but I didn't want to agree.

"I know Cal well enough ta know that she feels awful about what happened ta you, Grace. She's careful with her fledglings. She'd never want one of them ta do this ta anyone, believe me. So depending on how long ago she turned this Gavin fellow—and I'm guessing it had ta be recently—it's quite likely he had a lapse in control when he attacked you at the party. He probably panicked, after he realized what he'd done, tried ta bring you back, thought he failed, and tried ta hide the evidence. He might not have even known he'd successfully turned you until you showed up at the concert and started whaling on him. Imagine how shocked he must have felt. He's so young, he shouldn't have been able ta turn you, if he really is your maker."

"That's assuming he wouldn't have been one of the first people she interrogated, if Calliope really is his maker."

"Shit." He seemed to be pondering something.

I nodded at him. "She would have said something the night she found me."

"She asked if anyone at the party had seen you, not if anyone had turned you. There's a difference."

It was impossible to not be frustrated at how committed he was to ignoring what was obvious to me, and I wanted to scream. *Calliope called out to me by name, when she only saw me from behind, standing by the windows in her penthouse. She'd known my first name, and my last. Gavin may have turned me, I was certain of that, but Calliope had known...something. All along. And to think I'd thought I liked her.*

"Harold." I gasped. "Avie knew."

"The hell do you mean." It was a statement, not a question.

"She knew, when she shook my hand. She knew I was related to Calliope by blood. She knew *instantly*, Harold. And if Avie could tell, that means that Calliope—" I remembered the way Avie's entire demeanor toward me changed when she took my hand the first time, and how confident I'd been that Calliope was the one who'd turned Avie's maker. I didn't know how I knew, but I *knew*. We were related, somehow.

"No. See, this disproves your entire theory. The kid would have said something. Maybe not tae you, but she would have said something tae me. Either Gavin is Calliope's fledgling, in which case, he didn't turn you, or he turned you, but he's not her fledgling. There's no way—*no way*—both of them would keep me in the dark. I can't believe that."

I rolled my eyes, not sure if Harold was really that obtuse, or if he was protecting Calliope and, by extension, Gavin, as well. "He killed me, Harold. I'm dead because of him—"

Harold pressed his fingertips to his temples the way he often did when he was stressed or frustrated. "What's done is done. I'm sorry, but you have tae let go. Obsessing over what happened to you isn't healthy. You have time tae figure out what you want out of the life you have before you now. I know this isn't exactly the life you would have chosen, but—"

"*'Not exactly the life I would have chosen'*? Ladies and gentlemen, the award for understatement of the century goes to Harold fucking Laing. If that even is your real name. I don't know. I don't know anything about you." I spit my contempt as anger flared inside of me and threatened to boil over, exactly as it had that night at the Metro, when I saw my maker in the crowd.

He flinched. "You don't have tae be mean." His voice was the kind of soft that people reserve for talking to snarling dogs and cranky toddlers, and it did nothing to help my mood. "The night I was turned, I—"

I cut him off, acid and sarcasm flooding my tongue. "I'm *sorry*, but if you're going to be cutting off my head any night now, I'd really rather not know the story of your life, and how you chose to be a monster." *Not all choices have good options*, he'd said. But he could have chosen death. I wasn't even given that option.

"We all make choices!" He said, as if he could read my mind. "Wha's so difficult aboot dat tae understan'?" Whatever control he'd exercised to keep his voice low evaporated, and he stalked away from me toward the parlor, then stopped, when he realized the sofa wasn't there for him to sit on anymore, and spun around to face me as I followed him out of the kitchen. He seemed defensive, but also plaintive. "I've continued tae choose dis life ever night for a'most twa hunner' years, an' I refuse ta feel shame or regret for da tings I do ta survive. I enjoy surviving. I enjoy da night, an' da blood...I wish you would enjoy it, as'well. It could be better, if you let yoursel' enjoy it. Because I think you know you wann'ed dis. You wann'ed to live." He pointed his finger at me in time with his accusation, and I wondered what would happen if I bit it off.

"How can you say that?" I recoiled in betrayal, the violence of his words stinging like I'd been slapped. I wanted to slap him in return. *How dare he—*

He shrugged. "If you weren' meant tae be a vampire, you wouldna have resurrected as one."

I glared at him, but he was in a mood now, pacing in the spot where the sofa once was and going on, his accent growing thick alongside his frustration. "You survived bein' turned in one night—so few of us can claim dat. Your life is na some cursed mistake. Dere are dose would die for what you have. Dey'd kill for it. Dey have, and dey do—one in every tree fledglings we try tae turn, wi' all de care in de world, don' survive de process. Dey don' come back. An' yet you're so coo up in self-loathing an' resentment dat you canna even see de truth of de gift dat's right in front o' you."

"You think I should be grateful, to have survived for *this*?"

"*YES!*" He roared so loudly, the windows rattled—or maybe is was just a passing delivery truck and convenient timing. But I didn't flinch. I wanted to hold my own against him.

"I don't want to be a vampire! I can't go out in the sunshine anymore, I can't have pumpkin spice lattes, blood tastes horrible, by the way, and every time my fangs pop out I get a dumb embarrassing lisp and I hate it! I hate every second of this stupid vampire—" I choked back a lump in my throat, blinked away the crimson pinpricks accumulating at the peripherals of my vision. I wanted to stay angry. I didn't want to cry.

"And now the man who killed me has been getting entirely too close to my best friend, and you and Calliope both don't seem to have a problem with that!"

"Is Becca even your best friend anymore, Grace?" He shook his head like he was trying to dislodge water from his ears, and continued, his accent all but disappearing again. "She seemed rather upset at you via her last correspondence."

"Becca is my best friend forever. You don't know anything about us." I didn't think it was fair for him to bring up the Facebook posts. "And he's going to hurt her, too, and I don't know if—I don't know how to stop him!" The tears I didn't want to cry could not be held back a moment longer, and sobbed all the harder for it. "You say fledglings are chosen family, but I wasn't *chosen*. I wasn't *wanted*. Nothing about what he did to me makes sense. All I was to him was something to discard on his way to get to Becca, because she's the pretty one, the one who always gets attention from boys even when she's not wearing any makeup, the one who never has to even try to get told that she's pretty, and I have to try so hard, and it's exhausting!" My face was scrunched up and I was sure I looked like an absolute disaster, but once I started crying like that, the words kept coming out of my mouth and I had no way to stop the outpouring.

All the while, Harold just stood in front of me, dumbfounded and awkward in the face of my meltdown. "And, you know, whatever," I continued, sniffling a little and trying to pull myself together, "I think I'm fairly pretty too, if I dress right for my proportions and do my makeup and style my hair and remember how to stand so I don't look like I'm slouching or trying to disappear into the walls—I can be pretty, too, you know!"

I didn't even realize I'd had fallen into his arms until I felt the almost-warm itchy wool of his sweater wrapped around me, tight and comforting, and when my tears soaked into the yarn the wet fibers smelled awful, and I cursed my stupid heightened vampire senses. But after a moment or two of being held, I stopped crying, feeling even more foolish and self-conscious than I ever had in front of him.

He didn't say anything at first, but he handed me another fabric hankie out of his pocket to wipe my tears.

"Come, now..." he finally spoke up, resting his chin on the top of my head, his hands motioning small comforting circles at the small of my back. "There's no use in cryin' at da hert like so. I dunna think he abandoned you for not being pretty enough. That's...not likely. And I don't know what else to tell you, except: in two hundred years of being alive—or whatever you want tae call it—I have never known a pretty young woman wi' a pretty best friend who didn't each think the other girl was the prettier one."

"Oh yeah? And how many pretty young girls have you known?" I sniffled again into the hankie and wiped my eyes. Harold barely seemed social at all, let alone the sort of person to have a lot of romantic experience—with women or men, regardless of his claims to prefer "options." Whatever *that* meant. He was easy on the eyes, but no Casanova.

"Quite a few," He insisted with confidence. "It's a byproduct of where and how I've chosen tae get blood, at some times in my life."

I stood quietly in his arms, still pressed close to his chest, as the meaning of his confession sank in. "You did not just admit to me that you're some Jack the Ripper type who feeds on and kills—"

"No, no. But I've paid for sex, and I've paid for blood, quite a bit actually, and you can judge me all you like, but a man gets lonely, and the oldest profession in the world is still work."

He unwrapped his arms from around me and put his hands on my shoulders with another famous Harold sigh. "I've changed a lot over the centuries." He said softly. "We all do."

"Well, I won't change what I plan to do to my maker."

"You have tae be careful, Grace." He eyed me with cautious suspicion. "You have no idea what you could be getting yourself into."

⸺◄O►⸺

Chapter Seventeen

FLEDGLING

But I couldn't let it go. I became obsessed with Calliope Jones, tracking down every piece of information I could find about her online, every picture from every angle at every event she had hosted or attended where there was press coverage, as far back as I could find images. I used the internet archive, paid for subscriptions to digital newspapers and magazines, read every interview I could find that she'd ever given.

Becca wasn't the only one capable of detective work.

The first image I found him in was at Calliope's fundraiser at the Field Museum. There were no publicity pictures identifying Gavin by name, but I did find images where he appeared in the background (I also found a picture of the Roman artifact display with a suspicious-looking sweater-clad elbow obscuring the edge of the frame—but Harold had already told me he'd been at that event, and what he'd been most interested in at the time. Would he have even noticed or acknowledged other vampires at the museum, aside from Calliope?).

I kept scrolling backwards in time. Five years. Ten. The pictures got fewer and further between, and most of the links were broken, the image quality lower. It became difficult to make out faces in the dark backgrounds of the nighttime photographs. Calliope in 2001 looked shockingly like Calliope in 2015—she wore only slightly less makeup, a slightly different wig styled in a slightly different way. An old interview, deep in the archives of a local business magazine, mentioned a personal assistant: Ezra Richardson. No picture, and the name wasn't quite the same, but it gave me an idea.

"Ezra Gavin Richardson." I typed into the search bar. Pages of results, but nothing stuck.

"Gavin Ezra Richardson." The search results buffered for a moment, and then the page loaded. Nothing on the first page of search results, but something told me to keep looking.

The Loyola University Alumni newsletter. I had access to those archives already. "Search continues for Loyola Grad in Lake Michigan."

"Rescue workers are still searching for the remains of Gavin Ezra Richardson, Loyola School of Business class of 1998, now feared dead, after a boating accident over the weekend. A candlelight memorial is planned..."

The article was dated spring 2002, the picture from the article showed a young man with squinting eyes smiling in the sun, his dark hair obscured by frosted tips, a popped polo collar appearing from underneath an Ed Hardy t-shirt with a gaudy oversized American eagle motif emblazoned across the chest. I immediately wanted to send the picture to Becca with the caption, "things that are not aesthetic," but that didn't seem to be the best way to warn her.

Then again, Becca might actually dump someone over an Ed Hardy t-shirt... I zoomed in on the image. It was definitely him. I'd only seen him a handful of times before, but there was something about the cocky set of his jaw, his height, the way he carried himself...it had to have been one of the last pictures taken of Gavin before he died. *Before Calliope turned him*, I reminded myself.

It was easy to find out who Gavin had been, after that. He'd been involved in international studies, and the computer club, and finance club, and had been vice president of a political organization on campus. A former friend of his who made glowing statements about Gavin to the alumni newsletter now worked in the Cook County medical examiner's office. Another was the CEO of a local internet security company. The people Gavin had associated with when he was alive went on to have prominent careers. Clearly, he'd been ambitious long before he became a vampire.

I found his obituary online; he'd been born and raised in Wisconsin, just a few hours away. He had brothers and sisters and parents, all still alive. I found their profiles on Facebook; they seemed like a nice family. I wondered if he knew that he had a nephew named Ezra, or that his sister posted her favorite pictures of them growing up as children every year on his birthday in July?

I wondered if he still thought about his mortal family as often as they thought about him, and if he knew how loved he was. And I wondered how, if he knew any of that, he could have done what he did to me, without reaching out, without saying, "I'm sorry."

Unless what he did to me wasn't an accident.

Either he'd changed, after being turned, or he'd been a completely different person around his family. I thought back to the Ed Hardy shirt and decided that he'd probably always been a douche, but...

There was something afoot, and it involved me, it involved Becca, it involved Gavin and Calliope, and it involved Harold, too—how much he was involved, I didn't know, but I couldn't rule him out. Becca wasn't talking to me, and I didn't know any other vampires in the Community beyond a few given names—I had no idea how to get in touch with them even if I tried. I had vague ideas of what might turn up if I searched for "Chicago vampire community" online, and I didn't know whether to laugh or cry at the resulting mental image.

I considered my options. If I was going to kill Gavin—and I very much wanted to kill him, even if he had a nice-looking family in Wisconsin who loved and missed him—then I needed to know where to find him. Where he lived, where he hunted, where he got his blood.

I didn't even know all the places where Harold got his blood.

Well I was going to have to figure things out then, wasn't I? The truth was, the longer I stayed cooped up at Harold's, the more I felt something rising inside of me that was darker and...deeper, and more insatiable than ordinary hunger. Maybe I only felt that way because of the animal blood I'd been recently drinking. But—

Calliope was right to be disappointed that Harold hadn't shown me how to reliably source my own blood yet. Watching a single black market exchange in a dirty parking lot wasn't much to go on. I didn't want to kill ordinary people—just Gavin. But Harold wasn't going to put up with me forever, no matter how much he said he liked having me around. We both needed our own space—that much was obvious from the weeks that I'd spent with him. We were effectively strangers. He didn't want to get to know me.

And I said I didn't want to get to know him...I regretted the words I'd spoken in anger. Eventually, we'd part ways, probably sooner now than we might have before, and if I hadn't destroyed Gavin by then, I'd need to know how to survive on my own while I devoted the rest of my nights to hunting the fiend who had created me.

I hated Gavin Richardson. Hatred was a new emotion for me, but I embraced it, allowed it to envelop me. I turned my loathing into a cloak of protection around whatever was left of me that was vulnerable, and human. I needed to hate him if I was going to protect Becca.

Now that I had my car back, now that I knew who had turned me, there were things I could finally do.

<hr>

The next time Harold went out for supplies I waited five minutes, then pulled my car out of the garage and headed back toward downtown. It was a Friday, and based on Becca's recent online activity I had an idea what her plans for the evening might be. On the passenger seat next to me sat an opened Amazon Prime box—Harold wasn't happy about me getting packages delivered in my name to his house, and made me promise that I wouldn't do it again—but at least now I had my own bottle of peppermint extract to store in the glove compartment, and a decent pair of binoculars. My vision as a vampire was excellent, but I had to assume Gavin's was as well.

Harold didn't know about the binoculars. I'd told him the box contained a few novels. I'd guessed, from the lack of books around his house, that he wasn't much of a reader, and the way he immediately lost interest in the contents of my Amazon order when he thought it contained books was telling. Harold was pretty great in a lot of ways, but if he wasn't a reader, that was one more reason not to get attached.

Then again, at least with Harold, I'd never have to worry about him borrowing my copy of the Silmarillion, not returning it, and then posting a vain "beach reads" picture from some sunny Portuguese seaside town to Instagram months later, with *my* copy of the book in his hands. Unsavory rake, indeed.

As I neared Becca's apartment, I pulled the binoculars out of the box and slipped into a "loading zone only" spot about half a block away, crossing my fingers that I wouldn't be a sitting duck for the city's predatory meter maids very long. I didn't want another parking ticket, especially now that I was on Calliope Jones's bad side.

Only a few minutes later, the chaos monster herself waltzed out the main entrance, scanning the street, phone pressed to her ear. She was wearing the long black coat with all the buckles again, but she'd finally had the sleeves shortened, and the subtle difference in tailoring made her appear much more sophisticated than usual. Also, her hair was styled for once, instead of squashed down by a big furry hat. She looked like she'd gotten a professional blowout recently, and even her makeup was different. Becca was usually too impatient for more than smudgy black eyeliner and tinted lip balm, or black lipstick if she was going out to the goth club, but someone else had done Becca's makeup today. Someone professional, I'd put money on it. She was wearing bright red lipstick, and false eyelashes that fluttered so realistically, I wouldn't have known they were fake if I didn't already know every line and contour of Becca's face as thoroughly as I knew my own. A sodium flare of jealousy ignited in my solar plexus, and the hard plastic casing surrounding the binoculars cracked, just enough to get my attention.

I'd been entertaining violent thoughts again. *Focus, Grace.*

Seconds later, a bright green painted cab pulled up in front of the building, and Becca stepped inside. The older model Crown Vic had probably been purchased at a police auction—despite the new paint job, there were still a few bullet holes visible in the trunk of the car. I pulled out of the loading zone and began to follow the taxi. The vivid green sedan wasn't hard to keep track of, even with the driver zipping chaotically in and out of traffic. I hoped Becca was wearing her seat belt, and braced myself for another fender-bender if the damn cabbie pulled any more insane moves. Being a vampire only made navigating downtown Chicago traffic marginally less infuriating. Improved reaction times meant little when everyone else on the road drove like a maniac. I passed no fewer than three Calliope Jones Group ads on bus stops and billboards along the way, and tried not to imagine those porcelain blue eyes following me, judging me.

Screw Calliope Jones. I didn't think she was keeping a very good eye out for Becca at all.

I continued to follow the cab to a gated subdivision in River North where the condominiums started in the low seven figures, all ugly modern brick facades and scrawny young trees lining the sidewalks. I tried to watch where Becca was going as she exited the cab, but a car behind me honked, and I sped off before she could turn around. I wasn't certain she'd be able to recognize my dark blue Accord in all the other traffic, but I didn't want to risk it. I drove around the block a few times until a parking spot opened up nearby, and pulled out my iPhone.

Becca lost her phone constantly. Constantly. I'd had to use my phone to locate hers many times over the years. But I'd seen it pressed to her ear when she exited her apartment, so unless she'd left the device in the cab, it was safe to assume that she had it on her now. I made sure the sound was off before I ran the "find my iPhone" application, and watched her move around the inside of the condo for a bit, harboring more violent thoughts.

I could kill him. I could waltz right in there and—

But I couldn't, could I? Not without an invitation. Not without weapons.

Gavin's condo might as well have been a fortress. I could probably leap over the gate, I could probably locate his exact unit. But there was no way I was going to get inside without being invited—stupid vampire rules and limitations.

Becca's phone was on the move again.

I had to scramble out of the parking spot when I realized that she'd left the condo and gotten into another vehicle, and I thought I'd lost her, until a matte black Maserati GranTurismo roared past my inconspicuous little Honda. The pretentious Italian sports car looked exactly like something Calliope's fledgling would drive—I remembered her fondness for tailored Italian pantsuits. The Maserati's speakers blasted a familiar-sounding alternative rock band Becca sometimes liked to play when she was good and angry—she'd told me once that the lead singer owned a winery not too far from her family's. "A Perfect Tool," or something.

That seemed about on par for Gavin's aesthetic.

Under ordinary conditions, my life was no *Fast and Furious* movie, and my Accord was no match for a Maserati. But Friday night Chicago traffic was a great equalizer, and I was able to follow a few cars behind as Gavin and Becca made their way over to a trendy part of the Loop lined with upscale restaurants and late-night dance clubs.

The nightclub I tracked them to wasn't really the kind of establishment Becca and I tended to frequent, unless one of our service industry friends was working the bar or filling in for the DJ. Becca's grandfather might be rich, but he didn't give her "$300 bottle service at trendy nightclubs" allowance money. She bought her socks and underwear at Target like the rest of us.

So it was a little surreal to watch her get out of the Maserati at valet, with her expensive perfect blowout and makeup only slightly messier than when she'd gone in to Gavin's condo. Her long black coat was unbuckled, and when the wind blew it open, I recognized the Dolce and Gabana cocktail dress her Nonna bought for her on a shopping trip to Italy a few years back.

She'd tried to justify the price when she first showed the dress off to me.

"Italian clothes are a lot cheaper in Italy, obviously. And if you shop the seasonal sales, it almost makes up for the cost of the plane ticket."

Becca wasn't the best at math, but the price tag on that dress "plus the price of the plane ticket," even economy class, was equivalent to a month's rent and then some. It was a cute dress, but she rarely wore it. Becca hated being ostentatious.

Gavin stepped around the car and offered his elbow to her; the two of them were ushered past the velvet ropes and bouncers at the door with a casual, practiced efficiency.

They were such a ridiculously good-looking couple. It made me want to smash things.

I glanced at my own attire. I wasn't exactly dressed for a night out, but I had planned ahead. My black boucle miniskirt was a decent dupe for Chanel, if you didn't look too close, and the overall vibe was dark, understated, uncomplicated. Some people went out to socialize directly after work, didn't they? I wouldn't stand out among the other patrons. If anything, I'd slip past them completely unnoticed.

And that's all I wanted to do, really. I just wanted to step inside the club and watch them. I wanted to make sure he wasn't taking advantage of her. I wanted to know that she was going to leave the nightclub alive, heartbeat and everything.

"Not her."

I was handing my ID to the doorman when a booming voice behind me spoke up.

"Me?" My voice squeaked. I turned around to look at the bouncer, and a sinking feeling bottomed out my stomach.

"Yes, you, bitch. Go start trouble somewhere else." The bouncer was tall, broad-shouldered and big-bellied. He had multiple facial piercings, and "STAR WARS" tattooed across his knuckles, and I recognized him as one of the bouncers on staff at the disastrous show at the Metro.

I shook my head as innocently as I could. "I am not—"

"Remember I told you 'bout the fight outside Metro earlier this month?" The familiar-looking bouncer told the doorman. "She's the reason Ducky's out with a broken foot. She looks tiny, but she packs a punch."

"I just want to meet my friends. They're waiting for me inside." There was a $100 bill in my wallet. If I fished it out, maybe I could...

"Ain't no way, baby girl." The doorman glared at me. "If he says you ain't coming in, then you're not getting in tonight. There's lots of clubs in town, but you ain't getting into this one."

I looked at the doorman, and then at the bouncer. I felt a small twinge of guilt for breaking 'Ducky's' foot, but it paled in comparison to the anger and jealousy and frustration reaching a crescendo inside me, threatening to boil over. With peppermint up my nose, I couldn't smell their blood, but I didn't need to—the pulsing vein in the doorman's neck, just above the collar of his jacket, was enough to distract me. I clenched my fist.

I could force my way into the club, sure. Start another fight with my maker. Punch him in his pretty face a few times, revel in the carnage and bloodshed and chaos—but Becca was inside the nightclub. Through the closed doors ahead of me, I could make out a familiar pulsing beat, and I closed my eyes, remembered Becca dancing.

I was trying to protect Becca, not get her hurt. And I didn't want to want to kill anyone. I stepped backward, barely holding together my growing desire to crush skulls and tear out throats. I didn't want to be a monster.

Without another word, I pivoted on my heels and stalked off down the street.

I was just stepping out of my car when Harold pulled into the garage. He seemed surprised to see me there. "You coming or going?" He asked, eyeing me suspiciously. He had a brown paper bag with the logo of a local upscale butcher on it in each hand, and I wrinkled my nose.

"Just coming back. I went for a drive. That's not against the rules, is it?" I continued my stalking back into the house through the mud room.

"Grace, I thought we talked about this..."

I ignored him. I stalked up the stairs to my bedroom and slammed the door.

What the fuck was Gavin doing to Becca? She didn't even look like herself. She'd looked...fancy. Becca was anything but fancy.

I was going to need more than a pair of binoculars. I continued to stalk Becca's social media from my alt account, whispering a small, quiet prayer of thanks to my every time Becca posted an update that was timestamped with daylight hours. I knew where Gavin lived now, and what kind of car he drove. Maybe I could show up unannounced at Becca's apartment, ask to be invited in, come up with a story and—*no.*

That was too dangerous to Becca. I couldn't use her to get to Gavin. I was going to need to buy surveillance tools, real ones, and I started to make a list of the supplies I would need.

⋯⊶◆⊷⋯

Chapter Eighteen

Icarus and the Sun

Three nights later, Harold went out for blood again.

"You want tae come with?" He asked, casually leaning against the doorway to my bedroom as I tidied up the blankets. "I've got a lead on a batch of medical-grade human stuff at a small emergency room in Indiana. Bit of a drive, thought it might be nice tae have some company." His smile was genuine and inviting, no fangs this time, and I groaned. He had no right to be so damn charming when I'd already made other plans.

"Indiana? That's a ways off." I'd always wondered how far he had to go, and how long he had to wait, when he went to get supplies. Sometimes he was only gone an hour in the early evenings, and sometimes, like last time, he stayed away much longer into the night. It was good to know he was planning to be gone for a while this time, at least.

Harold shrugged. "I'm tired of visiting the stockyards. And I know you prefer the human stuff, too—"

"I don't have a preference." I lied, waving my hand.

Harold wrinkled up his nose in a passable imitation of the face I always made when he brought home animal blood, and I rolled my eyes. He was a shockingly good mimic, and I didn't want to add another endearing trait to the collection of things I didn't want to like about Harold Laing.

"You want to sit next to me in a car for several hours while we both insist we don't want to know anything about each other?"

The charming smile vanished from his face. "No, I suppose not. You've been upfront about your feelings, at least. I'll give you my thanks for that. Makes it easier than tae hope for—you know what? Nevermind." He turned around and left as silently as he'd arrived. I barely heard his footsteps going down the stairs.

"Harold, wait—"

But he was already disappearing into the garage when I caught up with him. "Just stay out of trouble for once, okay?" After that, he didn't say anything else. The car door slammed, and he backed out of the garage and drove off, leaving me alone in the kitchen, uncertain whether I should be sorry for hurting his feelings, or grateful to have several uninterrupted hours ahead of me to complete my plans. I settled on the latter.

As February crept closer to March, the days grew longer and the sun set later each evening, diminishing the nights by small, cumulative increments. When I'd first been turned, the sun would disappear below the horizon just before 4:30 each evening, but now we had to wait until closer to 5:30 to leave the house if we wanted to go anywhere. With each passing day, we lost precious minutes of darkness, and for me, that meant less time to work on my plans to protect Becca.

Ten minutes later, I pulled into the parking lot of a local camera shop just before its posted closing time, with a list on my phone and a general idea of where in the store I would find everything I needed. I'd taken a photography class for part of my journalism unit in college, and while I hadn't done any serious shooting since losing access to the camera rentals through school, I was relatively confident I still knew my way around manual mode. A midrange DSLR and a telephoto zoom lens were a step up from the binoculars, and with a camera, I would have evidence.

And if I could capture evidence of Gavin with Becca, or even of Calliope's involvement with Gavin, surely—

I wasn't sure of anything, actually, but I thought if I had indisputable proof, I'd be in a better position to demand justice from the Community.

I wanted Gavin Richardson dead.

I'd never killed anyone before, but I was confident I would have no moral com-punctions about letting Gavin ruin my perfect "no killing" streak. He deserved to die for what he'd done to me, and soon. The nature of my hunger was changing, and what emerged from the oozing rot of what once had been my soft heart was drenched in ichor, with teeth like knives. I needed less blood than I had when I was newly turned, but it was getting harder to slake my thirst with potable blood alone. I craved the hot pulse of something live and writhing in my clutches.

I didn't speak a word of this aloud, not even to myself, and certainly not to Harold. He was hardly a font of information about my condition as a vampire, anyway. Keeping me more or less trapped inside the house, with a hefty dose of peppermint extract shoved up my nose whenever I had the opportunity to leave or go anywhere, was about the extent of Harold's fledgling training duties, so far as I could tell. *No wonder the last time he'd turned someone, it hadn't gone well*, I mused. I liked Harold a lot—more than I wanted to—but I learned very little by way of practical advice about being a vampire from him.

'Don't get caught,' seemed to be his primary instruction. And I tried not to, I really did.

The staff at the camera shop were accommodating and helpful. A late-in-the-day sale of several thousand dollars always made management and commissioned sales staff happy. The employee at the register was younger than me, enthusiastic, and talkative. He was taking photography classes at the local community college, and he'd already won a few awards for his work at small regional competitions. His specialty was landscape photography, and he complimented me on my choice of lenses. I listened to him prattle on, and tried not to pay attention to the blue-green veins on his neck. He mentioned a girlfriend. I wondered what I would have to do to get him alone. He was hardly efficient while ringing up my items, and he apologized repeatedly for the difficulties he was having with the point-of-sale machine. If it took him much longer to figure out what the problem was, both of us would be dealing with an entirely different problem.

"Is something wrong with the card?" I asked, impatience and hunger fraying at my nerves. I was using the AmEx card that Calliope had given me. Well, given Harold. It was a business card, and it didn't have my name on it, but I was an authorized user.

...wasn't I? I hadn't used the card for much—mostly gas, new bedding, and the toiletries I'd needed to replace as they ran out, but I'd also used the card to pay for some subscriptions to online business magazines and archive databases when I'd

been finding out what I could about Calliope and her fledgling. That suddenly felt like a foolish mistake.

A balding hipster with a name tag that said "manager" and a handlebar mustache that gave him the unfortunate appearance of a cartoon villain walked over to help, while the employee pointed out something on the screen that only the two of them could see. That should have been my cue to leave; I didn't want Harold to worry if he got home before I did. I hadn't exactly promised that I'd stay out of trouble, but...

But even as irritation at the inexplicable delay started to gnaw at my self-control, I tried to remain polite and affable, even as the lights went out in the back of the store, and another employee took up a sentinel position at the door, informing incoming shoppers that the store was closed, and they would be welcome back tomorrow at 9:00 AM. I was too focused on managing my hunger. I should have been reading the room. I should have offered to pay for my purchases with cash.

Then, suddenly, everything was fine. The manager and the employee finished ringing up my purchase, they gave me a receipt and my packages, and I left the store, walking back across the darkened parking lot toward my car.

I never saw the police officers arrive—the lights were off on their unmarked patrol car as they pulled up to me from behind a massive pile of ugly gray ice and sludge in the far corner of the parking lot, and I was in a hurry to leave and get back to the house before Harold had a panic attack. I hadn't left him a note. I should have left him a note, at least.

And then I heard the store manager several yards behind me, standing outside the shop, instructing someone, "Yes, that's her, right over there—"

"Is there a problem?" I spun around, my voice quiet and cracked, my dead heart thumping over itself three times in a row—a new record. I tensed, poised to make a run for it. The lone employee at the entrance of the store was staring at me. The store manager outside was staring at me. Everyone was staring at me.

"Ma'am, you used a card that was reported as stolen tonight." The man with the mustache and the name tag nodded at the officers as he spoke, his tone clipped and businesslike. "And since this purchase is over a specific amount, okay, that's a serious charge, okay? You understand we have a procedure for when accounts are flagged like this…" he twirled the end of his mustache around his finger, and I half-expected him to let out a high-pitched evil giggle, but he remained almost offensively impersonal.

That was why they let me walk out of the store. I dropped the shopping bags.

"This is all a misunderstanding. The card was given to me over a month ago by—by a friend," I finished, not sure I wanted to name-drop Calliope Jones after the recent blow-up at the house. A creeping terror began to overtake me, rooting me to the ground when I ought to have been running, fighting, fleeing. My eyes darted fearfully between the officers, the manager, and my car at the far edge of the parking lot. In a gut-churning split second, I knew with violent, ruthless certainty that I could fight them all off if I needed to. The memory of bones crunching at the nightclub as I'd chased Gavin through the crowd washed over me, and my peripheral vision began to tinge red. I balled my hands into fists. "If you just let me go, I'll make some phone calls and come back tomorrow. This doesn't have to be a big deal. I live in the area."

One of the officers asked to see my ID. Like an idiot, I fished it out of my wallet instead of running away as fast as I could. I had never, not in my entire life, been stopped by the police for more than a minor traffic violation. I looked at my old Honda, surrounded by all the newer, fancier vehicles remaining in the lot. Nothing made sense.

"We checked her ID at the register, and it didn't match. The system flagged the card as stolen." The manager might as well have been talking on autopilot. "We see this kind of thing all the time, okay? And our system is very good. We always catch card fraud, and we prosecute to the fullest extent of the law. I'm afraid it's out of my hands now."

The second police officer got out of the patrol car and walked over to me with handcuffs. "We actually got a fraud alert from the cardholder right before your call came in. Someone hasn't been very careful." He spoke to the manager, but his shifty eyes kept looking back at me.

"They never are." The officer who had asked for my ID began to slip a pair of handcuffs around my wrists. The cold metal was heavier than I'd expected, and I practically snarled at him, fighting the instinct to bare my fangs. I jerked my hands away, but he held tight. I'd never been arrested before. I didn't know what to do.

"Don't make this harder on yourself, ma'am." (*Isn't that what Calliope had told me the other night? "Don't make this harder on yourself?"*) "You don't want to add resisting arrest to the list of charges we've already got started for you."

Even then, I thought, I still could have run. I still could have fought, fangs out, fingers hooked like claws, biting, tearing, smashing my way out the officer's reach, out of the parking lot, out of the village, with or without my car. I looked fearfully at the officers, the middle-aged mustached manager, and the teenage employee from behind the register who had betrayed me, just now exiting the shop to observe my arrest, and my fear was not for myself. *These people did not deserve to die*, I thought. *I'll figure this out. There's got to be a way to make this work. Harold. I had to figure out a way to get in touch with Harold.*

"I need to make a phone call," I said.

"You can do it at the station, sweetheart," the officer replied. I hated being called sweetheart. I was a vampire, dammit. Vampires shouldn't get called sweetheart.

⊰◆⊱

I'd known kids in college who got arrested for underage drinking at parties, and one time one of my dealers ended up with some serious charges, but I'd been unscathed in the incident. My own record was squeaky-clean. Becca and I had been much more discreet about our own underage shenanigans, sneakily injecting vodka into foil packs of fruit juice and re-sealing the puncture holes with a straightening iron in our dorm room, or soaking gummy bears in tequila. Becca even had a hair brush that functioned as a hidden flask. And when it came to substances Becca made sure we always hung out with the rich kids. They had the best supplies, and their parents could afford the kind of lawyers no one in school administration or law enforcement wanted to deal with.

All I knew about getting arrested came from the episodes of Law & Order Nana always used to have playing on the TV at her house. I'd always assumed that when you got taken into custody, they took you straight in to get...fingerprinted, or whatever they did at the station, and then you got bailed out and went home. It was still early enough in the evening when the officers put me in the back of their police cruiser, so I had plenty of time to fix the situation before sunrise, I consoled myself. All I had to do was call Harold, and he'd know how to fix things. He would be mad, of course, but he'd also said the Community looked after each other. There had to be resources.

But the officers who arrested me didn't go straight to the precinct. They drove idly around the suburb and stopped in various parking lots to listen to the chatter on the police scanner for *hours*. They even went through a fast food drive-through with me in the back seat. "You want anything, sweetheart?" the officer who had threatened me with resisting arrest asked. I didn't think he meant it, and anyway, I said I wasn't hungry.

I was starving.

The policeman laughed, harsh and callous, and sneered, "I guess the Golden Arches aren't good enough for miss priss back there. Hey, my partner wants to know, did you steal that fancy watch you've got on, too?"

I growled but said nothing.

"Yeah, you know, it's probably a fake, I think. Kids like you are always trying to be something you're not. I know the type. You think you can get away with stuff because you're young and stupid, and then here comes the consequences, and it's nothing but crocodile tears for days and days, 'I didn't do it! I didn't do anything wrong, it wasn't me, it was my friend, it was my boyfriend, it's all some big misunderstanding, blah blah blah.' You suburban punks don't know what real crime is, I tell you what. And you're fucking lucky to be learning this lesson now, huh? Straighten you out a bit? You got your whole life ahead of you, kid. You don't want to be doing this stupid stuff forever, trust me."

The officer rambled on the entire meandering drive to the station. I couldn't think of anything ton say that was clever enough or threatening enough to shut him up, but at least I didn't cry, either. It was bad enough to cry in front of Harold. I wasn't going to give these assholes that benefit.

It was after midnight when the officers brought me in to be photographed, fingerprinted, and charged. They took my phone, my watch, the faulty credit card, and all the cash in my wallet. Five hours til sunrise…I could still make it.

"What the fuck is this shit?" the officer doing my intake exclaimed when he saw the pieces of cotton shoved up my nose. His blue nitrile gloved fingers were rough as he reached up to pull out the peppermint-extract saturated material. "Christ almighty, you afraid of getting a bloody nose or something?" Another officer suggested that they needed to do a cavity strip search.

"And what, you think she's got stolen goods shoved up her twat?" Even the female police officers were crude. The others laughed in uproar.

"Don't worry, babe, they're just trying to scare you, huh? Lighten up a little. It's just a joke. I'm not gonna let them strip-search ya." A uniformed man who hadn't been one of the arresting officers tried to play the "good cop" role, but he wasn't very convincing. With the peppermint extract gone, there was no more buffer between me and the overpowering human stench of the officers processing my arrest, and I doubled over in the chair they'd told me to sit in, head bowed low. I tried to breathe through my mouth enough to continue the pretense that I was human, and I tried to block out the scent of their blood.

As they herded me deeper into the bowels of the police station, the completely fucked reality of my predicament became obvious. My window of opportunity for escape was long gone. If I ran now—if I fought to get away using all my stupid undead strength, they would shoot me. They would shoot me until I stopped moving, and then they would probably shoot me some more.

That was one of the ways vampires could be killed, Harold had said. At least I knew that much. But I couldn't die now. I had to take care of my maker and protect Becca; I wanted to know what was going on with Calliope Jones, and I had to tell Harold…I needed to tell Harold…

"Sorry, landlines only." A completely new official didn't even look up when it came time for me to use my phone call.

I thought that if anyone might still have a landline in 2015 it would be Harold, but I didn't know the number. There was a brutalized and torn-up phone book by the pay phone, but no listing for Harold Laing…*why would a vampire have a listed number under their real name? Did I even know Harold's real name?* I felt foolish even letting myself hope. It was almost 3 AM.

Two and a half hours til sunrise.

When they told me I'd have to stay at the station until my bond hearing at the courthouse the next morning, I nodded in hopeless resignation. I was going to die in police custody, then. The realization was almost comforting. Accepting my fate made me numb, and there was safety in that.

Just like after mom died.

Just like the night I found out I was a vampire.

They led me to a small cell with a narrow metal bed and no mattress—really more of a bench than a bed, jutting out from the wall—and a filthy sink and a toilet in the corner I was glad I wouldn't have to use. Thankfully it was a slow night at the station, and no one else in the cell with me. It had been too many nights since I'd had human blood, and I was pretty certain I wouldn't have been able to stop myself. I shuddered, unable to stop the intrusive thoughts that swarmed me, of tearing my teeth into someone's neck and...

I tried to redirect my thoughts. Kittens. I imagined a litter of orange tabby babies, warm and safe in their bedding, rolling over each other as they dreamed violent kitten dreams, and their orange color of their fur darkened to scarlet; their purrs turned to buzzing, like wasps. Swatting them away only made them angrier. The kittens wanted blood, and I wanted it, too. Wanted to claw and tear and...*oh, God.*

The imagined scene tore away in bloodied shreds; I couldn't hold on to anything solid, and reality slammed into me again, like the clanging of cell doors closing out any hope of survival. There was a single window in the cell, high up on the wall and recessed into the cinder blocks. I'd never had a particularly well-developed internal compass. Never been a Girl Scout, never been wilderness exploring or camping. Not even two months ago, I wouldn't have been able to tell a north-facing window from a southerly one. But this window, I knew, with a cold, painful certainty, faced east.

Less than two hours til sunrise.

I'd been Icarus, I decided, remembering the tragic Greek myth from my studies. Too bold, too brazen. I'd flown too close to the thing that could kill me, and now, I was falling, spiraling toward a deep dark sea.

I sat on the bench with my arms wrapped around my pulled-up knees, my eyes locked on the dark, grime-encrusted window above me, and rocked, waiting for the sun to rise and claim me. Harold had said death by sunlight would be painful.

I hoped it would be over quickly.

My internal clock, I knew, was deadly accurate. *An hour til sunrise. One hour til sunrise...*

I was so locked in focus, staring at the small block of reinforced glass through which my death would surely arrive, that I didn't notice footsteps approaching my cell, or even register the metallic clang of the door being opened. But I smelled the presence of a human wafting close to me, and spun around, eyes wild.

"Your friend is here to take you home," said a man I didn't recognize. I guessed shift change must have come and gone while I'd been counting the minutes toward my inevitable death.

Now, I didn't know what to think. "I didn't make a phone call..." I tried not to sound as confused as I felt.

"I don't know what to tell you, lady, but there's a man and his lawyer up at the front waiting to take you home, so hop to. You don't want to stay here all night if you don't gotta."

I indulged a hollow laugh in spite of myself, wondering what the officer would think if he had even an inkling of how true that statement was.

Harold was waiting for me by the counter where I'd been brought in, and I wasn't surprised to see him, I realized. Even though I hadn't been able to call him, I wasn't surprised at all that he had found me. He shook hands with a tired-looking man in a rumpled suit as I signed the rest of the paperwork securing my release, and his face was an unreadable mask, pale greenish eyes neutral, void of emotion. He stood still, very still, not even breathing still, as I retrieved my belongings—my wallet, my cell phone, my parka. They'd run the serial number engraved on the Cartier wristwatch, they told me. It wasn't reported as stolen, so I could have it back. They didn't return the cash or the American Express card.

I had a court appearance scheduled in two days. If I failed to show up, a warrant would be issued for my arrest. Did I understand? I nodded. There was no way I was going to be able to make my court appearance, of course, but that could be dealt with later. I just needed to get back to Harold's house, to climb into bed and under the covers and hide away from the sun.

I suppressed the horrible urge to grab on to Harold's hand and skip like an excited school kid on a field trip out the police station doors and over to his car, which was parked nearby. "How did you find me?" I whispered instead, breaking the spell of silence between us.

"I got fucking lucky, and I *guessed*," he spat. He paused for a beat before continuing, as if deciding whether or not to say anything else. When he spoke again, he did not hold back.

"When I go' back ta the house wi' de blood, and your car was'na in the garage *again*, I tried ta figure oot where you'd gone off ta, and you know wha? I didna have a *fucking* clue where you were, ya illcontriven almark. You didna leave your computer open dis time, and it's no laek I installed a tracking device on your phone—although, you know, in retrospect, mayhaps I should have—" He raised his voice, pulling out of the parking space and tearing through the nearly empty predawn city streets. I flinched.

"Whiesht! Ha'ee tongue! A'm klagget already—" he cut me off before I could utter a word in my own defense. I could barely understand half of what he said, anyway.

"So I drove aboot, tryin' to fix upon some notion of where you'd wandered off dis time, an' A happened to faa apon de lot where you parked your car. An' you were naught to be found, but I saw no sign o' a baffel, eider. A thinks to mysel' feich! Call de *police,* never there was a fledgling so fashious an' prone to running' off as dis one. D'ye know what an almark is? Tis a sheep at won't stay in its pen, dat's what you are! So I called central booking to see if you'd been picked oop by de cops, and de first time I called, you were na e'en in de system yet. D'you know how fucking lucky you were dat I called back once again? Dat I had a lawyer who could git you oot? Dat I had de muckle *money* t'git you oot? D'you know how absolutely, completely, impossibly lucky you fucking are?" Harold swerved around corners and sped through red lights. The sky was growing lighter, and I realized we weren't driving toward the direction of the house anymore.

"Harold, where are we going?" I asked as he blew through another red light, laying on the horn to alert ongoing traffic. A chilling thought occurred to me that if we got pulled over, we would both be in danger from the sun. But I didn't want him to slow down. The sun was approaching the horizon, and I could feel it in my veins and my bones and the small hairs on my arms and the back of my neck. The sun was rising, and we were both going to be caught out in it.

"We're goin' tae have tae git a room for the day." Harold made another sharp turn, and the familiar lights of a national motel chain's illuminated sign appeared on a low beige building at the end of the street. "If your ridiculous luck holds, they'll have a vacancy. I dunna know if we can make it back tae the house before the sun rises."

We parked the car, alerted the night clerk, and Harold paid for a room for two nights in cash. "I only have a king-sized bed available for the next two days," the clerk apologized, "and that's going to be an upcharge."

"It's fine," Harold responded through clenched teeth and tight lips. I knew it was because, like mine, his fangs were almost certainly extended. The primal, inhuman part of our nature was freaking out. Without the benefit of the peppermint extract blocking the very *human* smell coming off the motel clerk, I found my thoughts returning to visions of tearing out his throat, as if the violence of a bloodbath would save me from the impending flames. I clenched my fists and took several steps backward as Harold completed our transaction, and then we fled through the building toward the room we'd been assigned as the first vestiges of sunlight started to glow above the horizon. I couldn't see it, but I *felt* it.

Gripped by a full-on terror, I raced down the hallway.

⬩◆⬩

Chapter Nineteen

Whose Debt, If Not Mine?

Our rented haven until the next night had blessedly west-facing windows. That bought us time. Harold put the "Do Not Disturb" sign on the door, and I pulled the light-blocking curtains closed as far as they would go. With the room secured in gloom and the immediate danger of immolation past us, I felt the animalistic wild-eyed panic that had been driving me recede a bit.

Harold checked out the washroom. "The illbest place would be in here, with the door locked," he explained. "No windows."

But I felt my expression darken at the thought of spending the day hiding under towels in a bathtub, waking up tomorrow exactly as I had the night I resurrected. My head shook of its own volition. *No. Not that.*

Even though I didn't speak the words out loud, it must have been written across my face. Harold regarded me from across the room, and rubbed his fingertips across his temples. "So be it, then..." he stepped away from the bathroom door and over to the bed, pulling back the covers and examining them for opacity.

"The blankets seem thick enoo. We'll not be the worse for it under covers, so long as no one comes into de room an' opens up de curtains."

I looked at Harold, and down at the bed, and back at him, raising my eyebrows without meaning to. I hadn't had time to consider the implications of a single bed when we'd been racing for our lives against the sun. I reconsidered the bathtub.

"Lass, illhelt, git into the bed," he sighed.

A person might die of alcohol poisoning if they downed a shot every time Harold sighed in a single night.

"The sun is coming up, and A'm hed me a nicht." He removed his shoes before climbing under the covers, otherwise fully clothed, and I followed suit, doing as I was told because I was too tired, and too relieved, to argue.

With the thick winter blankets pulled up completely over our heads, we settled as best we could into the comforting darkness. The sun continued to rise in its arc across the dome of the sky above us, but I found myself unable to sleep, even though the weight of the day pressed down on me. The king-sized bed was large enough to provide both of us with all the personal space we needed, especially since Harold and I were not tall individuals. Restless, I rolled over from one side to the other, facing the middle of the bed, and was surprised to find Harold awake as well, and looking at me. His eyes in the darkness were enormous pools of black pupils dilated all the way open, no trace of gray-green iris visible. I guessed that my own hazel eyes must look much the same to him. I'd simply never noticed before.

"Hi," I said, feeling small and uncertain. "Can't sleep, either?"

"No, I suppose not." He seemed less angry than he'd been a while ago.

"I'm sorry I fucked up. I...I don't think you had to rescue me. No one would have blamed you if you'd let the sun take me. I was pretty resigned to it," I confessed.

"The sun is a horrible way tae die." He'd told me that before, on my very first night, the night he'd shown me the swords that he'd forged in his basement and promised to cut off my head if I really wanted to stop living, rather than let me face the sun.

"I guess I didn't realize before it came so close this morning. I've never been more terrified of anything in my life." I shuddered, and Harold reached out a hand to brush against my shoulder. "What would have happened to me?"

Harold's voice seemed very far away, as if he were remembering something when he spoke. "The light would have started tae fill the room you were in, dull at first, then brighter, and as the light got brighter, it would have started tae burn. No flames, not right away. The light would burn your eyes as it grew stronger, long before you ever saw sunlight, more painful than trying ta stare directly into a magnesium flame. Any exposed skin would start tae grow hot as the light filled the room, scalding hot. You would have tried tae find a way tae escape it, tae hide in whatever shadows you could find, but it wouldna be enough. Even if you curled into a ball in the corner of the cell furthest from where the light entered the window, the more sunlight filled the room, the more your skin would crackle and smolder.

"Then the burning would spread tae the protected skin under your clothes, and there would be smoke. Depending on the fibers in the clothing you were wearing, your clothes would start to singe and smoke, or maybe melt tae your flesh as your skin got hotter, and the sunlight filling the room would blind you, melting your eyes, and...you would start ta scream."

"Jesus Mary and Joseph, Harold—" came my horrified whisper, but he continued.

"...by the time the sun rose high enough in the sky tae shine through the window, you would be in...inescapable agony, no escape from it. When the sunlight directly hit your skin, flames would start tae lick away the flesh that was already blistered and blackened. No amount of water could quench those flames, no fire retardant...your skin would burn away, and then the underlying tissues—tendons, muscles, and sinews. It would burn you down tae the bone, Grace, and it would keep burning you, burning without stopping, burning for hours, and hours, and hours.

"And you'd be aware o' it all, the entire time."

I felt sick. Somehow, even in the goriest movies, it never seemed that bad. My stomach churned violently, and I wanted to throw up, but there was nothing to throw up but the bile rising suddenly in my throat. I swallowed it down, and as the burning pain receded, I understood, finally, that the all-consuming burning pain I felt when I was hungry was nothing like the fires of the sun. I doubled over on my side, curled in a fetal position. To think that I'd come so close to that kind of death was an overwhelming horror, and I shuddered and gasped and tried to process the graphic details.

I trusted Harold, absolutely. But it wasn't just my absolute trust in the vampire who had adopted me that made me certain he was telling the truth. It was the way every nerve and cell and fiber of my body had quaked in terror when the sun had been rising around us as we raced to the hotel room. Since becoming a vampire, I'd discovered that my body knew things long before my mind learned or accepted them.

"I didn't know." I was still shaking. "I didn't realize..." Somehow, without being conscious of it happening, we'd both drawn closer to each other, at the center of the bed, our knees and foreheads almost touching. "You could have died," I whispered, looking at him, realizing the kind of death he'd risked himself to save me.

"I don't..." Harold paused the way he often did, collecting his thoughts before speaking. "I don't want you tae die, Grace. Your life...it matters. Tae me. Please. Promise me you won't run off again. I'll teach you how tae hunt, I'll show you where tae get blood, I'll do everything you need me tae do tae show you how you can live for a long time as a vampire, I promise. And then, once you know everything there is to know, once you've experienced all of it, then maybe you won't want ta die so much anymore, either. Promise me you'll give me a chance tae give you that? I'll bring you up right. I won't hold back from you again."

"I don't want to live for a long time as a vampire, Harold." But I didn't sound as firm as I wanted to. I was so sleepy, and so hungry. I felt my eyelids flutter. The sun was crawling so high in its arc above us...

I began to drift off alongside him, limbs almost-but-not-quite touching, hands and fingertips almost-but-not-quite-brushing. Was I imagining it, or did Harold lean forward to kiss my forehead as unconsciousness finally overtook me? I slipped away into a dark and dreamless sleep for the rest of the day.

⚬

I awoke the next evening from violent, hungry dreams, groggy and disoriented. I didn't know where I was at first. Then I saw Harold sitting in a chair by the window, curtains still drawn, putting his shoes back on. He smiled when he looked over and saw that I was awake. "I didn't want ta disturb you. You seemed like you needed sleep."

I stretched out and yawned, like a big cat, fangs briefly bared, then rubbed my eyes. "What time is it?"

"Around eight-thirty," he replied. "You had a hard night last night, and I'm no surprised you slept in."

"It's three hours past sundown. Why didn't you wake me?"

"For what it's worth, I *also* had a hard night last night and slept in later than I would have liked."

"Fair enough," I admitted, trying not to look guilty. "Thank you again for...everything, really. I know we never would have met under ordinary circumstances, and I...I'm really glad I met you. I'm glad I get to know you."

Harold made a sound that might have been "pshaw," but wasn't fully formed, as though he didn't have enough air in his lungs to make the sound work—it happened to me sometimes, when I forgot to breathe, but I was mildly amused to discover that someone as old and experienced as Harold might also have the same trouble. He drew a deep breath, confirming my observation, and continued, "you don't really know me that well, ketlen." He finished tying his shoes and didn't say anything else.

"What if I wanted to get to know you better?"

"I'm not sure that you'd like the person you got tae know."

"Well, that's ridiculous." I got out of bed and started straightening the covers. I knew, intellectually, that housekeeping was going to strip the bedding in the morning anyway, but making the bed gave me something to do and helped me feel like I had a handle on things, even when I clearly didn't. "I don't have to know everything about your past to see that you're kind and talented, and generous and honorable and—" I ran out of air myself and had to stop, breathe, and start again, "—brave. What you did for me last night was very brave. And even if I lived for a thousand years, I'd never be able to pay you back."

"You dunna need tae pay me back for last night. Of all things. Of everything you think I've done for you, that one...keeping you safe from the sun, that one's on me. It's not your debt." He shook his head.

"Whose debt is it then, if not mine?"

Harold's half-smile was almost wistful, and he ruffled the sleep tangles out of his wavy brown hair and smoothed down his sideburns with his hands. He really did look ridiculously like an illustration of a Regency romance novel hero brought to life, with his hair like that, but I decided that I was never going to tell him so. "See, if you knew me...if you knew what I've done and all the ways I've failed, you'd know better than to ask that." His voice wasn't angry, just melancholy.

"What about the debt you owed Calliope? Isn't that the reason you took me in?"

Harold raised his eyebrows, startled. "How did you know about that? Did she tell you?"

I shook my head, surprised that he thought I didn't know. "No, I overheard her on the phone with you the night you came to get me at the penthouse. Vampire hearing, remember?" I tapped my ears and winked at him, and I thought, maybe, that he almost smiled again. But the look he gave me instead was flat and emotionless. "Anyway, she said you owed her this big favor after Macau. What happened in Macau?"

"You overhear too much."

"Okay, but you promised me last night you wouldn't hold back anymore, so I think I deserve to know. If I'm going to stay a member of the vampire Community—if, Harold, *if*—then I deserve to know if keeping a centuries-long tally of debts owed and to who is something I'm going to have to start keeping track of."

He looked like he wanted to say several things to me, but I appreciated that he answered my question instead of hanging on to my use of the word "if," which I already regretted. I didn't want to give him false hope. "No, it's not all vampires. That's just a thing with Calliope," he replied. "She's been very keen on paying and collecting on personal and private debts for as long as I've known her."

"Well, I guess that explains how she became a billionaire..." Certain things were starting to make sense. "Did you know each other before you became vampires?"

"Yes."

"Ah."

"It's not like that. Um. Whatever you're thinking, I promise you, our relationship is nothin' like that." He threw up his hands to defer further questions.

I took one brief, reluctant look in the mirror above the hotel room dresser and decided that I did not have the luxury Harold did of simply running my fingers through my own hair to neaten it. My brown hair was thick and long and prone to flyaways even after all the changes my vampiric transformation had brought, and tonight was full of tangles that only a strong hairbrush was going to be able to tackle, so I flipped my head over and secured my hair in a messy-chic topknot bun, and, after pulling out a few face-framing strands to make the style look more presentable, decided that that was probably the best I was going to get without styling tools.

Harold nodded approvingly. "That looks fainly pretty," he said as we exited the room and returned to where he'd parked his car early that morning. In spite of my gnawing hunger, I felt a spring in my step as we walked down the hall. Harold had told me I looked pretty.

The euphoria of his compliment didn't last long. My hands shook so badly back at the car, I couldn't buckle my seat belt, despite several attempts. "Did you drink last night before you left the house?" he asked.

I shook my head no. "I didn't think I'd be gone that long, and I wanted to wait for you." I didn't tell him that I'd grappled with a petulant refusal at the notion of drinking more animal blood. I just couldn't do it. I hated myself for it, but that was the truth.

"You have tae feed, Grace…"

"You going to take me hunting, or you going to take me home?"

"We're going home. Taking you hunting in your current state would be a disaster. You're a danger even ta my medical suppliers if you're this hungry."

I nodded in agreement. I wouldn't have been able to control myself in the presence of mortals at that moment, and I felt no shame admitting that to myself. Whether or not that was a sign of how far gone I was slipping was something I'd have to reflect on later. "You fed before you came and got me, though, right?"

Harold nodded. "I didn't want a repeat of what happened after the concert."

I remembered leaning against Harold in the kitchen, sucking the blood from his fingers, the delicate way he brushed the pad of his thumb up against my fangs, almost daring me to break the skin, the bloodlust rising up in both of us, I'd thought. Despite his claim that it didn't mean anything, it had felt real at the time. Ugh. The bloodlust was rising up inside of me again just thinking about it. I felt a low growl rise vibrating from my chest, and I balled up my fists, and bit down, hard, on my own hand. *Auto-vampirism.* I tasted a small amount of blood from the cut I made with my fangs, but it wasn't nearly enough to satisfy me.

Harold turned and looked sharply at me as he was changing lanes. "You all right?"

I shook my head, miserable. "I'm so hungry," I whispered. "I'm sorry."

"No, I'm sorry. I should have filled my flask. You can have whatever's in here, and I promise there's plenty of blood at the house. Good stuff, this time. We're almost there." The moment he spoke those words, all the brake lights ahead of us on the highway went red, and we hit traffic. We both sighed, long and exaggerated and in tandem.

It would have been funny under different circumstances.

I found a small amount of blood left in Harold's ancient dented hip flask, mostly congealed and clotting, disgusting, but still what my body needed, no matter how much I hated it. I tilted my head backward to drain every last drop and traced my tongue around the threaded seal of the screw-top lid, tasting the dried blood that had accumulated between the ridges.

"Give me that." Harold grabbed the flask out of my hands when he saw what I was doing. "I don't want other drivers tae look over and see you performing an oral sex act on my poor flask." I think he was only trying to sound shocked; I thought I caught an almost imperceptible upturn to the corner of his mouth—not quite a smile...or maybe it was. Vampire body language could be so much more subtle than mortals'. Not that I'd ever been any good at reading body language. But I didn't think he was mad at me for abusing his flask.

"Maybe the flask was enjoying itself as much as I was." I shocked myself by saying something so bold, but decided to take advantage of my inability to blush by meeting, and holding, Harold's gaze in the rear-view mirror. He grunted somewhat uncomfortably and shifted in the driver's seat. *What the hell has come over me?* I wondered. If I was being honest, I wasn't entirely sure if it was Harold I wanted, or just blood. I definitely wanted blood, but...

I lay back against the headrest and closed my eyes. I needed a pint of blood and a cold shower.

The awkward silence continued for a moment as the car inched along in traffic, and I wondered if I should say something to break the tension. Harold must have been having the same thoughts, but he beat me to it. I heard him clear his throat, and he began to speak.

"In 1985 or so, I decided I'd been in the United States long enough, so I sailed out of the country on a merchant marine vessel that had cabin space for passengers. Same way I came in, really, so it seemed like a good full circle. If I'm being honest with you, I don't think at the time I was planning on ever coming back. I hit up my old European stomping grounds, spent some time in France and Spain, and then I decided tae continue east because, well, why not? I'd never been there before, and I had a long life tae live, and why not fill it with seeing new places and experiencing new things? I was a bit of a monster in my feeding habits along the way. I feel like I should tell you. I didn't kill many people, before you ask—but I took what I wanted, when I wanted it, and I was rough, and sometimes I hurt people.

"Some people liked it, though…" Harold looked over at me with an expression that was almost hopeful. I glared at him, and he shook his head, clearing his throat again before he continued.

"Anyway, I learned a lot more about human anatomy in those years than I ever thought it was possible to know, and I figured out the places I could bite and drink from unsuspecting mortals practically in public, without them ever being the wiser…especially if they had drugs or alcohol in their system. I grew very fond of blood with certain substances flowing through it, and I got very bold and very…stupid. I moved through throngs of humanity in sweltering Southeast Asian cities, feeling practically invincible, unstoppable…

"And then I arrived in Macau. It's the Las Vegas of the East, you know. I don't know if you've ever been ta Vegas. But the city was full of lights and people from all over the world, every vice you could imagine available on the black market, and a shocking number of very respectable businessmen. I'll get tae that.

"I'd started accumulating money on my travels by getting very good at card games. It's something I picked up on ship back when I was mortal, even though the captain hated gambling, and we all risked whippings if we were found with playing cards in our possession. I suppose he would have rather we spent our spare time reading the Bible, but I've never been much of a book reader, never did like all those squiggly lines of ink across the page, s's that looked like f's and all sorts of problems. Never ask tae see my handwriting, Grace. It's horrible. But I could count cards. Some of it was natural ability, perhaps, a lot of it was practice, and more than a little bit of my skill came from being a vampire. You get very good at reading people, after a while. And the longer you do it, the better you get…"

Seeing a break in the bumper-to-bumper traffic, Harold navigated off the interstate and onto surface roads heading back to the house, then continued his story.

"Anyway. I was bloated on my own ego and string of successes, and I made the mistake of thinking I could get away with provincial tricks in a big city that takes gambling so seriously.

"And…I got caught. Quickly and embarrassingly, the casino security descended on me like a small army clad in businesslike black suits before I'd even finished two rounds at the tables. I'd heard stories of what happened to people who got caught trying to cheat the casinos in Macau, and the stories weren't pretty.

"I imagine you know what it feels like, now, tae be hauled off in handcuffs by more people than you can fight off without instigating a bloodbath. I probably could have torn my way out of custody and fled into the night, but the vampire Community in Asia is a lot more strict about keeping up appearances than they are in Europe and America, and I didn't want to get on their bad side, either."

I stared at Harold, unable to take my eyes off him, hunger almost forgotten—or at least relegated to a small, gnawing ache deep inside of me rather than an all-consuming need. I never would have guessed that the man was a born storyteller (or a card shark, for that matter—I was going to have to completely re-think my entire opinion of Harold after this), and it felt almost sacrilegious to interrupt his narrative with a breathless, "what happened next?" But it also seemed like he was waiting for me to interact with his tale, somehow.

Harold continued. "Right as I was about tae be hauled away into those infamous casino back rooms, Calliope Jones shows up out of nowhere. We hadn't seen each other since—well, that doesn't matter. And Grace—you are not the only one with good fortune in bad trouble. Calliope had no idea I'd been in Asia, much less Macau. She was only there for a business meeting with some Chinese investors. She's always been ahead of her time. Back then, she was only a multi-millionaire. But she saw me about tae get my ass dragged off the gambling floor and intervened, paying what I imagine was an enormous bribe tae keep me out of trouble. I was about as astonished ta see her there as she was tae find me, only to me, she was an angel sent from heaven, and tae her, well—I must have looked a sight. I'd been a wandering nomad for over half a decade at by then, and in a very real way, I'd lost myself. She could see that.

"She got me back tae her hotel suite and cleaned me up, got me off the bad blood I'd been indulging in for far too long, and then, once I'd detoxed, shipped me back tae her home here in the city in a big wooden box."

"She did what?" This time, my interruption of his story was entirely authentic.

"Shipped me back tae Chicago in a big wooden crate marked 'antiquities,' and probably paid another small fortune in bribes and customs along the way tae make sure that the box never got opened the entire distance." Harold let out a short laugh, and in spite of everything, he smiled, shaking his head.

I stifled a giggle and repeated, "Antiquities."

"I'm sure she got a kick out of that," Harold continued, and I couldn't help but agree. Of the two of them, I'd picked up on Calliope's sense of humor first. "It was the wildest coincidence in the world, couldn't happen again in a million years. Calliope saved my ass that night, and went on tae become an incredibly rich woman. And she never once called in on that debt, in all the years since...

"Not until you, Grace. And so when I tell you that I trust Calliope with my life, when I tell you that I am convinced she means tae do well by you, believe me. Calliope knows what it's like tae have a bad maker—just trust me on that—and I know beyond a shadow of a doubt that she is a good woman. A monster, yes, but a good woman."

We finally reached familiar territory, wending our way through suburban streets close to home, and I considered everything that Harold had just told me. He'd never been particularly talkative before, and suddenly I was seeing a side of him—and Calliope—I'd never previously imagined. It was very, for lack of a better word, *humanizing*. He might insist that I wouldn't like him if I got to know him better, but I thought that was something he said more for his sake than mine. Whatever had gone through his mind last night in the desperate hours before he rescued me from certain death, something seemed to have changed between us now.

"Do you want tae stop and pick up your car where you left it?" Harold asked. "It was still sitting there late last night when I drove past…You good tae drive?"

I nodded, only halfway certain that I was. The shakes had come back, and my peripheral vision was tinged with red that came and went when I blinked my eyes. But I'd been arrested only a short distance from Harold's house, so he navigated the detour toward the shopping center.

The parking lot was almost empty, except for a strange-looking dark gray car parked toward the rear of the lot, close to where I had parked my car the night before. At first, I was confused as Harold pulled his ancient BMW to a slow stop and rolled up next to the burnt-out shell of what had formerly been my midnight blue Honda. Then Harold swore in what I imagined was fifteen different languages, and tore out of the parking lot as I screamed, "What the fuck! What the fuck! Who did that to my car?"

A quarter mile away, I'd stopped screaming, but the red veil across my peripheral vision had grown stronger. An angry, hungry vampire was probably one of the most dangerous things in the world, I decided. I was shockingly confident that I would, without hesitation, kill any single mortal unfortunate enough to cross my path in that moment. There was no use trying to push back the rage and violation I felt, so I focused on clenching and unclenching my fists, feeling my body become taught, angular and sharp. All the softness that made *Grace* was gone, and in its place was something else.

"I've had that car since high school," I muttered. "My family got it for me on my sixteenth birthday."

I was staring out the passenger side window without looking at anything in particular when Harold's car rolled to a stop again at the corner of the street he lived on. Despite the lateness of the hour, the block was bustling with people, and my eyes darted from aimlessly wandering mortal to aimlessly wandering mortal like a cat watches cardinals flitting around a bird feeder. But it was the lights of the emergency services vehicles I saw next, flashing fire engine lights illuminating the whole sky, reflecting red off of drifts of snow. There were a lot of fire trucks, I realized. My eyes followed the line of emergency service vehicles down the block until I finally saw the same thing that Harold had been looking at the entire time: At the end of the quiet residential street full of colonial revival homes with stone facades and wide lawns, the last house on the block was an inferno. Flames licked the sky in an out-of-control blaze that had clearly been burning for a while.

I was still trying to process what I was seeing, what had happened, when Harold threw the car into reverse, then punched the manual transmission into drive, and sped off, wordlessly, into the night. His face was all angles and sharpness and rage. That made two of us.

⊸◆⊷

Chapter Twenty

Safe House

"Who the hell are you, Grace Cordero?" Harold pushed the BMW to the upper limits of the speedometer, racing along the expressway, careening around other vehicles, and barely avoided several accidents. His rage didn't frighten me. I'd run out of capacity to be frightened, or to feel anything at all.

He drove north, out of the city, toward the Wisconsin state line.

"WHO THE HELL ARE YOU?"

But I couldn't answer. My cracked lips and swollen tongue had gone mute. I shook my head, too hungry to even cry, too numb to even think. I stared at the road ahead and remained silent.

Finally, he let off the gas, slowed down to a far less lunatic speed, and said he had someplace safe, about two hours outside the city.

"How safe?" My voice was quiet and hoarse when I formed the words, but at least I was able to force them out. My mind was panicking again, remembering our race from the sun, uncertain where we were going to find shelter or blood now that his house and all our stuff had gone up in flames.

"Safe enough when you're dead, and you know you might have tae bug out of town." He gave me a sharp sideways glance, as if I ought to have known better. "Safe enough tae have kept me alive before, when I needed it. We can make it well before sunrise, and then...I don't know. We'll figure out what tae do next." His exhale was less of a sigh and more of a complete emptying of his lungs. I couldn't be sure, but I thought he spent the next several minutes not breathing at all, driving in complete silence.

We both jumped when my phone rang. Becca's number illuminated in the caller ID. I answered the call before Harold could stop me. "Grace? Grace? Oh God, can you hear me? Gra—" Becca's voice on the other end of the line was hysterical.

"Becca—" I couldn't speak above a whisper as I tried to respond to her panic, but Harold reached over before I could say anything else, grabbed the iPhone out of my hand, and hurled it out the window, where it disappeared into the darkness somewhere along the highway.

"You may have a death wish, but I don't," he snapped. "Someone wants one or both of us dead or completely out of the picture, and I'd rather accommodate the latter than the former, if you don't mind."

I didn't know how to react—I think I was so shocked I forgot to breathe as well and so, had nothing to say. The loss of my phone and all my other worldly possessions felt like a small distraction compared to my hunger—a blossoming pain in my belly that doubled me over with cramps so much worse than anything I'd experienced when I was alive. The hunger made me feel light-headed and distracted.

"Who the hell are you, Grace Cordero?" he asked again before we hit another brief traffic jam, red lights on the expressway as far as the eye could see, and he screamed again in frustration and rage. I was too out of it to even flinch at his outburst. I threw up my hands. I didn't know what kind of answer he was expecting.

"None of this is normal. Nothing about this makes sense. We don't just *turn* fledglings and abandon them. And now—not just your car, but *my **house***—who did you piss off? Why are you even here? What the hell is happening?"

"I'm no one special...I'm from Ohio," I whispered.

"Like hell you are." He scoffed. "How did you end up in Community crosshairs? Why are you being targeted—?"

"I don't know!" I shouted in return, my own anger rising up for an encore and giving me back my voice. "I don't know what's going on any more than you do. I'm just a girl who wanted to go to a fancy party with her best friend!"

"You keep saying that, an' I'm starting tae not believe you."

"Who would want you dead, Harold? Maybe this isn't about me at all."

"Here's the thing about my life. When you don't have many friends, you can't have many enemies. I've worked hard tae keep things that way."

"You're friends with Avie. And Calliope."

"Neither of whom want me dead, I can promise you that. Avie doesn't have a malicious bone in her body. She can't get her act together, but she means well to everyone she's ever met. Even her victims. As for Cal, she's no etterkap— She's saved my life multiple times over the centuries. *Multiple* times, Grace. She taught—anyway, not important. She's had numerous opportunities to see me dead, and at every one o' those opportunities, she's kept me alive. This is na her. It's not her style, and it's not...it's not in her character. She's na sae ill. It's someone else."

"There is someone who wants both Avie and Calliope dead though, isn't there?"

A chilled kind of silence settled over the car that had nothing to do with the temperatures outside. "She has no idea where I live..." Harold whispered. "I haven't seen Marie DuChamps since 1975."

"You've been sheltering Avie...if Marie could sabotage her plane, maybe she could, I don't know, track her car..."

"Sonofabitch."

"Avie said Marie set her house on fire..."

"More than once. It's...kind of her thing. Got her locked her away in some kind of a posh asylum for it, back when she was mortal. Cal didn't find out about that until later, though."

A psychopath vampire arsonist. Saints in heaven. Every one of those words made the one before it worse.

"That still doesn't explain what happened last night." I thrust my hands in the pocket of my parka, hoping to find something that might help my current plight, but even my pepper spray was gone, now. The waves of my anger swelled again like a rising tide, each crest larger than the one preceding it. "Why go through all the trouble of having me arrested? I was set up—whether or not the goal was to get me killed, but I think it was. And I think you were supposed to be in your house tonight, Harold. And I don't know who else, other than Calliope, who could have canceled the card and reported it stolen. *And,* the police knew where I was before the store called them..."

"So we're back tae figuring out who wants you dead."

"Gavin and Calliope are connected, Harold. Whatever's going on between them, I don't think either of us knows the big picture. If she's such a good friend, why didn't you know about her fledgling?"

"Calliope and I can go a long time without seeing each other. Especially since she started with the billionaire bullshit. She used tae just be into nightclubs and speakeasies and vice. You know, normal monster stuff. And we fought, pretty badly, when James went away. I left her house, and I never planned tae go back. Until the night you—I swear tae you I've never met him before. He's *got* tae be new—"

"He was at the Field Museum, the night of her fundraiser. The one with the Roman artifact exhibit? I know you were both there; I saw you in photos."

Harold flinched and stammered. "I never saw him. I wasn't looking for other vampires. The only reason I went tae that one event of Calliope's was tae get into the museum after dark, look at the swords, and snack on drunk society assholes."

"You *fed* on people at her party?" I don't know why I was shocked at this point; nothing Harold confessed should have shocked me.

"Why the hell do you think Calliope throws her parties? It's *Community service*, Grace. And it's probably the only reason the Community allows Cal to get away with so much. Yes, I fed at her party at the museum, and I enjoyed myself, too. But she never introduced me tae any new fledgling. Are you sure he was even one of us then?"

"You *said* you..." *How often did Harold feed on people?*

"I. Like. Being. A vampire. I don't always like that I like it, but I do. Sue me. I'm not some paragon of undead virtue. I keep telling you that." He shook his head. "You haven't figured out that's part of the reason you and your friend were invited up that night? You were there tae get fed on if somebody wanted you. You weren't supposed tae die, and you definitely weren't supposed tae be turned. You were just..."

The assault of his words left me reeling like a blow to my skull that struck me speechless again. I hadn't realized it, and I felt like an idiot for being blind to what was so obvious in retrospect. I leaned forward in the passenger seat, wordlessly rocking my body, trying to find comfort in the soothing rhythm. For a brief moment, I found myself imagining what would have happened if Harold *had* been at the party that night, and if he'd been the one to—I tried to push the mental image away, but I couldn't stop myself from imagining his teeth at my neck, instead of my asshole maker's, and I wondered with a sick, churning feeling, if I would have enjoyed it.

"Maybe I would have!" There was a defiant tone in his voice when he responded to the unspoken question hanging in the air between us. "...but you would still be alive, I promise you, if I had."

Inhale. "I know." Exhale.

I told Harold what I'd found out online about Gavin. I needed to redirect the conversation before I exploded. "He's been a vampire since 2002, at least. I don't know what constitutes 'new' in your book, but over ten years as a vampire seems like a long enough time to not be making stupid mistakes and 'accidentally' turning people."

"So you *were* targeted," he accused. "If it wasn't an accident."

"Sure, okay, maybe, if that's what you mean, but I have no idea why!"

He gave me a long, appraising look—as long as he dared to take his eyes off the road—and squinted at me. "Maybe you don't," he admitted. His tone implied that he might have an idea, but he kept it to himself.

We stopped at the smallest gas station Harold could find, and he pulled a shapeless tan overcoat out of the trunk of the BMW, along with a broken-in and boring trucker hat, and put on the coat and hat before he went inside the gas station to pay for filling up his tank in cash. Nothing traceable. He returned with his arms full of bags of salt and kitty litter.

After a few more minutes of driving in silence, he spoke again, his turn to change the subject. "No one knows about this house, Grace. I'm sure we all have our places tae disappear tae in an emergency, but this one is mine. You can never tell anyone about it."

"Who would I tell?" I mused, but Harold didn't answer. I had no cell phone, no computer, no cash, and there was going to be a warrant out for my arrest under my legal identity, and I had no other name to fall back on. I wasn't going to be talking to *anyone* for a long time, I despaired.

I must have dozed off, because I remembered nothing else until I felt the car pull off the smooth pavement of the interstate, onto less well-kept roads, and finally, a gravel drive that crunched and popped under the car's wheels like breaking bones—it had been cleared of snow fairly recently, but Harold still got out of the car to spread down salt and clay litter before proceeding. The long driveway led to a drab, ordinary-looking 1970s ranch-style house under some large overhanging trees that cast sinister shadows on the icy lawn. The semi-rural home was three shades of brown on the outside, and I guessed I would find many more shades of brown inside as well.

Harold stopped the car long enough to locate a key from a small leather case in his pants pocket, exit the idling car, and unlock the garage door manually. He stepped into the shadowy recesses of the garage, looking around, sniffing the air, just like I had done when we visited my apartment. After a moment, he returned to the car and drove it into the garage, closing the door after him and manually locking it again. I remained in the car until Harold opened the passenger side door with the same ceremonial bow he'd used the first time he invited me into his home, and led me into a time capsule.

Inside the brown house were even more shades of dirt, coffee, and manure than I could have imagined, punctuated by the occasional accent of harvest gold or avocado green. The whole interior appeared straight out of a 1970s JC Penny's catalog, down to the wagon-wheel patterned orange and brown upholstery on the living room sofa and matching loveseat.

However, on closer inspection, I noticed a number of small, unobtrusive, blinking lights, indicating at least some modern upgrades to the security system, and the interior of the home was well-maintained and uncluttered. It didn't look lived in, but it didn't look like a repository for decades of stuff, either.

In the living room, near the floor-to-ceiling blackout curtains that obscured sliding glass doors that probably led to a sun room, there was an ominous dark stain on the carpet. I don't know if mortal eyes would have picked up on it, but it was distinctive enough that I bet mortal equipment could identify what it was…or had been.

"Don't touch that!" Harold barked when I approached the stain. It was roughly human-sized, and I didn't want to get any closer than I had to.

After Harold finished his inspection of the main living area, satisfied that the doors and windows were all undisturbed and the blackout curtains in good condition, he led me downstairs to the finished basement, all wood paneled walls and orange carpet, where things started to get really weird. At the end of the basement, under a rectangular patch of carpet, a small steel rectangle appeared, recessed into the concrete floor, with a heavy iron ring welded to it. Harold lifted the metal plate, revealing a dark set of stairs that led to an even deeper sub-basement, and when he flicked on a series of lights, I realized we were inside an honest-to-god fallout shelter, complete with a small kitchenette, a bathroom, a bedroom with a single full-sized bed, and a couch in the common area that I assumed was a pull-out bed.

Harold busied himself in the kitchen area with a vacuum-sealed glass canister that made a satisfying "pop" when opened. I wrinkled my nose when I realized what the dark red powdery substance inside the canister was. "You can't be serious," I told him.

He added a small quantity of the powder to some bottled water in a cocktail shaker and thoroughly mixed it up. "Freeze-dried blood," he responded with an *unpleasant* seriousness. "It's about as foul-tasting as you can get before you hit rat blood, but it will keep you going in a dire emergency. I think this qualifies as such, don't you?" He poured the reconstituted blood into two harvest gold plastic tumblers that were definitely even older than his car, and held one out to me. The frothy film that rose to the top as the liquid settled, and the gritty, not-quite-dissolved texture, was familiar, as was the smell—too much iron, not enough salt. He'd prepared it for me once already, on the night I'd snuck out and tried to get to Becca, before Calliope stopped me.

And, yes, it still tasted foul. Even so, it calmed the aching, gnawing need of my hunger, sweeping over me in a brief but intense blood high that stopped the racing panic of my thoughts and tingled through my veins, all the way down to my fingertips. It didn't completely satisfy the hunger, but it helped. "Forbidden Nesquick..." I whispered, more for my own benefit than my companion's, but he still looked at me, confused. Becca would have gotten the joke. Becca would have—

"I...I don't know what that is," he confessed.

"Oh my God, Harold," I rolled my eyes and stuck my tongue out, peevishly. "You are so fucking old."

He ignored me, and pulled the bed in the small bedroom away from the wall, revealing the outline of a panel laid into the wallpaper, well-disguised by making clever use of the geometric pattern of the wall print. There was a safe set into the wall behind the panel, because of course there was.

Somehow, I wasn't surprised when Harold opened the combination lock, and multiple passports, papers, and small piles of cash slipped out and fell onto the floor. He reached into the safe to retrieve a handgun and a box of bullets, along with a new license plate and a fistful of documents. I bent down to help pick up the items that fell to the floor and briefly noticed one of the old IDs featured the photograph of a woman with what looked like strawberry-blonde hair, judging from the black and white photo. Harold grabbed it out of my hand and shoved it back into the safe with a roughness that seemed out of character for him, even given everything that had gone wrong that had led us to this place, so I said nothing about the woman in the photograph, but filed the information away in the back of my head.

He took the gun, the bullets, and a large amount of cash, along with the license plate and a small stack of other documents over to the table, and beckoned me to sit down.

"We have tae assume that both of our previous legal identities will be considered dead now." He started going through the passports and papers and piles of cash he'd removed from the safe, spreading items out on the table. "I think this one will do for you. We can get you set up with a new picture ID quickly with this."

I picked up a birth certificate and social security card held together by a paperclip so old and rusted, it discolored the pieces of paper it was holding together. Both documents looked authentic; the name on the birth certificate was "Angela Mercer," born at home in Indiana in November 1984. The name on the Social Security card matched. "Who is Angela Mercer?"

Harold shrugged. "She never existed. It used tae be fairly easy tae establish a legal identity by filing a notarized certificate of home birth, no hospital required. Then you waited a few years for the new identity to catch up with you and swapped. We picked these names out decades ago; never had a chance tae use them til now, so you might as well take Angela." Harold seemed to recognize his slip-up at the word "we," at the same time I did, and held up his hands, palms out to me.

"Don't," he implored.

Don't ask questions about the person Angela's birth certificate was meant for. Got it. Don't ask questions about the woman in the photograph—the one with the straw-berry-blonde hair. Got it.

The closer I got to Harold, the more secrets I was beginning to learn he had.

⚬

Chapter Twenty-One

TRYING TO FIX THE BROKEN THINGS

He went out the next night for real blood. "I know, I promised I'd take you hunting, but you can't come along this time. I'm sorry."

"Why not?" I demanded.

He pinched the bridge of his nose. "Because I might be gone a long while for this one, and I don't want you tae get the wrong idea."

"What would the right idea even be? You want to tell me you're not going to use the crate in the trunk?" I asked, sitting down on the sleeper sofa and staring ahead at the 1970's paneled wood walls that decorated even the utilitarian fallout shelter in the same brown-and-mustard rainbow scheme as the main house.

I don't know why I refused to look at him. We both needed blood, but I doubted he had contacts with black market medical suppliers this far out of Chicago. I remembered the funnel and the box cutters, and I was hungry enough to not care. "I suppose you know best. You've been doing this sort of thing far longer than I have or ever will." My voice sounded more bitter than I intended it to be.

Even staring at the wall, I still felt him flinch at those words. *Good.* Now that the house in the city was almost certainly destroyed beyond salvaging, there were no more swords to depend on for a pain-free sendoff into oblivion, and I reflected bitterly on my dwindling options. I didn't want to wait for the sun to rise anymore; the mere idea that I'd ever considered that an option was terrifying now, in retrospect. But there were other ways a vampire could die, after all. And now I knew that both Harold and Calliope kept guns.

"This isn't one of the fun parts of our existence, Grace. I'm sorry."

"Yeah, well, when we get to any of the fun parts of being a vampire, you let me know." I picked at a small imperfection woven into the rough fibers of the sofa's upholstery and tried not to think about the tools of the vampire's trade: the zip ties, black plastic contractor's bags, a bottle of bleach…When I felt my eyes burn and well up with tears again, I refused to allow them to fall down my face. *No more crying,* I decided.

"This doesn't have tae ruin your life. It's just a setback. We'll be all right."

"Harold, *everything* is ruined. That's kind of what happens when you die. Everything's ruined, and it all sucks."

"The sucking part isn't actually so bad, you know."

I twisted my entire torso to stare at him. "…did you—was that a pun? Did you just crack a fucking vampire pun at me?" *Unbelievable.*

"I thought we were at pun level friendship now." He shrugged, but I could swear he smirked at me.

"I could stake you."

"All right, so, not friends, or…not 'making jokes about being a vampire' friends yet?"

I rolled my eyes far enough back that the world disappeared into black splotches. "Just go already, will you?"

"Suck you later, gloomy." He chuckled, ruffling my hair before walking up the concrete steps that led out of the fallout shelter without saying another word, or even looking over his shoulder as I fucking growled in the direction of his departure.

I tried not to get carried up in the grim finality of our situation, Harold's attempt to lighten the mood notwithstanding. If we remained on the run, then God only knew when I'd ever have the chance to take out my maker. And Becca—I couldn't even think about that. I had no way of reaching her. What was I going to do—run off into the night in an entirely unfamiliar rural area? Knock on a strange family's door and ask to use their phone? Hitchhike back to Chicago? Do all of that, somehow, without killing anybody?

I got up from the sofa and wandered over to the cabinets in the kitchen area where Harold had gotten the freeze-dried blood and plastic cups.

Killing people was what Harold did.

There were too many cups in the cabinet above the sink, and they were all out of order. I clambered on top of the kitchen counter to better reach the overhead space, and started moving the cups around. There had to be a better way to stack everything. My hands continued moving even as my thoughts spun uselessly, like wheels churning in mud.

And if something really bad had already happened to her last night when she was trying to call me? She might already be dead. What if Gavin had already killed her, too?

I leapt down from the counter looked around the rest of the fallout shelter and felt the walls closing in around me; I was swallowed up by the earth. Might as well be in a coffin. I shuddered.

All my usual coping mechanisms felt hollow and inadequate.

On the night Dylan dumped me, I rearranged my entire bedroom. Becca took the L over to my apartment and helped me clean out my closet and makeup collection. Well, I did the clean-out and organizing. Becca made cocktails out of some boxed white Zinfandel and powdered calorie-free drink packets she found in my pantry, along with any other liquor she could locate in the kitchen.

"This. Is disgusting. You have to try it." She thrust an acrylic goblet in my hands, and I made a skeptical face at the aggressively pink concoction that smelled vaguely of artificial strawberries and lighter fluid.

"Did you use the entire bottle of rum above the fridge?" There was a chair propped up against the refrigerator and an empty glass bottle on the sink behind Becca, so the answer was rather obvious.

"I made a whole pitcher full of this stuff, so drink up. It tastes better the more you chug."

"That rum was Dylan's..." I said, gulping down the noxious offering with a grimace that demanded another sip. The drink was sweet and strong and tasted better once the goblet was half-empty. Becca topped me up as I moved my summer wardrobe items from the right side of my closet to the left, and I tried not to cry when I found one of his shirts hanging next to mine. "He loved this shirt..."

Becca grabbed it out of my hands and made an obscene wiping gesture involving the shirt and her rear end, grinning like a madwoman. "Fuck him. He doesn't get his shirt back. I wiped my ass with it. I own it now."

She made a big show of shoving a trash bag full of anything of his she could find, including a stupid ugly Sears Tower-shaped bong he insisted on keeping over at my place. I swear she threw it into the trash hard enough to shatter it on purpose, because her "Oops" sounded exactly the opposite of sincere.

By the time I needed her to hold the stepladder for me so that I could reach the upper shelves of my closet, we were both so tipsy that we thought better of the activity, and sat down on the floor, eating spoonfuls of Nutella right out of the jar and sorting through my collection of Instagram-trending eyeshadow palettes. Becca got carried away trying out the brightest colors on me until I looked like a parrot, and we dissolved into drunken giggles and passed out on the carpet next to my bed.

The memory made me smile, in spite of myself. My closet may have been immaculate, but Becca and I had gotten trashed. Isn't that what best friends were for?

I allowed myself a moment to mourn a future without bad cocktails consumed with a good friend, a glass of wine on a sun-dappled rooftop on long summer evenings, or a few too many vodka sodas on a night on the town. I did remember Harold saying something about being able to feel the effects of "certain substances" in the blood, and started to wonder what that felt like, if it was comparable to—

But I stopped myself. I did not want to imagine a future as a vampire. The problem was, once I started thinking about blood, it was hard to stop. I'd refused to drink any more of the freeze-dried stuff upon waking that evening; I'd thought freeze-dried coffee was bad enough when I was a mortal, but freeze-dried blood was levels of gross beyond that. Still, that meant that the hunger was creeping back in a painful way again, and I needed to do something to distract myself. The fallout shelter was relatively tidy, all things considered, except for Harold's paperwork, which didn't feel right to touch.

With a sigh, I pulled myself together and made my way toward the upper levels. Maybe one of the bedrooms had a sock drawer I could organize.

I'd seen a little of the ranch house the evening before, and as I wandered around the rooms, my feeling that the house had never been lived in grew. Thick layers of dust coated almost every surface throughout, but nothing seemed out of place. Nothing seemed like it had been touched for years; the house was sterile, devoid of personality. There were no pictures on the walls, no personal touches strewn about. It really did look more like a showroom than a place anyone had ever called home. It had been maintained enough that the pipes didn't freeze and the roof didn't leak, and electronic monitoring kept the property secure, but the safe house wasn't any place Harold had ever stayed for long. Maybe that was the entire point.

I decided that if Harold had never really used the house to live in, then it wasn't like I was combing through his personal possessions. And he'd trusted me to organize the common areas in his house back in the city, before—

There was no way the fire was an accident, and I didn't share Harold's conviction that Calliope wasn't involved. I wasn't even entirely sure Avie was innocent—the timing of her unannounced visit was too suspicious.

She and Calliope were the only two vampires who had been to Harold's Winetka house so far as I knew. Maybe neither of them had set the fire. But knowingly or not, they'd led the person who had done it right to Harold's door.

I tried to remember everything I knew so far. *Think, Grace, think.*

I knew of at least three vampires Calliope had turned: Marie DuChamps, James Medlock, and Gavin Richardson. If I included Avie and Calliope herself in my list of suspects, then there were five known vampires who could have turned me...but I *remembered* Gavin's teeth at my throat.

Harold said that James was tall and lanky and dark-haired. Avie was tall and lanky and dark-haired, too, if I wanted to go down that road. But neither of them was on good enough terms with Calliope to have been at her party, according to Harold.

That still left Gavin. And that had to mean that Calliope knew he had turned me. Instantly, the first moment she'd touched me.

So why the elaborate lie?

She wanted me hidden, somewhere out of the way. She'd sent me off to live with Harold. She'd offered to help me relocate—promised me a new name, and a new home. She didn't want the Community to know about me until it was on her terms. She needed time to control the narrative...I was still missing pieces to the puzzle.

Calliope wanted me out of the city, one way or another, and she'd warned us not to make an enemy of her. Regardless of Harold's opinion of the billionaire vampire ice queen, it was obvious to me that Calliope wasn't someone who could be trusted. I didn't understand her motivations yet, but Calliope Jones was used to getting her way.

I'd already been in her crosshairs the moment I entered her home. And Becca?

No one's going to do anything to Becca. I promise. I'm just...keeping an eye out for her. She was at my party, too.

I remembered the photo of Becca in the club, Gavin and Calliope chatting in the background.

Think, Grace. Think.

Why would Calliope Jones be interested in us?

In the first two bedrooms, I found nothing particularly interesting. A few moth-eaten wool socks forgotten in a drawer, a crumbling yellow newspaper from February 1985, an ancient frosted blue eyeshadow that turned to dust in my hands. None of it brought me any closer to the truth of Harold's past, or his missing fledgling. There were so many things I wanted to ask her, and I wondered where in the world she'd wandered off to, in search of the happiness Harold insisted she deserved. I wished I understood what had happened to them.

I finally hit the motherload in the third and final bedroom: Not a sock drawer, but an entire closet filled with men's and women's clothes, all so long out of style they might as well be trendy again. A judicious amount of mothballs and sachets had kept the insects away over the years, and several items of clothing were still wrapped in decades-old dry cleaning plastic.

I wondered if the dresses I found in the closet had belonged to the woman with strawberry-blonde hair and decided that they probably had. *Harold's fledgling*, I realized, as my hands brushed against the fabric. There was a subtle psychic certainty imparted alongside the tactile sensation that confirmed my hunch. They'd gone their separate ways a long time ago, maybe even before I was born.

Fledgling/maker relationships were still a bit confusing to me. Avie said she'd *thought* she was in love with Marie DuChamps before she was turned. I certainly harbored no romantic feelings toward Gavin Richardson. But Harold didn't seem like the kind of man to mislead someone before he turned them.

I stopped in my tracks, and tried to imagine Harold doing to deed—giving someone his blood, injecting a fatal dose of morphine to end their mortal life. I'd done morphine exactly once, before I died, and there was *nothing* romantic about that hangover. Becca and I stopped hanging out with that group of students, after the morphine.

Well, wherever the woman who had planned on using Angela Mercer's identity was, out there in the world, she had pretty good taste in clothing. I pulled a Dianne Von Furstenburg wrap dress out of the closet and held it up in front of the mirror over the dresser, then decided to turn on the lights to get an even better look at the pattern. The large-scale blue print dress was probably from the late '70's or early '80's, but that vintage retro look was back in style, and I could easily see a stylish woman pulling off the look today. With the right accessories...

I quickly stripped off my old skirt and blouse combo and slipped on the blue wrap dress. My own clothes were rumpled and unkempt from having been slept in for two days, plus my stint in the slammer. Wearing the same clothes for three nights in a row was giving me anxiety, and the anxiety exacerbated my hunger. Where was Harold, anyway? He'd been gone for hours.

I rolled up the sleeves of the dress to my elbows and tightened the sash. The other woman had been slightly larger than me—but then again, so were most people. The muted jewel tones in the dress went well with my coloring, I decided, and I sent a mental thank you out into the night, wherever the woman with strawberry-blonde hair was now. She wouldn't mind if another woman wore her dress after leaving it in a closet for thirty years, I decided.

I turned off the light in the bedroom, gathered my belongings, and went to explore a different part of the house. As I crossed the front room, I gave a wide berth to the dark-colored blotch on the carpet. I could guess at the cause of the discoloration—I'd watched enough crime dramas with Becca—and I didn't want to think about the circumstances behind the decomp stain any more than I had to.

That was just a thing vampires had to occasionally deal with, I guessed. The hunger clawing at my insides justified a horrible array of sins.

The window above the kitchen sink provided a view of the front yard, and I pulled the blackout curtains aside and peered out into the night, beyond the safety of the little brown ranch house. I could see no other structures, and the nearest road was almost obscured by hedges. No one was out driving this far off the beaten path, I realized. Probably another reason Harold had chosen this location. He seemed to like wide lawns and ample distance between himself and any neighbors.

The darkness outside the window was cold and still, large flakes of falling snow giving everything a muffled softness. I wasn't technically running off, I thought, if I only stepped out for some fresh air. I wasn't even leaving the property. I stepped out of the house in just my stockinged feet, not even noticing my lack of shoes as I shut the door behind me. I'd skidded several paces beyond mortal comforts, without realizing it at all.

The fresh snowfall in the yard dampened sounds, but if I closed my eyes and listened, beyond the night, I could hear the gentle "whoosh" of individual snowflakes as they fell around me, collecting on my hair and on my dress. I lacked the body heat to melt the snow, and my exhale left no trail of steam frozen in the air.

An owl swooped overhead, startling a winter white rabbit sheltering in a snow-covered hedge near the driveway, and the rabbit frantically darted across the snowbanks, propelled by primordial terror of being caught in the open. Without even thinking about it, I lunged for the creature, just like my childhood Labrador retriever used to do when rabbits came bounding into our yard, my own prey drive on high alert. I was mindless, skidding and reaching across the snow to drag the animal, and its precious few ounces of blood, out from its new hiding space deep inside an opposite hedge, the moment Harold's car pulled up to the drive.

"You wouldn't have enjoyed it if I'd hit you with the car," he warned me through the rolled-down window. I picked myself up from the snowbank and brushed myself off, the rabbit in the hedges momentarily forgotten as I leaned into the car through the driver's side window. Inches from Harold's face, I could smell the blood on him, see a faint warmth in his cheeks that hadn't been present when he'd left the safe house hours ago.

"You've already fed…" My voice had an unfamiliar husky quality to it as my fangs elongated, and I stood on shoeless tiptoes to get closer to him.

"I've got what you want. Just let me get out of the car." He sounded strained in a way that made me feel unsteady on my feet. I wanted blood. But I also wanted him. I knew it in that moment, completely. I licked my lips and clung to his body as he stepped out of the car, steadying me with one arm. He carried a large paper bag in the other. I tried to grab for the bag, and he held me tighter against him, holding the bag further away from me, at arms reach. "Git in de house," he said, low and direct, and he swatted at my rear end playfully as he pushed me toward the front door.

Immediately inside the entrance, he bent down and kissed me, setting the brown paper bag gently on the ground before putting a hand on each of my shoulders and pressing me up against the wall. I groaned at the release of pent-up desire and the taste of blood on his tongue, and I returned his kiss, my own tongue prodding his, exploring his fangs and letting the razor-sharp points nick the inside of my lower lip, feeling a small rush of pleasure mixed with pain. He pressed his tongue against my own fangs and allowed my teeth to cut into the soft flesh, flooding my mouth with the taste of our blood intermingling.

And oh, fuck, if this was what vampire kissing was like, I wanted more, I needed to taste more, to drink more, to know more…

We were both moaning then, our mutual excitement pressing me onward, my hands groping and tugging the belt around his waist, fumbling to undo the metal catches. I could feel how hard he was for me underneath his clothes, and my thighs were practically dripping from the wetness between my legs. His mouth moved from my lips to my jawline, tongue tracing a line toward the veins in my neck…and I froze. The world spiraled out in a cruel, disorienting vortex.

I was someplace else. Marble and chrome, white leather furniture, colorless winter blooms in a floral display, glittering bare branches styled to look like snow. A different set of hands pressing me against the wall, a different set of teeth at my throat…

"Stop. Just stop, please. I need a second," I gasped, desperate to hold on to the intensity of the moment with Harold even as he spiraled away from me, my brain on autopilot, replaying the moment Gavin first sank his teeth into me in Calliope's penthouse. My knees buckled, and the world was spinning, spinning, just as everything had been spinning when Calliope found me wandering around the next night, placed her cold fingers in my mouth to feel the place where my fangs were coming in. I sobbed and covered the evidence of my transformed monstrosity with my hands as Harold caught me and carried me into the kitchen, and sat me down in a chair.

He was calling my name, over and over, but even though I could hear him, I was miles away and frozen, paralyzed with fear, no different from the small white rabbit in the yard had been when I—

...count not my transgressions, O Lord, but rather, my tears of repentance. Remember not my iniquities...

My iniquities...my iniquities...

The words of the familiar prayer of contrition came unbidden to my voiceless tongue, and whether my lips burned from hunger or damnation, I could not tell.

I was only only vaguely aware when Harold stepped out of the kitchen for a moment before returning again, pulling a half-full plastic gallon jug out of the brown paper bag he'd brought inside with him. The blood in the container was almost warm, and very fresh, and I knew without knowing how that the blood had been inside someone's body until only a very short time prior. Maybe that would have mattered to moral, mortal Grace, but vampire Grace was blessedly detached. The smell of the fresh blood brought me back to the moment, and Harold held out a cup for me to drink, his eyes the color of sea glass, and full of quiet rage.

He refilled my cup when I was done drinking the first time, held it out again without touching me, keeping me at arms reach. His eyes flashed with something that might have been anger or guilt or worse, pity, and I swore, and apologized, for ruining the moment. For being a burden. For being stupid enough to get turned into a vampire in the first place. I didn't even know if I was apologizing to him, myself, or to God. All the arousal I'd felt only moments before reduced to a dull, throbbing ache.

"I hate him for doing this tae you."

"Don't make me cry again."

"It shouldn't be like this," he muttered.

I had no words. The world had barely stopped spinning.

He leaned back against the countertops, crossing his arms over his chest, and looked up at the ceiling, that distant sound he sometimes got in his voice when he spoke again. "After the storm, after I was swept overboard and cassen awa, I spent two days and two nights in the open water, clinging tae a piece of wood too small tae even be a life raft. I don't know how I survived. When I was rescued by Spanish fishermen off the coast, I was sunburnt about as badly as possible for a mortal tae suffer sunburn, and delirious from dehydration and thirst. Nothing like this...other, thirst, but I was close tae death.

"And for months, maybe even years afterward, the breeze could blow in a certain way, I'd touch a piece of wood with the same rough texture as the wood I'd clung tae, and it would all come flooding back over me—the night of the storm, the creaking of the ship's mast breaking, the waves crashing over the deck tae sweep me away, and I'd forget where I was, quaking with a fear caused by no immediate threat tae me.

"I know it's not the same as what you went through. But I do know that memories can play cruel tricks on us, sometimes for a long time...but they're supposed tae go away. Eventually. It won't always be so fresh, so...intrusive. But the fault tonight is mine. I got caught up. I fed too much before returning tae you, and the bloodlust? It overtakes all of us, from time tae time. But you shouldn't have tae suffer for it. I'm sorry."

Something about the way he confessed to feeding too much before coming back, the warmth to his coloring when he was still in the car, the manner in which the blood he'd brought back to the house for me was decanted into an ordinary repurposed plastic gallon jug, the grocery-store label peeling off the side, confirmed what I already suspected about where he'd been, and the source of my most recent sustenance, but I had to ask, in a quiet voice, "Where...did you get this blood tonight?"

He shook his head and our eyes held contact for a long, knowing beat. Of course I knew. I'd seen what he kept in the trunk of his car.

"Don't ask," he finally said aloud, and I nodded, amazed at how unbothered I was by the knowledge that he had killed someone tonight—a stranger—for me.

He gathered up the supplies, and rinsed out the bloodied cup I had drunk from.

"The kissing was nice, while it lasted…" I reached out my hand for his. I don't know why I ached, just then, to take his hand in mine, to hold it, to assure him that everything was going to be okay. Things were absolutely not okay. But I wanted to be able to tell him that they were. I wanted—

He jerked his hand away from mine inches before I reached him, and I flinched at the sudden movement. "I can't do that again, Grace. I'm sorry. I can't."

"Of course."

"It's not fair."

Of course. You're right. None of this is fair. I couldn't say the words. I stood, nodding at him. "Should have gotten rid of me when you had the chance." I forced an awkward, self-deprecating smile.

"No, that's—no. That's another thing I canna bring myself tae do."

"What?"

"I canna bring myself tae regret meeting you, either. I'm sorry I canna give you more."

"You've given up too much for me already." All his tools, his projects. Years' worth of work. It was unfathomable. All that money… "I'm nobody. I'm not worth it."

"Who is?" he asked with a shrug. "There's so much blood on my own hands." He glanced at me out of the corner of his eye, then lowered his face, staring down at his callused hands, flexing his fingers as he clenched and unclenched his fists. He didn't look up at me again as he spoke. "I wasn't anyone special. A boy who ran away from home. I got myself mixed up in a bad situation, and I can't scrub away the stains from every crevice under my fingernails, but I can cover up the old blood with engine grease, the evidence of honest work. I can tell myself it's not just about keeping busy, not being bored. If I can make broken metal pieces hum and stir and vibrate with life and power again, then maybe my own existence is worth salvaging, too. I am trying tae fix the broken things. I am trying tae fix—"

"But you can't fix…other people." *I'm sorry. I wish that I were fixable, Harold, but I'm not. You're right to push me away.*

"Sometimes people convince themselves that something whole is entirely unsalvageable when it's really only a small part out of alignment…why can't I try tae fix the small things?"

I didn't have an answer. There were no answers.

We went back downstairs to the fallout shelter. As I followed him, each descending footfall echoed off the concrete steps and arranged into a percussive pattern that my heartbeat should have sounded out, weeks ago. If I'd still had a heartbeat. Harold Laing was a good man; even the hollow void in my chest knew that, I realized. A monster, certainly—but a good man, as well.

I could hold both of those things to be true at once. For the first time, I almost wished that I didn't hate being a vampire so much. I wished that I was fixable. I wished that we had a chance at a future.

Chapter Twenty-Two

After the Fire

I laid awake in bed for hours after the sun came up, wishing Harold were beside me, but he'd insisted on sleeping on the pull-out sofa in the common area of the fallout shelter. I couldn't blame him for wanting to keep his distance. I was an emotional wreck; I wouldn't have wanted to be around my own self these nights, if I wasn't stuck inside my own damned body and my own damned mind.

I thought about blood, and killing.

When I was twelve, a classmate at school presented a report on factory farming, and I'd decided in an instant to become a vegan—a decision that lasted for about six weeks. Mom had tried to be supportive, Dad just shook his head, and Sunday dinners at Nana's eventually broke me. Italian-American families cooked with too much meat and cheese for me to hold out for long. It wasn't that vegetarian fare was a foreign concept growing up—of course, we never had meat on Fridays during Lent, but there was always fish and eggs. You couldn't escape the ubiquity of animal products in the food we ate, the clothes we wore. Leather shoes, cashmere sweaters, wool socks, and trousers.

I'd always loved animals, though. School trips to the zoo had made me deliriously happy as a child, the horses had always been among my favorite things at the Renaissance Faire with my parents. Even up til my first semester at college, I'd wanted to study zoology, until Victoria convinced me to switch majors. I loved Frodo, our family dog, loved the feral cats on my college campus, and yet I still ate meat, even long after learning about the awful cost and terrible cruelty of the food I put on my plate each day before I'd changed.

Maybe I did lack the moral fortitude to adhere to my convictions when push came to shove. It wasn't becoming a vampire that triggered this descent into endless justification in my mind; that part had always been there, looking back. My own actions and the things I claimed to believe, didn't always line up.

I mused over the cognitive dissonance experienced by most people I knew, who at the very least liked animals, but who also liked bacon and hot dogs. Weren't pigs supposed to be smarter than dogs, and have the emotional intelligence of a three-year-old human child? There had always been this separation in my mind between the food I ate, and the lives I cherished, and I guessed it was the same for most people, if they ever thought about where their food came from, and still chose to eat it.

How could you pet a cow on its velvety soft nose at an animal sanctuary, and know that it was a beautiful, sentient creature, and still eat cheeseburgers? But people did it every day. I had done it. Holding two things to be true at once. I liked this *particular* cow. But I also loved the way Nana cooked veal on Sundays.

Wasn't blood the same way? The blood that I had been given so far had either been medical grade, stored by the pint in typical plastic bags, or animal blood from a butcher. I wasn't sure if all vampires sourced their blood that way, but Harold and Calliope seemed to prefer to, for the most part. The blood they drank was sterile, divorced from its source. I never had to think of the human cost of the blood I'd been drinking; for all I knew, it had been donated, and no one was even hurt.

But the blood tonight had been *different*. There was a depth to it, and a potency, that chilled and filtered, screened and preserved medical-grade blood lacked, and I didn't feel guilty preferring the former over the latter.

I supposed there might be some vampires out there who subsisted only on animal blood, maybe even freeze-dried animal blood like Harold and I had resorted to last night; the same stuff Nana used to pick up at the garden center to put on her rose bushes. Harold had mentioned drinking rat blood, and I'd been very keen to catch that rabbit in the front yard earlier, when I'd been hungry. I tried to imagine night after night mixing up Forbidden Nesquick, drinking just enough reconstituted blood to keep me going, and trying to convince myself that I was being ethical, and cruelty-free. But how was it cruelty-free to depend on the byproduct of large-scale factory farming? It seemed less cruel, the more I thought about it, to take blood as needed, either out of the medical supply, or, even better, to hunt for it myself, killing only if necessary.

The more I thought about it, the easier it was to justify.

The difference between the people I might kill, and the people I still loved—Becca, Dad, Nana, all my cousins and aunts and uncles back home in Ohio—was as sharply delineated in my mind as the difference between Frodo, my childhood chocolate lab, and packaged ground meat at the grocery store. It was weird, maybe. And maybe it was monstrous. But was it really all that much more monstrous than the typical American diet?

There were many complicated things about being a vampire—not being able to go out during the day, having to legally disappear every few years or so before the mortal world started to pick up on the fact that you didn't age, and, of course, the loneliness. There just weren't that many other vampires out there, it seemed. The self-limiting factors of the difficulty in creating new vampires coupled with occasional intra-Community violence kept our population numbers low, and kept vampires paranoid of each other probably, to some extent. Those challenges seemed more complicated to me than the moral and ethical considerations of getting blood.

I *wanted* to hunt, I realized. I wanted to know what it was like to bite down on warm flesh with my sharp teeth and feel hot blood pour into my mouth.

I thought back to the night I'd been turned. I still didn't know why Gavin chose to bite me, when he'd seemed so interested in Becca, and maybe I'd never know. My relationship with my maker had thus far been limited to a handful of punches and insults hurled at each other outside a downtown concert venue. But I thought I might be beginning to understand his hunger, as I began to understand my own. It wasn't personal, what he'd done to me: selfish, irresponsible, thoughtless, risky—all those things, yes.

But he'd also tried, in the end, to save me, not knowing one way or the other if he'd even be successful if he did try. The meaningful implication was that he hadn't meant to kill me, and he'd attempted, perhaps the best way he knew how, to salvage his fuck-up by bringing me back. It didn't excuse what he'd done, leaving me alone for someone else to take care of—but it meant something.

Because, I realized, when Harold had killed for me tonight, he hadn't created any new fledglings in the process. I was absolutely certain, down to my bones, that he hadn't even tried. I lay back and let the realization wash over me, and discovered I was okay with that. I was okay with killing, in certain circumstances. For instance, killing Gavin, as soon as I could, and maybe Calliope for good measure, if I could manage it. And then, if Harold wouldn't help me, I'd find a way to take myself out as well. I didn't want to love him, and I didn't want to want the other things I wanted, either.

So that was the plan, then, and I finally drifted off to sleep under the weight of a hazy winter sun, satisfied to have figured out some of my feelings better.

<hr>

Underground, there was no way to tell when the sun went down, and I awoke sometime after sunset, according to the old mechanical clock on the bedside table. I dressed quickly in the dark, without turning any lights on. I didn't need any lights, and I liked the dark. To hell with whatever Calliope said.

I assumed Harold was still asleep in the other room, because I couldn't hear him moving around the fallout shelter, but when I stepped out of the small bedroom, the rest of the tiny underground space was empty, and my heart sank. Where had he gone off to now...?

Inside the tiny kitchenette's refrigerator, I found the rest of last night's blood, cooled and only slightly congealing, in the same plastic milk jug it had been in. I guessed Harold's crystalline chemical powder actually worked. I poured myself a cup and drank it cold, and quickly. It had been much better when it was still warm, but it was better than medical blood, and vastly better than the freeze-dried stuff.

Free range, wild caught really does taste different, I mused. The light from the fridge illuminated a piece of paper left behind on the small round table where Harold had sat, sorting through the cash and paperwork, two nights prior. There was one word written on the piece of paper in a coarse, uncertain hand:

"Ubftares."

I squinted at the single word for half a moment, before remembering what Harold had told me about his handwriting, and the letters fell into place. His penmanship was certainly lacking and his spelling might leave something to be desired, but the message got his point across, which was the important thing. He was upstairs, then, and presumably, he wanted me to join him. I found the note sweetly endearing. It was, more than the stories he'd told me about his life so far, somehow the most vulnerable part of himself I'd seen.

"Good evening." He looked up at me over a laptop he'd set up on the kitchen table, a brand-new cell phone next to it, providing a tethered internet connection. He held up the phone and said, "no signal downstairs, so no internet."

"Look at you…" I smiled, genuinely impressed. I sat down next to him and looked over his shoulder. "Using a VPN, too—Harold, I didn't know you were so tech-savvy!"

He cleared his throat and looked sheepish. "I've been using the internet since you were probably…what, four? There wasn't much online then, mostly message boards, always hard tae read, you know. But it's a useful invention, if you're careful."

I tried to hide my shock but was unsuccessful.

"Well, I mean, it's hard tae get anything done these nights without the internet…and online banking now, that's the best. You don't even need daytime intermediaries anymore for so much stuff—" he finally noticed the dress I had on and tilted his head to the side as though puzzled.

"Were you wearing that last night?" he asked.

I confessed where I'd found it, and the rest of the stored-away clothing. "I hope it's not a problem. I just didn't have any other clothes with me, and I'd been wearing the same outfit since before I was arrested."

Harold looked at me very carefully and, per usual, seemed to consider his words for a long while before he spoke. "It looks nice," he said at last. I halfway imagined I heard his voice crack, just a bit. "You had another one like it back at the house, didn't you? The green dress you were wearing when Calliope came tae visit?"

"I loved that dress," I admitted.

"I think the green looked better on you. But I suppose you can keep this one. She won't be looking for it any time soon."

"Is 'she' the woman in the ID photo I saw? I'm sorry, I wasn't looking, I just remembered, you did say you'd turned a fledgling before, and I wondered…if that was the same person?"

"Yes," Harold admitted, then abruptly turned his attention back to the computer screen. "I'm afraid I don't have good news tonight…but I thought you'd want to see this."

He pulled up the webpage for the local evening news station in the city, which featured an entire video segment on the blaze at Harold's house. The tethered internet connection kept buffering, and it was difficult to make out every word the newscasters said, but I flinched when I heard my name mentioned, and a recent picture of myself, taken by Becca early in the evening on the night I'd died, flashed across the screen. At least two bodies had been found in the ashes, one burned so badly that the lab was still attempting to extract a DNA sample. The other body had been positively identified as that of Grace Kelly Cordero, age twenty-four, from Toledo, Ohio.

The police were asking the general public to step forward if they knew anything about the fire, or the identity of the other victim. The report went on to mention that Grace Cordero had been in police custody twenty-four hours prior on suspicion of credit card fraud, and was last seen in the company of an unknown man who had used a fake ID to bail her out of jail. It was unclear if the person shown in the grainy police station security footage and the other body found inside the house were one and the same. Please call crime stoppers with…

Harold shut the laptop screen. "I thought there would be something in the news, so I stopped at a pawn shop last night for the laptop before…" He put his elbows on the table and clasped his hands together. "I told you I thought cutting all ties with your mortal life was easier, and still, I think it might be better this way—" he began gently.

My lower lip quivered, and I felt myself losing control of the situation again. All I could think about was my family, and how they would take the news that I was gone—really dead. "Better for who?" I asked. "My dad, my family, Becca? *My Nana*?" My unbeating heart broke for them. "They're going to think that I did something stupid and got myself into trouble before I—before I died."

"You didn't do anything stupid, Grace. You were in the wrong place at the wrong time."

*But it was still my fault, wasn't it? If I hadn't been so vain, choosing to wear that minidress and those stupid, uncomfortable shoes, I wouldn't have ended up freezing my butt off, susceptible to following strangers. If I hadn't had anything to drink at all, if I'd dragged Becca away from that fucking vampire, if I'd listened to my intuition...**he hadn't been wearing a jacket for Christ's sake!** I should I've known something was off. I should have run away. How was it not my fault, somehow?*

I shook my head. "My Nana is eighty years old. She always said she never had to worry about me, out of all of my cousins, because I was the one who always stayed out of trouble—or at least, I didn't get caught—and now this, it's going to break her heart!" *And Dad! Oh my God, my dad, this just isn't—it's not fair!* I snapped out of my own thoughts again. "Wait. Harold—where did she get the other bodies?"

"She? Your grandmother? I don't follow."

"*Calliope Jones* wanted me out of the city. Who else?"

"Stop trying to pin this on Calliope. If she wanted you dead, she could have destroyed you on the night you resurrected and saved us a lot of trouble—"

"Calliope is the only one we know for certain has the means, motive, and opportunity!" I ticked off my fingers, thinking back to the crime shows I binged with Becca. "She wanted me out of the city, she was protecting Gavin, and she threatened me when she knew I wanted to kill him. She's got the money and connections to make almost anything happen, and you know it. So, where did she get the bodies they found in the house!" I shouted at Harold, furious that I couldn't get him to see what was so obvious to me.

"We don't know what kind of connections Gavin has." Harold reminded me.

I remembered the friend of Gavin's who had been quoted in his memorial in the Alumni newsletter; the friend who had gone on to medical school; the friend who now worked in the Cook County Medical Examiner's Office...

A sudden and terrible thought descended on me, and I grabbed the laptop from Harold and clacked away furiously at the keyboard, logging in to my social media alt accounts. I prayed that no one would notice a log-in.

The first thing I did was load Becca's main Facebook and Tumblr pages. On each, there was a recent update, published hours ago, before the sun went down, eulogizing her friendship with...me, expressing heartbreak that she couldn't be the friend that I had needed at the end.

> *"Grace had more style and class in her little pinky than I could ever hope to aspire to, she was effortlessly timeless and self-assured. NO ONE could match her makeup game, I always felt less put-together next to her. Grace made me feel like a grown-up, even when we were still technically teenagers. Any space she occupied for more than 10 minutes magically became better, calmer, cleaner...she brought order to chaos everywhere she went.*

> *"I gave myself over to pettiness and judgement when my best friend needed love and support, and that's an unforgivable violation of every- thing that we held sacred in our friendship. I'm sorry, Grace, for failing you. You always cared enough to come rescue me when I needed you.*

> *"My heart goes out to her family..."*

As though she hadn't used exactly those things to throw me under the bus and imply that my tidiness made me unhinged not even two weeks ago. Still, I couldn't stop the tears from streaming down my cheeks when I read Becca's words, and even though I *knew* it was a bad idea, I scrolled through the comments under the Facebook post, noticing with a kind of nihilistic irony how many of the people who had such lovely things to say about me now that they thought I was dead were the same people who had called me untrustworthy and psycho after the bar fight. People were horrible and deserved to be fed upon by vampires, I decided. Not everyone, but definitely some people.

A mutual commented, "Are U alone right now? Do U need me to come over?"

Underneath, Becca replied, "My boyfriend is coming over in just a few hours, later tonight. We have a lot to talk about."

I looked at the calendar, counted on my fingers, as my dead heart echoed several ominous thumps in chest. "Becca's birthday is in four nights," I told Harold, toneless and hollow. "He's going to kill her on her birthday. I know it."

"Kill her, or turn her?" he asked, and I shot him a withering look.

"How do you know she doesn't want it?" Harold continued, persisting in spite of the daggers in my eyes aimed at him. "Maybe he's already told her everything, and she asked tae be turned? They've been seeing each other for a month now. I've known it tae happen a lot quicker than that."

"I don't trust Becca with Gavin as her maker. He's—" I ticked off my fingers again, wildly gesturing, though I did run out of air and had to stop to breathe, "selfish, a coward, and he's cruel. I know that already. It's not just that I harbor an intense grudge against him. It's that I don't trust him to not hurt Becca the way he hurt me—or worse."

Harold nodded, and seemed convinced. "Okay, you're right. I wouldn't trust him with a fledgling either, even one who was willing—which, given his track record, is dubious. What do you want ta do about it?"

"I want to go back to the city, and I want to talk to Becca," I told him.

"She thinks you're dead. And legally, you are. Known tae be deceased. How are you going tae talk tae her?"

I pressed my lips together and thought carefully before I answered. "If she's going to be turned on her birthday, then she's been drinking his blood. I don't think he's going to risk trying to turn her the same way he turned me. That means she already knows about vampires, so that won't be a problem, will it? Maybe I can convince her that she doesn't actually want this life, and then at least I can properly say goodbye." I closed my eyes. "You don't understand. Becca is *everything* to me. I can't let her get trapped in this hell, too..."

When I opened my eyes again, he was looking at me, unblinking, his own greenish eyes unreadable. I thought, for a moment, that he was angry with me again, but I was thoroughly unprepared for what he said next.

"You're in love with her." He didn't look away.

<hr>

"You're in love with her." He didn't look away.

Chapter Twenty-Three

To Vivisect Love and Loneliness

"No!" I brushed a piece of hair off my face and stammered. "Not—not like that. I do love Becca, more than anything...but she knows I can't give her that, and...I mean, we've talked about it. You wouldn't understand." I looked down at the wooden kitchen table, my eyes tracing the grain lines across the surface in an attempt to avoid his gaze.

"Do you think I haven't been in love before?" he asked softly. I tilted my head up in his direction, but avoided eye contact.

"I think there are a lot of different kinds of love," I countered. What could Harold possibly know about my feelings for Becca? What did he actually know about me at all? For all my complaints that I knew so little about him, what he knew about me was even more sparse, I realized. I'd been fed on and killed at one of Calliope's infamous vampire free-for-all-parties, I'd resurrected, I'd come to live with him, and I hated being a vampire. What else about me did he really know? A boyfriend had dumped me. My mom was dead.

I was used to letting other people tell me their stories. I was the sort of person people always volunteered their secrets to, and I wasn't so comfortable telling my own.

But Harold kept his secrets from me as fast as I held my own secrets from him. No wonder we tiptoed around each other in conversations. We were both full of land mines, but I'd been too focused on his to recognize my own.

I remembered the first time I saw Becca's face.

It was the end of the fourth week of my first semester at college, and temperatures were already plummeting fast in the evenings, despite the warm glow and golden light of the September days. One of the girls from my dormitory had said there was a litter of kittens in the shrubs behind the building. September wasn't usually the season for kittens, I knew from my weekends volunteering at the animal shelter back home, so I'd rushed outside, immediately worried that the babies would freeze to death overnight, when the frost came.

I remembered the crisp delineation between the warm light and the cool blue shadows as the sun sank low with bittersweet clarity, the sharp twigs and branches snagging my hair as I crawled on my hands and knees in the debris of the under-growth, making soft sounds and trying to lure the kittens, or at least the momma cat, out of their hiding. But I wasn't having any luck.

"Do you know those girls over there? I think they're laughing at you. Want me to punch them?" That was the first thing Becca Moreno ever said to me. I extricated myself from my flattened position underneath the shrubs and glanced over toward the dormitory. Sure enough, three of the girls who usually dominated the common room TV were leaning against the brick building, laughing and making meowing sounds. My heart sank.

"I wanted to help the kittens..." I said, feeling stupid and self-conscious. I hated the process of making friends, and I hadn't been very successful yet in college. Back home at my all-girls Catholic high school, I hadn't had many friends per se, but at least everybody knew me as the girl who was really good at hair and makeup, so people would talk to me about those things, and I'd felt useful and important, even though I knew most girls only approached me because they wanted my help or opinion. Chicago girls didn't have the same style sensibilities girls had back in Toledo, though. And no one had asked me about my eyeliner even once since school had started.

"I'm Becca," she threw out her hand to help me stand up. "And fuck those bitches. They're just mean and insecure. I know the type; they're basically worth-less—your eyeshadow is amazing, by the way."

"It's MAC," I said proudly, about to explain that there was a decent drugstore dupe of the palette I had used, but when I gripped Becca's hand to pull myself out of the bushes, I winced. "Your hands are like ice. Where are your gloves?"

She told me she'd already misplaced them in her room somewhere, and that's when I noticed she was shivering. She wasn't wearing terribly unseasonable clothing, but she didn't seem used to the weather, either. I asked her where she was from.

"California. *Northern* California," she stressed. "Napa. It gets cold there at night, but nothing like this. I think I'm going to freeze to death by Christmas." She laughed, but there was a nervous edge to her voice, and her arms were already wrapped around her shoulders.

"Didn't your mom help you plan for Chicago winter?"

Becca looked at the ground. "My mom died in a car accident when I was twelve. And my dad wears the same clothes whether it's forty degrees or ninety. Nonna made me pack a parka, but it doesn't seem cold enough for that yet. I'll figure things out." She shrugged.

"You need good thermal under layers when it starts to get cold," I chided, hands on my hips. I squinted my eyes a bit and peered at the girl named Becca, observing details. Her inky dark eyeliner was as smudged and messy as her black fingernail polish was chipped, but it was a look, at least. She was wearing a striped long sleeve shirt underneath her black T-shirt with a skeleton raccoon printed on it, which put me at ease, because I had a plush pillow up in my dorm with a similar design. Only mine was a cat. Becca seemed like safe people, but you couldn't lose your gloves when winter came to the Midwest, especially by the Lakes. I bet she didn't even own a pair of mittens.

"Hey—you're the one I keep getting confused for in Intro to English Comp—do you have the early class with Turner?" She pulled a small digital camera out of the front pocket of her studded black backpack. I recognized about three of the patches hand-sewn all over the canvas and leather, including a local band that had played near campus last weekend. I'd had no one to go to the show with.

"You're the 11:00 AM class, aren't you?" Suddenly it made sense—three times now, professor Turner had made an offhand comment about me being up early, even though I'd registered for his 8:00 AM class before school had even started, and

I knew my schedule. Becca and I looked at each other closely. There was something shockingly familiar about her. We were about the same height and the same build, same oval faces and hazel eyes. Our hair was even the same length—long and kind of straight and hitting the middle of our backs.

"This is unreal. I've got to take a picture for Nonna. She's gonna say we look like sisters." And Becca posed beside me and snapped a picture with her camera before I could say anything. "You're so photogenic." She smiled beatifically, showing me the resulting selfie in the small digital display. I didn't agree about the photogenic thing—Becca was clearly the prettier of the two of us—but we did, weirdly, look like sisters, same cut and design, only slightly different coloring. Becca was all high contrast and cool tones; I was warm and muted, plain as a sparrow. I held out my hand.

"I'm Grace. Grace Kelly Cordero. Do you...Do you need help buying the right clothes for winter? I've got a car, and I can take you to the mall and help you get what you need..."

Becca grinned and clasped her hands in front of her, jumping from foot to foot, exactly resembling the raccoon on her T-shirt. The very best-ever trash panda.

You'd think Becca and I would have been fast friends from that night on, but the first semester of college was a blur, and after that weekday night shopping trip, I only saw her a handful of times on campus until spring semester, when we both decided to try to rush for sororities during selections week. We didn't get in, but it didn't matter. We were a sisterhood of two. That was all I needed.

Becca was all I had ever needed.

And this—saving Becca—was important. I took a deep breath, sharpened my resolve, and vivisected my soul, right there on the kitchen table. "I was a really weird kid, okay?"

"I never would have guessed." Harold started to laugh, but stopped himself.

"Hold your tongue. There's weird, and then there's...something off. And that was me." Everything else came out at once. I told him about my family, how Mom and Dad were high school sweethearts who married right after graduation, and how

I'd been born early, just three months later, which was how they found out Mom had cancer the first time around.

I told him about how lonely I felt as an only child, even though Dad came from a huge family and I had more cousins than I could count. I always felt like there was a rulebook that everyone else got handed at some point that told them all the secrets of normal human interaction, but my copy must have gotten lost in the mail, or something. I liked animals more than people. All my friends were in books, the kind of heroines in fantasy novels who rode horses and wielded swords, mastered the magical arts and kicked ass.

I told him about the time I got detention for sharpening sticks on the concrete at the playground and brandishing my makeshift weapons against the mean girls.

"You threatened tae stake your classmates?" Harold grinned at that, and even I had to smile at the foreshadowing. Maybe the signs had always been there.

"Hush. They absolutely deserved it. I'm trying to make this make sense. I don't know if I can make *me* make sense." I always felt like I was on the outside, looking in, observing a world full of strange inscrutable rules that made no sense to me, not understanding why a person wasn't supposed to say this thing or that when sometimes things were just obvious.

"But then, when I was thirteen, my cousin Victoria got this makeup book. She's three years older than me. I guess she's kind of like my big sister..." Victoria had always tried to include me and look out for me, but until I found makeup and fashion, ordinary social interaction didn't make sense. I never felt like I fit in. I was always going through the motions. But with makeup, there was rules and techniques that made sense in my head. And finding the rules gave me leverage. At Catholic school, we weren't allowed to wear makeup, so a lot of girls didn't even bother in their off hours. But I did. And I finally had something I could offer, in return for something that felt like friendship.

"And I started getting invited to sleepovers. And to sit with the cool girls. And I could listen to them talk and figure out the code. The right things to say at the right time. The right tone. The right pitch. The right...gestures."

"That sounds exhausting. Couldn't you have just stuck tae swords?"

I rolled my eyes. Boys never understood how hard it was to be a girl. They just punched each other, called each other names, and went back to playing video games. "Girls don't get to have weird interests like swords and knights and jousting and *Lord of the Rings*." I let my eyes wander around the kitchen; the faded calendar on the wall had the right month, but the wrong year. No one had changed the page since February 1985.

"Girls have to do the right thing at the right time and say the right words to the right people with the right mannerisms, or else you're weird, and then they lock you in the school bathroom with the lights off and leave you crying in the darkness while they laugh at you on the other side of the door."

"And you think you're the monster..."

I pushed past Harold's pity. I didn't want his pity. I wanted him to *understand*. "All teenage girls are monsters, it's only that the worst of them don't realize it. But at least I got good grades." I said. And I told him, in as few details as possible, what happened when Mom died, my junior year. About how I went numb, and I never really felt the things everyone said I was supposed to feel when your mom dies, but at least I was still able to function. I was able to get into a good university after I graduated. I didn't feel anything, and for once in my life, I was grateful to be...weird.

But college wasn't high school, and all the social rules I mastered at a small all-girls Catholic academy didn't apply anymore. I was floundering, I was fucked. Everything was awful, and I almost dropped out and went home.

"Until I met Becca. Freshmen year. We both did rush week, trying to get picked for a sorority, but we didn't make the cut during selections—that was fine, though. Because she was a weird kid, too. Not weird like me, weird in like, all the opposite ways. She was loud, I was quiet. She could talk to people, understand people, get people...she was big picture, I was details. She liked *Harry Potter*, I liked *Lord of the Rings*. But, it worked. And being around Becca, it was like...breathing. Like realizing I'd been underwater my whole life and was finally coming up for air. It was like...the first taste of blood."

Harold nodded, gravely.

"For the first time, with someone, I didn't have to pretend anymore. I could just be me, and that was enough. More than enough. To be seen and understood. She's an only child from a big Italian American Catholic family, too. And her mom passed away a few years before mine did.

"I helped her remember her mittens, and her keys, and where she put her cell phone, and she helped me find more people who…weren't quite the same as she was, but who also just…saw me for me. And accepted me. Or at least, that's what I used to think. Becca made the world make sense, and as long as I had her, I was no longer invisible and alone, and that was everything. I would die for her, Harold—or maybe I already did. Maybe Gavin would have gone after her, first, if I hadn't been there, so…I'm glad. For that. She has too much to live for to let him take that away from her."

"I still think you're in love with her."

"Not like that."

"You're sure?"

"I'm…"

"I mean, you hear stories about girls in Catholic school…Would you feed off of a woman, intimately, if you got the chance?" He raised his eyebrows, and I was certain I was blushing, whether or not I was physically capable of it.

"Spare me the stereotype of the all-girls-Catholic-school lesbians." I rolled my eyes. "I knew a lot of girls who wanted to be nuns, sure. And there were the wild party girls that went both ways, or at least said they did for attention, but they almost always ended up dating boys anyway. I only ever dated boys.

"As to your lewd question, though: If you'd taken me hunting already, we'd both know the answer, but since you haven't, you're just going to have to use your imagination, I guess."

"I wasn't lewd! It was an entirely innocent query!"

I looked up at him with a pointed glance of my own. "I mean, you…with men? You said before that you like…options."

He shrugged. "Blood is blood. I've been known tae be peculiar."

"That's what I thought."

"Does it bother you now?"

"Now, what? After the kissing? I told you it didn't. And I meant that." I nodded, a bit thrown by his use of the word "peculiar," but I knew what he was saying…And he was right, of course. Blood was blood. The moment he said it, I knew. Grace from before would have been much more taken aback, but Grace of the present moment was surprisingly nonplussed to have my entire identity upended. "Feeding from is different than fucking, though," I insisted.

"I don't think we always get tae control who we fall in love with, is what I'm saying. And all your modern labels leave out a lot of nuances, from my perspective. When I was on the ship, I saw sailors who fucked each other in the dark below decks, then fucked women in the whorehouses on shore leave with the same fervor. Maybe I am just too old, but the way I see it, sex is sex, and love is love. And they don't have tae overlap...but it's nice when they do.

"What you described, being on the outside looking in, not being seen, trying tae keep up with changing social cues and trends and customs...that's what most vampires experience, as nights go on. Some of us struggle with that more than others, but you came into this world with experience, a head start you didn't know you had. Anyway, one of the first things we learn is that a lot of the old rules and expectations we lived our mortal lives by, don't really apply anymore. Especially when it comes tae sex. Or love."

I considered his point. Avie had said something similar, back at the Winetka house. "Becca is bi, and I'm...spaghetti," I begrudgingly admitted, remembering a handful of wild nights in college. Only kissing, though. And never with Becca. That would have crossed an unfair line.

He grinned like a feral cat with a wild bird in its jaws. "You'll have tae humor me. I never had a chance tae eat spaghetti when I was mortal."

"Putting aside how weird that sounds to my Italian-American heart—" I gasped in mock horror, clutching at my chest. "I mean, Jesus Mary and Joseph, who has never eaten spaghetti? That is legitimately weirder than freeze-dried blood, Harold. Stop distracting me. Spaghetti is straight until it's hot and wet. Does that answer your question?"

He howled with laughter and then, seeming to remember the seriousness of our conversation, pulled himself together. "I beg your pardon." The bird-eating grin still teased at the corners of his lips, and I didn't trust the salacious glint in his eye.

Harold Laing was hitting on me. I was pretty fucking certain this counted as flirting, for him.

I shook my head, glared at him, and continued. "Okay, now I believe that you're forever twenty-five. Sheesh. Do I interrupt you this much when you're telling me a story?"

"No, but I've only told you stories about myself when you were so distracted I wasn't sure how much you were paying attention."

"I pay attention." There was a not-uncomfortable quiet between us, and I softened, meeting Harold's gaze with as much sincerity as I could muster. "I pay attention..."

I continued. "Becca's the most important person in the world to me, Harold. We had plans, stupid, beautiful plans for the rest of our lives. We were going to have a double wedding, and raise our kids together, and grow old together in a dumb little cottage with like, roses growing over the porch, and I was going to raise chickens, and she was going to have geese because she's a creature of chaos like that, and now that's all fucked for me. But it doesn't have to be for her. She should have a choice—a real choice, and she can't make an informed decision if she's only hearing things from Gavin. She might not even know that there's a chance she wouldn't survive being turned. I can't let her take that risk. I owe her that much. As her friend. As her sister." I stopped, as the enormity of my vulnerable confession sank in. Crying in front of Harold was one thing, but telling him about what Becca meant to me, was something else. I already knew he thought I was broken. I didn't want him to know all the ways that was true, but here we were.

"Dammit, Grace..." He slowly exhaled before filling up his lungs again to speak, and then he threw his hands in the air in defeat. "An' if I told you that's all weel an' good, but I'm not going back ta the city, what would you do?"

"I'd figure out a way to get back to her on my own. I'd steal a car if I had to. Victoria taught me how to hot-wire."

That, for whatever reason, made Harold laugh. Then he swore, looked at me again, and said, "All right. We'll go back tae Chicago. I don't know where we'll stay; we'll have to risk a hotel. I don't know why I'm sticking my neck out for your death wish, but, the mellishon w' it."

"The what?"

"De devil." He gestured two little horns on his forehead and stuck his tongue out at me. "I thought you said you paid attention."

"I pay close enough attention to know when I can't understand what you're saying. How would you feel if I started going off on you in Italian?"

"*Vai avanti, soprendimi.*"

My jaw dropped. "How many languages do you speak?" I threw my hands up at him and flopped back in my chair. I didn't want to admit that most of the Italian I knew was curse words that would have Nana chasing me out of the kitchen with her spoon. I'd studied French in high school, and German for my semester abroad in college, but I wasn't fluent in those languages, either.

Harold shrugged. "As many as I need tae. You lose what you don't practice. I haven't practiced Italian much since the 19th century."

The 19th century. I shuddered, and looked down at my mom's watch. The time read a little past 8:00 PM, and I fiddled with the clasp, trying to anchor myself to something tangible. "Maybe I do have a death wish." I whispered, more to myself than Harold, at first. "I don't want to live as a vampire, to forget more than I remember." There was less conviction in my voice than there'd been before, but still enough. "I'm sorry, I know you've traveled the world and had grand adventures and lived for a very long time, and I'm glad that's made you happy. And I know you have this weird belief that I'm somehow suited for all of this. But I don't want the night. Not like this. Not alone, probably forever…I've been alone, and now that I've known what not being alone is, and lost it, I can't go back.

"Please," I begged him. "Just let me fix this, and then help me end it. I can't…"

Fix this. He flinched.

"I gave you my word…" he looked down at his feet before slowly looking up at me again; his green eyes were almost pleading when he did. "But, Grace…"

"What?"

"What if you didn't have tae be so alone?"

Neither of us had to breathe. Why did it feel like all the air had been sucked out of the room? I shook my head, disbelieving what I heard. "You don't mean that."

"Are you so certain?" His hand stretched forward to brush away a stray strand of hair that had fallen in front of my face. "I like having you around. When Calliope came over and tried ta take you away from me, and I thought you might say yes tae her offer, I thought, 'I've been a fool.' Your friends are right. You make things better. Not just rearranging all the clutter and making the house feel like a home, but you made me laugh again. You are *good*, and kind, and you care. And I know what loneliness is, too, Grace. But I don't feel lonely when you're around. I could be that for you, perhaps. If you'd let me..."

I parted my lips, uncertain what to say in response. Last night he'd pushed me away, told me in no uncertain terms that he couldn't...put up with me, I'd assumed. If there was any other way to interpret 'I can't,' I drew a blank. I didn't blame him for not wanting me last night, and now I couldn't understand what he was offering, but I leaned into his hand against my face without thinking, closed my eyes.

It could be nice, I thought, to be not lonely, together, with Harold...

He pushed the chair back from the table so fast I heard the chair leg rip into the linoleum floor, and he stood up, suddenly tense and alert and frightening. He moved with a quickness that was a blur even to me, and switched off all the lights in the kitchen. I closed the laptop again as soon as I heard the same sound Harold had. There was a car outside.

"Avie?" I moved my lips, but he shook his head.

"No, not her," he answered my question with equal silence.

Even though the brown house was terribly remote, and I hadn't seen or heard any other cars pass the entire time we'd been there, we could both hear it, moving slowly down the street at the end of the gravel drive. Of course, I hadn't been out during the day...

"You didn't park the car in the garage when you came home last night," I whispered.

"It's worse than that," he whispered in return, hands gripping the table until his knuckles turned white. "I'm an idiot tae have put it out of my mind. I invited Calliope into this house once, the night Irene died."

The vehicle idled to a stop, and the car door closed, and we heard footsteps approaching across the snow.

"Where's the gun?"

◆○◆

"Where's the gun?"

Chapter Twenty-Four

CALLIOPE'S ABSOLUTION

"The gun is in the car."

"Harold *fucking* Laing, you have got to be kidding me," I hissed through clenched teeth. We crouched down in the darkness on the floor of the kitchen, listening to the footsteps in the snow.

"For what it's worth, you were very distracting—"

"How? How have you survived two hundred plus years?"

"For all but the last two months of them, you haven't been in my life. Let's start there. Now, stay put. I'm going tae go to the car and get the gun." He started to crawl across the floor toward the front room, in the direction of the door.

"Harold—Harold, don't do anything stupid. Christ! You don't know who is out there! Harold!" We were still whispering, but I was getting desperate.

He reached the door and raced outside. I heard the BMW's door open and close, and for a short while, there was nothing but the sound of two pairs of footfalls in the snow outside.

I was expecting the gunshots, but I still flinched when I heard the blast, and I screamed Harold's name before running out the front door after him. To hell with staying put. I was the one with the death wish, right? I followed the trail of foot-prints in the snow around the house, flailing and stumbling where the accumulated banks were the deepest. *So much for vampires being creatures of preternatural grace and beauty...*

"Harold! Har—" I ran up behind where he was standing in the shadow of an overhanging tree as he fired off another round at a tall, dark-haired man stagger-ing past the hedges toward the road. I don't know if any of the bullets hit him;

everything that happened next did so very quickly. The car engine roared to life as Harold and I raced to the break in the hedges. Harold threw me to the ground as more bullets fired out of the driver's side window. The man I was certain was Gavin scrambled into the backseat of a black four-door sedan, and it drove off.

"Goddamit," he muttered, helping me to my feet. "I told you ta stay put—"

"What was he going to do, kill me? Again? You said it yourself, I'm the one with the death wish—I only saw him from behind, but that was Gavin, wasn't it?"

Harold nodded. "I recognized him from outside the nightclub, and the pictures you showed me from the internet. He was skulking around the house, but he ran off when he saw me."

"Did Calliope send him? Who was driving the car?" I felt out of breath, even though that was impossible. There was something about the make a model of the getaway vehicle that seemed familiar.

"Grace, I don't know what tae think—" he cut off, as a thick, acrid smoke began filling the air. We both swore at the same time.

Harold shoved the gun into the waistband of his pants and flinched. I guessed the barrel was still hot, but we had a bigger concern. Two empty red canisters, the type used for toting gasoline, were discarded around the opposite corner of the house, and whatever accelerant that Gavin had splashed onto the outside walls was already ablaze, flames licking the exterior of Harold's safe house all the way to the roof.

We spent several desperate minutes trying to heap snow onto the fire to put it out, but the wind picked up, and the flames rose higher.

Harold grabbed my hand and dragged me toward the entrance, instructing me to run and grab the phone and the computer in the kitchen and wait for him by the car. "I don't think he had time tae do anything to it. I got the bastard pretty good, but if he comes back—" He handed me the gun. "Shoot him and his friend until they stop moving, and enjoy yourself."

He raced into the house in the direction of the basement, and I heard him running down the stairs, shouting, "fuck. Fuck. FUCK," as he descended.

I made my own mad dash into the upstairs kitchen, where I grabbed the phone, and the computer and the chargers plugged into the wall. The house was already starting to fill up with black smoke, and I struggled to balance everything in my hands along with the gun, very glad that I didn't need to breathe, even though the smoke made my eyes water.

Harold exited the house a few minutes after me, just as the roof started to cave in. Off in the distance, I heard sirens. He carried the bloodied brown paper bag that had once held half a gallon of a dead man's blood in his arms. This time the bag was filled with piles of cash and papers.

We threw everything into the car and sped off, tires digging into the gravel and churning up ice and rock salt and kitty litter. For the second time in a week, I had no idea where we were going. I smelled blood. Harold's blood. I glanced over at him and noticed a large hole in the side of his sweater, the edges of the wool singed black and soaked with red.

"I didn't realize he shot you, too—"

"He's a coward and a terrible shot." Harold rolled his eyes. "He barely grazed me before running off. I should have been able tae get more than two rounds off before he got back tae his car, though. I'm out of practice."

"I thought swords were more your thing."

"Yeah, Master Santiago would be quite disappointed in me for adapting tae the twenty-first century." He rubbed his side gingerly. "It still hurt, though."

"Are you going to need more blood?"

"You volunteering?"

I flinched, but Harold didn't apologize.

As he drove, I did my best to organize the clutter that resulted from our hasty retreat from the not-so-safe house, and tried not to look outside the car windows into the distance behind us, to see the column of smoke rising up into the sky. Harold had lost two houses in three days because of me. I did *not* want to think about that, so I focused on the task at hand. There were more stacks of money in the brown paper bag than I had ever seen in one place before in my life.

"How do you have this much cash…?" I muttered, more to myself than to Harold. "I thought Calliope was the wealthy one…"

"How do you think compound interest works over two centuries? It's not that hard to imagine!"

"It doesn't work at all when you stash money in wall safes and mattresses, I know that!" I responded, irritated at his condescension. "I took business math in college, and I'm *not* an idiot."

"What you are is the most *agravatious* person I've known in—I honestly don't know how long. A very long time, Grace!" He kept his eyes on the road. So much for his insistence that I made his life better.

"I don't think I could meet anyone more infuriating than you if I lived to be a hundred years old myself!" I shouted in return. "And that's from someone actively planning to kill a man! I never know with you what I'm going to get—if you're going to hit on me or push me away!"

"Wi' me? Feich, I never know if I'm goin' ta be laughin' an' jokin' with you or if you're goin' ta be askin' me ta kill you again!"

"You volunteered!"

"I. Panicked. I panicked, all right? You were talkin' about goin' into the sun on your very first night. You have no idea what dat did tae me! No idea the tings I've seen!"

"You're right, I have no idea about anything with you, because you never tell me anything important, about *anything*!"

"Would telling you my life story really have made a difference? And—for what it's worth, I've told you more about my life than I've told anyone in *years*. How much do you want from me?"

"It would have been nice to get to know you—You've been the only company I've had since I—since he—" I stopped shouting.

"Well, the bastard made it personal now...you wanted my help eliminating your maker, fine. You've got it. Are you satisfied?"

Securing Harold's promise of assistance rang hollow in light of all that had happened. "Why did he do that? Who was with him?" I asked.

Harold shrugged. He had to drive slower on the highway, because of black ice. As a vampire, I could see the dangerous patches on the road that were frozen over in a way that would have been invisible to mortal eyes, but I still imagined that they were difficult to navigate. I let him focus on driving and resumed organizing the items he'd brought out of the house. He had multiple passports. At least one was Spanish. Another was Portuguese.

"I've had a long time tae put money away and get very comfortable, do you understand?" he finally said, once the road conditions had cleared up a bit. "Comfortable is what rich people say when they don't like admitting that they're rich. I have...I don't know, three more safe houses within a two-hundred-mile radius. I own the shell corporation that controls about four city blocks downtown, stocks, bonds...I don't even try tae keep track of it all. I've paid my accountants very well tae do that for a long time. I don't like thinking about money more than I have to, and I don't like showing off like Calliope does. But if you wanted a penthouse like hers, I could get you one. You want a closet full of designer dresses, you can have that. You want accounts of your own, I'll set them up. After one mortal lifetime, you'll have so much money accumulated in interest, you'd never have to touch the principle. I'd give you anything you wanted, anything at all, but the only thing you've asked me for is to cut off your head, so why does it matter?"

"You drive a ratty old car..." I was confused and exasperated. "And your pants are at least fifty years old."

"The 1985 BMW 7 series is an easy car tae maintain, the parts are still readily available, and I enjoy the maintenance. My car's not ratty or barloppin'. She's in pristine condition and drives like a beast. She might look clunky and square next tae your modern cars, but dis is a good car, and I'm allowed tae like what I like." Harold's defensiveness made me smile in spite of myself, in spite of everything. He was so much older than me, and yet, in so many ways, he was exactly like every other twenty-five-year-old man I knew.

"I shouldn't judge..." I soothed him. "I kept my car in really good condition, too. That Accord was almost ten years old and still smelled brand new, even though it was used when I got it. And I loved that car..." I finished, patting the BMW's dashboard apologetically. "I'm sorry I insulted your car. I don't really think that everything old is bad. I actually quite like...classic things," I finished, thinking back to my own wardrobe choices. I owned...well, I *had* owned, dresses in storage bags under my bed back at my old apartment that were from before I was born, and I regretted not packing up my springtime weight vintage Burberry trench coat from the back of my closet in the suburbs the last time I was there. Now that I was legally dead, my friends and family were probably going to pick through all my stuff and haul it away. Maybe, if I *was* going to stay a vampire, in a few decades' time, my own wardrobe would be as old as Harold's. But I didn't want...

But I did.

I fiddled with my late mother's Cartier wristwatch. You couldn't tell if it was made last year, or half a century ago. That's what I liked about it.

"I always liked that about you." He spoke softly, almost as though he were reading my thoughts again. "You take care of things, and you're timeless. A beauty in every age. You're smart, and you're brave, and...well, you're no fighter, but you're scrappy. You were doing all right for yourself against your maker at the nightclub before I stepped in."

"Scrappy."

"That's a compliment, in case you still couldn't tell if I liked you or not."

I had no idea what to say, so I didn't say anything at all. Harold let me sit in silence. I liked that about him. He seemed to know, instinctively, when I needed space, and when to talk. It was nice to feel so...seen. I'd spent most of my life listening to other people prattle on, everyone else's therapist. But Harold volunteered so little that it wasn't necessary to keep up the mask that I was actively engaged in conversation. With him, I could process things in silence, and he didn't freak out if I didn't respond to something right away. He let me *think*. I liked so many things about him, and it made me sad to think how much better this would have been, if I'd met him under different circumstances. If we'd both been mortal.

But then, he would have been dead long before you were born, I told myself. It really wasn't fair.

He pulled into a gas station, and we spent almost an hour combing over the undercarriage and under the hood looking for any tracking devices Harold was sure Gavin had planted at some point, probably before the Winetka fire. "I've only had tae deal with these once before, and I swear..." he reached under the rear wheel wall for the third time, finally eliciting a soft *a-ha*. "These things get smaller every year." He held out the small black object, tinier than a matchbox, for me to see. "And this is how I know it wasn't Calliope," he said. "She's a genius with numbers and profit and loss columns, but she's easily ten years behind the curve when it comes tae other tech. When did you say you thought Gavin was turned?"

"Sometime around spring 2002...so, not that long ago, I guess. How do you stay on top of all of this?" I asked.

"YouTube." He shrugged.

My jaw dropped.

"What?" he responded, casually reaching over to attach the magnetized box to an overhead streetlight illuminating the gas station. "There are car maintenance videos, blacksmithing videos, all kinds of stuff on new tech...it's like the website was created for a two-hundred-year-old jack of all trades who doesn't like reading and can't get out tae the library during the daytime anyway. Easily my favorite mortal invention in the last century, right after motorcars themselves."

Speaking of motorcars, there was something familiar about that car. I hadn't seen the driver, but... "Harold, what does Marie DuChamps look like?"

"Pretty. Brunette. Petite..." He stopped.

"Was it her? Driving the car?"

"I don't know. I didn't see well enough. But it could have been. Shit. Shit—we've got tae go. I want tae put miles between us and that little black box as fast as possible."

"If Marie DuChamps is working with Gavin—"

"I don't know what that means. I need tae think about things. And I need ta...take care of other needs, too."

"Are you going to kill someone again?" I tried to make my voice nonchalant, but a small vein of uncertainty crackled along the edges, and I was afraid I might shatter completely, like safety glass. I longed for the sensation of breathlessness I'd lost the ability to feel when I died; my heart should have been pounding—but it was mostly silent. I was terrified of the answer I refused to let myself admit I wanted. I looked away, hands shaking.

"That entirely depends," he said. We both climbed into the car. "Did you feed before you came upstairs tonight? Before the fire?"

I nodded.

"I don't need much, then," he said. "I fed…a lot, last night. If that bothers you—?"

"It doesn't bother me. What you did." I twirled a piece of my hair around my fingers and stared at it instead of meeting his gaze. "I don't think I'm the paragon of undead virtue you seem to think I am, either."

He gave me a strange, worried look. "I don't want—"

"But what if I do?"

He looked nervous. "I don't want tae force you into anything you're not ready for."

"You don't have to kill, do you?" I remembered what he'd said about Calliope's parties, his admission that he might have fed on me if he'd had the opportunity—if he'd wanted me—and his promise that, if he had, I'd still be alive.

He shook his head. "No. Not often. Not anymore. Last night was the first time in almost ten years."

"Why'd you stop?"

"Reasons."

I didn't pry.

We'd been driving for quite some time, getting closer to the city, when I felt the urge to speak again. I took a deep breath, uncertain if I really meant all of what I was about to say, but I wanted to say it anyway.

"Harold…what if I said I *wanted* to learn how to hunt? With you. Tonight, before I lose my nerve. And that, maybe, I don't know, when all of this has blown over, and I've done what I set out to do and saved Becca and all of that, then maybe I could try…to stay with you, a little while."

He liked me. I was sure of it. And I liked him, too. Maybe I even loved him. I knew in that moment that I could love him. Easily.

What had been done to me could not be undone, he was right about that. There was no turning back to life and all the possibilities I'd taken for granted before I'd died and become a vampire. It was as futile to imagine a meaningful future with Becca as it was with Dylan; those paths were severed now. But perhaps there was a different open road ahead that I'd been unwilling to see before. And maybe I really did have time to decide what I wanted to do with it all. I was shaking, but only a little bit, and I didn't take back my words. I wanted to hunt. I wanted to be with Harold.

He kept his left hand on the steering wheel and his eyes on the road ahead, but his right hand reached across the car to mine, caught it, and brought my hand to his mouth to kiss. His lips were cool, and soft, and trembling. Yes. He said...

"Yes."

CHAPTER TWENTY-FIVE

CINDERS

WE PULLED INTO THE parking lot of a generic suburban dive bar, and Harold killed the engine. There weren't many other vehicles parked nearby; temperatures were in the low teens, and a cutting wind howled outside the car windows. There were no insulating clouds in the sky above to temper the chill in the air, and despite not being affected by the cold anymore—at least, not in the way I had been when I was mortal—I sympathized with anyone who had decided to stay home that night. The weather in Chicago in February was no joke.

"Any particular reason you picked this place?" I tried to keep my voice casual. The bar seemed a little out of the way, and I'd never been to this neighborhood before, but Harold seemed familiar enough with the area that he'd practically navigated on autopilot.

"If I remember correctly...and admittedly, it's been a few years—this particular bar has a heated outdoor smoking patio." He drummed his fingers on the steering wheel. "Fuck, I miss cigarettes."

"Seriously? After two hundred years?" I side-eyed him. Cigarettes reminded me of my Uncle Davey, who chained-smoked European cigarettes he illegally shipped in by the case, and was always trying to puff up in the kitchen at Nana's, until she would chase him away with a wooden spoon.

"Smoking is a fine habit for vampires." Harold's tone implied that he thought it was obvious. "Helps you remember tae breathe when you're surrounded by people, makes it easy tae start conversations with strangers, get in close...very practical. Light a cigarette for a pretty lady..." he winked at me, and I remembered the story about how he and Avie met. "Feels like a million years since I've been here, though..."

"Back when dinosaurs roamed the earth?"

"Aye. Large beasties with wee tiny arms always frightening the women and children."

I giggled.

"Then all the cancer stuff came about, and it's just made hunting that much harder. I miss how easy it was when everybody smoked..." his voice trailed off, and he stopped talking. I wondered what—or who—he was really remembering.

"Well, I can't go in there..." I reminded him, twisting the clasp of my watch and trying not to look as nervous as I felt. It was one thing to talk about...*hunting*, in the abstract, but there were people in that building, and I wasn't entirely sure I was ready to act on my impulse to see people as...*food*. I shuddered involuntarily and continued, "I can't use my ID anymore, remember? I'm dead."

"Oh. Right." Harold shook himself off and reached into the back seat of the car for the tan overcoat, pulling an envelope out of one of its many pockets. "I took care of that last night, as well. Remember, the birth certificate and the social security card are real, so treat them accordingly." He handed the papers to me. "The ID is fake, but it's a good fake. I had my contact in Madison use the professional headshot from your old work's website and grunge it up a bit."

I was impressed. I'd seen a lot of fake IDs in college, but this one held up. "That 'professional headshot' was taken by Becca on her iPhone, because the damn HR manager kept giving me grief about not having one, and I wasn't about to shell out several hundred bucks just to have some creepy corporate photos taken. Three cheers for being cheap, I guess." I examined my new identity closely. 'Angela Mercer' would take some getting used to.

"You know, I don't think I can pass for thirty..." I raised my eyebrows at him, pointing at the birth date. "If anything gets this card flagged as fake, it'll be that. That's what always got the college kids into trouble, you know..."

Harold held up one finger and began rummaging around the driver's side door panel; it never occurred to me how much *stuff* he kept stashed in his car. From a hidden compartment next to him, he produced an eyeglasses case that contained an obviously vintage pair of horn-rim frames with plain glass lenses. They were a little masculine and oversized for my face, but they did the trick of making me look somehow completely different—and quite a few years older.

"Now do up your hair the way you had it the other night, with the—" He gestured to the top of his head, indicating the messy bun with the face-framing tendrils he'd called "pretty." I quickly leaned forward and adjusted my hair as Harold pulled off the remains of his damaged wool sweater, stripping down to his black V-neck undershirt, and put on the tan jacket to cover the hole in the side. We didn't look very warm for the sub-freezing temperatures outside, but we looked *different*, somehow, than we had just moments before. I thought I understood now how nobody recognized Clark Kent as Superman.

"We look like hipster scum," I observed.

"Yes, well—we are going tae be very hungry, very sneaky hipster scum—" he kissed me on the cheek as he reached over to pull the peppermint and cotton balls out of the glovebox and patted me on the knee when I wrinkled my nose at the sight of it. "We're *not* here to kill anyone. We're going tae scout out the clientele, I'll point out a few things you should look for, and then, if we're able tae get anyone alone—privately—we'll feed quickly and leave. The peppermint should help you from getting overwhelmed, and I'll be close by if things go wrong, so don't worry. You've got this." He seemed far more confident than I felt. Despite how badly I wanted to hunt, I was terrified—whether from fear of getting caught, or of crossing yet another point of no return on my descent into monster land, I wasn't sure.

"What if we lose control and kill the entire bar?" I chewed on my lower lip and tried to stop my hands from shaking.

"That only happens in the movies, kettlen. But, if it does happen, just like in the movies, we'll burn the place tae the ground, drive off into the night, and try again tomorrow somewhere far away from here." He was entirely too cheerful to be describing the potential wholesale slaughter of innocents, I thought.

But I remembered the two-faced comments from my so-called friends online, and thought, as we walked in through the door, *most people aren't that innocent, anyway...*

The interior of the bar was suitably dimly lit, with a low bank of booths toward the back, illuminated by mostly-red neon beer and liquor logos, a few dart boards on a back wall, and a pool table. It looked like the kind of place that attracted a neighborhood type of clientele, rather than tourists, or people passing through. There weren't many patrons at the bar, but a few groups were scattered about, engaged in conversation or quietly drinking alone. The TV was playing a recap of the Bulls game on mute, but no one seemed to be paying attention. I didn't immediately recognize the song coming from the speakers of the digital jukebox attached to the wall, but it sounded like something from the eighties or nineties my dad would listen to.

"Jack!" A man behind the bar shouted at Harold the moment we walked in. "Jesus fuck man, I haven't seen you in what—ten years? Holy shit, man, you look great."

I flinched at how easily Harold was recognized (*it's definitely the hair,* I thought. *Or the sideburns*), but Harold seemed nonplussed, fist-bumping the bartender like an old drinking buddy.

"Oh, I've been here and there," Harold—'Jack'—replied vaguely, leaning up against the bar. He pointed at me. "This is my friend, Gr—Angela."

"Grrrrangela, I like it!" The bartender winked. He didn't ask to see Harold's—'Jack's'—ID, but of course, he asked to see mine. I pulled out 'Angela Mercer's' card and handed it over with all the confidence I could muster.

"Grrrrr," I said, trying to approximate the same casual energy as Harold, but failing. It was like he had suddenly become a different person, and I was just awkwardly trailing along in his wake.

I thought I noticed the bartender raise his eyebrows slightly when he saw the date of birth on Angela's ID, but he didn't say anything about it. "I get you two something to drink?" he asked.

I shook my head, but the bartender ignored me, and put three shot glasses down on the bar, quickly filling them with Jameson. I'd had more than my fair share of Irish whisky at parties with Becca in college, and I definitely didn't want any now, with hunger gnawing at my insides. Harold and the bartender clinked glasses, and both downed their shots in one smooth, practiced gulp. I tried not to appear slack-jawed in my amazement. *That was an option…?* Harold caught my eye and smirked.

Never one to back down from a challenge, I picked up my own glass and did the same, much to my instant regret. *Not an option, not an option...*I coughed, like an amateur, embarrassing myself, and covered my mouth with my hands, feeling the fangs make an appearance as if to say, "do not like."

Harold slapped me on the back and laughed. "You doin' okay there, Angie?" he asked in a folksy lilting accent that sounded straight out of the Dakotas. I grimaced.

"Yeah, I'm fine," I sputtered when my body was mostly done complaining about the foreign invader. I could feel the alcohol sloshing in my belly like a dead weight, and I glared at him. Harold nodded his head to his left and started chatting with a bar patron a few stools down, leaving me on my own to converse with the bartender. I asked him how long he'd known 'Jack.'

"Jack used to come in here all the time after 9/11, then I stopped seeing his face around 2004, 2005. I figured he'd just moved on. I'm Keith, by the way." He held out his hand for me to shake. I got the immediate impression that he was a decent kind of guy, even though I couldn't have articulated, at the time, how I knew. "You two been together long?" Keith asked.

"Oh, we're not together," I corrected him, throwing up my hands in protest, but Keith smiled with the confidence of a man well-versed in wrestling deep dark secrets out of drunken patrons.

"Bullshit. I know a couple when I see one. Maybe you two haven't had 'the talk' yet or whatever, but he likes you...Is that what brought Jack back to this part of town? He showing you all his old hangouts?"

"I guess..." my eye flitted over to the conversation happening a few feet away. 'Jack' was mirroring the accent, body language, and mannerisms of his new drinking buddy with an accuracy that should have been terrifying, if he wasn't so damn impressive. I realized I'd been ignoring Keith, and returned my attention to the bartender.

"...he used to come in here all the time with a leggy lesbian—Abbie or something. Used to kill it at the pool table, those two. Always tried to get them to join the league—our team would have been unstoppable, but the selfish bastards refused to grace us mere mortals with their presence. You play pool?" he asked me, his voice piqued with hope.

I shook my head. "I'm usually the one who makes sure the players aren't cheating." It was true. Becca had dated an amateur pool player for maybe three weeks the summer after we graduated, prompting a brief fascination with the game on Becca's part that then spiraled into a full-on obsession for six months after the fling ended, and she made a point of showing up 'randomly' at all the billiards halls in the area wherever he was going to be. It got old after a while, but in the meantime, she'd gotten pretty good at the game, and I'd developed a keen eye for spotting illegal moves. Honestly, I think the fact that I kept pointing out *Becca's* illegal moves had been the primary reason she'd lost interest in the sport.

But I couldn't afford to think about Becca. I needed I focus on getting blood. I still had time. If Gavin was going to turn her on her birthday, she couldn't have had more than three nights of his blood. I could still interrupt the process, somehow.

"Well, Jack's good people, and you must be, too, if he's taking you to places that used to matter to him," Keith said. I smiled much more broadly than I meant to, and in an effort to make sure my fangs wouldn't show, I pretended to sip the cup of water he'd placed in front of me, as Keith the bartender moved down the bar to chat with other patrons. I made eye contact with Harold, who was deep in conversation about medieval weaponry with a different patron. This time he was chatting with a woman in a black sweatshirt that featuredthe logo of a local metal band. *Metal and metallurgy. Great combination.* Harold pointed to the open seat on the other side of the woman he was talking to, indicating that I should sit down, but I didn't want to interrupt his conversation with what seemed like an old friend, and besides, I didn't know enough about either subject to add anything meaningful to the discourse.

So much for giving me pointers.

I sighed and wandered off to explore the rest of the bar. It was dark and nondescript and unfussy, nothing like the pretentious, overpriced gastropubs and speakeasies downtown. Near the row of dimly lit booths at the back of the bar, I wondered how many times Harold had fed from patrons in those shadowy crevices, under that blood-red light, ten years ago. Probably lots. I could almost see myself doing the same, with a drunken stranger, luring him into the darkness and—

It was the sort of thing I had always warned Becca and our other girlfriends about. Don't get too drunk, don't go off into the shadows with strangers. You never know what kind of predators are out there. Now I was the predator, and after a lifetime of being petite and looking over my shoulder with my keys thrust between my fingers as I walked to the metro station at night, my pepper spray close at hand in my pocket...now that the tables were turned, it felt good. Maybe that did make me the monster. *Being a monster felt good.*

The woman with the sweatshirt approached, and thrust one of two shot glasses she had in her hands at me. "Here, honey, I'm gonna go take your boyfriend outside and smoke. Wanna join us?" Her thick Minnesota accent was only slightly slurred. I glanced over to see Harold waiting by the back entrance that led to the outdoor smoking area, and he raised his eyebrows and tilted his head at me, as if to say, *let's go,* so when Metalhead threw her head back and downed her shot, I did as well.

That was a mistake. I wasn't sure how I could have missed the difference, but with the peppermint extract up my nose, it was hard to smell anything. A shot of Jameson was bad enough, but Harold's new drinking buddy had just given me a shot of *Malört.*

I ran to the bathroom to throw up.

God damn Malört. That shit was vile, and the woman who bought me the shot was evil, I decided. *She definitely deserved to get chomped on.*

I rinsed my mouth out with tap water and spit. No more water, no more alcohol, tonight. I wanted blood, and I was going to have to figure out how to do it. Harold probably already had his new bar buddy under his thrall outside. "He is a very bad teacher," I decided aloud, casting a furtive glance at the monster in the mirror above the sink who happened to be me. The realization didn't completely alter my feelings for him, whatever they might be, but it did complicate my current predicament. Behind me, in one of the bathroom stalls, I heard crying, and I turned around, years of being the mom friend in my social circle conditioning me to look for a girl in emotional distress, regardless of the way hunger was growling at my periphery.

"Hello?" I called out to the crying voice.

"I'm fine," sniffled the girl on the other side of the stall.

"You don't sound fine," I countered. "You need someone to call you a cab or get you a bottle of water?"

I heard the pulsing of the blood in her veins before the girl unlatched the toilet stall and stepped out, seemingly startled to see me. She appeared to be about my age or older—maybe the same age as the nonexistent Angela Mercer. "No one here ever seems to care," she sniffed.

"You come to the bar to cry a lot?" I raised an eyebrow.

"Not a lot, just like, I live just around the corner, and this is kind of my hang-out...but my shithead boyfriend just dumped me, and I knew he was going to do it, but, like..."

I sighed and pushed my hunger down deep, deep inside of me. "Do you want to talk about it?" I asked. The girl nodded, wiping her eyes with the frayed sleeves of her thermal undershirt. I handed her a paper towel and appraised my options. Feeding in a dive bar bathroom did not sound sanitary, whether or not I could actually still be affected by illness.

"Let's go outside." I waited while the girl from the bathroom grabbed her coat and scarf and bundled up before stepping out the back entrance Harold and his drinking buddy had exited just minutes before, out into the chill. Even with the towering space heaters cranked up, the smoking patio was not entirely pleasant.

"You're not cold?" the girl asked, eying my lack of overcoat and thin long-sleeve dress with vague suspicion, but she didn't even wait for an answer before launching into her sob story about her on-again, off-again boyfriend of several years. She'd just found out was some other woman's baby daddy, when he'd promised on a stack of Bibles last time that he wouldn't do it again...

"Again?" I feigned shock, but also, I knew the type. How many other drunk girls had I comforted under similar circumstances? Harold's eyes followed me as I led my new friend over to a seat underneath a space heater, and I couldn't quite tell what he was thinking. I turned my attention over the woman from the bathroom. There wasn't a lot of exposed skin on her neck, and the specifics of what I planned to do were a little sketchy. She rambled on.

"He's got like, four kids, all with different moms, and I know he's no good for me, but he keeps crying and begging to come back, and I can't say no."

I glanced over at Harold and the Malört Fiend, who had begun "necking" in the corner of the semi-covered outdoor space. "Serves her right," I glared, without a trace of jealousy, only halfway paying attention to my new friend's babbling. I moved in closer to her on the low bench under the heater, and I wrapped my arm around her shoulders, patting and rubbing the other girl's back as she sobbed, stealthily unwinding and moving the scarf aside just a little...

Oh, God. What was I doing?

She looked up for a moment across the patio at Harold and his thrall in the corner. "Ew. Get a room," she muttered, all loud sniffles and chattering teeth. "You don't smoke, do you?" she finally asked me.

Focus, Grace. Focus.

"No. I have other vices." I shook my head with a small smile, leaning in closer, both arms tight around the girl's shoulders. "You know," I said, moving in to whisper in her ear, "You absolutely deserve better than him."

Then I opened up my mouth and bit down on the only part of exposed flesh on the girl's neck that wasn't bundled up in layers of clothing. *I don't even know her name*, I thought, before the reality of my fangs sinking deep into the skin and the blood bubbling up from the wound wiped my mind clear of thought. Her blood wasn't red on my lips, it was white-hot, burning to ashes the paper-thin facade that remained of my human morality. Once I tasted the life flowing out of her veins, the world disappeared, and knew I would not be returning to it.

I'd found myself in the roar of her heartbeat, like an incoming tide racing toward land across my tongue, wiping the shoreline clean of sandcastles I'd once placed so much value in.

My lips formed a tight seal against the puncture wounds my fangs had cut, and I suckled as gently as I could; the blood flowed freely but wasn't a gushing fountain inside my mouth the way I'd imagined it would be, and the girl didn't scream, or fight, or try to get away. I held on tight and drank, swallowing mouthfuls of electric copper energy down my throat, losing track of time, and I was whole. I was perfect. I had survived for this, been transformed for this. I was exactly where I needed to be. There was nothing else.

I lost track of time. Harold's voice whispered in my ear, but he was so far away. "Cut your tongue a little on your fangs and lick the wounds clean. They'll heal quickly. We've gotta go."

I barely heard him.

It took an enormous effort I wasn't sure I had in me to stop, until I did. But I pulled away, sucking at the wound as it closed beneath my bloodied tongue, lapping at the exquisite sanguine substance still staining her neck. Harold put his hand on my shoulder, and I pulled back more with strained reluctance, somewhat horrified at the limpness of the two women we'd brought out to the patio. We were otherwise all alone for the moment, but someone else might step through the doors any second. "Did we kill them?" My voice was hoarse.

Harold shook his head. "They'll probably be all right. They usually come around in about sixty seconds, then you better be far away unless you want some 'splainin' tae do." He leaped over the wooden fence that surrounded the smoking deck, and I followed close behind him. It wasn't as difficult as it should have been for someone my height, I discovered, and I quickened my pace until I caught up with him as he walked down the alley between buildings, around to where we'd left the car.

"There is—*so much*—you could have told me before we actually got started," I reprimanded him, wiping a small amount of residual blood off my mouth with the back of my hand. He took my hand in his and licked it clean, and a slow, shuddering chill ran down my spine. A faint whisper of frost escaped my lips from my sharp exhale, stolen warmth fleeing off into the cold velvet night. My head swirled in darkness upon darkness, the whole world sharp and vivid where things had once been dull and muted, before I'd crossed that fateful line.

Like finally ripping a bandage off all at once, I was stripped bare, at last, of all the illusions I had clung to about myself, my altered nature, my capacity to act on instinct. My body knew who and what I was—had known, all along. And now I could not hide from the truth my mind knew as well. I was not captive to my hunger. There was freedom only in submitting to it. My whole body was quivering and *alive*. I had stolen life and made it my own. Her blood. My blood. *Mine.* My heart meekly attempted a weak staccato, and I placed my open palm across my breast, in love with the shallow rhythm echoing inside me.

We collapsed in the car together, and Harold only drove as far as the next vacant suburban parking lot before turning off the engine again.

Our black eyes met in the dark interior of the car, and I wanted him.

"Well, I didn't expect you tae wander off and find your own mark so quickly—I was planning tae share. Could you do that again?" he asked.

I nodded wordlessly, overwhelmed by too much feeling all at once, and not sure how to communicate any of the thoughts and emotions stirred up by what I had just experienced. Of all the points of no return I'd passed since becoming a vampire—the terrifying first drink of blood under the guidance of Calliope's hands, the first time I'd felt caught up in the bloodlust in the kitchen next to Harold, the first time I realized that someone had died to quench my thirst—this one seemed the biggest, and most damning yet. If I hadn't been damned before.

I'd actively chosen to do this, to take blood from a stranger whose name I didn't know, and never would, even though I would carry the memory of her face for the rest of my existence, I was certain of it. Worrying about the state of my soul seemed futile and perfunctory. Taking part of her life had connected me to life on a scale so vast, I could barely comprehend it. That didn't seem evil or morally wrong. My place in the world, and the path before me now, were clear.

My vestigial heartbeat slowed to a murmur, and stopped altogether as the blood high dissipated, and I did not want to die anymore. My thoughts slipped towards darkness, envisioning the thrill of conquest alongside him, my mouth and my tongue, my lips and my fangs exploring so many other pulsing veins hidden away in dark, secret spots beneath layers of clothing and skin. I would become a fine connoisseur of the pleasures of the flesh, and apex hunter in the night, and perhaps, eventually, a ruthless killer. I wanted it all, to go on like this for centuries, for forever—

And *that* was why, I told myself, it had to end. The longer I lived as a vampire, the more I wanted it. And now that I'd tasted live blood straight from the vein, it would be even harder for me to walk away. Sadness flooded over me the way her blood had washed over my waiting lips. I wanted to live.

I looked down at my pale hands as I spoke. "I didn't realize it would be so intuitive, when it came down to the moment of truth." I shook my head, a small smile stretching the corners of my mouth as I revisited the instant my fangs broke human skin. "I thought I'd overthink myself into a corner, end up trapped. But it was completely the opposite, Harold. I don't know if I'm more thrilled or horrified.

I didn't think it would be so easy...why did we wait so long? I could have done this weeks ago...a month ago, I'm sure."

I couldn't decipher the look on his face, but if I had to put money on it, I would have said he looked guilty. I could not have fathomed the depths of that guilt in that moment, however.

"You're nothing like I—you're a natural," he whispered, so softly I could barely hear the words, and he didn't directly answer my question. When he spoke again, his voice was low, and vulnerable, but clear. "It was my fault. I was afraid. Tae revisit a hell of my own making, and I...misjudged you."

Whatever answer I'd been expecting from him, it wasn't a confession, and I wasn't sure I understood; I think I shook my head. My body was still practically vibrating from the blood I'd taken from the strange woman's neck. "How do you keep yourself from doing that every single night?" I asked.

"Kindness is a luxury I recognize the value of investing in." He said softly, as if that explained things.

I shook my head; his answer didn't make sense. He sighed.

"Vagabonds and nomads don't have much of an existence outside the pursuit of blood. But they hunt and they kill as they please, as long at they're careful. And Community blood allocations come with too many complications. But black market human blood is expensive. It's hard tae come by. Suppliers can be unreliable. Getting caught is always a risk. I'm old enough now, and settled enough, and I've had enough time ta arrive at a place where I see the benefit in spending that money, in taking that risk..."

"Because if the blood I drink is removed from the source, if I don't bother heating it up...the distance it affords me is worth it. I don't enjoy being cruel. And it's hard tae get live blood without cruelty, sometimes." He shrugged, and his hand reached out for mine again, gripping me tightly, as though he was afraid to let go. He was shaking, I realized.

I was, too.

Harold drew a deep breath and continued. "So it's a choice I make. I've made different choices in the past. But I'm a craftsman. I've always been a craftsman. I was a part-time smithy before I signed up with the Royal Navy, a carpenter when

I was in service, and I was a smithy again before I was turned. When I'm settled, I get tae make things and tinker and...I like doing that." He smiled at me like he had when he'd soldered the broken lampshades, the way I'd seen him smile to himself tightening nuts and bolts on the engine parts in the kitchen, the screwed up face of concentration he made when he mended his clothes, and I think I started to understand.

"You do beautiful work..." I looked over at him, trying not to let my guilt, or my regret over the loss of the swords, creep into my voice. "I'm sorry about the fires. I never meant any of this to happen. You'll set up shop again someday?"

"Someday," he agreed. "I'm not worried about the stuff right now. It's just things...you're more important."

I didn't know how to respond to that. "You still don't think Calliope had anything to do with either of the fires?"

"...No." His head shook with conviction. "The tracking device was absolution."

I peered at him, uncertain I agreed with his assessment. "What are you going to do about her? And Gavin? What about Marie?"

"I don't know yet."

"Then—?"

"I have a lot of thoughts in my head, kettlen. I'll let you know when I'm ready tae give voice to them."

Harold fired up the engine again and took off as soon as the windows were defrosted. "Let's go figure out where we're going ta stay for the immediate future." He tossed his most recently acquired burner phone onto my lap. "Find a suite at a nice hotel. Nothing too ostentatious, unless that's what you really want. But no more cheap motel rooms."

"No more getting arrested, then." I smirked and began scrolling through the online options.

"You're the one the one with a criminal record," he reminded me, with a smile of his own.

"*Alleged* criminal record. I never got my court date."

His laugh was short, but genuine. "I have done things that ought tae have seen me hanged. So let's both stay out of trouble while we're back in town, all right?"

"I'm going to save Becca and kill Gavin."

"Yes, but I'm going tae need you tae do that as quietly as possible."

"And then—?"

"First, I want tae finish what we started last night." He punched the car into gear and continued on, closer to the city. The blood I'd just stolen continued singing in my veins.

Chapter Twenty-Six

A Communion in Crimson

I FOUND A SUITE at a boutique hotel in an older brick building that was converted from a former warehouse in a rapidly gentrifying neighborhood, near the Loop. It wasn't too far from Becca's apartment or Calliope's penthouse, but not so close that we ran the risk of being accidentally discovered. The online reviews cautioned that the bedrooms in the mid-level suites tended not to have windows, due to the layout of the conversion—the perfect nest for two vampires. Harold nodded when I mentioned the property, as if he were already familiar with it, but offered no further information.

There was no desperate race from the sun to get inside the room this time, no quaking fear of death by daylight spurring us on. Our late-night check-in was quietly and efficiently handled by the front desk staff. Our footfalls were almost in tandem as we walked down the dimmed hotel corridors toward our assigned suite. Where we walked, power-saving motion detector lights flickered on, then off again, as we passed by rooms filled with sleeping tourists and travelers and trysting lovers. A small dog barked with enormous ferocity that far outstripped its diminutive size from inside one of the closed doors we passed, loudly alerting "danger! Danger!" to anyone awake enough to hear, but no one did more than stir at the yapping toy breed—possibly the only living creature in the vicinity to know that two vampires were nearby. Its warning went unheeded.

Harold opened the door to our rooms for me with almost exaggerated flair, and I swept inside with a half-swirl, anticipation making me giddy as I located the controls for the electronic shades that opened and closed the curtains on the floor-to-ceiling windows in the suite's sitting room and drew them shut, one by one.

I was acutely aware of his eyes on my body as I secured the suite from the sun that would eventually flood the room otherwise; gooseflesh raised the tiny hairs on my arms and back of my neck.

I wanted this. I had never been more certain of anything in my life.

When I turned around, he was standing inches away, and we faced each other for what might have been a heartbeat; his hand reached out to caress my face. "Are you sure—?" He asked. There was uncertainty in his voice.

I parted my lips in breathless anticipation, swallowed hard, and nodded. "I'm no virgin, Harold. I've wanted you since the night after the concert. The bloodlust wasn't meaningless. Not for me," I whispered, my voice hoarse and strained with desire. I leaned my face into the caress of his cool hand on my cheek. My body thrummed with excitement.

"I didn't want tae—tae take advantage." He cleared his throat. "Not of you, or the situation. But the first time I touched you, that very first night, I felt—"

"Shut up and kiss me already."

Our mouths and teeth and fingers connected with a force that knocked the wind out of me, but not for long. My hands found their way to his shoulders this time, pushing him against the wall with forcefulness I'd never been empowered to tap into before. I kissed Harold Laing madly, standing on my tiptoes, leaning my entire body weight against him. His fangs were not gentle when they tore into my lips this time, and I was shocked by how much I liked it when he bit me. I felt the blood start to drip down my chin, and I paused—for only a moment—to untie the dress I was wearing.

I neatly laid the dress over the back of an ornate armchair, and he let out a small, endearing laugh, then grabbed me by the arms and resumed kissing me. This time, when I reached out to undo the belt buckle on his pants, my fingers were far more sure of themselves, and I pulled down his pants and pushed up the top of his ruined T-shirt, leaving a ravaged trail of bloody kisses down his torso.

I sank to my knees, freeing his erection for the constraints of his thin cotton boxers. He was uncut, I realized, more surprised that I hadn't thought to anticipate that detail than I was at the presence of his intact foreskin. I'd never been with an uncircumcised man before, but I was confident in my abilities. I brought his pale member into my mouth, carefully shielding the sensitive skin of his shaft from my sharpened teeth. There was exquisite pain, and blood, where my fangs tore into my own lips, and this excited me, as I let my tongue and throat explore the length and girth of his sex, taking in as much of him as I could. He gasped and shuddered, leaning back against the wall, and then he moaned, low and guttural and inhuman.

He was looking at me when I glanced up at him, and when our eyes met I think we were both taken aback by my boldness. His hands shook when he reached down to stroke my hair as my mouth stroked his cock and hummed. Blood coated my tongue and escaped the corners of my mouth and I did not care. I could have kept going. It wasn't only my own blood that I tasted, and it made sense, of course, that there would be trace amounts of his blood in the salty fluid that escaped from his swollen, exposed tip. There'd been traces of blood in my tears, after all. We were creatures of blood, and pain, and pleasure.

Despite my own desire to keep tasting him, after what seemed like a very short amount of time, he grabbed me roughly by the back of the hair, begging, pleading for me to stop.

I was terrified that I'd done something wrong, when I pulled away, but there was a wicked glint in his eyes as he attempted to compose himself. "I dunna wan' tae embarrass mysel'...and *zounds*, Grace..." His voice was almost a whisper as he looked up at the ceiling. "'Tis been a while. Get on the bed."

Zounds. I wanted to giggle, feeling very pleased with myself. It wasn't every night that I sucked a man off so good, he forgot what century's slang to use. I obliged his request instead of giggling, though, and scrambled through the bedroom door, up onto the expansive king-sized mattress, watching him.

He moved so quickly to untie his boots that he snapped a lace in the process, but he ignored the momentary impediment with a quick shake of his fingers, before stepping out of his trousers and boxers. He left them where they fell on the floor just outside the bedroom door, and approached me as I lay back against the pillows.

I was already well-familiar with his muscular arms, and I'd been driven to distraction by the sight of his naked torso once already, but I'd seen him at a distance, then. I hadn't wanted to look. Now, my eyes drank in every inch of him, shocked that I had ever once told myself that he wasn't handsome. Harold Laing was rugged, underneath his clothes. There were more scars scattered across his body than I'd expected—softened by his turning, perhaps, but still there. Long, ragged white lines, even paler than his improbably pale flesh, criss-crossed his back, where he'd been whipped at least once, and badly. An almost-indiscernible horizontal line bisected his middle from side to side, as though he'd been cut open, and survived. He bore the faint evidence of twenty-five years engaged in hard manual labor well. He was strong and wiry and lean, and maybe it was his relatively small stature that made it seem so, but the erection I'd only stopped pleasuring with my mouth moments before was far larger than I'd anticipated.

There was tantalizing promise in his brazen smirk, and I self-corrected every doubt I'd ever had about his skill and experience as a lover. Maybe at one point in my life, I would have felt jealous, or insecure, of the two hundred years of "options" he'd had before me, but my own arousal and want and need were too overpowering for me to care. I wanted to to sear every one of his scars and markings into memory.

"You have tattoos..." I observed, not meaning to express my surprise out loud, but my eyes were drawn to the echoes of crude line art and symbols collected across his body. The outline of a ship with full masts occupied his left side, near his hip. A line of rope wound a sinuous spiral around his right leg, before abruptly cutting off, just above the knee. Here and there were dotted a nautical compass, a cross, and a crown. High up on the same shoulder as the faint smallpox vaccine scar he'd been so proud to show me I could detect the even fainter outline of what might have been a primrose entwined with thistle lingered, though very little of the original ink remained. He hadn't rolled his shirt sleeve up high enough for me to see it, that night in the kitchen. All of his tattoos, in fact, were coarse and faded, and a few seemed to be missing parts, like the rope that wrapped around his right leg. His lower legs, and his arms below the shoulder, were noticeably absent any ornamentation.

"Not as many as I used tae." He tilted his head to the side and rubbed his forearm almost absentmindedly. "I told you, I was a sailor...a man gets bored at sea, finds ways tae pass the time. And you?"

I shook my head. No, I didn't have tattoos. I'd always been too afraid of change.

He knelt over me, his eyes following the curves of my own flesh, fingers tracing lightly across my skin. After the euphoric agony of our violent kisses, the softness of his caress was almost unbearable. "I don't know..." he shook his head with feigned puzzlement, slipping a finger under the straps of the bra I still wore. "I canna see all of you now, can I?"

I hastily unlatched the garment and set it aside on the nightstand, as Harold started tugging at my other undergarments—pulling down my winter tights and panties, scattering my clothing around the room. I was too turned on to even care, and spread my legs beneath him, an invitation to what I assumed was the natural progression of events, but Harold didn't seem to be in a hurry.

"No. Not yet." He didn't say the words aloud, didn't have to, as he leaned over and inserted his fingers into my slick wetness, surveying my body from above with a hunger that went far beyond bloodlust.

My vocabulary disintegrated into swear words.

With every thrust of his digits, we could both hear how absolutely soaked I was, and I writhed and moaned as he curled his fingers inside me, unable to take my eyes off his face. His eyes were black in the darkness of the bedroom, his fangs fully extended, lips drawn back in a predator's grin that should have been terrifying, but a delicious, sinful pleasure coiled tight inside me. Dark blood—some of it surely mine—pooled from his open mouth and dripped down his chin, splattering onto my breasts, and I grabbed at my tits to smear the blood between them, a crimson film bathing my flesh. I think I heard myself call his name, or maybe it was only on my head—my mouth was open wide and bloodied as well, fangs aching to bite down, to break skin, to rip and tear and drink and devour. My hip buckled as he inserted a third finger inside me.

*Jesus **fuck**, Harold...*

Maybe he did hear me, because he leaned in ever closer and kissed me again, thrusting his tongue against mine in time to the thrusting of his fingers, the pad of his thumb pressed hard around my clit. The intensity of the pleasure sent shock-waves through my body as slowly, his mouth and his fangs and his tongue began to trace their way down my chin toward my jawline.

I tensed for a moment as he brushed past my carotid artery, but his voice was soothing and low when he murmured, "No, no, it's all right, I know..." and his lips were at the hollow of my throat when he almost purred, "Is this all right?"

"Yes," I breathed out, trusting him, and his mouth went lower, to the top of my breasts, where he paused and asked again,

"Is this all right?"

I moaned and nodded, so breathless I'd forgotten how to breathe, I couldn't have made the words if I tried. He licked away the smeared blood from my breasts, still propping himself up on one arm, still continuing his expert fingering with his other hand between my legs.

He put his mouth over my breast and paused there, the tips of his fangs pressed gently against the skin around my nipple, his tongue teasing the firm nub, but he did not bite down completely. He waited.

"Yes!" I gasped, remembering how my lungs worked again, and he bit down. The razor tips of his elongated teeth punctured and tore at my breast, and the sharp pain was both violent and exquisite as he suckled and lapped at the blood—*my blood, the blood I stole.* I wanted to reach down and stroke him, but my hands were balled into fists as I grabbed at the bedding beneath us, and I groaned, inching closer to a climax unlike any I had ever known. Whether by years of practice or some vampiric intuition I did not yet possess, or both, he slowed the intensity of his thrusting fingers, before withdrawing his hand from between my legs altogether.

His mouth moved on to my other breast, and he paused again, waiting for my breathless, barely audible "yes" before he bit down, and fed from me a second time. Now that his fingers were freed from the task of pleasuring my cunt, he brought his hand up to my open mouth and nicked his index finger against my fangs, flooding my mouth with the taste of his blood mixed with my own wetness.

"Oh God, yes, please..." He lifted his mouth from my breast and encouraged me to clamp down on his fingers. It felt good to bite, to taste the bloom of rust and copper on my tongue, and I sucked and moaned and begged him for more. I needed more blood, his blood, filling my mouth and flowing down my open throat.

He moved his lips further down my torso then, tongue caressing my soft belly in a way I would have been mortified to have allowed a lover to do before, but all shame about my body had gone away, vanquished along with the rest of my humanity, and I did not miss the shame. I gasped "yes," and "Yes," and "YES," each time he ask for permission before biting me. He pulled his bloodied fingers out of my mouth and sucked away the residual crimson with his own tongue, never breaking eye contact with me. I could drown forever in his pitch-black eyes, losing whatever remained of myself before I was turned.

Who was Grace Cordero?

She was dead. I was an amalgamation of blood and darkness. Pain was pleasure. I trembled and quaked as he rearranged his position on top of me, placing one hand on the mattress on either side of my hips and giving me one last, "is this...?"

And I said yes, yes, yes, over and over again as he went down on me, tongue prodding and licking and pressing along the length of my opening and sucking at my clit. Vampires, I remembered, did not need to breathe, and I arched my back against the mattress and surrendered to the climax building inside of me, hooking my legs over his shoulders. He sensed it the moment I came, I was certain of it, and he stopped what he'd been doing, took a deep shuddering breath, and when his lungs were full again, he asked me, "Grace...?"

"I swear to God, Harold, you can do whatever you want to me—" I panted, but whatever words I was about to say next were obliterated when he moved his mouth over to the side of my sex, and bit down—hard—into my femoral artery. I felt my blood gush from the wound; knew this would have been a death blow if I had been mortal. I wondered, through the vague fog of post-orgasmic bliss, if he was trying to kill me now, and I remembered what he'd said about vampires dying from too much blood loss.

*Hell of a way to go, after all this...*my mind wandered, but my lips mouthed the words, barely audible, "Baby, you'd better give some of that back."

I felt his tongue press up against the wounds he'd made to staunch the flow of blood, his cool, coarse fingers gently running over the sensitive places on me he'd just absolutely destroyed. He brought his head out from between my legs with a final, gentle kiss to the top of my pubic bone, and rose up, kneeling on the bed and grinning at me, blood trickling from the corners of his mouth. Just a few nights before, he'd been hiding his fangs from me as we fed together in the kitchen of his house in the suburbs, shielding me from any reminders of our shared monstrous nature, but he wasn't holding back now. He was reveling in what he was—what I was, alongside him—and I realized, with a comforting awareness, that I was no longer afraid, or ashamed, of what I had become. There was peace in the vivid clarity of blood-soaked darkness, peace in no longer loathing myself.

"You'll get your turn," he told me, holding my face in his hand, and I trusted the promise of blood in his voice. "But I'm going tae fuck you first."

And that's when I—

"...do we need a condom?" My voice was small and embarrassingly self-conscious. *Fuck.* He pulled his hand away, and I felt like an idiot again. *Why hadn't I thought of this sooner?*

"I. Um. Is that important tae you?"

If my life had a soundtrack, this moment would have been augmented by the sound of a record scratch.

"I mean, I've just um...seen the movies, and I don't want to—I mean, I don't know, we haven't talked about this part yet, and..."

"Your body can't get pregnant, and, um. We don't...I mean, our bodies aren't...there aren't any vampire, um, diseases," Harold tried to reassure me, panting. "But I've worn condoms before and...if that's what you want, we can call down to the front desk and..."

"No, I mean, it's okay, I've just never had unprotected sex before, and I guess..." I suppose it made sense, given my origins, to be at least a little bit concerned about unplanned vampire babies, and in my defense, the one in the movie had been super creepy. But still. I propped myself up a bit and tried to quell my swirling panic. The inconvenience of this particular upswell of anxiety was particularly unfair.

"Do you want me tae stop?"

"No! No, please, please keep going, I want this, I really do, I just..." I was babbling, embarrassed, frustrated, and overwhelmed. *No man had ever done that to me with his tongue like that before...*

He leaned in and kissed me on the lips, gently, running his fingers through my hair, and I relaxed a little, melting back into the pillows. "I'm a bit nervous, too, if that helps," he whispered in my ear. "I haven't been with anyone like this in...a while." A pause. "I'll stop if you want, but you were delicious." There was a faint thud in his neck where his pulse should have been, and my fingertips traced the lines of his throat.

"I'm sorry I ruined the moment..." I whispered back at him.

He reached out for my hand and guided it toward his cock, which was firm and erect between my fingers, and—in spite of myself—I did giggle, finally.

"Shall we continue?" He exhaled, and I nodded, planting another kiss on his lips as he finally entered me completely, and I rallied from my earlier orgasm and blood loss to fully engage my body with his, thrusting my hips beneath him. Just as I'd suspected, our bodies fit together and flowed in time with an easy rhythm that went beyond the physical. So much of our compatibility came down to chemistry. This—us—we were a good match for each other, and I felt the affinity in my blood.

I threw my arms around him, lips grazing his shoulder, and asked, with a shaking voice, "...may I?"

He groaned "yes," and I bit down, slowly; an eternity passed in the instant before my fangs pierced the skin, his blood filling up my mouth as my nails scratched scarlet rivers down his back, and I couldn't tell where his body ended and mine began. Our arms wrapped tight around each other, completely entwined as we fucked and convulsed and bled all over. His blood revived me, and it was as easy to discern his own impending orgasm as my awareness of my own had been—his blood told the story of his looming climax on my tongue, and I stopped thrusting along with his hips, prompting him to slow down long enough to ask if something else was wrong. I shook my head.

"I want to be on top when you finish," I murmured in his ear, and we rolled over together on the bed.

"Absolutely," he deferred, gasping, as I rearranged myself and began sliding up and down on his cock, controlling the speed and the depth and the angle of each thrust. I could feel a second climax of my own building, each thrust bringing both of us closer to the edge. I didn't need to be breathing so deeply, but I found myself doing so out of habit, inhaling the scent of our blood and sex and skin, tasting the air around us on my tongue. Every sensation was heightened to the extreme; I could see the sound of his gasps and hear the color of his blood on my skin, I could taste the sensation of his hands grabbing into the flesh of my hips and grinding my body on top of his; my hands reached down toward his to interlace our fingers in the last intensifying momentum of our savagery.

I wanted to say, "I love you," but I couldn't form the words. I loved him, though. I loved him, I loved him, I loved him.

He called out my name, moaning, and begged me to bite him again, stretching out and exposing his neck to me. "Please..." he gasped. "I want my blood in your veins..."

I bit down on his neck, harder than I'd bit the girl's neck at the bar earlier, and where I hadn't hit any major arteries before, this time I did, and the blood spurted out of the holes my fangs made on Harold's neck with a surprising amount of force for a guy with no heartbeat. I came a second time with a shuddering, violent intensity as I swallowed, gulping mouthfuls of the cold electric coppery fire, messily and carelessly consuming him, as he had consumed me, and I felt him come inside me only moments later. I pressed my tongue against the holes I had torn open on his throat, and the wounds began to heal, and I collapsed, rolling off of him finally and resting against his side. My fangs retracted, and my own cuts and scratches began to heal, the pain and the pleasure receding in slow, gentle waves; a tide flowing back to a dark and violent sea, and I was left spent, my head spinning at the horror of what I had just done, and enjoyed. I shuddered, too many swirling images and thoughts and sensations to sort out. Slowly, the overwhelm lapped away. Visions began to coalesce.

Calliope turned and looked at me, backlit by an inferno, and her face was monstrous, eyes black, blood dripping down her chin. I gasped.

"Grace?" I heard Harold call my name, but I was pulled back into another vision before I could react to his voice. I was drowning; the waves were too high; there wasn't anything solid to hold on to, and the ship was nowhere in sight. The salt spray burned in my eyes and my lungs, I couldn't go on for much longer...

Focus, Grace...

Calliope pulled Harold aside down a dark, wood-paneled hallway, whispering. Her hair was long, flaxen strands done up in braids that wrapped around her head;

she wore a functional dark brown linen dress that was almost black, and a blue apron pinned on top of it. "I think they sleep in the coffins." She lowered her voice at him, pointing to a locked door. She dangled a set of keys out of her pocket.

"You read too many novels." Harold laughed, then stopped when Calliope made a face. "What'll your Daa think if he finds out you've been going through guest rooms while they're away, huh?"

She straightened herself with an imperiousness that was the only part of Calliope Jones that I truly recognized. "*Ay, Dios mio*...My father is a drunkard, Blacksmith. You and I both know who runs this inn. So the question is, how will my father know, if no one tells him?" She opened the door as quietly as she could, and Harold peeked inside the darkened interior. The windows were covered with dark cloth; it was almost impossible to see inside the dim. On the floor, next to the empty beds, were three long wooden boxes.

"Trunks, not coffins...you imagine too much, Miss Jones..."

My entire body convulsed, pulling out of the memory, and I tried to wipe the taste of his blood from my lips, but I was too far gone in the visions and hallucinations now.

"You were friends...when you were mortal," I marveled, shaking the residual intensity of the vision away. I could smell the soap coming up from the clothes she wore; the scent of lemon trees and soot and ash. "Who was sleeping in the coffins?"

"I think you know..." Harold reached out to hold me, but I had no experience or perspective to help me process the disorienting experience of reliving Harold's memories. They were jarring, fragmented, out of order, crashing over me one after another with no relief. He'd wanted me to drink his blood. Had he wanted me to know...all of this?

The sun overhead was searing, blinding white, but Harold bobbed in the waves, draped over a small wooden raft, parched and blistered and mortal. Birds swirled in the air overhead, swooping and calling the alarm.

The beat of a wooden oar and flap of sails. Voices calling out in a language he did not understand, hand reaching out to pull him aboard, *agua, agua...*

When Harold opened his eyes again, there was a priest beside him, kind eyes and a tired voice. His country had seen so much carnage, and yet...he was soft, to a stranger. "You must rest. There is an Englishman and his daughter with an inn, some miles inland from here. You will be safe there. You are safe now. You must sleep, rest..."

"Stay with me, Grace." Harold's voice seemed miles away. "Focus on my voice. You had too much of my blood, that's all..."

I nodded, squeezing onto his hand. "Is this normal?" I asked.

Harold wrapped his arms around me tighter. "It's been a long time since I made love tae another vampire for the first time. I'd forgotten about..." He shook his head as though he were trying to dislodge intrusive thoughts of his own. "I'm...I'm in your blood, too. It's a lot. Just let it pass, I'm right here..."

But I didn't want Harold Laing in my blood and deepest secrets any more than I wanted to be inside of his.

"Harold, how...?" And I was spiraling through his memories again, and I didn't feel safe at all. Somewhere, someone was screaming.

⸺◆O◆⸺

CHAPTER TWENTY-SEVEN

REVELATIONS OF BLOOD

"I don't see why you think I should take on a half-drowned sailor. He looks like a rat. I've got a business to run, and my father...Padre, my father, means well, but we cannot afford—" Harold's eyes fluttered open as Calliope's voice rose out of the darkness. He was lying in the back of a cart, the sky overhead an impossible cerulean blue. The earth smelled of pine, and citrus, and sage. Coins in a leather purse rattled.

"He is your countryman. He speaks your English language."

"He's Scottish."

"Do as the Good Samaritan, child. This is the Lord's command."

Calliope sighed. Harold could hear her counting the coins. "Maria! Francisco! *Ven aquí!*"

Shouting orders. More hands. A bed. Clean linens. A room he would not leave for many months.

"...You nearly died." Calliope's voice was frank, almost bored. Sunlight poured through the open windows, and the breeze was fresh. "Not many people recover from pneumonia like that. I think you must have inhaled half the ocean. But you're going to get better, now. So. We should talk about your future..." She held a bowl of soup for him to eat. There were pieces of meat in the soup today. That was an improvement. For months he'd been given little more than broth. His hands still shook, holding the spoon...

...his hands shook, holding the small child in his arms; everything around him was midnight black and flames, and a terrible, delirious hunger was rising up inside of him. His face hurt; pain in his teeth and the roof of his mouth, radiating down his neck. Something had happened to them. *What happened to us?* The little boy screamed and writhed in terror, begging for his mamma, screaming out no, no, *por favor*...his mother's glassy dead eyes stared back at Harold from the fountain in the village square; there were so many corpses in the water that the flow rushed crimson red, and he could smell the blood, needed the blood, needed to tear and gnash at the tender flesh until the blood pooled into his mouth, hot and alive and...*oh, God*...arterial blood splattered his face and sprayed the air around him with the scent of rust and salt, and the child stopped screaming, dropped limply from Harold's arms. He needed to find more.

"I think they sleep in the coffins..." Calliope's voice reverberated.

Reality dissolved around me again. I was back in the sunlit room with Harold and Calliope, her crown of flaxen braids a halo that seemed almost to glow against the light from the window.

"...I think, since I saved your life, that you should work off your debt here at the inn. We've need of another stable boy, and if you're as good a carpenter as you say you are, even better. My father is often incapacitated from the injuries he sustained fighting for the resistance..."

The sun and the breeze and the soup were good. Looking out the window, far away on the rocky hillside, sheep grazed. At the very least, Harold knew how to wrangle and shear sheep. He could find work in southern Spain. Why not...stay here a while? The war was over; that trouble back on the ship was behind him. Napoleon was off to isolated St. Helena, wherever that was. And Calliope Jones was as beautiful as a painted angel in a chapel triptych. Even if that was idolatrous.

"Calliope Jones has saved my life...more than once, Grace."

I gasped. "Were you in love with her?" I asked Harold.

"I thought I was," he admitted, his voice quiet and strained. "Can you blame me?"

"She was so beautiful…"

"Still is, I suppose. She's never had trouble finding admirers."

"But you don't love her. Anymore."

"It's not like that. There was no room for that, after what happened."

"When you killed the little boy?"

"Do you hate me for that?"

"I don't…I don't understand what happened." I twisted my hands in the blood-soaked bedsheets, trying to anchor myself to reality. The blood memories had been so vivid…

I wasn't sure where Harold's mind was wandering, but he tried to answer my questions. Maybe he was grateful for the distraction from my own vivid traumas bubbling up in his head. I didn't want to think about what he was experiencing though my blood.

"Calliope Jones was the most beautiful girl I'd ever seen in my life up to that point. I thought, her father thought…it might have been a good match. She ran the inn, and I spent six months working for Calliope and her father, mucking stables, fixing the leaks in the roof, building a new fence…then they discovered that I could shoe horses, mend tin and copper pots, sharpen iron tools…The south of Spain was far away from things I wanted to leave behind. It could have been a nice life…" his hands traced the outline of my body as he spoke. I knew he wasn't thinking about me, but I wanted him to. Wanted to inhale the scent of our blood on his skin, anchor myself in his arms, forget about the things that were lurking in those long wooden boxes in the darkened room in the inn. But I couldn't shake the memories.

"Calliope had different plans, didn't she?"

"Calliope always has her own plans."

⸺◆⸺

"If you're going to insist on coming round and prattling on while I've work to do, then you can work as well, Blacksmith."

"Ay ay ay, Cal, my back is breaking. Master Santiago had me squatting with barrels of nails yesterday."

"The floors aren't going to scrub themselves. You can have my attention while you work." They spoke English to each other. It felt like their own private language; the only link they had to a world that he sometimes forgot existed at all. Calliope's English was excellent for someone who left Bath when she was three. She was a reader, though. One of those girls. Sometimes, on fine days, he'd catch her high up in the crook of the tree outside the inn, lost in some lurid story about ghosts or other nonsense. Sometimes in the winter, by the fireside, she read parts of her favorite books to him out loud. She liked stories about vengeance better than love stories. Harold had thought all girls liked love stories, before Calliope.

"There's a bookseller in Malaga who carries volumes by British writers, I've heard." They scrubbed the floors in tandem, and it didn't take long until they were clean. "And there's going tae be a fair in Malaga in a fortnight."

"And what am I supposed to do with this information?" Calliope stood up and arched her back; Harold felt a twinge of guilt for complaining about Master Santiago and his barrels of nails. Even with help from Maria and Francisco, she still put in hours of manual labor every day. Her arms and shoulders were strong from wrangling mattresses and fighting with the pump at the well. Not for the first time, Harold felt himself blush in her presence and look away. He'd been imagining what it might be like to playfully wrestle with those strong arms, and then...

"Master Santiago has promised tae give me the day off, and some money." He cleared his throat, trying to shake away the scandalous mental image. "We could make it there and back in a day if your father will let us use the horse and cart."

"So...do you want to go to the fair with me, or with my father's horse and cart?" She tucked an errant strand of pale blonde hair behind her ear before crossing those arms in front of her chest. She seemed impatient.

Get on with it, Blacksmith...

She'd taken to calling him "Blacksmith" since beginning his apprenticeship with Master Santiago, almost five years gone. Sometimes, Harold wondered if she even remembered his name anymore.

"I thought..."

"I don't know if it's safe to travel," Calliope interrupted. "I heard there was a murder at a farmhouse, not far from here. Whole family slaughtered. Highwaymen, I suppose…"

"All that trouble tae restore the monarchy, and what do the people get? A government that still doesn't give a damn about the ones who are starving." In the blood-memory, Harold's voice scoffed, and was bitter. "I'll bring swords and pistols then, Cal. I can protect you from banditos. I'll buy you a pretty hat, and a new book, if you'll go to the fair with me."

She didn't look entirely convinced. "Perhaps. *Maybe*, Blacksmith. Ask me again tomorrow."

But the strangers arrived in the village late that night. Three brothers, Calliope said, although they didn't look anything alike. They stayed in their rooms all day, and at night, they ate no food. They drank no wine.

"Blacksmith. They say you are the final pupil of Master Augustus Santiago de Martinez. Is that so?" The voice behind him, at the entrance to the forge, had an eerie quality to it that Harold could not place. He jumped.

"I did not mean to frighten you."

"Nae, it's not a problem, I just…wasn't expecting any visitors so late." He'd been planning to head over to the inn for a glass of wine or two with Calliope's father, if the man was still coherent, but the time had gotten away from Harold again. His apprenticeship was drawing to a close, and the sun had gone down while he finished up some of the pieces he'd been working on as part of his final project. The young man standing in the doorway was tall and handsome, with long dark hair pulled back in a ponytail, and fine clothing that didn't seem to fit him well—as though each piece of attire had been made for another man's body. He was a bit gaudy and overdressed, like a peacock.

"I have heard great things about the work of Master Santiago…to be his last student, that is quite the honor, no?"

Harold shrugged, uncertain around this strange man. His accent wasn't Spanish or French or German, so far as he could place it. Italian, maybe. He'd only ever met one Italian. And she…she did not act like this man. "I think Santiago was bored in retirement. He needed someone tae yell at. And me, I've been yelled at my entire life, so it's an acceptable arrangement for both of us."

"Dionisio Miguel de Mateos." The man stepped into the forge with a flourish, extending his hand. When his fingers grasped Harold's, they were cool, pallid to the touch, despite the summer warmth, and the heat from the forge. Harold's sense of uneasiness around him grew. There was something almost hostile about the strange man...this Dionisio. "I am a collector of fine blades myself. Perhaps you can tell me something of this one?"

He unsheathed a small sword, and handed it to Harold to examine. The fine engraving was instantly familiar.

"This is one of Santiago's pieces, that's his mark on the blade there, but...I've never seen one in this style before. Were did you get it?"

"It has been in my possession, in my family's possession, for a very long time. I believe it was forged around the year seventeen seventy?"

Harold examined the blade intently. "That would be an early piece, true that. I've not had a chance tae study much of his early work. The master has gone home for the evening, but if you want, I can try tae wake him. I'm sure he would be interested tae see—"

"No." Dionisio dismissed the idea with a wave of his hand. "I want to purchase an item from his final pupil, as a sort of companion to this blade."

Ah. That was the reason for the visit. "Well, I canna help you, I'm afraid. The terms of my contract with Master Santiago mean that I cannot sell work of my own until he releases me on my own merits, and he hasn't been terribly approving of my recent work, so..." Harold had been made to melt down three swords in the last week alone. The closer he got to the end of his five-year apprenticeship, the less Santiago seemed to consider his work worthy of even existing. It was discouraging. Harold's eyes flitted past the stranger to the door, and he wondered if Señor Jones was still waiting for him at the inn, or if he would arrive to find him once again in a wine-soaked stupor. He'd wanted to ask Señor Jones about borrowing his cart and taking Calliope to Malaga for the fair.

Dionisio looked up from examining a long sword Harold was almost proud of. If Santiago approved it, Harold wanted to purchase some semi-precious stones from a dealer in Malaga for the hilt...garnets, maybe. Deep red stones for the blood of an enemy. It seemed poetic.

"I have faith in your abilities, Blacksmith. I can wait for your Master to release you...it will not be long now."

Harold didn't like the way Dionisio said that.

"I think they sleep in the coffins."

"I heard there was a murder in a farmhouse not far from here. Whole family slaughtered. Highwaymen, I suppose."

"Did you hear? There's some sort of disease taking down livestock in the hills." Calliope put a glass of wine down in front of him, a worried expression furrowing her brows. "The last thing this region needs is another reason to panic. My father's drunk, by the way. You should have gotten here earlier."

"Miss Jones, why is everything a looming disaster with you? Plagues and coffins and murders...maybe you should read happier books or...I don't know. Don't most girls your age do needlepoint?"

She laughed, sharp and bitter. "Most women my age in the village have babies to keep them entertained."

"And you? You don't want bairns of your own?"

"I'd need a husband first."

"Well, aboot dat—?"

"It's such a shame that my father is too drunk every night when you stop by for conversation. I'm certain he really does intend to follow up on whatever it is the two of you were planning to talk about. It's just the old injuries, you know?" She squared her shoulders, and Harold peered at the pitcher of wine in her hands.

"Cal..."

"The men in the room upstairs sleep inside coffins during the day. I'm certain of it. And the sheep and cows didn't start dying until after they arrived. And Dolores, *en la farmacia*, says that there is an increase in women and girls asking for iron syrup to treat chlorosis. Don't you think that's odd?"

"I know that you and your father saw a lot of awful things, during the occupation…"

"Harold, please. I'm perfectly sensible. I've been running this inn on my own since I was sixteen. If you're going to imply that I'm somehow incompetent—"

"Nae! Never!" *She'd said his name…well, close enough.*

"Goodnight, Blacksmith."

In the morning, Harold found four small garnets in an envelope on his workbench in the forge, with a note. "Quick, tell me what it says before Master Santiago finds out that I'm not working." He was out of breath when he found Calliope overseeing laundry at the back of the inn.

"Blacksmith, for the love of—" her sharp exasperation faded to pity, which was worse, and made the heat rise up in his cheeks. "We've got to take care of your reading problem."

"I'm fine with printed stuff, usually. Mostly. But handwriting is different. Tell me what the note says, Cal. Please. Who left the garnets?"

"Dionisio Miguel de Mateos wishes that you would use these stones in your final project, which he will purchase from you at a fair price at your Master's earliest allowance. He also cautions you not to mention him to your Master. That's it. That's the note." She handed the paper back to Harold and returned to her laundry delegation. "Francisco! Be careful with the lye! You could burn yourself!"

The sword cut through Harold's belly, and he screamed, just once, high pitched and terrified, before the demon's teeth were at his throat, and in between the sucking sounds of rending flesh, he could feel the soft tissue of his entrails sliding out of the opening in his abdomen; he'd seen a man get disemboweled by a bullet, once, back on the ship. The injury sliced clean across the doomed man's midsection, and the injured sailor held his hand up to his gut to keep the intestines in place while screaming that he only needed stitches, someone get the doctor—he bled out before he could be carried below deck. Harold's vision grew blurry; he saw the face of the man who had just killed Calliope laughing like the Devil himself…

"I think they sleep in the coffins."

"I heard there was a murder in a farmhouse not far from here. Whole family slaughtered. Highwaymen, I suppose."

"Did you hear? There's some sort of disease taking down livestock in the hills."

"Blacksmith, how much longer before your master agrees that your work is as good as we both know that it is?" Dionisio lingered in the doorway of the forge, as close to the shadows as possible. Harold only ever saw him at night, when he was working late, trying to complete his master collection. The sword with the garnets in the hilt was almost perfect.

"Perhaps this week, Señor. Master Santiago is not well. I do not think he will put off releasing me much longer."

Dionisio made a dismissive sound and disappeared off into the early night.

Harold closed down the forge at the back of Santiago's small property on the edge of town, and contemplated climbing into the sleeping loft above the shed that he'd called home for half a decade, and calling it a day. The late summer sun had finished its descent below the nearby mountains, and in the valley where the village lay, cool purple shadows stretched far across the landscape, deepening under trees and rocky outcroppings. Soon the moon would rise, and the dimming sky would fill with stars.

He'd always found the nighttime peaceful; on the ship, he'd sometimes volunteered for watch. As the carpenter's apprentice, he was technically exempt from that duty, but he didn't mind. If a sailor was unwell, or if the trade was advantageous, he would often take position on deck after the sun went down, watching the night sky, the dance of the stars overhead, keeping time with the lapping of waves against the hull, and the flapping of canvas sails, the creaking of ropes. Nothing was ever truly silent on a ship, but at night, when most of the day's commotion had wound down, something akin to quiet, and calm, would settle over the HMS Minotaur.

It was the kind of peace he'd rarely known at home with his family, with all six of them cramped into their small stone one-room cottage, more of a hut, really, everyone practically on top of everyone else. Durring the day, little Roberta fussed and was frequently underfoot, and his unruly big brothers never missed an opportunity to pick on Harold for being short and lean and dark-haired, like their Daa. Ewen and Isaac were tall and blonde and broad-shouldered, like their Mam, like the Norsemen who came to the islands centuries before Harold was born. And Daa...with his whips and switches and loud booming lectures about hellfire and damnation whenever Harold displeased him, which was often...

Night was when all the chaos stopped.

Halfway up the ladder to his loft, he paused and inhaled deeply. The oleander was still in bloom, and some of the lavender that Santiago planted in his retirement garden. The heat of the day brought out the resinous sap of the fir trees, and the cool of the evening added the soft fragrance of the drying grasses, the straw from his mattress. There were sheep not too far off, and cattle, too. The scent of their bodies and dung was not unpleasant. As exhausted as he felt, the night was too lovely to waste on sleep. There was still a week to go before the fair in Malaga. Calliope hadn't given him an answer yet, probably because her father had been too drunk for conversation the past few nights. But it was early enough in the evening; maybe Harold would find him in a good mood, if he hurried over to the inn.

"I don't know where that careless girl is off to, young man. But if you can convince her to go to the fair with you, take the old horse and cart, and my blessing, for all it's worth." The innkeeper was not entirely drunk, for once, when Harold arrived. Probably because Calliope was not hovering around, refilling his wine glass whenever the man wasn't looking. The innkeeper would probably be deep in his drink most nights without Calliope enabling him; at least she kept him safe from harm, and managed the business well enough without her father. He was lucky to have her, Harold thought.

As to where she'd run off to on this particular night...

It was Monday. Didn't Calliope typically oversee laundry on Mondays? It was dark, but maybe something had interfered and kept her from bringing the bed-clothes in from the line. If she was busy, then Harold could offer to help, and let her know that her father had finally consented about the cart for Malaga, if she still wanted to go to the fair. With him.

Rounding the back of the multi-story wooden structure that dominated this side of the small village (only the bell tower of the local church stood taller than the inn), near the stables, Harold saw something that made him abruptly halt, and hide behind a rocky outcrop.

In the dark, he could barely spot Calliope, her dark dress blending in with the shadows, only her pale face and luminous blonde hair giving her location away. There was a man with her...he was no one Harold recognized.

"You still want this, then?" The unknown man asked Calliope. He receded into the shadows even further than she was; all Harold could make out was a faint silhouetted outline under the trees. Like Dionisio, the man had an accent Harold could not quite place. *He must be one of Dionisio's brothers...*

"I've made my choice. You know I can stomach it." Calliope's back was turned to him, but Harold well knew the proud set to her shoulders, and imagined the look on her face was stern and determined. Calliope did not like being questioned when her mind was made up.

"If we meet again tomorrow night, there will be no going back, you understand fully? What I am offering can not be undone, if you decide you are not happy with your new life."

"Give me the blood, Vincente, and get it over with. We made a deal."

It was difficult to understand what happened next. The man Calliope called Vincente stepped away from the shadow of the tree just enough for Harold to get a better glimpse of him. He was a sickly-looking man, with sunken eyes and gaunt skin, covered all over with moles and freckles, dressed in a simple black shirt and long trousers. If he was Dionisio's brother, they could not be more opposite, as different from one another as Harold was from Ewan and Isaac.

With a bit of a flourish that Harold would have better expected from Dionisio, Vincente rolled up the sleeve of his shirt and made a gash in his forearm. The cut surely ought to have been fatal, but he seemed unconcerned as he held a wineglass below the gash, letting the flowing blood almost fill the small glass to the brim. Before the cup was even full, the gash on Vincente's wrist closed up, the pale flesh healing perfectly, as though there had never been a cut or a mark on the skin, to begin with.

This is Devil magic...

Calliope took the bloodied glass from Vincente, raised it to her lips, and drained it down in three quick, disgusted swallows.

Harold couldn't run away from that place fast enough.

Calliope turned and looked at him, backlit by an inferno, and her face was monstrous, eyes black, blood dripping down her chin. The village was on fire, there were people trapped inside some of the houses, screaming and calling out for help. Vincente and Dionisio and their brother ran around laughing, grabbing at anyone who tried to run away, and...

Master Santiago was dead. The old woman who kept house for him found him in his bed when she came in in the morning. Died in his sleep, of course. Peaceful, she said. After such a long and eventful life, we should all be so lucky. She crossed herself, pulled the sheets up to cover the dead man's face, and waddled off in the scorching morning sun to fetch the priest, leaving Harold alone in the presence of death.

Master Santiago lived all alone in a small house a few blocks off from the square, where the lots were larger and mostly overgrown. The village had never been very large, and after the war and a smallpox outbreak some six years back, just before Harold arrived, the population was even smaller. There was a small stone church, a farmacia, and an all-purpose store that carried a few sundries, but mostly operated by orders—Harold knew this because Calliope would send Maria or Francisco over with the inn's grocery and material orders every fortnight or so, and about a week later, the wagon would pull up to the inn after a trek to Malaga or some other larger town's market day with casks of supplies. The inn was the largest attraction in town, and mostly served travelers passing through—it was one of the last safe stops before going through the mountains. Hardly anyone stayed in the inn more than a few nights, but Dionisio and his brothers had been there almost two weeks.

I think they sleep in their coffins...

Something wasn't right.

Harold looked around the small bedroom where Master Santiago's body lay in bed. The room was stifling, and already began to smell of death, but when Harold moved over to the window to open it, the sash was already cracked a few inches—Master Santiago always locked up at night, no matter how hot. He, too, had witnessed horrible things, during the war. That wasn't all. The crucifix that normally hung on the wall above Santiago's bed was lying on the floor, too far away from the bed to have been accidentally dropped by a dying man. It looked as though it had been tossed aside. On a sturdy wooden table nearby were a set of formal-looking documents, signed and dated only the night before. Harold recognized his name the way Santiago always insisted on spelling it—Señor Geraldo Laing—and gathered up the paperwork, shoving it under his shirt.

Something wasn't right.

There were bloodstains on the corner of the papers.

...An increase in women and girls asking for iron syrup to treat chlorosis. Don't you think that's odd?

Calliope drank the man—Vincente's—blood, the night before. Harold was certain of it.

Weren't Vincente and Dionisio brothers?

Merciful God.

Harold pulled back the sheet from Santiago's body and examined the face of his dead master. He didn't look peaceful, no matter what his housekeeper said. There was something unnatural about the position of his body, and the way the bedding was tangled. There'd been a struggle. Santiago hadn't been alone when he died.

Harold left for the inn before the priest and the housekeeper returned.

Calliope's father was drunk already.

"You won't find that worthless slut doing anything useful today." The old man slurred his words, but his tone and expression were sharp. "Don't waste your time on faithless women, boy." His head dipped low, and he dozed off, his quiet snores only audible for the complete lack of activity in the otherwise bustling inn. He looked so pale...

Harold brushed past Maria on his way upstairs. Calliope's bedroom was in the attic.

"She is ill, señor. Come back tomorrow…" Maria's voice echoed down the dark, wood-paneled hallway. Harold ignored her and continued to make his way to the third floor.

"Cal—Calliope—Cal!" he hissed through clenched teeth, pounding on the door. "Goddamit, Cal, open up—"

When Calliope opened the door, it was only a crack. There were dark circles around her eyes, and her lips were drawn and pale. "What time is it?" Her voice was hoarse, too.

"Late enough in the morning that you've usually been awake for hours. Are you sick? Master Santiago is dead, Calliope. What's going on? What's happening? Who are those men? Why—?"

Calliope opened the door to her room slightly wider. She wore a plain linen dressing gown, and her long flaxen hair was unbound, hanging in soft waves around her face. Harold had never seen her hair let loose before, and gasped in spite of himself. Even in the dark, her pale blonde hair practically glowed. He wanted to reach out and touch those strands, to run his fingers through the softness…

"Santiago…? But that's not what—" she stopped herself when Harold pulled the papers from Master Santiago's table out from under his shirt. "This is your journeyman certification. He released you?" Her eyes scanned the curling script on the page, confirming what Harold had already suspected.

"I think he would have, but he died sometime last night. I found this in his room. Cal, there was a struggle, I'm sure of it. Who would want him dead? This all started when those men—"

"Blacksmith, listen to me, please." Calliope thrust the papers back into his hands. "You have to get out of here. Leave town. Today. Before nightfall. Take my father's cart. He's drunk. Go to Malaga, go anywhere. Go to Seville, to Madrid, go to France, but you have to leave, you have to—"

Harold's eyes scanned the small room Calliope occupied through the crack in the door. She'd hung her blanket over the window, blocking out the light and making the already tiny bedchamber even more claustrophobic. A mote of dusty sunlight from a small window in the hall cut in front of the doorway to her room, and she flinched when her hands crossed the path of light.

"Calliope. Come with me. Marry me. I can get work anywhere, I can keep you safe. Whatever's going on, whatever arrangement you made with those men—"

"What do you know about anything, Blacksmith? Who said anything about marrying you?"

"I mean, I thought—your father thought..."

"I can't marry you, Harold Laing." She spoke as if it were the most obvious statement in the world. She shook her head, and the beautiful flaxen waves of her hair moved with her, but it did not soften the set of her shoulders, that determined look Harold knew so well.

"You could..." he began, even though he already felt the futility of it. Something small and fragile, that he hadn't even realized was hope, crumbled like rotted wood inside his heart. "I would be a good husband tae you, Miss Jones..."

"You deserve someone better than me."

"There's no one better than you. Not in this town."

"Please, leave. You don't know what they're capable of. Take the cart and go, before dark, before the sun sets—"

But Harold didn't leave the village that day. He packed up his meager belongings, the sword Dionisio had expressed so much interest in, and returned to the inn, drinking the day away with Calliope's father in the common room, while a handful of villagers Harold had made friends with over the years passed through, and expressed their condolences, and shared stories of Santiago bragging about facing down French soldiers and their pistols with a sword in each hand, even at such an advanced age...he was a legend, they said. Harold was lucky to have him as a teacher, no?

Late in the afternoon, Harold instructed Francisco to leave a note for Dionisio Miguel de Mateos:

"Tell him the sword he wanted to purchase is ready for sale. Tell him that the final pupil of Master Augustus Santiago de Martinez wishes tae have a word with him."

They sleep in the coffins...

"So you are no longer the master's apprentice." Dionisio appeared out of the shadows, still dressed like a damned peacock. Harold was even less charmed than he'd been at their previous meetings.

"Not sure how you'd know that." He kept his voice low, and peered at the pale man with the cold hands, the strange accent, who only came out at night.

If he was even a man at all. Harold wasn't certain anymore. He wasn't certain of anything. The wine made his head spin, made his suspicion sharper than the sword at his side.

"You're here to sell me what I came for. It isn't a difficult conclusion to arrive at. We are here to do business, yes? And I promised to make the purchase worth your time." Dionisio cocked his head to one side and narrowed his eyes; not a squint, but a warning, Harold thought.

He pulled the sword out of his rucksack and placed it on the table. The garnets glinted bloody fire in the light of the lanterns hanging overhead, and Harold wondered if the fires of hell burned with the same dark red light. Dionisio, for his part, seemed pleased, and examined the workmanship with the keen appreciation of a practiced buyer, balancing the blade in his hand, testing the sharpness of the edge.

"It is as excellent as I knew that it would be...Your late master did exceptional work, and so do you. Perhaps someday, I will purchase the first sword of your last apprentice, as well." He slid a leather purse heavy with coins across the table. "You will find that I keep my word regarding payment."

Harold shook his head, and the wine he'd drunk made the world blur and spiral. Even so, the amount was too much. Harold meant to be fair. He protested. Something wasn't right...

He counted the coins in the purse a second time. "You canna be serious." His intake of breath was sharper than he meant it to be, and a small, urgent voice in the back of his head compelled him to take the money, don't ask any questions, find Calliope and get the hell away from the village before things got any further out of hand. There was at least a year's wages in coin in the heavy leather bag. But when he looked up from the coins again, Dionisio had slipped away, disappearing into the shadows

Where was Calliope? Harold had to find her. Surely, now, with this much money...

He staggered away from the table. Something told him not to bother climbing the stairs to her room on the third floor again. He remembered what he'd seen near the stables the night before. Whatever Cal was planning with that man, Vincente, wherever she was planning to go, surely she would change her mind, now that Harold had money.

They only came out at night.

They drink no wine

They sleep in their coffins.

A family murdered, not far from here.

Livestock dying in the hills.

The farmacia ran out of iron syrup to treat chlorosis last week.

These men...these men...these men were not men. Harold was certain of it, in his bones and in his pounding heart and in his blood he was certain of it. In his blood...

They were drinking the blood.

He raced around the inn toward the oak-shadowed boulders near the stables, moving as quietly as he could, trying to use the dark to his advantage. The moon overhead was barely a sliver, as though it possessed some secret knowledge of the horror that was to come, and would only allow itself the smallest peek at the shadowed world below. The darkness of the night had an almost palpable quality. He crouched in the lee of a large stone outcropping, and listened for Calliope's voice.

"I had begun to think you would not return," Vincente's voice called out from the same spot he'd stood the night before, under the twisted overhanging branches of the gnarled oak.

Calliope stepped out of the stables, her shoulders squared, the same hard set to her face that she always took on once she had made up her mind about something. There was no one else who moved like that, stood like that, held themselves with that steel-edged determination. No one that Harold had ever met. And yet, nothing in the five years of knowing Calliope Jones as well as he thought he did, could have prepared him for the sight of her in men's breeches and her father's overcoat, her hair cropped short, almost shorn—all those beautiful flaxen waves cut away and discarded. Harold put his hand over his own mouth and bit down to keep himself from crying out.

"I told you that my mind was made up last night. There was no reason to think otherwise." The only emotion in her voice was iced-over disdain.

"And you've said your prayers? Made your peace with mortal comforts, the light of the sun—"

"I've better things to focus on than sentimentality."

"You still believe you can deliver? A fortune on that scale..."

"You keep your promise, and I shall keep mine. Give me the blood."

Vincente cut himself, then—exactly as he had the night before, and God only knows how many nights prior to that—and presented the same wine glass filled with his blood for Calliope to drink from. Harold watched, transfixed by horror, knowing he should call out, intervene, do something to stop her, and instead finding himself utterly unable to move. Calliope had swallowed the last of the blood in the wineglass, and Vincente, moving with a swiftness that was utterly inhuman, reached out from the shadows with his pale, mole-covered arms, and snapped her neck.

Harold cried out, too late to save her.

Hands reached out from behind him, grabbing his shoulders, twisting his arms behind his back. "You idiot," Dionisio hissed in his ear. "Drunken fool. Do you not think you've seen enough death today?"

Vincente stepped over Calliope's body where it lay in the dirt by the stables and approached Harold and Dionisio, joined by the third brother, whose name Harold still did not know. "Kill him already." Vincente shrugged.

The unknown man at Vincente's side wasted no time, the speed of his movements a blur in the darkness that Harold's eye's barely registered. In less than the time it took to draw breath, he drew Harold's sword from the scabbard at Dionisio's side and ran it across Harold's midsection. Harold screamed once from the pain, high and shrill, before the shock took away the hurt and the fear, and he stopped struggling against the arms that held him.

"What have you done?" Dionisio dropped Harold to his knees and lunged at the other man. "Bernard, you kill an artist—idiot!"

Harold looked up as the two men scuffled. "He will die tonight regardless." Bernard slapped Dionisio across the face. "You have more sentimentality than the dead girl. Drink your damned artist if you love him so much—don't waste the blood."

The demon's teeth were at Harold's throat, then, and his vision began to fade. Death was peaceful, Harold thought. Why was Calliope shouting?

"No, no, no no no—not him! Not him, you promised! Oh, God—the blood, the blood..."

Dionisio pulled away as though startled by the sound of her voice, and Harold saw her, rising unsteady on her feet, Vincente's hands on her shoulders, holding her back.

Bernard laughed, "Now this one is eager, *si*? When is the last time you saw a *novata* come around so quickly? Maybe we should turn the sweetheart, too?"

Calliope pounded her fists against Vincente, throwing him off-balance, but he held tight. "I can smell the blood, Vincente. Do something. Do something."

"It is what it is." Vincente shrugged. "You said you were not sentimental, no?"

"I'll double the debt."

"That is a lot of money."

"Twice as much. Everything. I swear. Don't let him—"

Vincente lifted his shoulders in a gesture that was less of a shrug, and more of a noncommittal acquiescence. "Dio...do you want to try? We could be wealthy men."

"He won't turn." Bernard scoffed. "I know the type. Do not bother, Dio..."

But Dio had already knelt by Harold's side, slipping off his ill-fitting embroidered coat, and rolling up the sleeves of his shirt. "If I am successful, this one is mine, Bernard. You've done enough..."

Harold's heart was pounding furiously in his chest as blood continued to pour out of the wound in his belly, and no matter how hard he tried to breathe, there wasn't enough air. He was drowning again. Gently, Dionisio pressed the crook of his elbow against Harold's mouth, and the saltwater was warm, and the sea consumed him, and the world stopped swimming, and he drank. Once again, he realized, Calliope Jones had saved him.

CHAPTER TWENTY-EIGHT

POISONOUS ROOTS AND VIOLENT THORNS

"Why didn't you tell me? That you hadn't been drinking the blood?" The vision faded, and as the overwhelming intensity of the blood memories released me, some bitterness that I couldn't quite put my finger on, flourished and took root near my heart. I'd seen so much, and yet…there was something he wasn't telling me, I was sure of it, still. "You were turned all at once, just like me! Why didn't you say so?"

"Would it have mattered?" Harold asked, but he was staring up at the ceiling, like he couldn't bear to face me. His voice was soft and sad, and I felt a twinge of guilt that we'd ended up like this. I wanted to wrap my arms around him this time, and tell him that it didn't matter, not really, how he'd been turned, but it did matter. Thorn-filled vines laced the hollows between my ribs.

He'd lied by omission, hadn't he? One more thing that he hadn't told me.

Poison tendrils wrapped around my heart and lungs.

"In my experience," Harold continued, though he still refused to look at me, "telling a person who is hurting that you've been hurt the same way they feel pain isn't exactly helpful. And, anyway," he paused to self-correct. "I've told you, I enjoy this life. I'm not in any denial about how much—"

"If you think being a vampire is really all that great, why have you only ever turned one other person?" I nearly choked getting the words out; there were ugly tattered blossoms filling up my throat; small green fruits swelled and ripened into something toxic. Almost sweet. I flapped my hands against my chest, but the gesture was futile. Not needing to breathe didn't save me from the feeling of something foreign in my lungs. I couldn't cough it all up if I tried.

"We should get under the covers," he deflected. "The sun will be coming up, soon."

I didn't exactly want to crawl under the blankets and spend the rest of the day with him when I was like this, but I still craved his presence, too. I wasn't sure what I felt or wanted, entirely, but in spite of everything, I loved him. Not because of the sex, or the blood—I'd been in love with him for a while now, I thought. I cleared my throat, but it did nothing to dispel the awful pain. I thought the thorns on the vines around my ribs should have poked through my flesh by now, begun tearing me to ribbons—but I also knew that the panicked sensation was entirely in my head.

My undead body finally figured out how to have a proper vampire panic attack. How delightful.

I coughed. I had to force myself to do it; I'd almost forgotten how.

"Are you all right?" He finally turned to see me doubled over, distorted and flailing.

I shook my head. "Don't touch me!" With effort, I dragged the blankets back and arranged the covers over my naked body, coughing and choking the entire time. The tendrils around my heart had sprouted thorns of their own. The pain made my eyes water, but I tried to get comfortable. The panic attack would pass. They always did. If I'd been mortal, I would have been more distraught at the thought of sleeping without any clothes on. But I wasn't mortal, anymore. And it wasn't our nakedness that bothered me.

"Grace, you're scaring me."

I flapped my hands harder, but it didn't soothe me. Everything was awful. I'd *felt* it, when Harold remembered drowning in his blood memories. Now my body was replicating the same sensation, my lungs filled up with vegetation, all spikes and poison fruit.

"What happened to Irene?" I wheezed. I'd seen her face flashing through his memories, too—I was certain of it. "Why don't you want to talk about her?" I needed to know. Oh God, the pressure in my chest would go away if he'd only tell me; my imagination ran off in horrible directions. I needed answers. I needed reassurance that he wasn't—that Irene hadn't been—

"How much did you see?" Harold's voice was far away again.

"I don't—kn-kn-know w-w-hat. What I saw." I stuttered. "M-m-mostly, I saw the n-n-night you w-w-were turned, and...Everything is j-j-jumblededed. I saw..." I closed my eyes and tried to piece together the half-remembered fragments of his memories that didn't fit with the rest of the narrative puzzle I'd assembled.

"The w-w-oman w-w-w-ith the strawberry blonde hair. The woman with all the d-dresses, in your closet. The woman whose face I kept seeing in your memories—" I paused, and the remnants or recollection slid in place, flashes of his life and experiences like murderous shards of glass reflecting disconnected glimmers of light. The rotting fruit surrounding my heart exploded outward, all the pressure building up inside me releasing all at once, and I recognized that the bitter thing which had taken root inside of me had a name.

Betrayal.

"She wasn't just your fledgling, Harold." Toxic ichor seeped into my voice. The blood-memory congealed into a series of crystalline images: *Irene in a sepia-toned picture postcard, scantily clad in a flimsy collection of scarves and holding a prop scimitar, every line of her body unmistakably a dancer's. She wore a Juliette cap with a long filmy veil trailing down to the floor on their wedding night, clutching a poisonous bouquet of lilies—the very picture of flapper chic. I saw her again, laughing at night outside a farmhouse, perched on the running boards of a brand-new Buick, its Art Deco lines instantly evocative of the late 1930's.*

She volunteered the both of them to knit socks for the neighborhood Red Cross chapter during the war, and the look on her face when Harold (eyepatch and all) won the prize for 'fastest knitter' was a thing of beauty. Christmas, sometime in the 1950's, judging from her full red skirt. She was kneeling beside a lit-up aluminum Christmas tree, making a present of a familiar-looking flask. Her wedding ring was engraved with owls.

"Grace!" Hands reached out to grab me, but I buckled, pushing myself across the mattress, away from him.

...She was bent over a newspaper dated 1964, tears streaming down her face, moved by some new national tragedy. Irene had the biggest heart. She always had the biggest heart. There she was again, a few years later, restoring an old Victorian house in the 1970s. Even in paint-splattered denim jeans and a worn-out men's shirt, she

was chic. She wore frosted blue eyeshadow, and her short bobbed haircut had become stylish again. My hands were shaking. *She was slumped in the passenger seat of the gray BMW—Harold's car—something horrible had happened. Her eyes were vacant and—*

"Goddammit." My voice was a whisper.

"Get out o' those memories, kettlen," Harold said, softly. "We can talk about it tomorrow night."

"She was your *wife*," I hissed the accusation through clenched jaws. "How—how long were you married?"

He didn't say anything. I could feel him from several feet away, clamming up. But the shared blood in our veins connected us yet, and that was the worst of it. Intermingled with my own rising magnesium-flare rage I felt his pain, and grief, the anguish of his loss, and I hated this stupid vampire blood communion bullshit.

"It's a pretty important detail to tell a person before you fuck them, in case you hadn't realized," I went on, my hands grabbing onto the sheets like they were a lifeline.

"Grace, she's dead—"

"So's my mom!" I shouted, fury and betrayal unlike anything I had ever known spewing from my lips.

"She's been dead since before you were born!" He raised his own voice at me, anguished and defiant.

I rejected his attempt at explanation, throwing up my hands to keep him further away from me. "That doesn't matter! When you *marry* someone, you promise forever—that's what love means! You don't replace them!"

"You are not a replacement for Irene—!" Once more, his hands reached out for me. Once more I moved aside. I was almost teetering at the edge of the bed. Any further and I'd end up sprawled on the floor.

"I thought I was falling in love with you. I really fucking did, you asshole." I choked back intractable sobs. "But I guess it all makes sense now, why you refused to tell me. All this time, you could have said something, and you chose not to. You with all your fucking *options*," I spat. "You really are nothing special, you know that? You just wanted to fuck me, just like...Like Dylan wanted to fuck all those hot European girls or whatever. I can't *believe* I let myself get used like that again." I scrambled out from under the covers before something even more humiliating could happen.

"Grace—Grace!" Harold called after me. "Where are you going? There's too much daylight inside the rest of the suite!" He sat up and tried to grab on to me one last time. I avoided his grasp.

There was a bright band of winter sunshine glowing under the bedroom door, and even that diffused light was enough to make my eyes burn and water. I ran to the mercifully windowless en-suite bathroom and locked the door behind me.

Harold pounded on the door until the hinges rattled. "You're not being fair! How long do you think a person should grieve? I never *wanted* tae love anyone else, but I met you and I—"

"Leave me alone!" I wept. There was no stopping the tears now. "You knew what you were doing! You're just like my dad. My mom deserved better, and so does—so did Irene!" I spat the name of Harold's dead wife through the door at him, and he went quiet. After a few minutes, I heard him shuffle back to the safety of under the covers. He might have been crying. *Let him.*

He'd tasted my blood, he knew. He knew how much his lies of omission would hurt me. Hell, he'd known long before that, even, what a sore spot my dad's betrayal of mom's memory was for me. He had no excuse. Everything between us had been a lie from the start.

I gathered together all the fluffy hotel bath towels I could find, and made a nest for myself in the large, jacuzzi-jetted bathtub. It wasn't comfortable, but I didn't want comfort. My dead heart ached with a sadness I could not articulate, and I sobbed into the bath towels for hours, as the sun traversed its daily path overhead, sank below the horizon, and the world plunged back into the darkness of another cold, February night.

I missed my mom.

◄O►

Chapter Twenty-Nine

BECCA

I WOKE WITH A start the next night all alone in the bathtub, confused and disoriented, naked and caked with dried blood. I thought I'd heard a door slam, but maybe it was just my disorganized frame of mind inventing sounds out of the ceaseless rush of noise that always threatened to overwhelm my capacity to process any sound at all. It was inevitably the worst when I was drifting in or out of sleep; I imagined all sorts of things

I'd imagined that he loved me.

Well, to hell with that thought. My stomach lurched violently, and for an awful moment, I thought I was going to be sick, exactly the way I was last time I woke up in a bathtub, but the queasy sensation dissipated once I worked up the courage to leave the washroom.

Harold-the-betrayer was nowhere around. Not that I wanted to see him, after what happened last night, but I called what I thought was the number to his burner cell phone from the hotel room telephone, to at least be able to say I made an attempt to check up on him. But of course, he hadn't set up voicemail, and I didn't want to leave a message for someone who might be a stranger, when Harold never checked his messages anyway.

Fuck.

It occurred to me that I was back exactly where I had started as a vampire, waking up alone under a pile of bath towels in the marble washroom of a swanky building with floor-to-ceiling windows affording yet another breathtaking view of the city, and no idea what to do next. It would be traumatizing if I wasn't still so goddamn angry.

A shower was definitely a priority. I was still covered in blood—mine and Harold's—and I wanted to scour away the remains of him from my body as soon as possible. I returned to the washroom and fumed some more, folding up the towels that I had used for bedding during the day and stacking them on the sink in neat, tidy hotel-folded piles. That made me feel marginally better.

Cleaning myself off helped enormously as well. I wasn't sure what I was going to do about clothes—I definitely didn't want to continue to wear Harold's dead wife's dress. That was gross. I walked out of the bathroom wrapped in a complimentary hotel terry cloth robe that was several sizes too large and tried not to look at the bloodstains on top of the bedding, where Harold and I had done *it* the night before. That felt gross, too. Vampire sex was gross.

"*But you enjoyed it...*" my own voice inside my head reminded me, and I growled at the voice to shut it up. The things I enjoyed now were gross. I had to reach out to Becca, to warn her what she was getting herself into before it was too late.

A small pile of familiar department-store shopping bags set just inside the door to the suite caught my attention on my second walkthrough, and I was torn between curiosity about what might be inside those bags, and an unwelcome territorial anger that someone had been inside my (temporary) domain.

Curiosity won. There was note attached to the outside of the largest bag, penned in neat, thoroughly modern handwriting but presumably dictated by Harold:

"*I woke up late this afternoon and called downstairs to the concierge to get some clothes for you. Hopefully they got the right size. I will see you later tonight. Harold.*"

The note didn't say, "love, Harold," but it did say, "*I woke up late this afternoon...*" He'd woken up before sunset, to call downstairs to the concierge desk and make sure I had clean clothes to wear, and if that wasn't love, what was? The thought made me angry. He had no right to love me. But I needed clean clothes. I sighed, and began sorting through the packages.

Whoever had done my shopping had good taste in the kind of classic silhouettes that suited my petite figure, and the sizes were surprisingly accurate. It occurred to me that Harold had spent more than two hundred years measuring and crafting and making things with his hands; he could probably estimate each of my measurements in centimeters and inches with shocking precision. Even the bras fit. Of course. He'd already sized up and memorized the exact volume of each of my breasts.

...the memory of his teeth at my nipples the night before came unbidden, and unwelcome. I pushed it aside and got dressed, and because I couldn't help myself, I took the rest of the clothes that fit and hung them up in the bedroom closet, leaving the few items that weren't quite right in the shopping bags, hoping that someone had saved the receipt. When I finished blow-drying my hair, I picked up the hotel phone again, and, with shaking hands, dialed a California area code I had memorized forward and backward since my freshman year of college.

Becca.

The call went to voicemail. Becca usually didn't answer the phone when she didn't recognize the number. I called again without leaving a message, praying Becca would make an exception the second time.

A familiar voice came on the other end of the line. "Hello? Who is this?"

"Becca?" I responded, voice trembling. "It's Grace..."

✦

I found an envelope containing quite a bit of cash in the drawer of Harold's bedside table. I guessed that the rest was locked up in the safe, and I didn't have the combination, but what he'd left behind for me to find was more than sufficient. I ran downstairs to the lobby and palmed the doorman a $20 to hail me a cab, and instructed the driver to take me to an out-of-the-way late-night restaurant in a less trendy neighborhood where no one Becca or I knew might be expected to show up. I'd told Becca to come alone, and I didn't know what I was going to do if Gavin showed up with her.

She was sitting by herself at the restaurant bar with a glass of red wine, and she gasped when I walked in the doors, jumping out of her bar stool to embrace me, but I pushed her back to arm's length. I hadn't had time to find any peppermint extract, and I was hungry. I didn't want to think about eating my best friend.

"How is any of this real?" Becca asked, fear and wonder making her voice shake. "They told us you were dead, that you died in the fire..."

"Are you really alone?" I needed to know.

Becca nodded, and I suggested we get a booth.

"First of all, I'm glad you came alone, because I really needed you to," I said, as we both slid into the shadowy recessed seating. "Second, you've got to stop being so stupid about things like this, going off alone after dark to meet dead people is how you end up in a bathtub full of ice with your kidneys stolen—or worse," I chided. I'd always been the one cautioning Becca to not be so trusting of strangers, but when it came down to one of those strangers eventually being a real monster, I'd been the one who'd gotten targeted. Not fair, but better me than Becca, I decided.

Becca tried to disguise her nervous laugh with a big gulp of wine, then made a face, and set the wineglass down.

"Since when are you a red drinker?" I asked, more pointed than I intended. For as long as I'd known her, Becca's distaste for wine had been practically a part of her personality...and an endless excuse to quote Dracula.

"Oh, you know...I guess your palate changes with...new experiences, and...people." Becca made an attempt to be vague, and I arched my eyebrows at my friend across the table until she cut the bullshit.

"It tastes nothing like blood, you know." I kept my voice low, but casual. We might as well have been discussing a dull work meeting. I reorganized the sugar packets at the end of the table by color and hummed a few bars to a song I knew Becca would recognize. 'Our' band had played it as their opening number, the night of the concert at the Metro. Becca looked like she might faint, and voicelessly mouthed the words, "Oh. My. God." But did not speak.

"What has Gavin been telling you?" *Blue packets belong with the other blue ones. The yellow packets all go together.* It was a struggle to keep my tone light. Having something to do with my hands helped.

"I—he—I mean...well, how much do you know?" Becca finally found her voice, but sideswiped the question. She fidgeted, fingers toying with a fine gold chain around her neck, moving a small winged pendant back and forth across the links. Some kind of delicate owl motif...it wasn't her usual style. Becca tended to prefer clunkier silver pieces of jewelry. It looked expensive, though. Like a gift.

I peered at her, not wanting to think about the person who might have given her such an out-of-character present, and expected her to wear it. "Assume that I know much more about vampires than you do, Becca, because that's all that I've been dealing with since New Year's Eve when I died, bestie."

I could practically smell Becca trying to process what I told her. She looked confused, but a shy smile crept across her face after a moment.

"He's been letting me drink his blood, just a little," Becca leaned in and whispered, as though it were any other girlish secret between friends. "I feel amazing."

"How many nights?"

"I don't—?"

"How many nights has he been giving you his blood, Becca? This is very important!" I hissed, and Becca leaned back against the seat of the booth, startled.

"Five times, tonight," Becca whispered. She was frightened. I could smell the fear in her blood from across the table, too. "We'd just finished, when you called and...I told him I had to run. He didn't know about you, I promise."

Five times. That was too many. I'd miscalculated. Fear gripped my stomach, driving up the tempo of my hunger.

"You need to stop," I insisted. "You need to break up with him, tell him you never want to see him again, leave the city, and never come back! Go home to California to your family!" My fury at Gavin was threatening to undo my self-control, and I fought to keep from slipping. The monster inside of me wanted blood. I held my breath for several moments, struggling to retain composure. I felt the familiar itch as my fangs began to poke out of my gums, and willed them to recede back into place. I didn't want Becca to see me like this, no matter what she knew.

"Grace—you're not breathing," Becca pointed out.

I exhaled. "Has Gavin told you what he's planning to do to you in two nights?"

"It's my birthday," Becca said, as though she needed to remind me. "He said he's planning to do something really special." She touched the pendant around her neck again. It was definitely an owl, stamped in yellow gold, with two small diamonds for eyes.

I didn't have time to analyze Becca's jewelry choices. "He's going to kill you, I think."

"You're lying."

"You already know he's a vampire. You've been drinking his—*blood*." I sneered. "What do you think vampires do to people?"

I'd never seen Becca look so frightened, and I wished to hell she didn't. The fear plastered across her face made me want to take her in my arms and—*no*. Under the table, I dug my fingernails into the palm of my hand until I felt the skin break. I focused on the pain, and stared at the menu. Literally nothing sounded appetizing anymore. *How had I ever eaten all this crap before?*

"Grace, for real—are you really one of them?" Becca chewed on her cracked cuticles, and I prayed that she didn't start bleeding. I kept telling her she needed to use better moisturizer in the winter...

I nodded in answer to her question, and stretched out my hand across the table for Becca to feel just how ice-cold I was. I knew she couldn't pick up the subtle vibrations from skin-on-skin contact that I found myself able to perceive now, but I wished she could. I needed her to know how bad it was.

"Prove it."

"My hands are ice cold, Becca, come on."

"Show me your teeth."

"No!"

"I want to see. Gavin showed me his, so it's nothing I haven't seen before. Prove it."

I didn't even have to think about it for my fangs to come sliding back down, and I carefully pried open my lips enough for Becca to shut the fuck up about it. I didn't like how excited she seemed, how eager.

"Have you killed people?"

I shook my head. "No, not yet. At least..." I remembered the plastic jug of the dead person's blood Harold had brought back to the safe house. "Not directly," I corrected myself.

"Okay, so, what if Gaven's planning to turn me, instead of kill me?"

"Same difference."

"No, it's not, Grace. Look at you! You're here, and we all thought you were dead! It's a miracle! And I want that too, I want to be miraculous and powerful and strong and beautiful forever, but now this is even better, because we can still be friends, don't you see? We really can be best friends forever, isn't that what we always planned? How is this not perfect?"

"Because it's *hell*, Becca. It's *awful*. You're trapped inside all day by the sun, getting the blood you need is not easy, it's expensive and clandestine, and there's always the threat that if you're caught, you have to flee your home and run away and start over from scratch somewhere else. And the hunger…This thirst…you don't want this, Becca, I promise you. You'll never have cheese fries again. Ever."

She rolled her eyes. "Oh no, not the cheese fries. You know, I think I can learn to live without them."

"Sunsets?"

"I've seen plenty. And it's not like I couldn't look at pictures online."

"Your family?"

"Nonno is a homophobic racist. Nonna only cares about me marrying rich and making Catholic babies. My dad and stepmom are alcoholics. Next."

"Your *soul*, Becca. I know you're not the most devout, but what about that? Are you that willing to choose damnation?" I knew I was grasping at straws, but there had to be something. Becca wasn't confirmed, but we'd still gone to Mass together, sometimes.

She scoffed. "Let me tell you something about hell. Hell is spending your twelfth birthday in a pediatric psych ward because your mom just died, and your own fucking father doesn't understand how emotions work.

"Hell is watching your Nonno lose a little bit more of himself every day as he gets sucked into angry propaganda on the TV, til he's full of nothing but rage and resentment toward anyone who doesn't think like him, hating immigrants and gay people, as if his entire business didn't depend on the work of one and the business of the other, as if his own grandfather wasn't an immigrant.

"Hell is drinking yourself into a stupor every day and night like dad and his wife, because if you stopped for even a *second* to actually process how fucked up your life has become, that reality would destroy you faster than the wine in your bottle.

"Hell isn't a place you go to when you die. That's just some ancient allegory that people have decided to take literally so they can abuse and manipulate the hurting and the powerless. Real hell is something you live through and carry around like a weight around your neck, and I know what that's like.

"I'm not afraid for my soul. I've seen enough hell in this life, and any god who would want me to suffer more because I chose love isn't a god powerful enough to damn me."

"How many people are you prepared to kill? How much blood do you want on your hands?"

"But you said yourself you haven't killed anyone. It's not impossible. Gavin doesn't kill people, I asked him. He swore to me he doesn't."

I let out a hollow, mirthless laugh.

"I want your blood right now, Becca." I leaned forward and spoke with a conviction that frightened me, and Becca's eyes widened, her pupils dilated. I could hear her pulse quicken.

She licked her lips, a hitch in her breath. "Grace, that is the hottest thing you've ever said to me." Her voice was suddenly low and tinged with arousal. I could *smell* it on her.

I stopped breathing again, internally screaming. Becca was *very* turned on, and this was *not* going the way I had planned.

"Ask me who turned me," I growled. I wanted her in a very different way than she wanted me, and I hated myself for it.

"Grace..."

"Ask me."

"Well...I assume it's that guy you were with the night of the concert when you attacked us, so, whatever, if he's your type now, I'm not really going to judge, but whatever his grudge against Gavin is, he's going to have to let it go if we're all going to remain friends after my...birthday."

"NO!" I shouted, pounding my fists on the table and attracting the attention of several other patrons. The waitress came over and asked, pointedly, if we were ready to order. I handed Becca my menu and told her to order dessert, at least. The waitress rolled her eyes but took Becca's order for tiramisu, and left us alone again.

"Gavin turned me. On New Year's Eve, Becca. I didn't hook up with him, he attacked me and left me for dead at the party he took us up to. He killed me..."

"No." Becca shook her head. "That's not how turning someone works, he told me—"

"…violently, Becca," I continued slowly, forcefully, stressing every word. "He violated me in the worst way imaginable and left me for dead in a stranger's bathtub. He is not a good man. He's not even a good vampire."

"You're full of shit," Becca's entire demeanor shifted, and it wasn't hard to imagine the anger flashing in her eyes now was the same as it had been when she made her bitter post about me after the concert. I knew my friend well, and braced for the worst. "Let me remind you what happened on New Year's Eve, because you seem to have forgotten some crucial details in your self-righteous tirade right now, and I am not going to argue about this with control freak Grace. You showed up at my apartment in a bad mood, moaning on about your ex-boyfriend from over six months ago, and your dad's new girlfriend—which, by the way—"

She stopped, peered at me, and then continued, "Never mind that. You were grumpy, and I practically had to drag you out. And then we go to this bar where Miguel's friend works, so at least we could drink for free, and who else is there? Gavin Richardson, the same man I had been crushing on for *months*. And you knew how I felt about him! Even before I knew he was really a vampire, and not just a nerd who dressed up like one for Halloween. And running into him on New Year's Eve was some kind of magical coincidence, you know? The sort of thing that happens in movies, I just knew this year was going to be amazing, and you couldn't be supportive even when he invited us up to this amazing party, you were all, 'blah blah stranger danger' like the mom friend you love to be, just sulking in the corner on your phone like a wet blanket—"

"I was *not* a wet blanket, I was trying to text my dad and wish him Happy New Year, but my battery was low, and my texts weren't going through because he was in Cancun—"

"Whatever. I was trying to flirt with Gavin, and we were actually having a great time, but then it was getting closer and closer to midnight, and I was like, 'I have to find Grace, I have to find Grace, this moment in time is just too amazing to be without my best friend in the whole world, and Gavin got upset that I wasn't paying attention to him anymore, so I started wandering around the party looking for you, and then I saw the *both* of you in the hallway together just before midnight, and you knew I had a crush on him but there you were, making out with my man on New Year's Eve, and then the two of you wander off, and no one sees either of you again, and then the party's over.

"And I *never*, Grace, never would have thought you were capable of going that low. I can put two and two together, you know, even *if* Gavin hadn't confessed to me, when we first started actually dating two weeks later, that he'd slept with you after you drunkenly came on to him at the party. And by then, you were already acting really weird, so I forgave Gavin because at least he was *honest* with me. I can work things out with people who are honest and communicate…

"Anyway, the part about him being a vampire didn't come up until after the concert, when he healed so quickly after you and your boyfriend beat him up, that he kind of *had* to confess the whole truth to me.

"So I am *not* going to let you destroy my current and future happiness by throwing my boyfriend under a bus and pretending that he is some kind of a rapist predator when he's not. He is *hot*, ambitious, very wealthy, and he treats me like a goddess. I am going to be young and gorgeous and rich and powerful forever, and you can join us if you want, or you can walk away and sulk that Gavin still chose me *after* you threw yourself at him."

I listened to Becca, dumbfounded, a weight in my chest like wet cement. This wasn't right. We shouldn't be fighting like this. I choked back a strangled cry, anger and frustration and betrayal gnawing at my ability to stay calm. If I lost control of the restaurant, there would be casualties.

I'd always known Becca to be too trusting. She took people at face value, and she believed them, and she believed them, and she believed them, right up to the moment that she didn't. Becca was kind and intelligent and creative, but she could be hotheaded, too.

And I'd lied to her. From the beginning. I'd told her I had the flu. I'd told her I was hanging out with new friends she didn't know. I'd told her I was fine when she knew I wasn't, I'd stood her up, I'd ghosted her. But I was me, Grace. The Feral Anxiety Cat to her Trash Panda. That had to count for something. "Gavin is a liar, Becca—"

"Is he?" She paused when the waitress returned with the dessert and the check, and waited until we were alone again. "Of the two of you, I know who's been there for me in the last two months. He didn't lie to me about sleeping with you or about being a vampire when I confronted him. He's been *honest* with me, Grace—you couldn't even manage that. 'The flu.' Fucking really? As if I wouldn't have understood? Me, of all people! But you lied, and you let me worry. You let me think you were dead for three whole nights. Your dad thinks you're dead now. I mean, at least you still have a dad who cares about you. I would *never* have thrown that away—"

There weren't many other patrons in the dining area, but my and Becca's melodrama was obviously the height of the evening's entertainment for a few nosey faces I caught craning their necks to catch snippets of our conversation. I tried to reel in the tension.

"Becca. Please. Stop. You have to listen to me. Did he tell you that you might actually die? That you might not survive being turned? Lots of people don't. Do you even understand the real risks you're taking?"

Becca was already shaking her head. "I can't trust anything you say anymore. I'm sorry."

"He *hurt* me, and it kills me to see you taking his side of the story over mine. I thought you were better than that." Tears burned in my eyes like acid, and my fangs nicked the inside of my lips as I tried to control my emotions. The faint taste of my own blood extended my teeth further, and I knew I'd have to get fresh blood soon. Not Becca, though. *Not Becca...*I was staring down at her, unblinking. Inhuman.

She winced.

"Well, it's hard to kill something that's already dead." Her voice was cold as she started to scoot herself out of the booth, tiramisu untouched.

"I'm going to kill him, Becca. Did he explain the rules to you? No one bats an eye in the vampire Community when a fledgling kills their maker, and he *is* my maker, and I'm going to destroy him."

"Don't be a psycho bitch, Grace. Enjoy the rest of your very long life. I plan to enjoy mine." Becca stood up, grabbed her ridiculous velvet and brocade coat, and stalked toward the door.

I bolted up after her, leaving enough money on the table to cover Becca's wine and dessert, plus a generous tip to the waitress for putting up with us, and followed Becca out onto the street.

"You're making a mistake!" I shouted after my best friend in the whole world, who was ignoring me, already jaywalking to get to the other side of the avenue. "Becca! Listen to me!"

Becca finally turned to look back around, just before she reached the curb, her face distorted with indignation, and took two angry steps forward, as though she was about to say something important, right as a roaring matte black sedan sped up out of nowhere, and plowed directly into her.

Chapter Thirty

IS THAT A FREAKIN' SWORD?

It happened fast.

I was powerless to act; in the movies, the vampire always steps in with superhuman speed and strength at just the right moment and rescues the girl, and I would have *flown* across the street, leaped in front of the car to save Becca, if I'd known how to fly. But there wasn't enough time. One minute she was about to tell me something, get one last word in before heading off into the night to pursue her own damnation with my maker, and the next thing I knew, the black car was practically aiming for her, slamming into Becca with an awful, splattering impact, before peeling off down the street. She didn't even have time to scream. Neither of us did.

A woman wearing a turquoise hijab jumped out of a nearby vehicle, shouting that she was a trauma nurse at the hospital. Her head covering was the exact same color as a dress Becca had worn to the winter formal, senior year at Loyola. Little details seared into my mind. The broken neon light above the restaurant flickered. Two men jumped off of the sidewalk to direct traffic around the accident, clearing space so the ambulance could pull in close when it arrived. A dog walker with a cell phone started recording witness statements. Their beagle mix whined and strained against its harness.

I stood there paralyzed, watching drivers slow down and bystanders shout to call 911, and my brain was a dial tone. Through the stupor of shock and the fog of my hunger, I could smell the ominous dark stain spreading out from the sad, misshapen form in the street, saturating the frozen blacktop. And I knew, with a detached, preternatural certainty, that there was nothing I, or anyone else could do to save her life. The angles of her body were all wrong. The nurse in the turquoise hijab held Becca's hand. She was gone before any ambulances could have made it.

Something snapped, a survival instinct I didn't know I had, and I tore off running before my body betrayed me, before I threw myself to my knees in the icy gutter to lap up Becca's spilled blood. My feet were moving before my mind caught up, racing away from the restaurant as fast as I could manage, easily slipping around pedestrians and scooter rentals littering the sidewalk. I ran past bars and shops and corner convenience stores, past a dark and lonely elementary school, waiting for the new day to bring children back to the playground, and onward still, until I couldn't run any further, not because I was out of breath, but because my thirst had become something frantic and inescapable, and I was all alone without blood, without Harold, and I was *hungry*. I moaned, softly, leaning against a cold brick building, shivering in spite of myself—not from the chill, but from the *need*.

Everything was fucked, unfathomably worse now than ever before. I'd intended to stop Becca from becoming a vampire, but not like this. Not like this.

Harold had been right all along, and I almost hated him for it. I should have left Becca alone, and let her think that I was dead. Cut all mortal ties, just as he'd kept telling me to. Thoughts of Harold brought with them feelings of betrayal, and anger. He'd had no right to use me like that. He'd had no right to make me think I could love him.

I steadied myself against the wall and tried to *think*.

My resources were limited to some cash, a hotel room key, and...whatever instincts my vampire nature gave me. The weight of all I knew I didn't know felt unbearable.

"Thanks, I hate it," I muttered, throwing my head back against the brick.

"You all right, baby girl?" I smelled the blood belonging to the man walking up behind me before I heard his voice, and then I smelled the rest of him. He was middle-aged and unhoused by appearances and accessories, carrying his belongings over his slumped shoulder in a big blue shopping bag that was fraying at the seams and edges from overuse. But his face was kind underneath his knitted wool hat, and he smiled a sweet, nearly toothless grin at me when I looked up at him.

There's no way it's this simple... I closed my eyes.

"I didn't mean to bother you, ma'am. I'm not asking for much—I'm just trying to collect a few dollars to get something to eat before I go to the shelter tonight, is all, and you look like a nice pretty lady with a big heart, and I thought, such a nice pretty lady doesn't need to look so sad, that breaks my heart, and I know people. You live on the streets, you know who a good person is and who isn't, ya feel me?"

I reached into my pocket with shaking hands and pulled out a few $20s, holding the bills out to him. He took a step back from me and threw up his hands, as startled as if I'd pulled out a gun.

"Oh no, ma'am, it ain't like that. I ain't trying to rob you or nothing. I'm just trying to get me a bit to eat at the fast food place over there, that's all. You don't have to give me all that. I ain't threatening you—"

"No one deserves to be hungry," I told him with whispered conviction. *Kindness is a luxury I recognize the value of investing in,* "Harold had said, *as if that explained things.* "So I want you to have enough that maybe you don't have to worry about food for a few days, okay? It's cold outside."

His dark eyes lit up, and he slowly reached out to take the gift I had to offer, as if he were afraid I'd grab it back. I made sure he pocketed the money before I spoke again.

"I have just a small favor to ask." I gave my best closed-lipped smile. Inside my mouth, my fangs were screaming at me to do what I'd already resigned myself to happening next.

"What you want, sweetheart?"

"Can I have a hug?"

Of course I could have a hug.

⸻◆O◆⸻

I left the man sitting on the sidewalk, after I double-checked to make sure that he was still breathing, and that the wound I'd made on his neck had closed. I was concerned that I'd taken more blood than was safe to take from him, but a few moments later, he started to groan and stir on the icy pavement, and I quickly looked both ways to cross the street and rounded a corner before my dinner could realize where I'd gone off to. I hoped he'd get a nice dinner himself after that.

Feeding was too easy, I thought, wiping my mouth with the back of my hand. Although I was going to have to learn to be a less messy eater. I spared a brief glance at my reflection in a parked car's side mirror to make sure I'd wiped away most of the blood and continued on to the nearest major street, where I hailed a cab. I didn't want to go back to the hotel, and I knew I couldn't go back to my old apartment. I wanted to find and kill Gavin, but I had no idea where to look for him now, and with Becca...*dead*, I told myself firmly, I might have lost my only opportunity to find the vampire who had done this to me. To Becca. A familiar comforting numbness shielded me from the immediate pain. I welcomed it.

Harold implied that he had killed his makers with dynamite in 1870. He'd been turned in 1820. Fifty years seemed like a long time to wait for vengeance. But I owed Gavin the death that was coming for him now. I owed it to him for Becca.

I asked the cab driver to drop me off at a cross street close to where Harold's house used to be.

"That's a long ways out of downtown," the driver complained. "I've got to make rent in three days."

I promised the driver I'd make it worth his time, my hand reaching for the still-large stack of bills in my pocket. Mortal Grace would have been terrified walking around after dark in Chicago with that much cash on hand.

Somewhere in the back of my mind, Vampire Grace laughed, and laughed.

⸺◦◦◦⸺

I had the driver stop a few blocks away from Harold's house, and as I paid my fare and exited the vehicle, I had a thought.

"Wait for me here for an hour, tops." I handed the man a hundred-dollar bill. "If you're still here when I get back, I'll give you another hundred dollars, plus whatever your normal metered wait time is, okay? And If I'm not back in an hour, go back downtown, and you never ever saw me."

The money seemed to cheer him up, and the cabbie promised to wait with a chipper, "Whatever you say, lady! You're the customer!"

I slipped through backyards when I could, and hid in the shadows of the large, leafless trees that lined the residential streets as I made my way back to whatever remained of the burned out house, concerned not just about the peering eyes of suspicious neighbors but also, their security cameras.

But it didn't take long to find the house again. There remained a few pieces of scorched framing rising into the sky out of the snow-covered ground, and tarps and police tape still surrounded what remained of the house, while an unsightly chain-link fence had been erected around the perimeter to keep the crime scene intact. I jumped over the fence neatly, once again impressed at how easy so many things were as a vampire. If only heartbreak and loss were easier to manage when you were dead.

I found my way inside the ruined basement with ease, vampire senses helping me to see in the dark, to navigate the hazards of the scorched interior. *The fire didn't start in the forge*, I realized. I was no arson expert, but I didn't think the blaze had started inside the house at all.

Still, the flames had destroyed almost everything they touched, throughout the house, rendering the world inside what was left of the walls charred and unrecognizable. I exhaled an almost silent prayer that forged steel had survived what so much else had not. My guardian angel had been asleep at the wheel for a bit too long. They owed me this much.

Poking my way through the charred debris of the home that had sheltered me in my first nights as a vampire stirred up emotions I wasn't sure I wanted to spend time processing. I had felt that Harold's home was a prison sometimes, but through the lens of hindsight, the house had been my haven. I just hadn't allowed myself to realize how much I'd needed it. The stone walls had kept God only knows how many people, myself included, safe until I had mastered the degree of self-control I now had. It wasn't much, but it was better than what I'd felt those first nights, even with peppermint-extract-soaked cotton balls shoved up my nose. I chuckled softly in the dark, remembering my revolted reaction the first time Harold had told me what I was going to do when I had to spend time around mortals—and then I frowned, because I wanted to stop thinking about Harold.

*I should probably get out of his house, then...*I reminded myself, redoubling my efforts to search through the rubble. My hands found the hilt of a blade before my eyes saw it, but when I picked up the sword, the blade was broken off, leaving less than ten inches of steel extending past the guard. *Fuck.* I shuffled around in the ashes for a few more minutes before fumbling onto success again. This time, the broadsword I found had been somewhat protected under a big sheet of metal that had fallen on top of it, keeping the weapon miraculously intact, in much better condition than the other sword. Even the scabbard was only singed a little bit, from what I could tell. Perfect. The weapon looked better with a little battle-scarring on it. We'd both already survived what should have destroyed us. I had faith in the sword that had passed through a fire and remained intact.

I stood up to leave, trying to brush soot off my knees but only really succeeding at smearing ashes across my hands and clothing, despite my best efforts. As I stepped forward in the darkness, the toe of my foot made contact with a small object—something hollow-sounding and metallic.

The flask.

Much like the sword with the scabbard, it had been sheltered by the fallen sheet of metal and was mostly untouched by flames—well, compared to everything else. The cardboard packaging was a bit charred, and there was a discolored spot on the shiny polished pewter surface, probably caused by heat, but otherwise, it seemed fine as I turned it over in my hands. I decided to take the flask with me, too, on the way out. A good flask, I had discovered, was a very useful thing for a vampire to have.

The cab driver was still parked and on standby when I got back to the intersection, I'd left him at. "Yo, lady—is that a freakin' sword?" His eyes flicked from the sword in my hands to my newly soot-covered attire, and seemed on the verge of asking several other questions I didn't want to get into.

"You didn't see nothin'," I answered, handing over the second bill I'd promised the driver as I climbed inside the backseat.

"Okay, okay, I didn't see no sword, but I'm gonna have to charge you extra for the cleanup. You've got shit all over you, hun. It's making a mess back there."

"You're going to make rent early and then some buddy, I promise. Relax, okay?" I met the cab driver's eyes in the rearview mirror and grinned recklessly at him, flashing my fangs.

The driver laughed and started to navigate back toward downtown. "As you wish, lady. I'm not into the freaky stuff, but you do you."

No one believed in vampires anymore.

⸺◆⸺

I got back to the hotel with less than an hour left before sunrise.

The only agent at the desk at 5:00 AM practically squealed with nerdy delight when I entered the otherwise empty lobby. "Hey! Is that a freakin' sword?"

"You didn't see nothin'," I responded, holding up my room key and stalking toward the elevator without another word. Behind me, I could hear the desk agent let out a low whistle.

"That is so freakin' cool..."

Harold was not in the suite when I got back, which was concerning. His note had said that he'd meet me later that night...

But it was nearing dawn, and I'd been out for hours and hours with no way to call him. What if he thought that I'd run off and done something reckless again?

Hadn't I?

What if he was driving around, desperately looking for me, as the sky grew lighter and lighter? The thought stopped me in my tracks and filled me with a sickening terror. He'd already risked his life for me that way once. I reached for the hotel room phone and called the front desk. Was Harold's gray 1980s BMW still parked in valet? It took ten anxious minutes for the answer to come back: No, ma'am, its owner took it out to go somewhere early the previous evening. Did I need the bellman to call a cab for me?

No, I thanked the helpful person on the other end of the line, absentmindedly wiping away at the dirt and oil obscuring the face of my mother's watch. Was this how Harold had felt when I hadn't come home after getting arrested? I had no idea where to look for him—a knot in my gut suggested that maybe I should call central lockup, but I didn't know where I would find that phone number without a smartphone. The hotel was modern, and I couldn't find a phone book anywhere in the suite. Wait. There was a laptop, wasn't there? I'd rescued it from the kitchen of the Wisconsin house.

Wherever Harold had put the laptop, I couldn't find it. I wasn't even certain I remembered bringing it in from the car.

Now approaching full-on panic, I picked up the receiver to the room phone again, about to call downstairs, when I noticed the blinking red "message" light on the base of the telephone blinking, when it hadn't been before. I must have missed the call when I was on hold, asking for the whereabouts of Harold's car. I hit the correct buttons to play the message, and was relieved to hear Harold's voice playback in the recording:

"Grace, I'm with Calliope. Call me." No other details.

I quickly dialed the number for his cell phone. No answer. I called again. No answer. I screamed and kicked the armchair where I'd laid Irene's dress after taking it off the night before, and the armchair busted and fell over, taking Irene's dress down with it. I left the mess as it was, and retreated to the bedroom. I was going to bill Calliope for those damages, too.

Somehow, I was convinced, this all came back to Calliope Jones. And now Harold was trapped with her for the whole day. If she harmed a hair on his body...

I didn't want to sleep on the bed alone; somehow, that was worse than the bathtub. I hunkered down again with my towels in the dark for the second morning in a row, and for the second morning in a row, I cried myself to sleep.

⚬

Chapter Thirty-One

THE OWL AND THE WINTER WHITE RABBIT

THE FIRST STEP IN salvaging the laundry debacle was acknowledging the reason for the laundry debacle, and the reason was, *Becca didn't know how to do her own laundry*. That was one of the first surprising things I learned about her, when we moved into the dorms together as roommates sophomore year. I was incredulous.

"How have you been getting your clothes and sheets clean?"

Laundry service, she said. Amazon prime deliveries for things like socks and underwear, if she ran out.

I stared at her. On-campus fluff and fold service was mind-bogglingly expensive. "You know, you can do a load of laundry at the student center for like, seventy-five cents..." I did the math on a scrap of ruled notepaper with one of Becca's ridiculous glitter gel pens, and the calculation smelled faintly of blueberries when I finished. "You're wasting so much money!" I threw the pen down on the desk, triumphant.

"You don't have to yell at me!" Becca looked ready to cry.

"I'm not yelling!" I shouted. "I'm just—don't you know how to do your own laundry?" I'd never met anyone who didn't know how to run a washing machine. I'd started washing and ironing my school uniforms in the third grade—admittedly, because I was a perfectionist and Mom could never get the pleats right.

Becca just looked at me, lost and trapped like an animal in a cage that hadn't realized yet that the door was unlocked and open, just steps away from them—

I was determined to teach Becca the right way to wash and fold clothes. How to do her own grocery shopping, so she could prepare food in the dorm room instead of just buying meals on campus, how to budget her allowance, how to check out books at the library, and how to make coffee, real coffee, in a normal coffee maker.

"The fabric softener goes in this compartment here, but you don't have to use it for every load of clothing. And just because there's a space for liquid bleach—"

"Well, how was I supposed to know it was going to ruin all my T-shirts and make them orange and splotchy?"

"It's called 'bleach'…" I sometimes wondered if Becca's family ever taught her anything useful, but I held my tongue. The small laundry room adjacent to the campus student center wasn't crowded on a Friday night, but it wasn't exactly private, either.

"All of this is very stressful…" Becca looked over her piles of sorted laundry, and it sounded like she was on the verge of tears, but I had to hand it to her for determination. She'd already developed strong preferences for how to fold her T-shirts. It was the wrong preference, but it was a start. She sighed, and reached into her backpack, fishing around until she found an only slightly-crushed package of pop-tarts, tore open the foil packaging, and bit off a frosted corner, dusting crumbs all over the freshly washed and discolored shirts she was supposed to be folding.

I shook my head, trying to ignore the urge to brush away the crumbs and mess. I couldn't make the situation better by doing everything for Becca, even though part of me wanted to. "It's not your fault for not knowing what no one taught you," I reminded her, for what felt like the millionth time.

"I just feel so dumb. Everyone here knows loads of stuff I don't. I can't do laundry right, I'd never taken public transportation before I came to Chicago, and no one ever told me that Froot Loops are all the same flavor! Like, what? I don't know, I still think the purple ones taste different…"

"*You're* a Froot Loop." I laughed as she flicked a T-shirt in my direction, getting crumbs all over my blouse. "Anyway, didn't your mom pass away when you were like, ten?"

"Twelve. Car accident."

"Sixteen. Cancer. Same year my dog died."

"My mom died a week before 9/11."

"Our lives have the best timing." I twisted a lock of black-dyed hair around my finger and made a face. The choppy layers didn't look as good on me as they did on Becca—my hair was finer and prone to too many flyaways. It took forever to straight iron it into submission every morning. But if I grew my hair out, Becca and I wouldn't look as much like sisters anymore...

We hadn't talked about our moms yet. 'My mom's dead, too' was a perfunctory conversation we had the night we first met, and then, all through the rest of freshmen year—the disaster of sorority selection week, midterms, spring break, finals, and a whole entire summer spent thousands of miles apart—neither of us had brought up the subject again. It was like a secret, an unspoken thread that connected us, something the rest of the girls we were friendly with on campus couldn't begin to fathom. Chloe Kristoff, who lived in the dorm across the hall, called her mother, crying, at least once a week. When that happened, we'd close the door to our room, and Becca played angry music at the loudest volume she could justify, and we both tried to pretend that we couldn't hear Chloe complaining about the weather and boys and how impossible her physics class was.

"I used to believe, butterfly effect and all, that if she hadn't died, the terrorists wouldn't have been able to fly the planes into the buildings," Becca said softly. "I know it doesn't make sense."

"Twelve-year-olds believe a lot of weird stuff. When my dad was twelve, he believed that if he played the right guitar chords, he could summon Bessie out of Lake Erie, take a picture, and sell it to World Weekly News for a million dollars." I thought about all the irrational things I had once believed. What if I hadn't been out partying with Victoria the weekend before Mom died? God wouldn't have punished me by taking her away. But that was too hard to talk about. Dad's story was funnier.

"Your dad is so weird it's actually cool."

I smiled and shook my head vigorously. "Not when he tells the same story every time a certain song comes on the radio..." I scrunched up my face. Dad had gotten a girlfriend over the summer. Her name was Shellie, and she smoked blue American Spirits and made me turn off *Lord of the Rings* when it came on cable, because she wanted to watch some reality show on E!

Mom would never.

"Were you in the car when the accident happened?" I asked.

"No...it was pretty bad. There was a rock slide, she overcorrected, went down a ravine. Californians don't know how to drive in the rain." Becca stopped trying to wrangle her shirts and instead, pulled herself up onto the folding table and stared into the spinning contents of the dryer, watching her underwear tumble. I wondered if her thoughts were tumbling, too.

"My mom had breast cancer, but they didn't catch it in time, and it was already in her brain by the time doctors found out. I mean. They found out the day she had the stroke."

"The best timing," Becca repeated softly. "I always hated it when, afterward, people would try to tell me that everything happens for a reason. I remember one of the nurses at the psychiatric hospital used to say that, and like, I don't know, it always felt like that was the cruelest outlook to have. To think that Mom had to die for something else, something presumably better, to happen. I didn't want anything better to happen. I was just a kid. I wanted my mom, you know?"

"My AP English teacher used to say that we create reasons out of the things that happen to us, and faith is the pen we use to connect the dots."

"All my faith ever got me was a six-month lockup in a juvenile psych ward…I don't believe in all of that anymore. Not the saints, not the supernatural, nothing. The Goblin King isn't coming to take me away. There's no reason for anything. But I like Pop-tarts and cheese fries, so…gotta stick around for something, right?"

⬧✦⬧

I wished I'd never mentioned cheese fries last night. Maybe, butterfly effect and all, if I hadn't brought it up, Becca would have left the restaurant in time to just miss the car. I imagined it racing down the street again, black body gleaming under the street lamps, the blinding glow of its headlights, the weight of the air as it flew past, and Becca, just out of reach, spinning back toward the curb, running off into the night. Safe.

There were no reasons for anything. We had to make those up for ourselves. The only way to clean up this mess was going to be by taking out Gavin, and possibly Calliope. She knew too much to be innocent. I didn't care what Harold thought.

I showered quickly to wash away the soot from my misadventures the night before, putting my unwashed hair up into a bun and pulling out a few face-framing tendrils, the way Harold had said he liked. Not that I was styling myself for Harold...but I wanted to know that he was safe. The harsh edges of my anger and betrayal had settled into a dull, hollow ache that drummed at the periphery of my frayed emotional state. I'd lost too much; I had no bearings anymore.

I wasn't human. Whatever future I thought I'd imagined with Harold lay shattered like so much glass at my feet. There was no house in Winnetka to go back to, and my own apartment in Oak Park was no safe haven. And Becca—

Once again my mind's eye replayed the sick wet thud of the car hitting Becca's body, memories returning to that awful moment I knew she was gone, the color of the steam rising off her blood that seeped across the icy asphalt—and the whole world collapsed inward again, compressing reality into a singular, catastrophic horror: It was my fault. *Everything was.* I'd tried to save Becca from a fate I considered worse than death...but I'd failed, and Becca was truly dead.

Almost would have been better to let her become a vampire then... the monstrous voice inside my head had been growing bolder.

No.

But maybe. Possibly. I didn't know.

I knew I was hungry, and that there was no blood in the suite.

I scrunched up my eyes to keep tears from falling; the ache in my belly was equal parts hunger and grief, impossible to know where one began, and the other ended. I wanted to unravel the whole world, like one of Nana's crochet afghan blankets, when she decided to start over. There had to be something salvageable in all this mess that had become my life.

I wasn't sure what the future held, but destroying Gavin was the only focus I had left—my sanity and sense of self clung like bloody tatters on the shards of all that had broken around me.

The clothes from the night before were too stained and smudged from stomping around in the ruins of Harold's old house to wear again, so I hung them up on the shower curtain until they could be dry cleaned, deeply ingrained habit one of the only facets of myself I could still rely on, and I put on a pair of jeans and a thick, soft green sweater from the closet where I'd put away the rest of the department store clothes last night, double-checking that I had what remained of the cash, and my hotel room key. As for the sword...I wrapped it up in a bath towel. It was a poor disguise, but the best I could do with the materials I had on hand.

The flask, sadly, would not fit in the pockets of any of my clothes (why couldn't girls have functional pockets, too?), so I left it in the center of the bed where I wouldn't forget it later, after doing my best to straighten the covers. The bedding was still a bloodstained mess, but at least now it was a tidy blood-stained mess.

I thought I remembered the general stretch of Michigan Avenue that intersected the street Calliope's high rise was located on—the large windows had overlooked the lake and a number of other downtown landmarks as well, and I remembered that there was a popular gastropub on the ground floor nearby. I also remembered that we had walked there from Becca's apartment on New Year's Eve, which narrowed things down considerably, but it still took several aggravating, traffic-gridlocked circles around the Magnificent Mile with my increasingly frustrated taxicab driver before I was certain I'd found the right building.

I'd never been so glad to get out of a warm vehicle in my life. With the heater cranked up inside the cab and no windows open for ventilation, the scent of the driver's blood was becoming overwhelming, and I didn't want to think about what I could have done to him if we'd had to make another circle around the block. I paid my fare and all but jumped out of the car—only to immediately land on a patch of ice and skid, arms flailing, across the sidewalk toward the private, residents-only entrance of Calliope's building.

The doorman was not amused.

I imagine he'd seen all types, even vampires, but I imagined that the other vampires visiting Calliope Jones' penthouse didn't make fools of themselves slipping on ice.

"I'm a guest of Calliope Jones." I steadied myself with as much dignity as I could muster, although I'm not sure how effective of a recovery I made.

"Password?" The doorman gave me an arched, appraising look. In my thin winter clothes and lack of an overcoat, I was suspiciously ill-prepared for the windy Chiberia temperatures.

"I don't know the password. I have an appointment."

"You don't have an appointment without a password. No password, no appointment."

"I swear, she knows me. I've been here before. You need to let me in."

He shook his head and took a full step toward me, effectively blocking me from entering the lobby any further. I could have forced my way past him. I could have broken every bone in his body, ripped his still-beating heart out of his chest, and danced in the rain of blood before it froze in the icy air.

But that would have been cruel. I'd decided I wanted to avoid cruelty, if possible.

The doorman threatened to call additional security, and I didn't want to get arrested. Again. I started to wonder how long it would take me to climb up the exterior walls of the skyscraper to reach the penthouse. Maybe, if it hadn't been so windy, I might have attempted it. I took two steps backward to examine the ornate exterior of the high rise, then settled on a better idea. I reached into my jeans pocket and pulled out the rest of the cash I had on hand.

"I'll make you a bet." My voice dripped honey. "Call up to the Jones residence, and inform her that Grace Cordero is here to see her, and if she doesn't let me in, I will give you all this cash and walk away, and you'll never see me again." I tried not to stare at the throbbing pulse of the doorman's neck, visible just above his tightly wrapped scarf. I held my ground. Behind the second set of doors that led into the lobby, the receptionist was already picking up the phone.

"Ms. Jones says that Grace Cordero is on the approved list," she informed us.

I flashed the doorman a tight-lipped smile and palmed him a large bill for being a good sport about letting me pass. He escorted me over to the private elevator and entered the code, still squinting at me suspiciously. His eyes fell to the blanket-wrapped item I carried in both arms.

"Is that a freakin' sword?" he asked.

"You didn't see nothin'," I shot back as the elevator doors closed, and I began my ascent back to the place where everything had started.

Calliope Jones was waiting for me in the foyer, and welcomed me into her home with a hug I was not expecting.

"Grace, what are you doing here?" Her voice, so uniquely sharp and soft whenever we'd spoken before, now cracked, and I didn't know what to think about the almost palpable sense of relief radiating off of her.

"You keep asking me that question." I blinked, rooted in place, briefly transported to the moment Calliope had first found me standing next to her windows. I blinked again and returned to the present, shaking off the vestiges of memory like snowflakes from my shoulders. Calliope looked tired, stretched too thin. Her eyes darted back to the elevator behind me, as though she were expecting someone else to come up. No one did.

"What's with the owls?" I asked. When she'd leaned in to hug me, I'd noticed the small jeweled and enamel pin on her lapel.

"Did Harold bring you back here?" she asked. Her hand darted, briefly, to the antique jewelry, but she didn't answer my question.

I shook my head. "I haven't seen him since the night before last. He left me a message, at our hotel. That he was here. So where is he? And why—?" *Owls. I was seeing them everywhere.*

She seemed startled, and the effect was jarring. She looked much as she had the first night I met her—no wig, no heavily stylized makeup. She wore a light blue blouse that was perfect for her coloring, tucked into a pair of loose-fitting chino pants secured with a simple designer belt. Even her casual clothes probably cost more than I earned in a month at my old job, and I couldn't help but notice the subtle, skillful tailoring that rendered the few curves she had almost invisible. Her short-cropped hair was tousled with some kind of styling paste, and the overall look would have been completely androgynous, if not entirely masculine, absent the perfect smear of matte red lipstick she wore. It was a curious concession to femininity, but I didn't have time to think about that.

Harold left almost an hour ago to get back to the hotel, she insisted. She couldn't have kept him if she'd tried, she swore. But why didn't she help me try to reach him? She dialed the number to our suite on a hard plastic landline phone situated on a marble console table near the foyer. Of course she knew the number of the hotel. It was one of her properties.

How much of the city was under her control?

I did not trust Calliope Jones.

The phone she handed me rang multiple times after I entered our suite number, but no one picked up. I left a message.

"Um. Harold. Hi. I'm at Calliope's now. I guess we missed each other. Call me at her place when you get this message, okay?" I disconnected the call and handed the phone back to Calliope.

She gave one curious glance at the towel-wrapped package I was toting under my arm, but didn't say anything about it. "When word got out in the Community about the fire, when I couldn't reach either of you—I cried for nights. I still don't know everything that happened, even after what Harold told me, but I'm so glad you're all right." She reached out her hand as though she was going to touch my face again, but I stepped just beyond the stretch of her fingertips, shaking my head, remembering what Nadia had told me about vampires and touch. I wished she'd given me a heads up about vampires drinking each other's blood, too, but it was too late for that.

"Why can't I reach Harold's phone?" I asked.

She let out a long-suffering sigh and shook her head. "He had a meltdown last night, recounting your falling out—"

"He *told* you about that?"

"Harold Laing and I have known each other for a very long time—I think you might have some idea now—and we don't keep secrets from each other. His temper can get him into trouble sometimes, and he threw his phone like a petulant child. It broke. The sun started to come up, and he had no choice but to spend the day in my guest room. It's not like he hasn't spent the day here before. He used to live here, you know."

"What exactly did he tell you?" I asked, indignation torching through me. I hadn't known that he'd lived with Calliope at the penthouse. I didn't know anything, and Calliope seemed to know everything. *He had no right to tell her anything about us.*

Calliope walked toward the modern kitchen I had seen before, with all the appliances hidden behind panels meant to look invisible. "Are you thirsty?" she asked, avoiding my question. "I know you're always thirsty, when you're young..."

I shook my head no, then nodded yes, and Calliope laughed, not unkindly. She was already heating up water and pulling familiar-looking bags of crimson liquid out of a discretely hidden refrigerator.

"The owls are a bit of an inside joke in the Community." She said, finally volunteering some information, even if it wasn't very much. "Nocturnal birds of prey, all that symbolism. It's all very silly, but common enough to exchange owl-motif items as gifts, between makers and fledglings...I'm surprised—but I suppose there was no reason for Harold to have told you that, since you aren't, in fact, his actual fledgling..."

In the memory that wasn't mine, I recalled the image of Irene, her full-skirted red dress, the aluminum Christmas tree glowing behind her, and the owl-engraved flask, wrapped up in a box with a bow. *No wonder he didn't like the plain version I had given him.* Irene had put so much more thought and effort into her gift. She'd been his fledgling, after all. My version had just been picked up as an afterthought. It was nothing special. Just like me.

"Well, I guess you're just going to have to stay here for a while until you get in touch again. Isn't this like old times..." Calliope chuckled for a moment, then turned and said, very seriously, "I hated the old times, actually." There was a hard set to her jaw that spoke volumes. From what I knew of Calliope's history, her loathing was justified.

I looked around at the penthouse while waiting for the blood to warm up. "I like the way you've redecorated," I said. I didn't want to think about the necklace Becca had been wearing last night. *He had been planning to turn her, after all.* They'd both wanted it. The idea of Gavin grieving over Becca made me sick. He never should have touched her. He never should have come near either of us.

Calliope seemed confused for a moment, scanning the room for anything it of place, then smiled, a sound that may have been second cousins with a laugh escaping her lips. "Oh, you mean the mess from the last time you were here…Yes, I had that cleaned up right away, I can't stand clutter."

"Me, either," I agreed, as she handed me a mug of warmed-up blood, just as she had my first night as a vampire. Calliope, stripped of all the artifice of her public persona, at ease in the comfort of her own home, seemed like a genuinely pleasant person, and I was growing confused about the assumptions I had made about her.

Calliope answered a cell phone call, made some notes on her tablet, and did a few more business-related things, leaving me to my own company. I only paid enough attention to her business to determine that it had nothing to do with mine, before wandering over to the baby grand piano I'd noticed on my first night. I'd wondered if it had just been for show…

I lifted the lid and tested a few keys. It was in tune, as perfectly maintained as everything else Calliope Jones owned, but as my fingers brushed the black and white piano keys, I picked up no vibrations of Calliope's energy, radiating off the instrument. There was something tantalizingly familiar about the vibrations I did pick up. Something that felt like home, and belonging.

I sat down on the bench and tried to remember the pieces of music that Nana had forced me to commit to memory. Alberto Ginastera's Danza de la Moza Donosa came to mind. It was a dark, melancholy composition that suited my mood. Nana had always liked Ginastera. "He's like us," she told me. "Italian, but not from Italy." I think he was born in Argentina.

It was a pleasure to play on Calliope's piano, and my fingers moved across the keys less falteringly than I would have expected, after so much time out of practice. Muscle memory, and my morose frame of mind, made the notes come easily—and if my timing was slightly off or a note or two misplaced, who was there to judge me?

I doubted that Calliope had much working knowledge of twentieth-century modernist composers.

"I didn't know you played piano." Calliope's soft voice came up from behind me.

"Not sure how that's something you could have known." I shrugged. She sat down next to me on the piano bench, ran her fingers across the keys.

"It's been a while since anyone here played music."

"James?" I asked. Calliope looked taken aback.

"How do you know James?"

"Harold told me, a bit." I shrugged. For what it was worth, it felt good to return a little bit of Calliope's own medicine.

Calliope shook her head. "No, James was..." she looked like there were several things she was trying to decide between saying, but she was quiet for several minutes, saying nothing instead. She looked even sadder than she had before.

"What did Harold tell you about...us?" I asked, changing the subject.

Calliope looked up sharply. "He said that you found out about...his wife, in what must have been the worst way possible. He's never been able to control what comes out in his blood, even as old as he is, and I told him he was an idiot for not being upfront with you about her, and he didn't take my lack of sympathy very well." She sighed. "He says it was a long time ago, but it really wasn't. Not for our kind. Not for us..."

"Do you think that's why he hasn't tried to get in touch or called back?" I fidgeted with the corner of the towel that was wrapped around my sword that was propped up against the piano bench.

Calliope shrugged. "Harold has a history of running off when life gets difficult. I wouldn't be surprised."

My heart sank. I wouldn't blame Harold for running away from me. He shouldn't have been so cagey about his past relationship, but my rejection might have been...slightly disproportional. I didn't know how I was supposed to feel about things. But it didn't feel respectful to his dead wife to have done the things we did in bed. You weren't supposed to replace people after you'd promised them forever. I was certain of that much. "Do you live here all by yourself?" I asked, changing the subject. The penthouse was as immaculate and impersonal as a hotel. Calliope might occupy the space, but there was no sign of her anywhere inside it, other than the white-on-white and clutter-free decor, which seemed consistent with her preferences overall. "I guess you don't need staff..."

"I have a crew come in once a week the dust and vacuum and keep the chandelier sparkling, that sort of thing. " Calliope shrugged. "I don't need a chef or a personal trainer. My toilets hardly ever need cleaning...having mortals up here more often than they already are would be too risky. My secretary works in her own office nearby, and my entire business can be run remotely, anywhere in the world. So I don't mind keeping my own space tidy, to answer my own phone when the doorman calls, or welcome my own visitors." She smiled and looked around at her lovely home, and seemed to be very much content.

"It's just a lot of space to be all alone in, I guess."

"Most of us live alone, Grace. That's the nature of our existence," Calliope said, with a touch of sadness.

"I think it's probably better that way." I agreed, a sudden sullenness descending on me. We stood up and walked back toward the kitchen. I carried the mug of blood in one hand and the sword in the other. Calliope still hadn't said anything about it.

"Now you sound just like Harold."

"Proximity, I guess..." I finished the blood that Calliope had given me with a gulp and a shudder of pleasure that left gooseflesh on my arms under my sweater sleeves and set the cup next to where I thought the sink was. Bagged blood, even heated up, was nowhere near as fulfilling as... (*wild-caught, free range*, said the voice in my head). I didn't argue with myself, but vowed to stick to the processed stuff as often as possible.

"*Human blood is hot, Grace.*" I could hear Harold's voice in my head now. "*If I'm used tae drinking blood chilled, or even stale, then I won't be as likely tae see people as food every time I step foot outside the house.*"

"I think it's more than simple proximity..." Calliope mused. "I think you two have quite a bit in common."

"Harold and I have nothing in common," I insisted.

"You were created in the same way."

My jaw dropped. *Of course she would know that...*I remembered.

"It's more than that, of course," Calliope continued, resting her chin on her hands and gazing at me intently with her ageless blue eyes. "It's obvious now. Both of you have a penchant for trying to play the hero for the people you love, or think you love, and you both get burned for it."

I swallowed a lump in my throat that was all shards of broken mirrors. "You mean like...Becca? And...you?"

Calliope nodded. "I found out about her last night through the grapevine. I'm so sorry, it was a terrible accident. I can only imagine what it was like to watch that."

"I don't want to talk about Becca," I insisted. *I should have done more. I should have moved faster. If I'd only caught her by the arm on her way out the door, delayed her crossing the street by three seconds...if I hadn't distracted her while she was walking away, if I hadn't wasted time, hunting and fucking the night before...*guilt gnawed away at my sanity. What the hell was I doing, wasting time with Calliope, when I ought to have been looking for her fledgling so I could murder him? My fingers twitched as I gripped the sword tighter.

"Harold's foolish heroism in regards to me got him killed. Did he tell you that? As if I wasn't perfectly capable of making my own decisions and pursuing my own agenda—"

"He didn't tell me, exactly, but I saw...in the blood. You bargained for him."

She nodded.

"Did you do it because you loved him?"

Calliope rolled her eyes. "Harold was in love with me the way a man will decide that he's in love with any young woman who nurses him back to health when he's sick. It's all very romantic...but, you see, I am not and was not a romantic, regardless of what Harold and my father seemed to believe. I suppose to the outside, it was a good match. Harold was skilled at many things, I was good at running an inn. Wouldn't we have made a charming provincial couple, running a prosperous roadside inn next to a blacksmith's shop, helping out travelers and shoeing their horses and raising a half dozen children? He couldn't even read, you know. Not at first. I would have died slowly, every day, trapped in that life." She sighed, but not the way Harold sighed. She wasn't exasperated, just...wistful.

"I wanted more opportunities than a woman of my era was afforded. Particularly, I wanted business opportunities. I was interested in commercial shipping operations and banking and, oh, all sorts of things women weren't supposed to be interested in. And so when I figured out Vincente's little secret, well, I made a deal. It was a simple as that."

"Did you know what you were getting into, really? What you would become?"

She nodded and leaned forward, whispering, almost confidentially. "Turn me, I said, and be the male identity I need to front any business venture I might undertake, and I promised them...a lot of money. I was so confident I could make us all wealthy, with enough time, and the right business partner—mostly one who stayed completely out of the way. Vincente and his brothers were growing tired of ravaging and pillaging the countryside. I offered them stability.

"And then, once we were turned and everything behind us had burned to the ground, I paid my debt." Her voice lowered even further as she continued, "It took me almost fifty years."

I raised my eyebrows; I'd misinterpreted Harold's story by the bonfire in the backyard. "*You* blew them up after you'd paid them off, didn't you?" Three vampire brothers who got the wrong end of a stick of dynamite...

"I paid the debt I owed. And then I made them pay, for what they did to me. Fifty years of hell...They deserved it, all three of them. I booked us passage to New York. Harold and I in one stateroom, Vincente, Bernard, and Dionisio in another. We shouldn't have all traveled together. That many vampires on board one ship was too dangerous. Everyone was sick, multiple people died. The captain started to get nervous. But that made him easy to manipulate. I told him enough—that they were monsters, that the sickness would go away if he got rid of them. He was a superstitious man. I'd already arranged for a small shipment of dynamite in the hold, and it was easy to convince the captain. He ordered their steamer trunks removed from their cabins at mid-day, loaded onto a raft piled with explosives, and—"

"Boom!" We breathed in unison, surprising me. Calliope's eyes met mine for a brief, startled moment, and then she looked down, smiling softly. She was beautiful, I realized, like an ancient porcelain vase. Maybe a little crazed on the surface, but more durable than you'd think. She'd survived for centuries, after all. I didn't want to like her, but she was very difficult to dislike.

"I even paid a photographer on board to take some glass plates. I wanted proof. The plates are in the Smithsonian collection," she went on. "I finally donated them sometime in the nineteen thirties. Of course the curators don't know the true story behind the image, but I like knowing that it is safe."

I thought it was odd that Calliope would brag about killing her maker, when she knew that I was planning to kill the vampire who had turned me. I'd even brought the weapon I was planning to use into her home, carried it right in front of her, and she hadn't said a word about it. But neither of us said Gavin's name, either. It lingered unspoken in the air, the proverbial elephant in the room.

Calliope glanced at her phone again.

"Are you waiting on someone?" Given her attire for the evening, whoever Calliope had been planning to meet certainty wasn't a mortal who would expect to see the more advanced version of Calliope Jones. She'd definitely been planning on meeting with another vampire.

"After...everything that's happened in the last week, I thought it best if I take the night off," she said, by way of non-answer. The nervous, haunted look returned to her eyes.

"What have you done with Harold?"

"For the love of God, Grace, please. Harold is the one person, man or vampire, I could never harm. You must believe me. I have no idea where he is, but I know that he's an idiot, and that you hurt him, badly."

"It's complicated..." I tried to explain, but there were no words.

"Harold has a history of running away from his problems, I told you. If you only knew the extent of it. Maybe he's decided to run off again. For his own sake, I almost hope he did. I hope he's far away from Chicago, by now."

"What's going on?"

"Oh, It's all rubbish, and mostly deals with events that ought to have nothing to do with you. I tried to protect you, you know. I sent you away. And, when that wasn't working, I tried to bring you back here. Sadly, I can no longer extend that invitation...But there's still time. I can get you out of the city tonight. My secretary can drive you anywhere you want to go—"

I shook my head, determined. No.

"I don't want you to end up like Becca..."

"Someone hit her. On purpose. I'm going to find out."

"And then what, Grace?" Her tone was nothing but exasperation. "You still don't know anything about anything. Consider yourself lucky. I was planning to receive another visitor tonight, but it no longer looks like they will be stopping by."

Something excited and violent and bloodthirsty lurched inside of me, and I knew, with complete certainty, that Calliope had been waiting for Gavin to show up.

I took a deep breath and let it out in a trembling exhale, trying to steady my shaking hands. I doubted I'd have the opportunity to ask Calliope my next question ever again. "What happened to Irene?"

Chapter Thirty-Two

AN INDELIBLE STAIN

I MUST HAVE CAUGHT her off guard—I think she swayed, ever so slightly, before she pressed her hands together and brought them to her lips, as though considering her options. "I thought you knew. He said you'd seen it all, in his blood. He said you wouldn't look at him after you found out about it."

"I saw pieces. Fragments. He's the one who said she's dead, but I don't know what happened, not really, and—still. There's lots of things he didn't tell me. And I don't know if he's coming back. Maybe you're right. I think he would have by now, if he was going to. But I think I deserve to know."

"Irene was my best friend. You probably didn't know that, either, did you, Miss-I-Don't-Want-To-Talk-About-Becca-Moreno."

I flinched, and Calliope softened.

"I'm sorry," she corrected herself. "It's just that it's a terrible memory, and I don't like revisiting it or what happened to bring it about, if I can help it."

"Harold said you were there. It happened at the Wisconsin house, right?"

"Oh, God. That's where the two of you disappeared to. I don't understand why he still keeps that shrine..."

I remembered the human-sized stain on the carpet near the patio windows.

Calliope must have figured out what the look on my face meant, because she sighed and placed her hands very carefully on her lap. Much like Harold often did, she appeared to consider her words with precision, before she spoke.

"Where to even begin? He used to feed on prostitutes. I think something about exchanging money for what he needed appealed to his moral code. Or maybe he just enjoyed hanging out at brothels. They could be entertaining places, you know. I've owned several establishments myself, over the years. But Irene wasn't one of my girls. I never would have allowed that kind of thing. He met her down in Kansas City, I think, about a decade after his hopelessly misguided infatuation with that Irish cop ended badly...but that's an entirely different story. Harold Laing really knows how to pick them..." Calliope rolled her eyes, and I wasn't sure if I should be offended.

"And Irene was a lovely creature, truly, but she was also broken, and Harold couldn't do anything about that. He fed from her, he fell in love with her, he married her, and then...he turned her. Which only exacerbated a problem that had been there long before they met. Between you and me, I think he believed he could fix her. I've never heard of anything more foolish. We're all responsible for our own demons..."

I tilted my head in half-hearted agreement, wondering how much she knew about Harold's conversations with me. *He'd called me broken...*

Calliope continued, her voice growing softer, less judgmental. "I'm not saying I don't understand her appeal. Irene was a darling, and she doted on him. He obviously loved her. Even I adored her. Years before we met in person, she was always sending cards and letters, keeping me informed of where they were living, what they were up to, and I wrote back...she was my friend. I'd never had a platonic female friendship like that. Not that I wouldn't have minded something less platonic. But Harold would have killed me, and Irene was as straight as they come.

"But I used to have a film projector, and we'd have movie nights. I'd show up at his house in my Cadillac and call out to him, 'I'm kidnapping your wife,' and she'd come running down the walk in the silly high heels she wore that always made her taller than him, and...anyway. The details aren't important." Still, I thought I saw an almost-smile tease the corners of her mouth before her face became sad again.

"She had a real gift for people. You just don't find that very often with us. That kind of warmth. She never forgot a face or a name, an anniversary or a detail or...Everyone in the Community loved her. I loved her completely, in my own way."

She sighed and waved her hand dismissively when I winced. "It's not that you're not charming and attractive on your own, Grace. I hope you'll realize someday just how many—but I digress. I could see the writing on the wall years before Harold did. I knew it was all going to end in disaster...

"Because he wouldn't *let* her hunt. I think maybe a few times they'd go out into the woods together and...feed off of animals or something. Deer, I guess. They fed on a lot of animals for a while. It was a phase. But she never hunted on her own or went out and got her own blood, so far as I know. Harold did that for her. And at first, of course, we all do that for our fledglings, but Harold just...never stopped. If she wanted blood, he got her blood. If she wanted a farm in the countryside, he bought her a farm, no matter how far out he had to drive to find hospital blood, or hunt down hobos on the train tracks, or whatever. Just ridiculous. He was besotted with her."

I didn't mean to catch my breath, but she gave me a penetrating glance when I did. "That's why you were so angry at him for not taking me hunting," I said, the foundations of their argument at the house suddenly clearer to me. "Well, that's fixed now."

Calliope seemed to appraise me for a moment, something about her expression reminding me of a dressmaker's shears sliding through silk, cutting down a large bolt of fabric into manageable pieces. She cocked her head slightly to the side, offsetting her otherwise preternatural stillness. I still wasn't convinced vampires were incapable of mind-reading, especially after some of my conversations with Harold, even before the blood and the...fucking. He'd said it was just practice and intuition. But when my eyes briefly locked with Calliope's before I looked away, I knew she knew I'd crossed that threshold, and I'd liked it.

*...the wash of my victim's blood over my tongue, hot crimson rivers pulsing down my throat to the beat of his pounding heart, the way he grew limp in my arms as I set him down gently on the icy sidewalk...*I'd done that, all on my own. I couldn't imagine denying myself that pleasure, now.

The last time I'd sat on her sofa, I would have averted my gaze entirely and spiraled inward at the very idea I'd be capable of such a thing, much less want it. But that Grace was dead. Maybe she hadn't died completely on New Year's Eve. But the Grace I'd been before was surely as dead as Becca was now. I was a monster, and I didn't think I minded so much.

"Good, I'm glad to hear it." Calliope leaned back, looking up at the soaring ceilings of her penthouse, and got on with her story. "Irene had a baby when she was thirteen. I never knew the exact circumstances, except that she was rather young. And the nuns made her give the baby up for adoption, you know. That's the way they did it in those days. As if a runaway street urchin barely out of childhood herself was in any position to care for an infant, it's ridiculous to think...

"But Irene never got over that child. Ever. Harold turned her in...nineteen twenty-four? When Irene was maybe twenty-three years old, I think. And for the next sixty years, she obsessed over finding the little girl. She never could. She was still looking for her baby when that baby ought to have been an elderly woman with grandchildren of her own, and I braced the inevitable disaster for years...but I never expected the fallout to be so grim." Calliope was quiet for several moments, unmoving. When I looked closely, she seemed to be trying to swallow a lump in her own throat, and I gripped the leather sofa I was seated on, already knowing, in my gut, what must have happened.

"Who did she kill?" I whispered.

"Oh, she did more than kill someone, sweetheart." Calliope's laugh was colder than wind rising off the lake. "In the winter of 1985, Irene lured a pregnant teenage girl into her house while Harold was away, off getting blood to feed the both of them, and she *slaughtered* that young girl and her baby. I don't know what she was thinking. I don't know if she was thinking. She lost control, is what happened. Her hunger got the better of her, and the scene was gruesome, from what I was able to get out of Harold. Six decades she had been shielded from her true nature, coddled, like an innocent, instead of the creature that she was. That we all are. Of course she was going to blow it eventually, and it was always going to be messy. You could see that coming a mile away. Inevitable." Calliope clicked her tongue and looked at the time, stalling.

"The stain on the carpet..." I insisted, feeling sick again. Calliope gave me a sharp look.

"You've seen how Harold gets, in a disaster. You can guess what he did when he came home to the mess. There was no salvaging their life on that street after what she did, so he set the crime scene on fire, as one does, and drove off...you know the place. A kind of 'just in case' getaway...we all have them. He should have torn up that rug decades ago. I don't know how he can stand returning to that spot, as often as he goes there to keep the windows caulked, and the shingles on."

She spoke of the house in the present tense, as if she was unaware what Gavin and his accomplice had done the night before. I considered the possibility that she didn't know; that despite her assertions, there were secrets Harold kept from her. I decided there was no point in bringing up the fate of the house. I didn't want Callipe to stop talking. An abrupt and awful thought descended and plunged me into ice water, and I realized that I already knew who, not what, had caused the human-shaped dark spot on the floor in the living room, right next to the sliding glass doors that led...outside. "She didn't." I whispered.

Calliope nodded. "She did, poor thing. It was winter, around the first week of February. And it was snowing that day...that Irene walked out into the sun."

I gasped in spite of myself, in spite of knowing what was coming, but Calliope continued, as committed to her story and all the gruesome details as I was to hearing her tell it.

Look at me, getting everything I thought I wanted, recently. I was going to have to stop wanting things.

"She called me, just before sunrise. So close to sunrise...James was already out like a light; normally I wouldn't have even picked up the phone. She was babbling, hysterical. Said that she could never face him again, never face herself. She wanted me to know where she was. I begged her to go back to bed. I don't know if there was anything I could have done. They were hours outside of my circle of influence in the city.

"The yard was north-facing; it didn't get a lot of sun throughout the day, not beneath all those trees. And winter days are short. And if it was overcast...but, you see, all that made everything worse, I think, in the end. I started driving as soon as the sun went down...the sky still so red on the horizon, I could barely see at first. But I knew. I knew when she'd called me, sobbing, what she was going to do. She was Harold's wife, but she was *my* friend." Calliope continued staring up at the chandelier; her eyes glistened, but no tears fell.

"...Harold found her in a snowbank, long before I got there; she'd been outside for hours. I don't know how long it took her the courage to step outside. Did she slip out the door when the sky was still dark, and wait for the sun to meet her? Or did she have to work up her nerve? Did it take her a while, I wonder, to drum up the courage to do it? And did she try, perhaps, to crawl back inside after she started burning? Or did she just lay there in the light and take it? I can't tell you how often I've been haunted by those thoughts, especially after what happened in Australia...

"What was left of Irene was charred and blackened all over when I came around the back of the house, and found him cradling her in his arms. He'd dragged her inside the glass doors, as if getting her shelter at that point would have changed the outcome. She wasn't ash yet, though, and he was pouring his blood into her mouth, trying to heal her. I think he would have emptied himself out for her, if doing so would have stopped...

"Nothing would have saved Irene Laing." Calliope shook her head, and her voice grew quiet and strained as she went on. No mortal ears would have heard her horrifying whispered memories. It was hard enough for me. The background roar of the skyscraper was a monstrous accompaniment.

"I was shouting at Harold to invite me into the house, he was shouting at me that they needed blood, more blood...but you could see already that it was too late. Sunlight is awful for us; once the fire starts, the chain reaction is unstoppable, all the blood could do was delay the end. He finally invited me inside, and I...sat with him, for some time, hours maybe, while we waited for her to fully die, and her body to turn to ash. Sometimes, her fingers would twitch a little before they fell off. She was still there. She could hear us. She knew, in the end, that we loved her...And then she was gone." Calliope shook her head and exhaled completely, but it didn't stop her lower lip from quivering. If I'd had tears of my own left to cry, I would have sobbed beside her, but we sat in unnatural silence instead for several minutes.

I finally drew in breath to speak, my voice a whisper barely louder than Calliope's had been. "I'm sorry. I didn't know..."

"Well, you wanted to. So there you go." Calliope didn't look at me. I had no more words. After what seemed like a long time, she stood up and wiped her sweating palms on her slacks with her typical brisk efficiency, trying to regain composure; we both reacted with shock when faint smears of blood appeared on the fabric where Calliope's hands had been, and she sighed, contemplating the bloodstains.

"Obviously, it's still a very painful story. But I don't think I've ever told it before to anyone else, either."

"Thank you…" I whispered, my voice hoarse, my stomach leaden.

"I don't know what the hell you're thanking me for. But at least you know now. What he wouldn't tell you. Though why he'd want to relive that night for anyone is beyond me. Did you think you were in love with him?"

"It was stupid, really…"

Calliope scoffed. "Harold Laing is a fool, too. I don't know what to do with either of you. Give me a few more decades, and I'll figure it out. But Grace…? Take care of yourself? Don't get too preciously obsessed with what you left behind in your mortal life. Don't live in a fantasy world where you can pretend to be something you're not. Don't get too attached to people, or things."

It made sense to me now, why Calliope lived alone in such sterile comfort. The penthouse was nice, but nothing inside of it was irreplaceable. No fine art master-works of centuries past, no tapestries or original sculptures or engravings. All of the art and decor was high-end, but not original. Reproductions and mass-produced corporate art. *Calliope's most treasured possession is in the Smithsonian*, I remembered

"And Grace…" Calliope looked up at me, pleading, "if you do see Harold again, don't tell him I told you all of this. He tries so hard to forget. He wouldn't want to know you were carrying this memory alongside him."

"I don't think you need to worry about me and Harold," I replied. "Actually, at this point, I don't think there is a me and Harold. Not anymore. I shouldn't have said the things I said, and…he probably just decided to keep driving, like you said. That's why he hasn't called. I'm able to hunt on my own now, and I'll figure out the money thing I guess. I don't really need him." I shrugged, realizing as I spoke the words that it was all true. Of course, Harold had left the city. He had other houses elsewhere. Places that wouldn't get burned down, if I wasn't with him. I would have left, too, if the tables were turned, just like I'd run away after Becca was hit by the car.

"Maybe that's for the best, sweetheart," Calliope mused. "I've known Harold a very long time. He's the closest thing I ever had to a brother. My dumb, brilliant, chaotic, hopeless romantic of a baby brother. It was my fault he got dragged into this life, and I've tried to look out for him, all this time, but I can't stop him from running off and being an idiot. He married on a whim, he turned his wife when she begged him to without thinking it through, and you see where that got him. I'll admit there were moments when I grew concerned about the two of you getting entangled. I should have taken you off his hands when I had the chance. Like I said, you're very much alike, in a number of ways. But I could never put myself on the receiving end of that kind of heartache. I wouldn't wish it on you or on him...not again."

She straightened her shoulders and forced a thin, unconvincing laugh. "There are always other distractions. Honestly, I've had more lovers than you can imagine. They come, they go, men, women, other, neither...the last fledgling I turned didn't quite work out, but life goes on. You get used to the pain, and it stops hurting so much. I promise."

"You should put some seltzer on those bloodstains before they set." I stood up and looked around, trying to get my emotional bearings, at least. It had all been so vivid, the story that Calliope told, and when I closed my eyes, I could see the charred and blackened form of what had once been the woman with the strawberry-blonde hair, Harold's blood and her ashes embedding the carpet with a dark, indelible stain that would only ever be washed away by fire. How could anyone love someone else again, after that?

Gusts of wind rattled and howled outside the enormous plate-glass windows like a wounded animal, and I wanted to cry out as well, to scream into the winter gale until my lungs were empty and void, my screams carried away by frigid drafts and absorbed into the roar of the storm. There were clouds on the horizon that promised snow, and lots of it. I wanted to bury myself in a snowbank the size of a mountain and not emerge until spring; maybe by then, I'd be transformed into something that could survive this life. *But not even a snowbank had saved Irene from the sun*...I swallowed down more shards of mirrored glass embedded in my throat.

"Do you have any mixers left over from your party, by any chance?" *Focus, Grace.* Bizarre to think that the event at which I'd died had been less than two months ago. I longed to hit a reset, to erase eight weeks of my life.

Calliope stood up from the sofa and stretched, leonine and elegant, twisting her head back and forth on her neck as though she'd ever feel a crick there; she could pass so perfectly for human, she didn't even need to try. Every gesture, every nuance was practiced to the point of second nature. Again, I found myself unable to take my eyes off of her.

Am I attracted to Calliope Jones? That thought seemed like a disaster. As if things with Harold hadn't gone bad enough, bedding my maker's maker felt…not incestuous, exactly. But more dangerous than I cared to contemplate. Even so, I didn't think the attraction was one-sided. I didn't trust her, but that didn't mean that there wasn't some part of me that didn't want her. I quickly turned away toward the windows again, watching the storm clouds roll in closer from across the lake. Calliope started walking toward a hidden cabinet in the kitchen that contained an ungodly number of small, plain glass bottles.

She smiled and winked at me as I raised my eyebrows, thoroughly impressed.

That is one very prepared vampire. I was starting to like Calliope more and more. I didn't want to like her.

She twisted the seal on a small bottle of seltzer that opened with a hiss. "I knew I liked you the very first night we met, even though the circumstances were less than ideal." She dabbed on the stains her bloodied palms had let on her slacks with a damp paper towel.

"Really?" I squeaked, instantly humiliated. I coughed and cleared my throat, and Calliope laughed in the delicate non-laugh I thought was the least practiced—and most authentic—thing about her. *She had the most commanding presence I had ever known.*

"Why did you cancel the credit card and report it as stolen, then? Why did you go through all the trouble of having me arrested?" *Focus, Grace.*

She wrinkled her forehead at me. "I have no idea what you're talking about. I gave you that card to cover your expenses. Why would I cancel it?"

"And about those bodies they found in Harold's house? Where did they come from? Because it obviously wasn't us."

"Grace, I swear to you, Harold had the same questions. I can only tell you what I told him, it wasn't me, I don't—" but Calliope looked frantic.

I pressed on, gripping the sword at my side tighter. "...and the last fledgling you turned, the one who was supposed to meet you here tonight but didn't show up...what was his name?"

"I never told you my fledgling was a man. I never brought up details about any of my fledglings." Calliope arched a cool eyebrow and stared at me. I started right back, both of us unblinking.

Her cell phone made a chirping sound, which we both ignored, and I hoisted the sword, still wrapped up in the towel, taking a single step forward. As I did, the wrapping came undone slightly, revealing the hilt of the weapon that Harold had forged in his basement. Calliope looked at the sword and looked at me, her voice once again the polite scalpel edge when she said,

"I think you should leave. Now."

⸺⸺◆⸺⸺

I had time to think, as the elevator slowly made its way down to the lobby. I knew Calliope was hiding something that had to do with Gavin. I should have been in incendiary with rage.

But, I also knew that Calliope cared deeply for Harold. The bond they shared was definitely love, of some kind, even if it wasn't romantic. Calliope had cared for Irene, too, and in her own way, I knew she cared about me, not necessarily for any commonality we might share (although that might have been part of it), but mostly because Harold cared about me. Like he'd cared about Irene.

No. Not anywhere near like he'd cared for Irene. There was no way I could hold a candle to Harold's universally beloved late wife. That much was obvious. I was self-absorbed and insecure, no force of conviction holding me to any of the values I ever pretended to have. Archimedes might have been able to move the world with a long enough lever and a fulcrum, but it never really took more than a nudge to send me spiraling down dark trains of thought. Grace the monster never needed more than the right lever. So much less complicated than moving the world. All I'd needed was a few weeks of nudging.

Maybe I was a sociopath. Perhaps I always had been. I'd never felt truly connected with people in a way that made me keep in touch with old friends and acquaintances after...years and years. I was no sender of birthday cards and holiday letters. I'd known Becca for almost seven years, and that made her the longest friend I had.

Had had, I reminded myself. Becca was dead.

I was going to enjoy making Gavin Richardson pay for that. My hand caressed the hilt of the sword.

Harold had told me to let go of my mortal life, and I'd been so hesitant, so resistant. But how connected had I been, really? I had one close friend in the city—everyone else I'd known was really more Becca's friend than mine. I'd seen Dad and Nana less than a handful of times a year, over Thanksgiving and Christmas or maybe once during the summer, since graduating college. Since growing up, I'd only seen most of my cousins at holidays or weddings or funerals, and I hadn't kept in touch with a single acquaintance from elementary through high school. People tended to like me—at least, now that I was an adult and less plagued by mean girls and bullies, people were always telling me that they liked me...but looking at the evidence, I didn't really seem to like people very much.

I made the perfect vampire, didn't I? Unassuming, pretty without being threatening, so nice you just wanted to pour your heart out to me. And I could give...a little reassurance, a little money, a little hope, to people who came to me with their needs, and I could take what I needed in return. There was no violence when I hunted. People came to me. It was that easy.

The elevator door opened to a commotion outside the lobby, the doorman trying to stop someone else from getting in. I wrinkled my nose and smelled the copper bloom of blood—a lot of it.

"Hey, sword lady, my night's already weird as hell. Maybe you know this weirdo too! She says she needs to get up to the penthouse!" The doorman shouted as I strode across the lobby. The receptionist was already on the line with 911. Outside, in the first line of driving snow, a flailing homeless woman in ill-fitting green hospital scrubs screamed, almost incoherently, above the roar of the blizzard that was almost directly above the city. I took a few steps closer to get a better look at the trouble, and unsheathed the sword.

...she was covered in filth and soaked in blood, although none of it was hers, barefoot and bareheaded in the snow, her thick brown hair lustrous even matted with gore, monstrous screaming face beautiful, even without a stitch of makeup.

Becca.

CHAPTER THIRTY-THREE

PICTURES ON THE WALL

I LET OUT A slow-motion litany of curses as I raced over to the commotion, arrivingI at the door with a speed that felt supernatural. Maybe it was. I can only guess what I looked like as I positioned myself between Becca and the doorman while still, somehow, keeping one hand on my sword.

"It's okay. I've got this. We're good!" I shouted at the receptionist, who was still on the phone with emergency services, her eyes round orbs of confusion and fear when she looked at me. I dragged Becca down the street and waved goodbye to the beleaguered building staff. It wasn't their fault they were having a very weird evening…they were both just lucky to be alive, judging from the state Becca was in.

For her part, Becca seemed to recognize me, almost going limp as soon as I arrived to take charge. I pulled her into a shallow decorative alcove along the building's exterior, probably intended to hold planters full of flowers in the warmer months, but the space was empty now, except for the smell of piss that reeked even in the snow. The wind had picked up considerably, and temperatures were plummeting as thick heavy clouds rolled in, obscuring the tops of the buildings. Snow fell horizontally, stinging our faces, but it wasn't intolerable—and it was the least of my concerns. Becca was almost catatonic, and I needed her not to be, if we were going to make it to safety.

"Becca. You gotta help me out here." Pressed so close against her, I could smell the blood soaked into the fibers of the thin scrubs she was wearing, and my nostrils flared, my fangs extended. Even half-dried, the scent of the blood was stronger than the reek of urine rising up from the dirty sidewalk, and I inhaled, deeply. *Wasn't this fun?* I shook my head to dispel the voice of the other Grace, took Becca's face into my cold hands, and forced her to look at me, not as gently as I would have liked to. She blinked at me slowly, several times, her eyes focusing and unfocusing on my face.

"You're going to be okay," I insisted. "I'm here now. I've got you."

It started with a quivering of her lower lip that turned into full-body trembles, and Becca collapsed, throwing herself into my arms. "He wasn't—it wasn't—I was left in the dark, and I was all alone!" She wept breathlessly, still trying to figure out how to get her lungs to work well enough to make words, now that she wasn't breathing automatically anymore.

I threw my own arms around her shoulders and held tight. "I'm sorry. I'm sorry." Except, I wasn't. I was holding on to Rebecca Danielle Moreno again, and nothing could dampen that relief. "But I've got you and you're with me now, Trash Panda, and we've got to get you home. We can make it to your apartment, if you can trust me and *focus*."

Becca clung to me for a moment longer and whispered, "I could smell the blood in them!" into my ear, nodding her head in the direction of the building entrance we had just left behind us.

"It's like that. At first. It gets better in a few weeks." I didn't know what else to say. I remembered the way I'd lunged at the cleaning crew back at Calliope's my first night. Arms that held me back, from what I'd wanted to do. I'd wanted not just to feed, but to kill. Arms had held me back.

There had been no arms to hold Becca back when she rose, by the looks of things. That, too, was my fault.

Another frigid gust of wind blew in from the Lake, and I had never been more grateful for the hellish cold of a Chicago winter storm before. There were few cars on the road, and even fewer pedestrians on the sidewalk. I assumed Becca had fed on at least one person already, judging from the quantity of blood on her, and whoever it had been was probably dead. But at least that meant Becca was well-fed for the moment. I could worry about the moral complications later. I pulled her out of the alcove, grabbed her hand, and started walking in the direction of her apartment. The luxury high-rise that housed Becca's shoebox studio apartment was in the same general neighborhood as Calliope's high rise.

I didn't find navigating the distance back to Becca's place to be difficult, even with visibility approaching white-out conditions. I should have been shocked, but...it was a building I knew as well as the one I paid rent on, a place I'd slept at more nights than I could count. *Home.* Becca's apartment felt like home. It was the only safe place I knew anymore, and my feet remembered the way, all on their own.

I hoped the inclement weather had delayed the arrival of Becca's family to deal with the situation surrounding her recent demise. She'd only been dead since last night, after all. Maybe her family hadn't even been notified of the accident yet.

I used Becca's code to buzz us both into the main lobby through the side entrance, avoiding the doorman, because of course Becca didn't have her keys, and my own key ring had gotten lost somewhere between Harold's car and Wisconsin. All of Becca's personal possessions were probably still down at the Cook County Medical Examiner's office, where it looked like Becca had woken up. I shuddered. That was definitely worse than Calliope's bathtub.

There was a cabinet or a drawer near the concierge desk that contained copies of the keys to every unit in the building, I knew, because on more than one occasion, I'd had to sign for a copy when Becca was plastered after a night out.

I needed to be able to access that cabinet without being seen.

I left Becca on an out of the way bench in the lobby and marched a few steps closer to the concierge desk that was supposed to be manned twenty-four hours. "Don't breathe!" I whispered over my shoulder as I walked away, praying she heard me, and would do as I told her. I would have given my kingdom for some peppermint extract. But I trusted Becca to listen to me in a crisis. Becca always listened to me in a crisis, and this? This was a Crisis.

A curvy woman in her mid-thirties emerged from a small storage closet behind the desk, carrying a fresh cup of coffee and a stack of newspapers. She didn't seem to anticipate a busy night helping residents go anywhere or do anything—not with the weather outside behaving as badly as it was. I'd dealt with her before. Her name was Ruth, or something equally soft-sounding, but she was not a fan of Becca's frequent forgetfulness. Last time I'd had to sign for a key, she'd lectured both of us at length about building security and tenants' contracts. My stomach sank.

"Ruth? I hate to ruin your night, but someone's dog made a mess in one of the elevators. Jesus, I hope it was just someone's dog..." a man's voice called out from down the hall.

Ruth swore and ambled over to document the damage, and I said a silent prayer thanking my guardian angel for actually looking out for me. I wasted no time slipping behind Ruth's desk, frantically trying to discern where the spare unit keys were kept.

She'd left her own key ring behind on top of the stack of newspapers when she'd stepped away, but none of the keys seemed to match any of the cabinets at her station. Panic started flooding in. I could not afford to panic. I glanced up at the row of security monitors the staff had access to—Becca was still looking down at the floor, probably distracted by the reflections of the lobby lights on the marble floors—*good.* The concierge was still down the hall with the other tenant, but either of them could stop what they were doing at any moment, and we could not afford that trouble.

Focus, Grace.

One of the keys on the ring was the kind that opened a standard door lock. I darted over to the storage room behind the desk, and tried the key in the lock. It worked.

The small space behind the door was just large enough for a minuscule desk, cubby space with a purse and other personal belongings, a coffee maker, and a few courtesy umbrellas branded with the property's name, reserved for residents and their guests. But behind a musty-smelling, motley collection of staff parkas, I saw the edges of a row of grey metal cabinets set into the wall.

Becca lived on the seventeenth floor.

With barely seconds to spare, I rifled through the cabinets, located Becca's spare key, and locked up the closet.

The concierge returned almost immediately after I walked back to Becca. I glanced over my shoulder, and she seemed none the wiser for the intrusion.

I exhaled, slowly and completely.

"Gotcher key," I informed Becca, dangling the fob in front of her. "Let's go." I picked up my best friend and the sword from the bench where I'd left them both, and navigated us toward the stairs, avoiding the sight line of the concierge. There was no way in hell I was going to risk the elevators.

"Tell me what happened, but tell me quietly," I prodded Becca, as I pushed open the door to the stairwell, and we began our ascent. At least neither of us had to worry about being out of breath when we reached the top.

Before all this had happened, when I was still mortal, I'd refused to take the stairs, even if I thought I needed the exercise, terrified of predators lurking in the dim stairwells of my friend's lavish, security-coded luxury complex. That was no longer a problem. I didn't need to worry about people who might mean to do me harm in dark and lonely places; would-be predators needed to worry about running into me and Becca. I felt something like a grin crawl across my face, and I knew my smile was unpleasant and inhuman, and I didn't care.

Becca gave a recount of what she remembered—fighting with me in the restaurant, walking out onto the street...mercifully, she remembered else until waking up in a body bag on a slab in cold storage. "You'd think I would have taken the opportunity to at least enjoy the unique experience," she quipped with a wink, and I remembered her prized collection of antique toe tags she used often as bookmarks. If anyone was equipped, psychologically, to resurrect under those conditions...

"Anyway, after what seemed like hours of shouting to get me out of there, someone finally did come and open up the locker I was in," Becca continued, "and I guess he was pretty shocked when he found me, because, uh...whatever killed me hadn't been pretty about it."

"It was a hit and run," I said, bluntly. There was no point in trying to soften the truth. "It was pretty gruesome."

"So, what, you watched it happen, but you couldn't use your vampire super-speed to rescue me?" Becca pouted, and I wanted to throw my arms around her again, and kiss those pouting lips right there on the landing between the sixth and seventh floors.

"I think that sort of thing only happens in the movies," I said, instead of kissing her. "The car came out of nowhere and was going really fast."

"Damn Chicago drivers..." Becca shook her head with a rueful smile. Now that she had stopped screaming and was back in somewhat familiar surroundings, she was chatting as easily as anything. I'd been an absolute wreck the night I resurrected. For Becca, it could almost have been any other Wednesday evening.

Until it wasn't. "He was right there. The assistant medical examiner, or whoever he was, and…" She went quiet, and the light disappeared from her eyes. When she continued, her voice was dull and toneless, so similar to what my own had been, that first night. "…and his *neck* was just right there in my face, the veins were pulsing in his throat, and I was so hungry, I just…"

"He's dead. I killed him," she finished, without any discernible emotion. "I'm really sorry, but like also, I'm not sorry? Because, I mean, the blood…" She stopped, and trembled. Even recounting the experience made her fangs reappear, and I watched as she paused, ran her tongue over the razor edges, and seemed to quietly process what she had become.

"Yeah," I agreed, quietly. There was no need to elaborate on what we both knew.

"I never thought it would feel like this…" She shook her head several times, as if trying to dislodge a stubborn thought. I couldn't tell what she was thinking, or feeling. But she was still Becca. I touched her, and I knew.

"It wasn't just him, though," Becca went on. "After I sort of started to realize what had happened, we were both on the floor, the man I'd killed and I, and I wasn't wearing any clothes. So I stole his scrubs, and I ran out the emergency exit, and the alarms started to go off, and I just started running, off into the snow, and I wasn't as cold as I should have been, and after a few blocks of running away, I started walking, and a woman pulled up next to me, and told me to get into her car…"

"She was very nice." Becca looked pained. "She told me I was lucky she found me, she was going to take me to a hospital, because I shouldn't be out in the snow…And you know, for maybe three seconds, I actually thought, if I get to the hospital, they can fix me, the doctors can make this right, and I won't actually have to feel like this…

"But then it happened again, I couldn't stop myself, it was like I was outside my body looking in, and I threw myself at her, and…I think I killed her, too. I don't know about that one. I got out of the car, and I ran off again. But at least by that point, I had a better idea where I was. And I knew I needed to find Gavin, that he'd know what to do…but when I got to his complex and rang at the intercom, he wasn't there, or he wouldn't buzz me in, and I couldn't...I knew the code to his unit, but I couldn't get in. It felt like this *weight* on my shoulders. I couldn't go inside. I don't know why. So I continued on toward Calliope's, thinking maybe she'd be able to help me...but I honestly don't remember much of the last stretch before you found me."

Two people. I tried to keep my head from spinning. Becca seemed to be holding up, at least. Climbing the stairs gave us something to do. It was good to have something to do when the world was falling apart.

We finally arrived on Becca's floor, and I poked my head out of the stairwell into the hallway to make sure things were all clear, that no mortals were wandering around, and I gestured for her to follow me down the passage to her apartment. I pressed my ear up against the door and couldn't hear or smell anything unusual inside. I didn't think any of Becca's family had been there. But it was hard to tell. I mostly felt weird and unwelcome, with my ear pressed up so close against the threshold to a residence I hadn't been invited across. I handed Becca her keys.

"After you go in, you have to invite me in. That's the way it works now, okay?"

"This is so fucking weird..." Becca took the keys and unlocked the door, shaking her head in amazement.

"That's not even the weirdest thing," I told her. "What til you see what happens when you *yawn*." I winced, hoping my own fangs wouldn't show up and make an appearance just because I'd thought about yawning, and assumed they'd been summoned. I followed Becca inside at her invitation, an enormous sense of relief sweeping over me; I hadn't realized just how tense I'd been until suddenly I wasn't, and for the first time in what seemed like ages, I relaxed. I propped a chair up against the door for good measure, though. I wasn't sure if Becca had ever invited Gavin into her apartment, or how such invitations worked if the person initially providing said invitation had technically died. Better safe than sorry.

I glanced around the tiny, familiar space. Becca's messy bed, her art supplies and reference books strewn all over, a canvas on an easel in the corner containing an unfinished acrylic painting that might have been my portrait. I winced. On the row of hooks on the wall by the door, my vintage Burberry trench coat was casually draped next to the Standord hoodie Becca had been given for Christmas, and I gasped in spite of myself. I'd paid quite a bit of money to have the classic item tailored to fit me perfectly, and I didn't like to see it treated so carelessly. It should have been on a padded satin hanger to help keep its shape.

"Hey!" I cried in mock indignation, "That's mine! The trench coat was not on the approved list of things for you to steal when I died!" I clutched at my beloved thrift store find and glared at Becca. "You...you scavenger!"

"You were dead!" Becca threw up her hands, clearly still bothered by the memory of thinking I was more dead than I actually was. "Blame your dad, actually, he's the one who begged me to take anything of yours that I liked when we packed up your apartment!"

"Daddy was here?" I staggered backward and sat on the floor on top of a pile of scarves.

Becca nodded. "I helped him and Celeste clean out your place after we found out about the fire. It was awful, Grace. We all cried buckets."

"Celeste, huh? I guess I was going to have to learn her name eventually." I feigned disinterest only somewhat successfully. I didn't like the idea of dad's girlfriend going through my stuff. Why did he have to bring her?

Becca's voice took on a warning tone. "Grace...don't be like that. You don't even know her. She's nice. And she loves your dad. They're going to have a baby."

"What?" My eyes widened, even as the words barely registered. If I hadn't been sitting down, I probably would have fallen over.

"Celeste is pregnant. They've known for a while, I think, but they posted the announcement on Facebook the day before...before the house fire. It's a boy. I guess you didn't know. I thought so, the other night at the restaurant. I'm sorry I didn't say anything."

"I'm going to be a big sister?" Nothing could have prepared me for this moment. I sniffled in shocked disbelief, rocking back and forth on the musty pile of scarves on the floor...*I'd wanted a baby brother since I was four years old.*

She threw her arms around me. "Celeste is going to make a great mom, Grace. I know she's not your mom, but she's really lovely. And she's so excited. She's like, thirty-five, and it's her first."

"...are they going to get married?"

"Have you met your Aunt Francesca?" Becca raised her eyebrow at me, and we both giggled, because laughing was better than crying, and we were hysterical, either way. We laughed until we were sobbing, until we ran out of air, until we remembered to breathe, and started all over again.

Finally, we both calmed down, and I stood up first. My head was still spinning, but I had a better grip on being a vampire, and Becca and I needed to figure out what we were going to do next.

"We need to talk about Gavin," I said, re-focusing my priorities. "We need to get you cleaned up, and then, we need to figure out what the fuck our options are."

Becca showered, and I tidied her apartment. It had been almost two months since my last visit, and Becca had certainly been Becca in the interim. And I was still Grace, after all. I found two pairs of my shoes under her bed, and wasn't sure if I had accidentally left them behind or if they were also victims of Becca's scavenging. I lined them up neatly by the door, and I straightened out my thoughts.

Celeste is pregnant.

Well, that was convenient timing for my dad. He got to start all over again with a brand-new family, just replace the old one completely from existence. Mom was dead, I was dead. We were easy enough to replace.

Except...I remembered the last fight Dad and Shellie had, when I went home to visit for Christmas break, sophomore year. She'd tried to take Mom's pictures down off the walls, and put up new ones, with just her and Dad. It hadn't gone over well.

"Christ, calm down Christopher! It's not like I was going to throw them away!" Shellie took a drag off of her blue American Spirit cigarette and reached for the wedding photo again. "I got nothin' against your late wife, but all these gilt and rhinestone picture frames are tacky, anyway."

Shellie was tacky. Mom's gold and crystal picture frames had made her feel like royalty. At least Dad understood that much. He was still shouting at Shellie, practically screaming, as she pulled her car out of the driveway and took off into the evening gloom. She didn't come back.

"Goddammit..." Dad muttered, after she was gone. He looked up at me where I'd perched on the top of the stairs. I hadn't meant to eavesdrop on their fight. And I hadn't meant to gloat, either. But Dad could see the look on my face. "Your Mom's pictures stay on the wall, kiddo. There's room enough for more photos, if someone wants to add to them. But Oriana's pictures stay put."

I knew he wasn't just talking about the photos themselves. It was the memories the pictures stood for—Mom making a silly face, trying to pose on the hood of Dad's first car, Mom and Dad at prom, on their wedding day, with me at the hospital...Dad never took the pictures down. He wasn't going to. Wherever he went, wherever his life took him next, there'd always be pictures of me on the walls, too. He'd add more picture frames next to them—Celeste, my baby brother...

Love was more complex than a linear equation solved by substitution. It was multivariable calculus, a measure of continuity and limits; sometimes the results could be counterintuitive, but love and mathematics both had to account for the irrational.

Harold had offered to put my picture on his wall, and I'd rejected him, without thinking. Without processing. Without understanding. I imagined him driving his gray BMW down the highway somewhere, headed off to a different safe house, and a new life, in a new city...maybe even a new country, without me. I hoped he was safe from the storm.

I washed the dishes in Becca's sink, wiping the tears from my cheeks on the sleeve of my shirt as I did. I wiped down her electronics. I clung to whatever semblance of control I could muster.

I gave wide berth to any of the candles or various saints' medallions or prayer cards I discovered strewn about her apartment in random places like booby traps. The religious paraphernalia was less evidence of a still-practicing Catholic and more "I'm just here for the aesthetic," and I knew that, but I wasn't taking any chances. I didn't want to touch the relics of my former faith. I didn't want to be reminded that God had turned His back on me.

I wasn't certain where, exactly, vampires fit into divine ineffable plans, but I was certain I was in no state of grace, and I was unlikely to enter one.

A cheap black plastic rosary dangled from an upside-down bouquet of roses left out to dry above the radiator, and I wondered if Gavin had given Becca the roses for Valentine's Day, like he'd given her the owl pendant.

A token, for his fledgling.

It made me sick to think of him doing anything nice for her. Gavin was not nice. He'd left Becca to wake up alone at the medical examiners. She'd had to walk across town in the snow. He'd given her his blood, so he should have taken precautions. I would have taken precautions, if I had been in his shoes.

I was still mulling over all the reasons I hated our shared maker when I finally heard the water in the shower stop, and the only sound left was the howling of the winter storm outside Becca's windows.

She looked much better after she'd cleaned off the blood and put on fresh clothes, and I was glad to be free of the distraction—all the blood covering my best friend had been starting to give me feelings I still wasn't ready to process—not that I think Becca would have minded knowing what those feelings were, but I kept them to myself.

I glanced at Mom's watch. For everything that had happened so far that night already, it was barely a few minutes past midnight. Thank goodness for long winter nights. There was still so much to say.

Becca broke the spell first, her voice quavering. "Grace, if you'd been really dead, I don't think I ever would have been brave enough to get over that."

"You still drank Gavin's blood, though." I flinched at the resentment in my own voice.

She looked away. "I didn't want to go through life as I knew it without you, so I chose a different one. It's not that hard to understand."

"Where is he?" I asked.

"I don't know. I don't even know if he knows about the accident—"

"He knows," I cut her off. "Calliope knew about the accident, and if she does, so does Gavin. He is her fledgling, after all—isn't he?" I didn't tell her the car that hit her was a matte black sports car. I didn't want to crush her more than she already was.

Becca slowly nodded, confirming what I'd already been convinced of for some time. "She turned him a little over ten years ago, he told me. He wanted it. He wasn't really into vampire stuff before he met her, but he wanted the power, and the strength, and—he wanted to be with her. She's kind of awesome, actually. We talked a few times, when we went out. She knows a lot about art and music and weird underground history that, like, no one ever teaches you in school—"

"Becca. We're talking about Gavin."

"Right. They met at a nightclub. But maybe she was already stalking him. Because he worked for her company in the IT department. It was his first big job out of college. And Gavin likes brunettes, and she used to go out wearing a brown wig to a lot of the after hours clubs, early in the morning before sunrise. They dated for a while, and then she, you know, dropped the vampire bombshell on him, and made him her personal assistant, except she wasn't CJ anymore, she was Calliope Jones. But when she offered to turn him, he didn't say no. And he told me he didn't regret it, even though they fizzled, romantically. I think she wanted something he couldn't give her, and he got tired of her, you know, sleeping around."

"What?" My eyes widened. I mean, Calliope had told me that she...but hearing it from someone else was seeing a side of Calliope Jones I had not expected. I had to readjust so many things in my brain, starting with: CJ?

"Oh yeah," Becca continued. "She likes to get dressed up and hit the after-party clubs real early in the morning, after all her work is done, she's got like, a million wigs or something, and she goes out and...picks up other men. And women. And like, anyone hot, really. You should see how she dances. She can get anyone she wants, it's kind of amazing."

"She's probably feeding, too."

Becca considered this for a moment, presumably through the lens of before and after becoming a vampire. "I mean...yeah, probably." An evil, clever glint flashed in her eyes, and she leaned forward conspiratorially. "A THOTsferatu, if you will."

I groaned in actual agony at Becca's horrible pun. "You're grounded. Jail. Jail for Vampire Becca."

"I've already been to vampire jail," she reminded me. "It's called the Cook County Medical Examiner's office." She pantomimed a Y incision across her chest, and I froze.

"They didn't—" a horrified whisper escaped my lips.

Becca shook her head at me. "With this city's backlog? If I hadn't woken up this evening, I would have been on that slab for weeks, if not months, and you know it."

I shuddered at the sobering thought, but tried to veer Becca back on course.

"So why isn't he with you?" I pressed on. "Why didn't he come get your body from the morgue, or pay someone to do it? You know he has connections. Why didn't he tell the Community you'd been given the blood for five nights, that there was a chance that you would rise, and someone needed to do something to get you out of there before you did wake up? He should have been there for you. Where is your maker, Becca?" My line of questioning was more pointed than I meant it to be, and Becca broke all over again, and started crying.

"He told me that he loved me..."

"He lies."

"Yeah. I know." Becca deflated. "It feels foolish now that I believed him, when he said all those things about you seducing him and being on drugs—"

"I mean, to be fair...that last part wasn't much of a stretch. You said so yourself. It's why you hated Dylan."

"I hated Dildo because he wasn't good enough for you, and it pissed me off to see you settle for someone so mediocre."

"Also because we did a lot of drugs."

"But the point is that you weren't what Gavin said you were. And I took him at face value instead of giving you the benefit of the doubt, because I was so caught up in my own perfect vampire romance fantasy. If he'd actually just come out and told me he accidentally turned you on New Year's Eve—"

"It wasn't an accident. Attacking me was removing an obstacle keeping him from you, and creating chaos for his ex. I think he was very calculated."

"I should have believed you."

"Yeah, well, he's throwing up all kinds of douchebag predator red flags, and being an actual bloodsucking vampire is the least of them." I crossed my arms over my chest and tried not to sound too sarcastic. Becca had gone through a lot. I still had questions. "You said, last night, you had his blood for five nights. But the house fire was five nights ago tonight; so he had to have started giving you his blood before that." It wasn't that I didn't believe Becca's profession of not wanting the life she had before if I wasn't going to be a part of it, but something wasn't adding up.

"He wanted to turn me as soon as I found out." Becca offered. It was the kind of non-answer I would have expected from Calliope, and I raised an eyebrow at her. She shrugged a little, and stood up on the tips of her toes to reach the bouquet of dried roses above the radiator. She wrapped the black plastic rosary around the stems without so much as a pause, and tossed the whole bouquet into the trash.

"Things moved kind of fast after the concert. Maybe he wanted to take advantage of the fact I was so angry at you, but I said no. And I kept saying no. I wanted a chance to patch things up with you, before I became...this." She slammed the lid on the trash can shut, and wandered over to the fridge, still chatting. "Do you think any of this is still good?"

"Good as in, 'not spoiled' or good as in 'I can still eat this even though I'm a vampire now'? Because I wouldn't, Becca..."

She wrestled with the lid on an expensive jar of imported olives, took a whiff, and made the most ridiculous expression I'd seen ever cross her face while sober. It was impossible to tell how much she was hamming it up; nothing about the smell was appealing.

I rolled my eyes and tried not to gag. "Warned you..."

"No, really, you have to sniff this; it's horrible."

"I can smell it all the way over here by the door and that's more than enough. You know I hate olives! Close the lid! Close the lid!" I frantically waved my hands in a futile attempt to waft the stench away. I'd *never* liked olives, and Becca knew it. Why did I put up with her brat shenanigans again?

"Repelled by olives...how tragic." Becca wrinkled her nose and made the sign of the cross, burying the offending jar in the back of the fridge. She slammed the stainless steel door shut and leaned against it like she was afraid the abominable olive jar might try to escape, even bouncing against the fridge a few times for emphasis.

But she was stronger than she realized now, and the appliance rocked in a precarious manner I didn't like. "But I suppose it could be worse. It could be...*garlic.*"

Our exaggerated expressions of disgust and horror mirrored each other, and in spite of everything, I laughed until my sides split, long after my lungs had run out of air, and I had to lean the frame of Becca's bed to keep from falling over. Eventually, I lowered myself to the floor, while Becca clung to the granite countertop of her kitchenette, wheezing until she, too, had no more air to laugh out loud with.

"Trash Panda. Stop goofing off. This is serious." I drew in a long shaky breath and tried to pull myself together, but seriousness seemed impossible at the moment. Everything was ridiculous and awful and wonderful all at once.

"Missed you," Becca grinned, when she'd stopped laughing long enough to breathe again. "Gavin never laughed at my jokes. And like I started to say, if I'd known you were already a vampire, there would have been no hesitation when he wanted to turn me. Zero." She steadied herself against the counter and regarded me for a long, unblinking beat, before turning away.

"He wanted you all for himself, Bec."

"Twenty-four hours ago his possessiveness seemed really romantic..." the slight shrug of her shoulders was almost dismissive. As if she could hide her pain from me. "Mind gameth," she lisped softly, as she examined her new reflection in the polished sheen of a black charcuterie stone on her kitchen counter, willing her fangs to extend and retract. "I didn't know who to trust. Gueth I'm going to have to thtart trusting you, babe." But it was her own reflection she kissed, not me.

"Becca..."

She spun around to face me, and her movements were delicate, controlled. Like the dancer she'd always been. "He finally convinced me to start drinking his blood so I could become a vampire on my birthday," she said. "He made it sound so romantic...But the first night, his blood was gross and overwhelming, and I freaked out. I said no, I changed my mind, I needed to find you first before we could do it. He got mad at me and threw a fit, and said...really mean things."

"Like what?"

She shook her head, and the next minute she was sitting next to me on the floor by the bed where we always sat, her arms wrapped around me like they always did.

"It doesn't matter what he said. It wasn't true. But he calmed down, and promised to hire a private eye to track you down, and he insisted I'd have plenty of time to make amends before I turned. And I wanted to believe him...

"The fire was the next night, but I didn't find out about that until after he gave me his blood again, and it wasn't as bad the second time. I didn't throw up like I thought I was going to do the night before. He told me his investigator already had a lead on you, that you were at some drug house out in the suburbs, and there was going to be this grand rescue, or something. Maybe that was why the blood was better. I actually started to feel really good. My senses were sharper somehow, and my brain felt clear. I started planning all the things I would say when we saved you from the drug house.

"But then he got a phone call. And the woman on the other end told him to turn on the TV. And the fire was on the news, and he told me that the investigator had tracked you down to this mansion in Winetka. And the breaking news said it was some kind of drug lab fire. And then he told me...you were dead, and I wasn't going to get to say any of those things I wanted to say, after all. So that's when I decided I was really going to go through with it, no looking back." She sighed. Slowly, as though it were the most natural thing in the universe, my hand reached up to hers, intertwining our fingers.

"Becca..." *I love you, Trash Panda.*

"...Grace?"

I started to say it. I almost did. But something else came out of my mouth, instead. "Wait. If Gavin was with you when the fire started..." Nothing made sense. "Who was the woman on the phone? Calliope?"

Becca shook her head. "No, someone named Marie, I think."

I stared at her, slack-jawed, before I found my words again. "Marie DuChamps..."

"Who?"

"Another one of Calliope's fledglings from, like, a hundred years ago. She's a psychopath."

Becca giggled. "Oh, no, not another vampire psychopath..." But then she stopped. I knew her well enough to recognize the look she got on her face when she was suddenly putting things together. It was one of her ADHD superpowers.

She gasped, eyes so wide they could split her face in half. "Grace. Oh my God. We have to stop him. Them, maybe—I don't know."

"Them?"

"Tomorrow night—my birthday. He said he had it planned so I'd resurrect on my birthday, and were going to go travel the world together forever. And I don't think you were the only obstacle he wanted to eliminate first. I think he wanted his maker out of the picture, too. And I think...I think he was planning on having help."

Time decelerated like a roller coaster at Cedar Point easing to a stop, and I felt all my blood rushing to my head, a dizzying realization making me suddenly ill.

Calliope was planning on meeting Gavin at the penthouse that night. Before the storm. My own thoughts started racing again—I'd spent enough time with Becca to foster my own intuition. I grabbed her shoulders.

"I think one of them is over at Calliope's right now. I think she was expecting someone to show up any minute, just before I left. There might still be time to—" I stood up and unfurled the sword from its hotel towel sheath, and it crashed onto the bed.

"Oh my God. Is that a freakin' sword?" Becca asked.

"Yes, it fucking is. My vampire boyfriend made it, and I'm going to use it to cut Gavin's fucking head off. Hand me a belt and my trench coat."

I wasn't sure if Calliope needed saving, or if I even wanted to be the one to do it. But I had a score to settle. I wasn't going to miss my opportunity.

⸻◆○◆⸻

Chapter Thirty-Four

GAVIN

It took less time to navigate our way back to Calliope's than it had when we stumbled away from it only a few short hours before. We ran, with inhuman speed and precision, all but invisible to anyone who might have been out on the street in those wretched winter conditions. We didn't encounter any pedestrians, though, and Becca kept up right alongside me, a natural. I didn't have time for awe or envy.

We pivoted as we approached the block to avoid the resident entrance, and opted instead to go around the back alley. It was dumpster-filled but otherwise empty; the inclement weather kept everyone else inside. Becca was only momentarily distracted by the tinsel that sparkled on the desiccated corpse of someone's belatedly discarded Christmas tree.

"I mean, really," she muttered, skidding to a stop and cocking her head to one side. "Even I managed to take my tiny little Trader Joe's tree down by February first. There's procrastination, and then there's..."

"Becca. Please. We have to get upstairs." I pulled her away by the elbow until we located the service entrance at the back of Calliope's address. The door was heavy, reinforced steel, and solidly locked from within. There wasn't even a handle on the outside.

"Well, fuck. Do we climb? Can we fly?"

"We can't fly, Becca. I thought you said Gavin told you things?" I rolled my eyes and pulled her back. It was different when I'd asked Harold the same question, of course. It's not like I'd known I was going to end up a vampire beforehand. If I had, I would have done my homework first, before I got my fangs. But who was I to anticipate Becca doing her homework? Silly me.

Even though I wasn't keen on the idea, climbing the exterior of the building was starting to look like our best option, until the sound of footsteps approaching on the other side of the door gave me an idea. "Hang on—" we melted into the shadows just as a skinny young man in black cargo work pants and an over-filled down parka stepped outside. He wedged a small brick between the steel door and the door frame to prop it open before sheltering a cigarette and a lighter between his hands. He didn't see us as he leaned into the space between two dumpsters, trying to stay out of the wind.

Next to me, Becca growled softly. I gave her a warning look that must have been more formidable than I'd intended, because she took a step away from me, mortification marring her otherwise lovely face. I held up my hand, silently signaling, 'stay back', and approached the smoker. I hadn't intended for him to see me, but he was apparently jumpy, and I was inexperienced at vampire sneaking.

"Is that a freaking sword?" he asked as I came near.

I looked at him, and at the sword and scabbard at my waist; the trench coat covering both fell to mid-calf on me, and the sword was so long it practically dragged along the ground; I wasn't exactly inconspicuous. "Um. Yeah."

"Go on with your bad self, shawtie Highlander." He grinned at me as he exhaled his cigarette smoke. "You need something? You ain't coming for my head or nothin'?"

I felt my fangs extend.

The act of actually grabbing onto him to feed was a bit more complicated than I'd experienced before; he fought back as I got close, and I think he saw my teeth before I lunged for his neck, but he didn't have time to scream, and I didn't have time to think as the fire of his blood filled my mouth and burned my throat; I hadn't thought I was thirsty, but the bagged blood from earlier in the night had only done so much, and I wanted more, needed more, to bathe in the rain of blood til I was as soaked in death as Becca—my eyes flew open.

Becca stood steps away from me, watching, breathless, as I fed, and I stopped. I cut my tongue on my fangs to heal the evidence of my violence and listened for the hum of his pulse. He was still alive, but as limp and unconscious as the other two victims I'd fed on had been.

"You can do that?" Becca asked, incredulously. "You can just stop?"

"I think it takes practice," I told her, wiping the blood from my mouth. Becca licked her lips, and for a moment I wondered if she was going to try to kiss me—I wondered what I was going to do if she did.

But instead she reached out to grab the unconscious man by the armpits. "We should drag him inside, at least." She moved him as easily as dragging a plastic chair across a summer lawn. "It's so cold out here. I don't want to cause another—" She stopped talking, and I didn't have anything to add.

I held open the door so she could wrangle the unconscious man inside. All this took only a few seconds, but Harold had said victims normally came around after a minute or so. We didn't have much time. I scanned the interior of the service bay for any inspiration for getting upstairs. There was a service elevator that went directly to the penthouse, I was sure of it.

Becca located the industrial elevator that read "penthouse" before I did, and hit the call button. *This felt too easy...*

The padded interior was a very different experience from the brass and mirror elevator that had ferried me up and down the skyscraper before. There was a magnetic key card reader by the buttons that would send the elevator car up and down between each floor; Becca and I exchanged worried looks. No. Definitely not easy. But there was a small covered panel under the normal buttons with a handwritten label that read "override" in bold, blocky lettering. I stared at the number pad in silent frustration, trying to figure out our next course of action. Could we climb up to the top floor via the elevator shaft? Maybe there were stairs we could take instead? Not far away, but just out of sight, I heard the young man I'd fed from beginning to stir and call out, disoriented, "Hello? Is anybody there?"

Becca tilted her head to one side, as if expecting another one of her sudden bursts of inspiration, and then, she hit a random series of numbers, and the elevator doors closed, and the car began to rise, not a moment too soon. The man I'd fed on was just around the corner.

"What did you do?" I asked her.

"It's the same as the code to Gavin's condo complex." She shrugged. "Only in reverse."

My brilliant, beautiful best friend.

When the elevator reached its destination on the top floor, I stepped out into the foyer with ease. The large double doors that served as the security entrance to the interior of the penthouse were cracked open, and I could hear shouting from somewhere inside. Becca, who had not been invited up to the penthouse since becoming a vampire, was stuck in the elevator. "Another invitation?" she wailed. "I've already been up here. It isn't fair!"

"Hang on, I'll find her. You stay right there!" I assured, zooming across the marble floors. Something monumental had gone down since I left the penthouse earlier in the evening. Furniture was overturned, and indentations marred the walls; artwork was askew, and several modern, minimalist marble sculptures were knocked over and shattered. The beautiful bouquet of flowers that had greeted visitors at the entrance to Calliope's home was on its side, hothouse blooms and greenery strewn about the room. From the sound of the raised voices arguing above me, the fight had moved upstairs.

It was easy to follow the sound.

"—why should I tell you?" Gavin shouted. "If she wanted to be here, she would be here. What have *you* done with Becca?"

"I haven't the slightest idea under heaven where she is! You're the one who lost her! If you think I had anything to do with the accident, you're more delusional than I thought." Calliope sounded exasperated.

"Don't you dare try to shrug off your responsibility here, too. You turned me. The Community will come for both of us—"

"The Community will have your hide, not mine. I'm tired of covering for you. This is the second one that you've abandoned, you careless, selfish idiot—"

"You don't get to call me careless, you fucking slut—"

It sounded like a nasty conversation, but then again, I'd expected nothing but nastiness from Gavin to begin with. *What a piece of work.* I threw open the doors to what appeared to be a private study and interrupted Calliope and Gavin in their quarrel, feeling like I ought to have been out of breath.

"Becca's here, and you need to invite her in because she's a vampire now, and we really need to talk to you!" I blurted out all at once.

"Becca? Becca's here?" Gavin looked at me like he'd seen a ghost.

I couldn't resist throwing him a toothy grin. "Hey there, vamp daddy. I'm going to kill you."

"Who the fuck let you in, bitch?" He recovered from the shock of seeing me in Calliope's study quickly, but he took a step back anyway when he saw my hand move toward the sword under my trench coat. *He really is exactly the kind of coward Harold said he was*, I thought.

"I let her in, earlier tonight, when you were driving all over the city looking for someone Grace was able to find in a few hours, fool." Calliope turned around and swept past him with typical imperious scorn, but I was the one who took a step back. There was a horrible purple bruise surrounding her eye, and her artfully tousled hair appeared as though it had been roughly grabbed at. Her blouse was torn at the collar where her jeweled owl pin barely remained secured to the lapel, and more blood on her clothing than the faint stains she'd dabbed at with a damp cloth earlier.

"This isn't what it looks like," she insisted, waving her hand in front of her face. She seemed relieved to see me, relieved something had interrupted the tension between her and her fledgling. She tried to exit the study, all brisk business and cool, collected self-assurance in her movements, but Gavin threw out his arm in front of her.

"Of course this isn't what it looks like! You hit me first! You always hit me first!" He caught her violently at chest level, and she staggered, the air knocked out of her lungs. For several wide-eyed seconds, Calliope was unable to speak. I took a another step backward, out into the hallway, jaw dropped at his casual display of violence.

Gavin laughed at Calliope's temporary defeat exactly the way he'd laughed when he kicked me outside the Metro, and shoved her aside. She shoved him back, pushing him into a wall of bookshelves, and shouted loudly down the hall, "I invite you in, Becca! You are welcome to enter my home!"

I turned around to sprint back downstairs as their fight continued, mostly muffled, punctuated by a flurry of epithets and curses. A loud crash that sounded like an entire shelf full of heavy books toppling over reverberated through the apartment. I tried to ignore them, and focus on getting back to Becca, but I wasn't fast enough. I returned to the foyer just in time to see the elevator doors close and begin their automatic recall to the ground floor. Becca wordlessly waved to me as the doors shut and the car descended, while I frantically hit buttons on the elevator keypad until the car returned.

Several tense moments later, Becca was able to step out of the elevator. "Weird," she said again, because it *was* weird.

We were approaching the stairwell together when Gavin's voice, suddenly calm and triumphant, practically sneered, "My sister sends her regards." A gun went off, and Calliope screamed exactly once.

The deafening echoes of the gunshot caught us both off guard, and we threw our hands over our ears and doubled over, sensitive hearing overwhelmed. I recovered the quickest, grabbing Becca's hand and dragging her down the first-floor hallway, hiding in the washroom. The bath towels had been freshly laundered, I could tell, and the distinctive scent of the detergent triggered instant, nightmarish recollections of my first night. I gagged, panic and terror threatening to overwhelm me, even as I tried to be brave. For Becca.

"So this is it, huh?" She deadpanned, surveying the luxurious white marble space as we huddled together in the bathtub, gesturing to the potted orchid still blooming on the sink. "The place where you died...Wow, so tragic. I died in the gutter after a hit and run and woke up in the morgue." Becca, for all that every part of her experience resurrecting as a vampire had been so much worse than mine, seemed utterly unflappable.

"Well, it was really awful at the time," I hissed, but I had to admit I felt better with Becca there to provide some perspective.

"Of course it was." Becca leaned in closer and hugged me. "You had no idea what was going on or what had happened to you. I at least had some notion. And I wanted it. You didn't. There's a difference. But I'm glad you're here with me now. Even if we are hiding in the bathroom from my douchebag vampire ex-boyfriend with a gun.

"Wait—" She asked, "Can guns kill vampires?"

"Calliope had a gun holster under her dressing gown the night we met, and I could tell from the silhouette it was a pretty big gun."

"That is so hot," Becca said with a shudder. She'd always had a complicated relationship with firearms. I blamed it on being raised in California, and shushed her.

"Harold told me that if you get shot enough, and you bleed enough, and there's not a blood supply nearby to replenish you, you can die, yeah. It's a thing."

"Fuck."

"I know."

"What do you want to do?"

"Me?" I squeaked. "I don't know, Becca. This all played out a little differently in my head."

"But you're Grace. You always have a plan!" Becca insisted.

"He said his sister sends her regards…" I furrowed my brows and tried to think. *Focus, Grace.*

"…but his sister lives in Madison, I know because I looked her up online, and she's not a vampire, she's—"

"Grace. Grace," Becca interrupted me with her hands on my shoulders. "His *sister*. You said that Marie DuChamps woman was also Calliope's fledgling, right? The one who—"

"Set the fire. Jesus Mary and Joseph—"

I was berating myself for being an idiot when I began to smell smoke.

"Run," I said. We fled the hall bathroom and scrambled off in different directions. So far, I knew of one fire that had probably been set by Marie DuChamps, and another that had probably been set by Gavin, but Harold had said fire was more Marie's calling card, and I had no desire to encounter her and Gavin teamed up together.

The grand, open floor plan of the penthouse didn't offer much cover. I ducked behind support columns and doorways and tried to avoid the fires erupting from wastepaper baskets and small pieces of furniture. The flames weren't spreading fast, and I couldn't smell any accelerant. Mostly, they produced a lot of smoke. There should have been alarms going off and fire suppression sprinklers engaged, but I bet someone had disabled the security systems.

Gavin stalked from room to room, muttering to himself. "Goddammit DuChamps, where the fuck are you? You said you'd help..." He upended the contents of drawers, and opened up a wall safe with a single violent blow with his bare fist, throwing paperwork and passports and other valuables into a large black duffel bag slung over his shoulder. I was equal parts terrified and impressed at his strength. I didn't know that was a thing you could do as a vampire, but it made me feel much better about the punches Harold and I had been able to deliver to Gavin's stupid pretty face the night of the concert. Shame we weren't able to do any permanent damage.

The phone on the console by the elevator doors started ringing; Gavin picked it up. "Marie? Where are you? I did it, okay? I shot—" a muffled male voice that didn't sound like it belonged so someone named Marie DuChamps began to speak, and Gavin uttered a single, "fuck you," into the receiver before throwing the phone against the wall, where it shattered completely. Nearby, Becca let out a loud yelp at the sound of the impact, giving away her location.

Shit.

"Becca? Honey? I was wondering if you were going to show up tonight..." Gavin called, attention turned away from plunder. "Baby, don't be scared. Everything's going to be all right, I can explain..."

"You left me to wake up in a fucking body bag!" she screeched and leapt out at him, no longer trying to hide. "You said I was your goddamn queen of the night, and you left me on my own in the fucking morgue!" She threw a vase at him, but he sideswiped the flying pottery, and it shattered on the floor, instead of his head. "You could have come and got me. It's not like you don't have the fucking money to bribe people." It was good to see Becca's anger directed at someone who wasn't me, for once.

"It's not like that princess, I promise..."

"Oh, now I'm a princess, huh? Is that a demotion?" I didn't have to see Becca to be able to picture the indignation plastered across her face, and I stifled a giggle.

"Don't get it twisted..." Gavin's voice was level with accusations, all of them aimed at Becca. "You ran off. You left me. We were planning our future. You were *drinking my blood*—do you remember that? What was I supposed to think? You didn't even tell me where you were going. What were you doing in that part of town, huh?" I watched him from down the hall, but he stepped out of my field of vision. Becca let out a yelp of pain, and Gavin reappeared, dragging her by the hair into the center of the great room. Her arms and legs flailed, trying to catch on to something, anything, until he stopped and released her, knelt down, and put his hands on her face.

"I said, what were you doing in that part of town, babe?"

Becca babbled something incoherent and wounded.

"Were you off meeting with Grace? After I warned you about her? After I told you she lies—"

"You HURT her, Gavin! What the fuck?"

He scoffed. "I hurt her? I gave her everything you wanted. Everything you *begged* me for, remember? You even got down on your knees and…"

Becca slapped him.

Gavin caught her hands roughly and grasped them between his, looming over her like an ogre. He was so much larger than she was. "Don't start fights you can't win, babe. That's no way to start off eternity together, I promise you."

"I don't want to be with you for eternity. I changed my mind. Let me go. What did you do to Calliope?"

"Calliope Jones is dead. Just like your little friend is going to be, babe. I tried to make her go away without killing her, I knew you wouldn't like that. But she can't take a hint, and I'm not going to let her come between us. She and her dumb blacksmith boyfriend are no good. Grace is violent and unhinged, Becca, I told you. Her boyfriend shot me, did she tell you that?"

"That's not true. Grace isn't like that—"

"DON'T CALL ME A LIAR!" he screamed in her face with unbridled fury. Becca struggled harder to free herself of his grasp, and Gavin yanked her to her feet. My hand went to the hilt of the sword. *Not now.* I needed to make sure I didn't hurt Becca, too.

"If your psycho friend isn't dangerous and violent, why does she have a sword with her, baby? What kind of normal person carries around a sword? All I ever wanted was for us to be together, Becca angel, you and me. I wouldn't have gone after her if you'd just paid attention to me, like you were supposed to."

The smoke was getting thick, and started burning my eyes, when Gavin struck Becca upside the face, hard. She cried out in heaving sobs, begging him to stop, please stop—I slid down to the ground and bit my own knuckles to keep from crying with her.

I didn't know what to do.

I didn't know what to do.

I didn't know what to do—

My eyes fell on the baby grand piano. The lid was still up from playing it earlier, and somehow it seemed to have missed the worst of the violence that had happened downstairs. The longer I stared at the piano, the more thoroughly unhinged my ideas became. I prayed my intuition about Gavin was correct. Becca and I might not be able to out-punch him, but I could *absolutely* out-crazy him.

I cracked my knuckles, mostly to psych myself up, and began a familiar, eye roll-inducing composition...nothing like playing up the vengeful vampire stereo-type.

He'd called me a psycho bitch—

He didn't have the slightest clue how weird I could be. My hands trembled a little as my fingers slowly danced over the keys, but I hit the right notes in the right order. Fifteen years of Nana's lessons had to count for something.

"What. The fuck. Are you doing?" Gavin stopped shouting at Becca and turned his attention to me as music echoed off the marble—the acoustics were actually quite lovely. He looked deeply unnerved.

"Moonlight Sonata," I answered, keeping my voice light. "It's by Beethoven." I winked at him, and he fucking flinched.

"I know who wrote the fucking Moonlight Sonata, weirdo. I asked, what the fuck are you doing?"

"I saw this in a vampire movie once. It seemed appropriate...you did try to set me on fucking fire," I continued playing, not even looking at the keyboard. The Moonlight Sonata was easy. I'd played it a thousand times; my fingers knew the notes by heart. I didn't break eye contact with my maker, even when he pulled the handgun out of his waistband and pointed it at me. His hands were shaking more than mine.

"Why didn't you just go away? All you had to do was leave, and everything would have been perfect."

"Why did you turn me and abandon me in a bathtub?"

He looked unexpectedly crestfallen. "I didn't know that would work. Fuck, I'm sorry, okay? I didn't mean to—"

"You didn't mean to kill me? That's nice, I guess..." I kept playing and tried to ignore the gun. His apology meant nothing. Not at this point. Calliope was dead, and heaven only knew where Harold was. I had to protect Becca. I needed time to come up with a better plan.

He fired, and a bullet whizzed past my ear. I didn't flinch, but I stopped the music, a cold, sickening chill flooding my veins. I slammed my hands down on the keys, creating a discordant sound that made Gavin jump.

"You're a coward and a terrible shot," I said, remembering Harold's assessment.

He didn't shoot again. I cocked my head to one side, allowing a slow grin to stretch across my face, eyes wide and unblinking, staring at him. He took a step back and lowered the gun, ever so slightly.

Crazy? I'll show you crazy...

I leaped off the piano bench and lunged at him, shrieking and clawing like a CGI velociraptor. I saw that in a movie once, too. I definitely caught him off guard, because Gavin screamed, and dropped the gun. It clattered to the marble floor and slipped beneath a low bench.

"What the fuck is wrong with you?" he continued screaming as he backed away from me. There was fear in his eyes, and I liked it.

Becca scrambled to retrieve the gun before he could pick it up again, but he shoved her roughly aside, and my stomach dropped. Gavin probably wouldn't fall for the "suddenly a dinosaur" trick a second time. In my experience, it only worked on street catcallers exactly once.

"Gavin Ezra Richardson, you're a piece. Of. Shit." Calliope enunciated each word as she limped down the curving staircase, leaving a smear of blood on the chrome handrail behind her as she descended. My face fell at the sight of her. Blood ran down across her head and face, and it was impossible to tell where her smeared crimson lipstick ended, and the blood around her mouth began. Her clothes were tattered by bullet holes and equally bloodied, but the wounds on her pale flesh, visible through the scorched fabric, were healing, slowly. She carried an ugly sharpened three-foot-long wooden stake in her free hand, and I had no doubt as to what she intended to do with it.

Neither did Gavin. He aimed the gun he'd wrested out of Becca's hands at Calliope, but it did not fire. Something must have gotten stuck when he dropped it. He screamed again, violent and wordless, trying to unjam the mechanism.

Calliope kept talking, kept slowly making her way down the staircase. "Of all the fledglings I've ever turned, I think you might be the biggest disappointment. Once upon a time, I thought you were handsome, and smart, and charming…"

"Spare me," he muttered, slamming the heel of his fist into the butt of the handgun several times. "I was never going to be anything but a disappointment to you, CJ. It had nothing to do with me. You were never going to love me, because I was never going to be *him*." He spat the last words at her.

"Who told you that?" Calliope stopped in her descent, pausing between treads, almost swaying. It was impossible to tell if the pain in her voice was from his words or her injuries. "That's not true. I loved you."

Gavin laughed, sour and hollow.

"Where is she, Gavin?" Calliope looked around the smoke-filled great room, at the small fires littering the space, and there was fear in her eyes, too. "If it's Marie you've been listening to, if she's here, Gavin, I can explain. Whatever she told you—"

Becca let out a pterodactyl scream of her own, grabbing Gavin from behind, right as he tried to shoot again, and he misfired wildly. Calliope continued her approach with the stake, as Gavin grappled with Becca, violently grasping both her hands above her head in vice-like grip. Her feet brushed against the floor, almost dangling. He was well over a foot taller than her, and brutal. She didn't stand a chance against him.

"Put her down, Gavin. You're angry at me, not her." Calliope reached out, almost gentle in her pleading. "I loved you," she repeated. "I loved all my fledglings—"

"Back off." Gavin raised his arm higher, lifting Becca off the floor completely. His other hand still gripped the gun, and Becca whimpered in pain like a small wounded animal. "He was a bartender, CJ." Gavin scoffed. "A gay fucking bartender. I was fucking upgrade. A goddamn upgrade! I was *better* than him—"

Calliope cut him off with two quick steps toward him. "You're nothing." She whispered. "A disgrace. Jimmy would never hurt me like you do," her words were like icicles, as deadly and pointed as the stake in her hands.

"Oh my God, stop TALKING!" Gavin released his grip on Becca and dropped her, unloading the remainder of the bullets into Calliope's head and torso. Her body crumpled at the base of the stairs with a splatter like rotten fruit.

Becca screamed, and I rushed to grab the stake Calliope had been holding before Gavin could grab it. I was pretty sure the gun was out of bullets.

His foot crashed down on my hand so hard I felt several small bones snap, and I cried out in pain, reflexively cradling the injury to my chest.

"Oh, boohoo, does that fucking hurt?" He taunted. I loathed him, viscerally. I wanted him dead. But Gavin got to the stake first, and thrust it at me, stopping a mere fraction of an inch from where my broken hand still clutched over my heart, and he laughed.

I tried to scoot away from him.

"Leave her alone!" Becca cried. "Just go away and leave us all alone! You're scaring me. Why did you shoot Calliope? She was nice to me. You didn't have to kill her. What's wrong with you?"

"Me? What's wrong with me? You don't know anything about anything. You're just a fledgling. You don't know what that thing—" he pointed at Calliope's body, "is capable of. What she's done. I'm not the monster here! I'm not the monster!"

My good hand found the hilt of the sword of its own volition—my sword, I thought of it now—*not a sword to be used on me, but a sword that I could use.* I flexed my other, injured hand, gratified to discover it had already mostly recovered, and hardly hurt at all. Everything seemed to happen slowly and impossibly fast, all at once. My grip tightened on the hilt as I pulled it out of its scabbard, and for the first time in a long time, maybe since I was fourteen years old and told my parents I was too old for the Renaissance Faire, I felt absolutely, perfectly, *myself.*

"I fucking hate you!" I screamed at my maker, lifting the broadsword above my head and charging at him. I swung my arms to bring the blade down on his stupid, pretty face.

I was so fast. Inhumanly fast. Impossibly fast. Gavin was faster.

The single blast from the last remaining bullet in the handgun's chamber hit me full force at close range, and I skidded backward, slamming into the white leather sofas by the window that Calliope had been so concerned about me spilling blood on. *I'm sorry, Calliope…*but Calliope was dead, and I was an explosion of crimson. A waterfall of blood poured out from chest where the bullet ripped through me, my hands stained red as they tried to staunch the lethal flow.

My mind drifted.

"Could a gun do it?" I asked Harold, standing next to him by the bonfire in the backyard.

"I suppose a gun could do it." He turned and looked at me, his voice solemn, his face an unreadable mask. *"If the bullet rounds were large enough, modern hollow points, maybe, depending on how many times you got hit, and whether or not there's an escape, route and access to a source of blood nearby."*

I didn't think there was any escaping this. I didn't think there was enough blood to save me now.

Morbid curiosity overwhelmed my fear, and I raised my head enough to look down at my ruined chest, at the massive hole in my torso. Another fraction of an inch to the left, and the bullet would have hit my heart, but it didn't matter. I knew with a peaceful kind of clarity that my aorta was shredded, and all my blood, all that stolen life, was spilling away…the world started to go dim around the edges.

It felt…peaceful. I felt good. I wondered where Harold was now, and if he was going to be happy. Wherever he was, he deserved to be happy.

Through the thickening smoke, and the narrow field of my dying tunnel vision, Gavin's face loomed above me, his lips a sneer of triumph. "At least you didn't try to punch me this time, bitch!" He was laughing again.

I wasn't angry at him anymore. He didn't matter.

And then he turned to Becca. "You see, baby? It worked. The blood worked, there was just a little complication. You're here now. We can be together forever now, just like you wanted. You can have anything you want now. We're safe, the Community won't come after us, it's going to be okay." His hand caressed her cheek.

Becca flinched, panic coloring her words. "Don't touch me!" she screamed. "You *are* a monster!"

Gavin laughed again, practically a giggle. "Guess what, babe, so are you!"

Her sobs became an anguished gurgle, and I heard, more than I saw, her slap him across the face again. *Should have punched him...*I drifted further into oblivion. I think Gavin hit her upside the head with the empty gun, trying to get her to shut up. Becca was still screaming in pain as the world went dark.

Chapter Thirty-Five

BETWEEN THE SPIRIT AND THE DUST

I don't make it through the final night of selections; none of the sororities on campus want me. Becca doesn't get a bid for the Loyola chapter of her grandmother's sorority. I tell her it has to be a mistake. She's legacy—sororities love that, don't they? Becca wears her rejection like a badge of honor and doesn't wait five minutes before breaking out the black box dye she's been saving for the occasion.

"I will never, in my entire life, encounter anything creepier than the knowledge that intimate details of my life have been discussed in a dim campus basement by a bunch of college Stepfords wearing Greek life sweatpants," she announces, heading toward the communal bathrooms back at her residential hall.

I roll my eyes but scramble after her. "Mother of God...if you're going to dye your hair with black box dye, Becca, let me help. You'll never get even coverage on your own..."

Back in her dorm, she cuts her own hair in an asymmetrical, choppy style. Mall goth hair. I sit on the edge of her unmade bed, mesmerized as Becca peers into the mirror above the tiny sink in the corner of the room, wreaking havoc on what had formerly been almost waist-length tresses. Her bangs now cover one eye completely. She looks like a MySpace celebrity, I want to tell her. I don't tell her how beautiful she is.

"You should tell everyone that your new name is Ebony Dark'ness Dementia Raven Way." I twist a piece of my own coffee-brown hair around my fingers and make a face, remembering the awful piece of fan fiction Becca made me read last weekend. I'd actually put off studying for bio to read...whatever that was.

Becca laughs and drags the scissors down the length of the hair that frames her face. More pieces of freshly-dyed hair hit the floor. "That would be hilarious. I wonder how many professors I could convince...?"

"Tell that cute guy from your film studies class. Tell him that's your name now. Enoby Dark'ness Dementia Raven Way—" **AN: look up 'My Immortal' (fanfiction). If u don't know what that is get da hell outta here! Credit to the infamous unknown author, wherever they are.**

She squeals, drops the scissors, and throws a bag of potato chips at me, scattering the floor with crumbs, and I shriek, holding up my hands to shield myself from the incoming mess. "Sorry!" Her eyes grow wide in shock and embarrassment. "I didn't realize the bag was open, I promise!"

I glare at her and grab the whisk, broom, and dustpan. "Fifty points from—from whatever house the goths belong to."

"I'm not goth, Grace. Goth is for people who can't get over the nineties. I'm emo." Becca rolls her eyes but kneels down to help me pick up the mess she's made. "Anyway, I'm glad that farce is over."

"What, selection week?"

"The whole bit. I never wanted to do the sorority thing. I just went through the motions because Nonna and Parker wanted me to. It felt so fake. And the color-matching, I can't. I just can't. Bury me in black lace, please."

I'd wondered how serious Becca had been about the whole sorority process. Even in the first round of introductory meetings, she'd seemed out of place, like she didn't want to be there. I'm not sure I'd wanted to be there, either, but it had seemed like a good way to make friends, at the time. I'm still struggling in the friend department at Loyola. The RA at my dorm has pulled me aside for a couple of insincere heart-to-heart "talks," but I remain the weird girl no one wants anything to do with. In retrospect, it was probably dumb of me to think that joining a sorority would have helped any. At least Becca likes me.

I'm pretty sure she likes me.

"I don't think you made any bad decisions to get us here, by the way. It's not your fault that all of this happened. Sometimes the wrong turns in life take us to the right places, you know?"

I nod.

Wait. That's not how that conversation went.

The Cordero family pre-Thanksgiving spaghetti dinner takes place every year the night before turkey day. Dad says it started back when my Nonna was still alive—that was Nana's mom, she died when I was 8—because all the women are busy in the kitchen the days before Thanksgiving, cooking and baking and all, so the Cordero men get together to make red sauce and spaghetti for the night before, and there's always foil-wrapped garlic bread heating on the grill. Maybe the tradition is a bit sexist and old-fashioned, but it's always been one of my favorite family holiday gatherings, and this year, sophomore year, I get to share it with my new best friend and roommate, because Becca doesn't want to go back to California.

On the five-hour drive to Toledo to Nana's house, Becca chooses the playlist, and the car snacks.

Somewhere midway across Indiana, I choose not to make her ride in the trunk over some of her song choices. But if I have to listen to another track with a paragraph-long title and screaming vocals...

"What if they don't like me?" Becca asks. Actually, she asks, "Wah eh hey oneike eh?" Because her mouth is full of goldfish crackers. I can tell she's nervous, because she keeps scrolling through her iPod, looking for songs that don't exist: The kind that will magically make her feel more confident about meeting my family. I don't know why she's so nervous.

Before I met Becca, most of the music I listened to was Dad's '90's stuff, or movie scores. Hans Zimmer and John Williams, usually. Becca voraciously consumes music like she breathes air—a song for every mood, a lyric for every inside joke. My dad is going to love her. He already knows everything about her. Calls her his "other daughter" when he phones to check up on me.

"And how's my other daughter doing?"

Becca's going to be fine.

Cousins and aunts and uncles are already spilling out of the house and onto the expansive lawn when we arrive, their faces all a blur. The entire front yard is taken over by several enormous pots set up over a motley collection of propane campfire cookers pulled out of various relative's garages and basements. Red sauce recipes that have been closely guarded secrets for generations get the star treatment every Wednesday before Thanksgiving, and competition amongst brothers and cousins runs deep.

I look over at the crowd of relatives for Dad, but he's not outside. All around, people I've known my whole life have suddenly become strangers to me—I don't know who anyone is, familiar faces all rendered in soft focus pushed to the extreme, like Vaseline coating the camera lens, all distinguishing features washed away.

Something isn't right, that's not how this is supposed to happen—

I grab Becca's hand and run into the house, looking for Dad, for Nana. We stride down the hallway toward the kitchen, past all the family pictures hanging on the walls. She pauses in front of a particularly cringe-worthy picture of me from Homecoming, ninth-grade year.

"Ooh, you never showed me this one—!"

I try to drag Becca by the elbow, away from the incriminating evidence. "I was young, and I didn't know better, I was still learning—"

"No, no, no, bump-its and an orange tan. I'm getting evidence of this—" she pulls out her iPhone and snaps a picture of the framed print. Fortunately, it comes out blurry, like all the other faces around us.

She examines the resulting image with the concentration of a movie archaeologist deciphering ancient hieroglyphics, regardless. "They say that blood is thicker than water," she reminds me, "but the original expression is, 'The blood of the covenant is thicker than the waters of the womb.' I think too many people forget that."

I stare at her, open-mouthed and confused. *I don't think that's something Becca's ever said to me.*

She's sitting fully clothed on the thoroughly unsanitary tile floor in the shower at our residential hall, lukewarm water drenching her in a weak spray from the mineral-encrusted shower head above. She hasn't moved in four minutes and thirty-seven seconds. I've been counting the entire time, watching her breathe, watching the tears stream down her cheeks.

"Becca?"

She doesn't respond.

I kneel down next to her at last, and the water sinks into my dark rinse skinny jeans and soaks the crisp white cotton of my oxford blouse until the fabric softens and clings against my skin, and I don't even notice, because Becca Moreno has been catatonic in the showers for over five minutes now, and that's just since I found her.

I don't know how long she's been this way.

"Why am I like this?" she asks, finally, staring at her hands.

"You're exactly who you're supposed to be," I tell her. I know she had a date tonight. A girl from her media illustration class. They've seen each other a few times now. I don't know what went wrong. "Becca?"

A strangled sob she can't choke back escapes her, and my heart collapses, bottoms out, a basket full of red summer berries bruised and splattering crimson on the tiles. If my emotions had form and shape, they'd be visceral, thick like spews of blood.

"I want," she whispers. "I want, and I want, and I want, but no one ever wants me, so it must be me that's the problem, then. It's always my fault, always has been...Why am I *like* this?"

I throw my arms around her shoulders, lean into her. "Shut up. You're perfect," I whisper. *Perfect. Perfect. Perfect.* My lips brush up against her cheek. *You're perfect, Becca. I'm the one who's full of flaws.*

I think about my darkness, the way I don't relate to people, the shame I've always felt about my...strangeness. The problem has never been other people. It's always been me. I was always the stranger...until Becca. When we sit in silence, there is peace in her presence that washes away loneliness. I watch the water swirling down the shower drain, tinged indigo from the dye in my jeans, dark blue, the color of sadness. Of course when I'm around her, it leeches out of me and stains everything it touches.

How could Becca think that she is anything less than perfect, when she sees all my brokenness, and never flinches or looks away?

I've held her close like this before. There's nothing between us, romantically. There couldn't be, because what I feel for Becca goes beyond feelings of romance. I would die for her if she needed me to, and that's not romance. That's self-sacrifice. It's a different kind of love altogether. So I don't understand what happens next.

When her face turns toward mine, I don't expect it, and suddenly our lips are almost touching, and if I kiss her now, I feel like reality would cave in on itself; my mind is a flock of birds scattering as they rise with the morning sun. She exhales like the breath of life against my skin, and I breathe her in, expanding my lungs to hold on to this gift that my brain can't comprehend, and this is the most intoxicating moment of my twenty years of existence. I am no stranger to intoxicants by now.

I want and I want and I want—

I don't know what I want.

"Grace..."

I don't want to ruin my best friend, burden her with my shadows even more than I already have, simply by existing in her light.

I pull away, rearrange our limbs, now my arms are under her shoulders, and I'm lifting her to her feet, dragging her up from the communal bathroom floor. "Come on, Bec. Let me get you to bed. Tomorrow is another day, I promise. Tomorrow won't be so broken."

...but I don't remember ever being so certain. I don't remember ever telling her those things.

They say St. John Cantius Parish Church in River West is "the most beautiful church in America." I've wanted to come to midnight Mass here on Christmas Eve ever since I first moved to Chicago for college, but every year, I've spent Christmas at home in Ohio with my family. Even though, year after year, that "family" seems to grow smaller. Cousins grow up. Move away. No one stays close to home anymore. Even Victoria is spending this Christmas with her fiancé's family in New Jersey. Dad and Celeste are off in Cancun...

I call Nana to make sure. That she doesn't need me. It's the holidays, after all. She says she's spending Christmas volunteering at the soup kitchen this year. "It's a lot less work than cooking for all of yous...this year, I only gotta make five dishes, and I get plenty of help!"

So I've stayed in Chicago. I was supposed to go to Mass with my coworker and her family, but they cancelled last minute. Some last-minute emergency. So I'm going to Mass on my own on Christmas Eve.

I'm not sure I know what I'm doing, to be honest. Faith has seemed like something terribly far away from me, recently. But the Christmas story...even if I'm not sure what I believe, I'm anchored by tradition. Familiarity. Going through the motions is an act of faith in and of itself, sometimes.

So I go through the motions. I genuflect, slip into an empty pew. Actually, all the pews are empty. But they're not. The church is crowded, filled to capacity, spilling over out the doors. I had to wait in line for over an hour just to get a chance at a decent spot before the doors even opened. I can hear the low murmur of voices surrounding me, parishioners shifting in their seats, and the familiar creak of the kneelers being set in place. The air is hot and thick with the crush of humanity, the smell of incense and candle wax.

But my pew is empty. And I can't make out any faces in the blur of the crowd that surrounds me. Confusion swirls in my brain. I know that something's wrong; I've felt this sense of disorientation before, the night I...

The night I...

"You are a very difficult person to get ahold of," Becca genuflects, slides into the pew beside me.

"I'm sorry, I've been busy. I've been dealing with...a lot of stuff." I peer at Becca. She's solid and distinct, corporeal against a shallow depth of field.

"You think there's anything you might struggle with that I can't handle? If you talk to me?"

"What is there to talk about?"

"Blood doesn't lie, Grace."

Her words are a lit match to accelerant; everything dark is suddenly illuminated and clear, purified by flames. "Are we dead?"

Becca lifts her shoulders, not quite a shrug. Like I'm asking the wrong question.

"But isn't that what this is about?"

"I don't think I know what death is, anymore. The old concept I used to hold onto no longer applies."

"I don't know what you mean."

"What if Emily Dickinson was right, and Death is just, 'a dialogue between the Spirit and the Dust?' Then I'm pretty sure all we are is taking part in a complicated conversation...that's going to stretch out long into the night. That's my take on things, at least." She gets up to leave again.

"Where are you going?" I reach for her, but she's already fading. My hands grab on to nothingness.

I don't want to be left alone.

"It takes two to have a dialogue, Grace. Communion and Community share a common root." She disappears into the faceless blurred crowd that surrounds us, losing all distinction, until I can no longer find her in the swarm of life that fills the center aisle, shuffling toward the altar for the Sacrament.

Body of Christ.

Blood of Christ.

I make a half-hearted move to follow her out of the pew and into the shimmering gilded congregation, to dissolve completely in the same murmuring haze Becca has evaporated into, to lose myself alongside her, wherever she has gone to, but I am anchored in place by a momentary overwhelming memory of iron and salt on my tongue.

Blood of Christ.

A roar fills my head like a train engine as the world decomposes into swirling black. The golden light of the church grows dim and cold; red stars swirl in my peripheral vision.

I prayed for oblivion not too long ago. There's a peace that comes with surrender to this void, where my darkness and my shadows have always found a home, and I crave the soothing comfort of that peace like a craving for the rush of blood. I am torn between two desires, and the roar that fills and surrounds me is the thunder of a summer storm, my inner conflicted turmoil as potent as warm earth meeting cold atmospheric pressure.

Winds whip at my tattered, bleeding senses. The whole world is nothing but ichorous dark clouds bathed in eerie red light.

Some vague, distant part of me knows that I'm hallucinating all of this—my memories, Becca, all the things we never really said. My unraveling consciousness merely trying to create order out of the pandemonium of dying, and I wonder if this is how my mother felt in her final moments, when the stroke that killed her ripped through her skull. Did she even have time to know she was leaving us behind?

Dull rumbling from the storm clouds rises in pitch as the whirlwind picks up, and all sound distorts to a scream that cuts through the tempest that defines the edges of death. I can still hear Becca screaming, even as I'm bleeding out. Even as I fade away. I've always known that I would die for her.

I never imagined how badly she would need me to live.

Death is a dialogue between the spirit and the dust. My mother has passed beyond that point, and I'm balanced on the precipice. That's why it's not my mother's face I see as I lay dying: It's Becca's.

Becca's voice overwhelms every other audio vibration, every other sensation in my fractured reality, and it suddenly becomes so beautifully, perfectly clear. Life, after all, is for the living.

And if Becca is still alive, then so am I.

CHAPTER THIRTY-SIX

GRACE

Pain.

Darkness. Smoke and flames. Screaming.

Becca.

Dying in reverse felt…strange. Nothing Harold had told me about being a vampire could have prepared me for that. My mind willed it, and my body became a sponge, absorbing all the blood pooled on the marble floor around me. My blood, of its own volition, started to find its way back, re-entering my emptied-out capillaries and veins and arteries, knitting my body back together again. I felt the skin growing fresh over new bone and tendon and muscle where it had all been blown away, and after a few moments in the black, my vision returned to me, and I could fill my re-formed lungs again.

I opened my eyes.

Focus, Grace.

It took an enormous, shaking effort to sit up, then stand, where I had fallen. Rivulets of blood traveled up my legs and torso as I swayed but did not topple. I willed my body to stop shaking, and it did. The tremors in my fingertips went still.

Focus.

I did not have enough blood inside what had re-formed from my broken body to miss this chance. If he shot me again, there would be no more getting up. The knowledge made me curiously detached, watching my movements from outside my body. Part of me was still floating, not quite tethered to the world of the living.

The fires Gavin started in the wastepaper baskets had nowhere to spread; they smoldered and churned out noxious black smoke and half-hearted flames that sputtered as they ran out of fuel. For a man who had been involved in two house fires in the last week, his arson inside Calliope's penthouse seemed perfunctory, unenthused. I wondered how far he'd thought any of this through.

His back was still turned to me, looming over a hysterical Becca, trying to calm her down, cajoling her in one sentence, threatening her with the next, manipulative entitlement on full display. He didn't notice I was standing; he was too busy trying to find the magic words that would render her compliant.

I saw my maker in that moment, fully. He was incompetent and reckless. Insecure. Not only a coward, but unfit for the rigors and challenges of an extraordinarily long life. His self-obsession made him a danger to himself and others. I did not understand why Calliope had been so keen to protect him; was her reputation really so frayed that she was in danger simply for bringing him into the night? I shook my head; decided I didn't care. It was easy to know what to do.

The sword had fallen a short distance away from me when I dropped it as I skidded backward, and I picked it up with a smooth fluidity of motion that didn't seem to belong to me; my movements were inhuman, alien, *other*.

It felt good, though—the heft of the blade in my hands, the tightening of my grip on the hilt.

It felt right.

"Goodbye, Gavin," I said. Every shredded and rebuilt filament in my being stretched taut with deathly anticipation as I lifted the sword in my hands.

He still had Calliope's stake, wielded it to parry the first blow as he spun around to face me.

"Fucking hell, won't you just die?" He thrust the stake. His reach was far greater than mine, but I blocked him, just barely. The sword grew heavy as I held fast against the sharpened wood; I wasn't sure I could hold out against him much longer. "Why do you have to make everything so difficult?" he whined. "You ruined everything."

For just a split second, our eyes met, and once again I saw the fear in his eyes. I spit at him. "Coward."

"Bitch."

I stepped forward. "Asshole."

"Whatever." But he took a step backward. That was his fatal error. Becca grabbed his ankle and pulled down, hard, taking Gavin down with her. He toppled to his knees with a screech of terror, and dropped the stake.

He only had a fraction of an instant to look up at me; I think he might have been about to say "please." I think he might have begged me for mercy, but I had already started to swing. The downward momentum of the blade cut time in two; I swung the sword with uncanny precision, as though I'd been born for this moment, every second of my existence leading up to this singular purpose.

The world paused, the storm outside the windows went still, the ever-present hum of the living, breathing skyscraper grew silent. Even though I knew I was imagining it, I heard music coming from the baby grand piano. Schubert's "Ave Maria." Nana had played it at Mom's funeral.

Ave Maria, gratia plena

...gratia plena

Perhaps there was more than one way to exist in a state of grace.

And then Gavin's head separated from his body in a smooth, sweeping motion, landing at Becca's feet.

She was battered and blood-spattered about the face and hands, but she would heal, I knew with a gratifying confidence. Becca picked up her ex's severed head and screamed at his face, wordless and full of violent rage and betrayal, then lobbed the revolting thing away from her as far and as hard as she could throw it. Gavin's head made contact with the reinforced floor-to-ceiling windows with a satisfying "thwump," and skidded down the glass, leaving a bloody trail behind it. Before the head could reach the floor, it, and Gavin's body lying half a room away, disintegrated into ash.

"I'm going to outlive Twinkies and cockroaches with you." Becca breathed, looking up at me with awe. I smiled, straightened my shoulders, and I was perfect. She was perfect. Everything in this moment, all of it—was perfect. Her injuries were already starting to look better.

"I love you, too. You know that, right?" I helped my best friend in the whole world stand up, and she leaned against me. I drew in a shaking breath, still lightheaded from the blood loss, still uncertain how I'd managed to pull myself up again. But

Becca was safe, and nothing else in the world mattered. "I will one million percent admit that your first night as a vampire has been a thousand times worse than mine was."

"I can't do the math, but I'll take your word for it." Becca giggled until she snorted, wild and deranged, which made me laugh too, all the stress of the horror we'd just survived rendering us incapable of any other response, and we collapsed against each other, barely holding each other up as we dissolved into hysterical laugher, surrounded by carnage, oblivious to the smoke from the trash fires filling the room.

Becca came to her senses first, or maybe she got distracted, and she gazed around the room in awe, halting over the prone figure by the staircase. "Calliope didn't disintegrate like my ex-boyfriend just did. Is there still time to save her?"

I pivoted my eyes to the crumpled form fast enough to give a person whiplash. Calliope's body was bloodied and broken, and her fingers were twitching in the electric rhythm of death, but she wasn't entirely gone—not yet. Maybe there was time. "She needs blood," I told Becca knowingly. "Probably lots of it. I think I know where she keeps her hospital stash."

I raced to the kitchen. Every single stupid panel looked exactly the same. I opened the microwave drawer in the center island twice before I found the refrigerator Calliope kept her hospital blood in—the refrigerator was also a drawer, secured with a biometric lock. I decided I hated it. I yanked on the drawer pull with all my strength, and the electronic locking mechanism catastrophically failed, swinging the drawer open so far, it would never close correctly again. I hardly felt bad about the destruction—Calliope's place was already trashed, and I'd seen the aftermath of her parties. What was a bit more damage?

I filled my arms up with bags of blood, then realized I didn't know where Calliope kept her scissors, so I dropped the blood and looked around for a drawer the scissors might have been in, before I remembered I was a goddamn vampire and I'd tear the blood bags open with my teeth, if I had to—and raced back over to where Calliope had fallen.

Becca sat cross-legged on the floor, Calliope gathered into her arms and suckling from the inner crook of Becca's elbow in a scene blasphemously reminiscent of medieval religious art. She looked up at me when I approached. "You said she needed blood," Becca shrugged with a sheepish expression on her face, "and I thought, if hospital blood is good, maybe vampire blood would be better? And hey, look, I'm a vampire now, and anyway, I guess I was right. I think it's working." She gently stroked the back of Calliope's head with the hand that wasn't feeding her, and I watched the fractured, jagged bits of Calliope's skull reassemble themselves, sliding back into place and reconnecting with a slow, wet sound.

It was very impressive, but also very gross. I threw my hands up in the air, and the bagged blood toppled to the floor around us, plastic bags bouncing on the marble but thankfully not rupturing. "Okay, sure, all of this is still new to me too, but why not?" I walked a few steps over to my sword and picked it up off the floor where I'd dropped it after beheading Gavin, and used the edge to open up one of the blood bags. My stomach instantly lurched at the smell, but I handed the bag to Becca. "You're going to need this, then."

"Definitely," Becca agreed. "I can smell it from here."

I sat next to her on the marble floor and tore open a bag for myself, and when Becca and I turned to look at each other, we smiled fangy, monstrous grins at one another and laughed again until Becca stopped and looked up. The chandelier above us both shook softly, dancing cascades of prismatic light falling over us.

"There's someone in the vents," she whispered.

I strained my ears, and the crawling sound above us stopped briefly, then continued. Our eyes tracked the distance to the ventilation grating, cleverly disguised among the ceiling panels. Becca gripped Calliope tighter and began to scoot away. My hand gripped the sword at my side again, thoughts returning to the threat of Marie DuChamps—she still had her head attached to her shoulders, and I didn't like knowing that.

"Hello? Grace? Calliope—?" The vent grating popped away as an arm punched down, and Harold toppled out of the ceiling, flailing for a moment in mid-air, before righting himself and sticking a competent, if inelegant, landing. He was covered with dust and soot from the vent, dirt streaked across his face, and his hair was a mess. I decided that he was the kind of man who looked better a little bit grunged up. It suited him.

He scanned the room, took note of the fires, and darted off toward the kitchen, wild-eyed, before saying anything to either of us.

Becca gave me an apprehensive, sidelong glance. "That's the guy who beat up Gavin."

"That's Harold. He's all right." I assured her, but she didn't seem entirely convinced.

Harold came back into the room with a fire extinguisher in one hand, carrying the broken sword I had left behind in the charred remains of his old home in the other. He still didn't say a word; he just aimed the nozzle of the fire extinguisher at the nearest trash can that was still on fire, and pulled the trigger.

"That was Gavin," Becca offered, by way of explanation, as the flames smothered, and went out.

Harold raised an eyebrow and seemed to find his voice. "Gavin was a trash fire?"

"No," Becca said. "I mean, yes, he was, but also, he's the one who set the fire. I think there's one burning in the other room, too."

Harold squinted at Becca, and then at me, and then back at Becca. "Are you Becca?" he asked her, as if it wasn't perfectly obvious who she was. Becca nodded, and Harold cast me a single, curious glance before he walked off to extinguish the rest of the small fires in the apartment. Thankfully, nothing had spread.

I called after him, confused, "How did you get up there?" more relieved to see him than I ever imagined it was possible to be.

He returned to where Becca, Calliope, and I were still clustered together on the floor, and surveyed the chaos wordlessly for another beat. The penthouse was full of smoke, there were bloodstains and bullet holes on the floor and walls, and an ominous streak of blood across the windows was the only evidence of where Gavin had once been, aside from the dark pile of ash smudged and smeared across the floor. His eyes finally returned to me, and the sword he had forged—but it was my sword now, I'd already decided—lying across my lap.

"I thought you might have been the one tae take the broadsword." He put the broken sword down. "And I guess I won't be needing this." He took his own gun out of the waistband of his pants and set it aside; it was identical to the one Gavin had been using. I guessed Gavin had been using Calliope's own firearm, and it amused me that Harold and Calliope had matching BFF guns. He threw his hands up in the air.

"I'm not very good at this hero thing, am I?" Harold asked

"Never have been," Calliope's weak voice was muffled, because her mouth was still nuzzling the crook of Becca's elbow.

Harold rolled his eyes. "I'm glad you're feeling better," he told her.

I giggled again, giddy and overwhelmed and exhausted—but also strangely content—and tried to stand up, but I was barely conscious from all the drama. And blood loss. I opened another bag of blood and made a very messy job of replenishing myself. Harold knelt beside me, put his fingers to the skin of the new flesh through the gaping hole that had been blown through my clothing. The vintage Burberry trench coat I'd only just been reunited with was a total loss, but it had died a truly epic death.

"He shot you." Harold's voice cracked, quietly furious.

"He shot Calliope, too. Many times. Then I cut off his head and Becca threw it at the window, and it went whoosh. Splat." I gestured to approximate a recreation of events. "I tried to call you," I said. "Lots."

Harold sighed, and I had never been so happy to hear him sigh since I'd met him. "I shouldn't have left you alone for so long. I should have tried tae send you a message sooner. I'm sorry, I should have..."

"I shouldn't have said the things I said that night. It was all overwhelming and—"

"You don't have tae apologize. I know. I saw it in your blood, how hurt you were, and—" He hung his head low.

"I didn't mean to hurt you, too."

"I can take the pain, as long as you're safe." He reached out a hand to brush the hair away from my blood-streaked face. "When I got back tae the hotel, and the flask was on the bed, I thought that was some kind of message, from you. Telling me where you were—"

I felt all my giddiness evaporate, replaced by guilt; it had never occurred to me he might interpret the flask on the bed as anything significant, and really, I—of all people—should have known better.

"I spent hours in the wreckage of the old house, looking for you, looking for more signs, looking for...anything, really. I found the swords in the basement finally, and realized one was missing, and if only one was missing, there was only one person who could have taken it, and there was only one place you would go, and I was so afraid—I didn't want tae be too late..." he took my face in his hands and broke, silent tears streaming down his face. "I dunna want tae lose you, kettlen."

I swallowed a lump in my throat and blinked away tears of my own. "I don't want to go anywhere. I want to be with you." I sniffled, throwing my arms around him and refusing to let go. "I thought you'd left me, after everything I said."

Calliope finally had the strength to sit up, but Becca kept her arms around her, and Calliope did not seem to object. "How come we're the ones with crappy luck with men?" Becca asked her.

Calliope chucked, taking Becca's hand in hers. "You have no idea. Let's not do that again."

I looked over at my best friend and at Calliope Jones, whom I had had many conflicting thoughts about during the night, and raised my eyebrows. *What is going on there?* I wondered.

There was a powerful intimacy in the blood.

Harold spoke up, tilting his head to one side. "I don't want tae sound the alarm, but I believe that's the fire department I hear coming up the stairs. The elevators have already been disabled. Do you want tae stay and explain this away, Cal? Or..." He gestured outside.

Calliope gave him a knowing look, and sighed. "Well, we've done this sort of thing before, haven't we?" She glanced around at the destruction the night's misadventures had wrought on her lovely home, carefully standing up and brushing herself off, as if the gesture would do anything to remedy her destroyed designer attire. The jeweled owl pin had miraculously survived, hanging on by a thread. Similarly, we all looked like hell.

She walked over to one of the plate glass windows and gazed outside, tracing her fingers on the glass. The worst of the storm seemed to have passed, and while the world outside the windows was shrouded with thick clouds, the white-out conditions of earlier in the night had died down, and only a few flurries of snow remained, borne aloft by gusts of wind that howled much less frequently than they had before.

"I have enjoyed it here, high above the world. But it's been almost two decades, and that is entirely too long. I was getting greedy," she admitted, quiet sadness washing over her. She appeared to give herself a moment to mourn, breathing in and out deeply as though the unnecessary gesture would prepare her for something she didn't want to do. Then she punched through the plate glass window, and it shattered, raining shards into the penthouse and far down onto the street below. A cold winter wind filled the interior space, and the smoke began to clear away.

I was aghast at Calliope's strength, and looked down at my own hands in quiet wonder. I'd had no idea that was a thing I might someday be able to do...but then I remembered how Becca and I had run back to the penthouse faster than any car and how I had torn open the electronic refrigerator lock...vampires were clearly badasses.

"You're not actually suggesting what I think you're suggesting?" Becca looked alarmed, but she also sounded very excited. I rolled my eyes at her oh-so-typically Becca reaction. *Everything really was going to be okay*. Gavin had been right about something.

"The fire department isn't parked on this side of the building," Calliope said, looking down. How she could know that through the thick cloud cover was beyond me, but I trusted her. "We should go now." She stood on the window ledge and held her hand out to Becca, who stood up, took two steps toward Calliope, then paused, before she stepped across the floor to where Gavin had dropped the black duffle bag before he died, and slung it over her shoulder.

"I think there's some good stuff in here. Waste not, want not, right?" She took Calliope's hand with all the faith in the world, and they jumped out into the night.

A freezing gust of wind blew directly at me, messy tendrils of long brown hair adhering themselves to my lips and eyes, and I sputtered, wildly rubbing my hands over my face to dislodge the errant strands, without much success. It was even windier outside, and I didn't like thinking about what was going to happen next. Harold grabbed my hand and squeezed tight.

"Are you...you're okay? With things...?"

I knew he meant the part about Becca ending up a vampire anyway, despite my ridiculous efforts, and I nodded, drawing in a deep breath of frigid air. My heart was silent, still, and calm inside my chest. *Content.*

I stood up, and the sword clattered out of my lap and onto the floor one last time. My sword—a sword for me to use, not a sword to be used on me. I left it where it fell, and let Harold lead me over to the window. We didn't have much time before the fire department would burst through the doors.

"Are you sure you want tae leave the sword behind?" he asked, grabbing me by the waist and pulling me close to his side. He'd acquired a new wool sweater in a similar Fair Isle knit pattern as the others he usually wore, and I buried my face in the itchy, dust-coated yarn. It didn't smell vintage yet, but I knew, in time, it would.

"I'm leaving a lot of stuff behind tonight, I think. I was holding on to too much anyway, and I don't want most of it, if I can have you." I was afraid to look down; the height still made my head spin and my anxiety spike. I was still Grace, after all. "Take my hand and help me do this, Harold. I can't watch."

He did, and we took a leap of faith all our own.

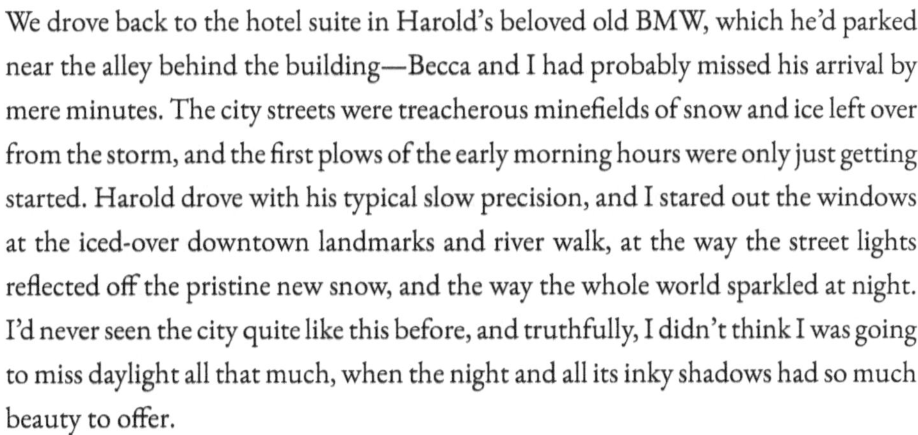

We drove back to the hotel suite in Harold's beloved old BMW, which he'd parked near the alley behind the building—Becca and I had probably missed his arrival by mere minutes. The city streets were treacherous minefields of snow and ice left over from the storm, and the first plows of the early morning hours were only just getting started. Harold drove with his typical slow precision, and I stared out the windows at the iced-over downtown landmarks and river walk, at the way the street lights reflected off the pristine new snow, and the way the whole world sparkled at night. I'd never seen the city quite like this before, and truthfully, I didn't think I was going to miss daylight all that much, when the night and all its inky shadows had so much beauty to offer.

"I can't believe you risked street parking," Calliope spoke up from the back seat, where she and Becca were still curled up in each other's laps, limbs tangled so completely they seemed like conjoined twins. I was the only person in the car wearing a seat belt.

"Who was going tae tow me? A vampire tow truck driver, out for a pleasant late night drive in the middle of a lake effect snow storm?"

"...reckless as always."

"I don't hear you offering better suggestions..."

I stifled a giggle as Harold and Calliope bickered on in their characteristic manner the entirety of the drive. I wasn't certain, but was beginning to think that was how they told each other, "I love you. I'm glad you're safe."

<hr>

Later, as it got closer to sunrise and we'd all hunkered down for the day in the suite, I lay under the covers with Harold, holding his hand, trying not to actively listen to the quiet murmurs, giggles, and occasional wet, sucking noises, coming from the bathtub in the adjacent washroom. Technically the king-sized bed was big enough to shelter all four of us, but Calliope and Becca had opted to sacrifice comfort for the illusion of privacy in the windowless en suite.

"I'm so confused." I chuckled, but I really wasn't, knowing Becca. She'd thrown herself head over heels into new romances at the drop of a hat for as long as I had known her, and it wasn't like she hadn't been crushing on Calliope Jones for almost as long.

"I'm not confused at all," Harold said with confidence. "Your Becca is exactly Calliope's type. I'm honestly surprised she didn't try tae turn your friend herself."

I paused for a moment, letting his words sink in. For all our differences, Becca and I were still very much alike. *And Calliope had known my name the night she first found me wandering around her penthouse*...I was beginning to formulate a theory, but I didn't have enough data points. Yet.

I rolled on my side to face him in the dark. "Maybe it's better she didn't turn Becca," I mused. "I imagine there are a lot of complicated feelings, between a maker and their fledgling, even if love is there. And that can distort things in really harmful ways." I didn't mean to give away what I'd learned about Irene from Calliope, but I felt him flinch, next to me.

"I'm sorry you saw all that. It shouldn't have been that way. I'm sorry I didn't have better self control, I'm sorry—" he said, softly.

"I didn't. See…the worst of that, in your blood. I think I mostly saw happy memories. Calliope told me the rest. I asked her to, don't hold it against her—"

He exhaled, went still for a moment. "She told you everything?"

"Enough. I mean, it was a lot. But it was also enough. I'm sorry…" I paused for almost as long as Harold sometimes did, but I found my words. "I'm sorry that happened. To all of you."

"It was a long time ago…" Harold insisted, as he always did. "I don't like talking about it, or thinking about it, or…but I should have told you. And I shouldn't have let you find out what you did learn, that way—"

"It still happened." I shrugged. "And it still affects you. And that's all right. I wouldn't love you so much, I don't think, if it didn't affect you. Love doesn't stop just when a person dies."

"No, it doesn't," he agreed.

"My dad's girlfriend is pregnant." I changed the subject slightly. "They're going to have a baby boy. I'm going to be a big sister." The sigh escaping my lips sounded sadder than I meant it to. "I'll only watch from afar, don't worry. I'm not going to get obsessed. I just think it's neat. My dad is a good person, and I think he deserves to be happy. He's had enough heartache for one lifetime. I'm happy for him." When I spoke the words, I knew they were true. I held Harold's hand tighter. "I think you deserve to be happy, too. And…I want to be happy. With you."

His free hand caressed my hair, and I closed my eyes, allowing myself to be lulled by the soft sensation. There were other things Calliope had said the night before, too, that I wanted to talk to Harold about, but the sun was rising high, and I could feel it in my veins, and I was so sleepy. "I love you…" I whispered.

"I love you too, Grace Kelly Cordero."

I yawned, then, and my fangs popped. "Fuck me," I complained.

"If you say so," he replied.

And he did.

Chapter Thirty-Seven

SANGUIS INTERRUPTUS

CALLIOPE AND HAROLD WOKE up so much earlier than Becca and I did. I heard the sound of their voices, low and murmuring, outside the bedroom when awareness nudged at my consciousness again, but it was the creak of the en suite washroom door opening that woke me from my slumber. I'd been dreaming about fountains filled with blood in a burning village.

I sat up, rubbed the sleep grit from my eyes, and saw Becca tiptoe slowly out of the washroom, approach the bed, and climb on top of the covers.

"Are you awake?" she whispered to me in the dark.

"Clearly, no." I resisted the urge to yawn, the needle-sharp tips of my fangs hovering just below the surface of my gum line, an exquisite pain that dragged me the rest of the way out of the blood-soaked dream world and back to reality. I reached over and turned on the lamp on the bedside table. "Were you waiting for me to wake up?"

Becca shook her head. "I only just woke up myself. I was all alone in the bathtub—" She winced.

"Yeah, how do you like it now?"

"Still better than the morgue."

"Fair." I noticed the hollow circles under Becca's eyes and reached out to touch her face. Those hollows should have been dark, pooled with the faint blue shadow of blood below the surface, but her face was bloodless and wan. Even her lips were cracked and pale.

"How much did Calliope drink from you last night?" I was worried about how drained Becca looked.

"She gave me plenty back in return, really, don't worry about that."

"So I heard." I smiled at her, and she looked away, rueful.

"I'm so hungry, Grace..." Becca really did seem miserable.

"So am I," I whispered in return, reaching out to hold her hand. "And it can get a lot worse than this. I tried to warn you."

Becca nodded. "I know. Maybe, if I hadn't been hit by the car, I would have calmed down, and listened to you...maybe not. But I don't feel the same way about being a vampire as you do, I think."

"Probably not..."

"I mean, really, it's not that we didn't have that conversation in college when I was on my vampire melodrama kick..."

"Oh, God..." I shook my head, remembering those nights. "And you dragged me to the midnight release of the last sparkling vampire movie, and I couldn't hear anything that was happening on screen because the teenage girls and their moms were just screaming the entire length of the film."

"Good times," grinned Becca. "Even with everything that happened last night, I feel...good. I don't regret my decision, even if things didn't work out the way I planned. And I know I'm better off without Gavin...I never would have had the nerve to do to him what you did, last night. So, thank you. Because you did save me, in a very real way."

"And you and Calliope?" I arched an eyebrow. "You saved her, I think we all know that. But the two of you hooked up pretty sudden-like..."

"We could hear the two of *you* through the closed door too, you know." Becca traced her finger across some of the bloodstains on the bedding and shrugged, "I don't feel so guilty about what happened to the towels in the bathroom now."

"Hotel management is going to be so pissed off. I don't think we're ever going to be allowed to come back." I was thinking about the armchair I'd destroyed in the other room and giggled in spite of myself. I'd said I was going to bill Calliope for the damages without even knowing that the hotel was one of her properties.

"I don't think we're going to be allowed to stay in the city, Grace," Becca said solemnly. "Calliope told me last night. Or maybe it was sometime during the day.

She has the resources to pay off whoever needs to be paid off to keep things mostly out of the news and public records, but that doesn't mean that we aren't in trouble.

"I think there are some Community members coming over tonight, and we'll find out how bad it is."

I shivered in spite of myself. I'd never met any of the older vampires.

Becca and I got dressed as best we could, salvaging what was left of the clothes I'd already worn and what was left of the department store purchases, and helped each other fix our hair, since we didn't have access to any styling tools. If I was going to be facing down an angry Community of vampires, I at least wanted to look as presentable as possible. I didn't tell Becca about the small bald spot at the back of her head. She couldn't see it, and the hair would grow back.

"...do you love him?" Becca asked me, nodding toward the living room of the suite, where Harold and Calliope were still talking, but the timbre of their low conversation had returned to their more familiar pattern of not-quite arguing. I could have listened to them if I wanted to, but I didn't. Vampires probably had to navigate a lot of nuanced, deliberate ignorance when it came to being aware of other vampires' private conversations and activities.

I returned my attention to Becca. "Yes, I think I really do. I mean, you know, the age gap is really inappropriate..."

"A red flag even I can see," Becca agreed with a knowing smirk, helping me straighten the covers over the bed. "Those are some hella unbalanced power dynamics. You've got to be careful."

"And you?" I asked. "You and Calliope, I mean, was that just last night or are the two of you...? I think you've have a crush on her for a while, haven't you?"

"I mean, I'm not convinced that it's love, but...we shared a lot of blood last night. It was amazing. Like, wow. And the things that woman can do with her tongue! Holy shit!" Becca flopped down on the freshly made bed and sat right back up again. "...I told her my family would disown me if they found out I was in a serious relationship with a woman, and she just hugged me and said I'm her family now, so...where she goes, I will follow. Until she decides that she's sick of me, I guess." Becca shrugged. "...but I guess this makes us sisters for real now, huh?"

I hadn't thought about it that way. "I mean, Gavin did turn both of us, so…" I smiled. Sisters. That was comforting. "That alone makes up for a lot. Not everything, but a lot." I picked up Becca's hand and held it, imagining the both of us, in 200 years, like the elder vampires in the next room. Even if something happened to Harold or Calliope, we'd still always have each other, always be bound by that blood.

Becca cleared her throat. "What I really want to know is…?"

"What?" I asked.

"The other night, at the restaurant, you told me that you could smell my blood, and you wanted it. Do you? Still, um…want it? Because I would absolutely be down to bite you just a little bit, if I could, um…"

I looked at the hunger in Becca's eyes; felt it reflected in my own. I was still young, and I needed to feed at least once, preferably twice, a night. Becca needed so much more blood than that. And, as an older sister—technically, I was the older sister, now, because I'd been turned first, right? I felt protective, of Becca, still. Sharing blood with Becca wouldn't be like what it was between Harold and me, or what Calliope and Becca did…I licked my lips, watching as Becca bit down on hers, and nodded.

Blood is blood, Harold had said, after all. "Not on the neck, though…" I whispered, holding up my wrist to Becca. Becca handed her own pale wrist over to me, and my fangs slid out from my gums the rest of the way, extended in anticipation. My heart was trying its best to produce a rhythm, as was Becca's, and if you didn't know better, our heartbeats almost sounded like one, seriously fucked up, heartbeat.

"Grace…" Becca whispered and bent down, her teeth caressing the sensitive skin where my veins were closest to the surface. I was shocked to discover how much I welcomed this, how much I wanted…

There was a knock at the hotel suite door that startled us both.

"That's the Community," Becca whispered.

I groaned.

"Sanguis interruptus," Becca grunted. "I hope they brought snacks."

⬦

"Thank you, Hannah. That will be all for now." Calliope turned away from the visitor at the door and walked back into the suite carrying a banker's box and a rolling Globe Trotter luggage set.

"I thought—"

"You thought what?" Calliope snapped, the edge to her voice sharper than I'd anticipated. I followed the line of her gaze back to the bedroom and took an involuntary step back.

I hadn't anticipated her being the possessive sort, but there was something in the fixed line of her jaw that made me feel like I'd been caught doing something bad.

I turned toward Harold, who shrugged and tilted his head but said nothing. At least he looked marginally amused, I thought. I brushed past both of them and pushed aside the curtains that were still drawn over the large windows—I thought I'd noticed a balcony, the night Harold and I cleared my throat. "I'm just going to step outside and, uh, get some fresh air."

"You do that." Again, I couldn't tell, but Harold seemed amused.

As I closed the hermetically sealed door behind me, I heard Calliope call out, "Becca, darling, come here. I want to show you something."

Darling, huh? Calliope only ever called me "sweetheart."

It was impressive how nearly soundproof the glass was once the door was fully shut. Even straining my ears, it was hard to make out the details of the conversation happening inside. Not that I wanted to pay attention to other people's conversations. I gazed down onto the bustle of the Chicago streets below and exhaled slowly. The echo of the faint heartbeat stirring in my chest just moments ago faded to memory, but it had been real. Not even Harold made my heart do...that.

I wondered if Calliope had heard. I wondered if that's the part that upset her.

"Hello, Grace Cordero. Isn't this serendipitous? You're just the person I was hoping to see."

On the balcony one floor down and to the left of mine, a woman leaned against the icicle-draped black iron railing, smoking a pungent fat cigar. I was shocked I hadn't noticed it until the moment she spoke, and I pivoted to get a better look at her. She was taller than Harold, and absolutely regal-looking, in her deep plum overcoat. It made her copper skin and ink-black hair almost seem to glow.

"I don't know you," I said, keeping my voice low and warning.

"Think of me as a friend." The woman exhaled a perfect series of smoke rings and extinguished the cigar, sliding it back into a silver case that she placed inside her coat. When she did, I caught a brief glimpse of a shoulder holster beneath the satin flash of lining, and I knew, instinctively, that I had not been given that information on accident. The woman's smile was all sharp teeth. "I know who you are. I know who turned you. And I can help you, if you let me. Gavin Richardson was a wealthy man. I think you're probably entitled to the lion's share of that, wouldn't you?"

"Who are you...?"

"I've been going by Esther Red Willow these nights. Have you heard of me?"

"No."

"Pity. Come on over to my room. I'd like to ask you some questions—privately. I believe you may have insight into a matter that I have a deeply personal interest in."

"I don't know you," I repeated.

"We're Community, Grace. I'm not going to hurt you. I just want to ask a few questions."

"My friends are on the other side of this door. If I call to them—"

"Gavin used full metal jacket ammunition last night."

I stopped in my tracks. "How—"

"Shell casings and spent bullets, back at the penthouse. Now, if any one of you had been shot with a hollow-point round, which is exactly what I have loaded in my firearm...do you want to guess what a .38 could do to your heart? And I am a very, very good shot. I would not miss."

Some friend.

"What do you want me to do? Jump from my balcony to yours? That's over ten feet." I swallowed hard and looked down at the street again. I wasn't as high up as Calliope's penthouse was, but I still didn't like the distance between myself and the ground below.

"That is exactly what I want you to do. Come on over to my room. Look at some pictures. Answer my questions. I promise I won't hurt you if you help me."

"And if I refuse, you'll blow me to smithereens?"

"I'd hate to have to do that, child. I surely would. Now jump."

I climbed up to the balcony railing, balanced precariously for a moment, and leaped off as hard as I could. I crashed onto Esther's balcony with an inelegant tumble, dislodging the icicles, and landed at her feet. Her tall black boots, I discovered, were classic Celine, and I relaxed just a little, in spite of myself. No one with taste in clothing that impeccable was going to kill me unnecessarily, I decided.

But she didn't extend a hand to help me up, either. I pulled myself to my feet and followed her through another hermetically sealed glass door into her own room. It was smaller than our suite but nicely appointed. The bed was stripped of its comforter and pillows, and I guessed that she had slept the day away in the bathtub. Apparently, that was a thing that vampires did a lot.

On the desk next to the TV, she'd laid out a series of photographs, all taken with a telephoto zoom lens. The blown-up images lost some detail in the enlargement, but the subject matter was obvious. Gavin Richardson appeared in several of the shots, as well as a woman I didn't recognize. Esther swept the images out of my line of sight and looked at me intently.

"See anyone you know?"

"My maker."

"And?"

"I didn't get a good look at the pictures."

"Then I want you to think back to the night of the hit and run. Your friend wasn't struck by accident, was she?"

I shook my head. "No, Gavin hit her. And then he drove off."

"You're sure?"

"I'm sure. She was hit deliberately."

"You're certain it was Gavin Richardson who hit her?"

"Who else—?" I pulled out the desk chair and sat down, memories of the awful scene rising up and flooding me. The car was too fast, I was too slow. Becca didn't even have time to scream. The thud of her body hitting the asphalt, her blood leaching out into the slush. I closed my eyes and tried to will the images away, shaking my head. Beyond the hermetically sealed door to Esther's balcony, I could faintly hear Harold outside, one floor above us, shouting my name. "I have to get back," I said.

"Calm down. I need you to think. Get as deep into the memory as you can. Who was driving the car? You witnessed the impact. Tell me what you saw."

"She killed my friend…" I whispered, feeling nauseous. I was still so hungry, and my knee ached and throbbed where I'd landed on it, jumping down onto Esther's balcony. My body was trying to heal the injury, but I needed blood. "She drove straight into Becca, and she killed her. Why?" I didn't mention that Becca was a vampire now as well, sitting in the suite above us, probably wondering where the hell I'd disappeared off to. "Esther…who was she?"

She slid a photograph onto the desk in front of me. Even though the image had been taken from a considerable distance and the angle was less than perfect, there was something about the particular set of the subject's shoulders, the curve of her jaw, the straight line of her nose…She brunette and average-looking, otherwise unremarkable. "Was it this woman?" Esther asked.

I nodded. Yes. I'd seen her a thousand times. I'd never seen her before in my life. I'd know her anywhere, now. "That's her, isn't it? That's Marie DuChamps."

"Unfortunately. A thorn in our side for decades."

"Whose side? The Community?"

"The Community isn't a monolith, child. That's both a blessing, and a burden, that DuChamps is well-equipped to exploit. There are many who want her dead but, she is very difficult to locate, if she does not want to be found. Do you have any idea what she might be doing in Chicago?"

"None."

"Harold Laing is a known associate of her fledgling. Did he tell you anything, anything at all, about what Marie DuChamps might want?"

"He told me she's a certifiable psychopath, and that he never wanted to see her again."

Esther laughed softly. "At last, Mr. Laing is in agreement with the sensible side of the Community. A momentous occasion, to be sure." Her cell phone rang. "Yes.

Are you ready?" She didn't waste time when she accepted the call. I heard a low, gruff voice on the other end of the line.

"Where are you?"

"I'll be right there." Esther ended the call. "Come on. I told you I wasn't going to hurt you. Let's get you back to your people. The rotational council's representatives are about to arrive."

Another person I didn't know—a redheaded vampire in a dark green suit—leaned by the door to our suite, leonine and disinterested, as Esther and I approached. They barely glanced up at us. I couldn't tell if they were a woman or a man, and quickly decided that wasn't my business. More important to me was the red and white plastic camping cooler resting at their feet, which I tried not to stare at. I desperately hoped there was blood in there. I doubted it contained beer.

"Piff..." Esther welcomed, air-kissing them once on each cheek. "Who else are we waiting on?"

"Just Iqbal." 'Piff' replied.

From down the hall, a man's voice called out, "I am coming! I need just a moment! There is a damnable pebble in my shoe..."

I turned to look at the owner of the voice, which belonged to a lean, broad-shouldered Black man kneeling down in the hallway, completely engaged in the act of removing the offending pebble from his footwear. He had an accent I couldn't place, but I didn't think he was American. Nevertheless, he wore a well-tailored but conservative dark three-piece suit with a matching tie, and looked every bit the stick in the mud that Nadia had warned me about.

"Who is this?" he asked, looking at me as intently as I'd looked at him.

"I believe...that this is Gavin Richardson's fledgling," Esther answered, placing her hand on my shoulder, digging in with her fingernails more than was necessary.

Chapter Thirty-Eight

THE COMMUNITY

"*Hostia puta*," Calliope swore, and I'd spent enough time around Carlos and Miguel to decode her blistering blasphemy. I silently crossed myself out of reflex, and did not burst into flame. Calliope's eyes flicked from me to Esther, standing just behind me, to the other Community members flanking either side. She took a small step backward, steadied herself, and when she spoke again, the strangled sound like cracking ice was gone from her voice. "Is bringing her into this really necessary?"

Esther squeezed my shoulder even tighter, and I winced.

"No one is here to kill you, Calliope Jones," Iqbal insisted, entering the suite without an invitation. Calliope and Becca hadn't needed one the night before, either, and I filed that information away as probably very important.

Piff followed close at his heels but paused, leaning their forehead against Calliope's as intimately as a lover might. "But you are in trouble." And Piff kissed Calliope softly on the cheek before walking further into the room.

Just past them, I could see Harold standing in front of Becca. I couldn't read the expression on his face when his eyes met mine, but he wasn't happy. "Hi. I'm fine," I insisted, but my assurances felt meek, with Esther still gripping my shoulder. I'd decided she wasn't my friend.

"Move it!" Becca hissed under her breath, trying to get around Harold. "I can't see! Where's Grace?"

"I found this one outside," Esther said, releasing her grip and pushing me forward. I staggered just a little, but caught myself before I collapsed into Calliope. She held out her arms to catch me.

"What on earth were you doing? Where did you go? Did you jump off the balcony? You can't do that in front of people. What if someone saw you?" She took me by the arms and shook me, lightly.

"I didn't—" but one sidelong glance from Esther told me to keep my mouth shut. I walked into the suite the rest of the way and sat down on the sofa, poking at the sore spot on my knee. It still wasn't entirely healed, and the shakes were starting to get bad again.

Piff set the cooler on the table in the middle of the room. "Brigid and Jennet would be here tonight instead of Esther, but Brigid just tried to raise a fledgling who by now is quite obviously not coming back, poor thing, and Jennet is staying with her for a few nights in solidarity. Brigid is taking the loss hard, as I understand it. I don't think she's tried to turn anyone in over a century. So she sends the blood, since she won't be needing all of it, and her condolences to the one who was turned without consent. Esther is merely joining Iqbal and myself as a Community observer, that is all." Then, addressing Calliope directly, they continued. "If we were going to send an enforcer of Esther's caliber after any of you, you never would have seen her, and you know it. What the hell have you done, Jones?"

"Piff—" Calliope began before she was cut off.

"Arailt. I heard you died in a fire." Iqbal greeted Harold with a deprecatory smile I did not like. There was an undercurrent of animosity like frayed electrical cords between them that practically crackled. Harold stiffened at the elder vampire's hostility, but did not respond to it, and Iqbal turned to survey Becca and I with an arched eyebrow. "*Two* fledglings, Calliope Jones? Which one is the girl from your party?"

"And does anyone know where Gavin Richardson is? No one from the Community has been able to reach him, and if he's involved as well..." Piff asked, as Esther kept her unblinking eyes on me, and I dared not speak.

Becca, however, was not impressed by the newcomers, ancient vampires or not. "Okay, like, yikes! Is it typical of Community house calls to open up with an interrogation or something? I don't even know these people." She plopped down on the couch next to me, hungry face fixed not on the other vampires, but the red and white cooler occupying the table.

"Becca!!" I jabbed her in the side with my elbow, but she didn't flinch.

"I'm *sorry*, I died in the gutter and woke up in a body bag last night. I've got the manners to show for it. Is there blood in that cooler? I'm shaking."

"There's your rogue." Esther nodded at Iqbal, who pulled a cell phone from the inside pocket of his suit jacket and made a call to someone named "Corinne," informing her that the search for the rogue from the medical examiner could be called off now, the fledgling was found safe, and he'd provide an update later. He sounded equal parts furious and relieved, and when he disconnected the call, he sat down in one of the dining chairs, shooting daggers at Calliope with his gaze.

Calliope whispered some vital information about the Community vampires in Becca's ear. It was nothing I didn't know, or couldn't guess. Piff and Iqbal were centuries old, far older than either herself or Harold. Esther Red Willow was younger, but...her *unique* skills kept her highly favored by Communities all over.

Piff lowered themselves into the armchair I hadn't destroyed, one leg draped over the upholstered arm, occupying the seat with the liquid and implacable air of a house cat. "What I don't understand, Jones, is why you allowed another situations with one of your fledglings to get so out of hand—if, in fact, what Esther says is true, and Grace is both Gavin Richardson's fledgling and the unfortunate girl from your party—"

"The children are starving, Epiphanie. Let them feed." Iqbal held up a long-fingered hand to hush his colleague.

By the time Esther was able to open the cooler and hand over a stainless steel thermos to Becca, she was too far gone in her hunger, and needed assistance holding the canister to her lips. Maybe I would have thought back to my own early attempts to navigate the disorienting torment of my thirst as I watched Becca drink, but I was too preoccupied with unscrewing the lid to the thermos I'd just been handed to pay much attention to Becca. Harold had to help me get the lid off before I could drink and, in the absence of any hope of privacy, I closed my eyes and surrendered to the waves of relief washing over me, my tongue and my lips welcoming the damning scarlet pleasure; iron fire in my belly, copper flowers on my palate. Electric energy in my fingertips. The blood was still warm, but it wasn't fresh—I could tell the difference, now. Still, it was enough to soothe the straining tension in my face and neck, and I leaned against Harold, who welcomed me into his arms.

Everything was different, now.

I thought for a moment about what Piff had said about Esther. I did not doubt she was as formidable as both of them claimed; not after our encounter outside on the balcony, but I was struck by how incongruous the idea of Esther as a deadly assassin was, in her $2,000 boots and equally expensive tailored overcoat. She wore a simple A-line skirt that stopped a few inches below the knee, and a beautiful cable knit sweater over a crisp white blouse. The dove gray fibers of the sweater had a subtle sheen, like silk. She looked like she would have preferred to spend her evening drinking blood from a bone china teacup in front of a roaring fireplace, in an expensive townhouse filled with art and antiques. I wondered why she chose to work with the Community. I wondered what her beef with Marie DuChamps was. Everyone, it seemed, appeared to despise the woman.

I looked up again, and Esther was seated next to Becca, leaning in close; comforting, protective. I wanted to warn Becca about letting strange vampires touch her, especially this vampire, whom even Calliope seemed to be afraid of, but Esther was already brushing hair away from Becca's cheeks with a soft hand. "Who turned you, then?" Esther asked, her voice gentle, brow furrowed.

"Gavin Richardson, I guess…" Becca gave a sad shrug, and starred ahead into nothingness, with a glazed-over expression I recognized well. It was the look Becca always got when she didn't want to think about something—a painful memory, an embarrassing moment she couldn't avoid.

"You guess?"

"I'd only had his blood for five nights before I got hit. So I don't know—"

"If he's been giving you his blood, then he's responsible for you. Do *any* of you know where he is?" Piff interrupted.

"What's left of Gavin Richardson could probably be sucked up off the floor of Calliope's penthouse with a shop vac," I said, so harshly I heard a small wounded cry escape Calliope, and even Becca balked. "Sorry," I offered. But I wasn't sorry. It had felt good to cut off the bastard's head. He'd shot Calliope. He'd *hit* Becca.

"I see." Iqbal nodded. "Then there was no need for our investigation and inquiry into the matter of who turned you. We were on the lookout for an outsider who had infiltrated our Community, violated our most sacred laws, and put us all at risk, and yet—Calliope Jones must have known her own fledgling created this one the moment she found you. Isn't that right?"

I glanced over at Calliope, who brushed off his accusation so casually, I knew she was fighting panic. "I wasn't sure. At first. Of course I recognized she was of my lineage, but I never would have imagined Gavin would dare such a thing. Not at my event. Not under my roof. Not after—" she stopped, presumably before she could incriminate herself.

"Marie DuChamps, Elvira Pearl, and now, Gavin Richardson..." Piff recited each name with the enunciation a judge reading off a sentence. I wondered if Piff was French; I couldn't place their accent with any certainty. "And how many more times are we going to have to cover up for your get? Do you have any idea how many security cameras these two were caught on last night?" They gestured at Becca and me.

I looked back at Becca but avoided eye contact. "I didn't know what to do. I didn't have anyone to reach out to, and I didn't know who to trust and—"

Iqbal pressed his long fingers together in front of his face, his expression unreadable. He continued to conspicuously ignore Harold, but when he spoke to me, his voice was—almost—kind. "None of this is your fault, do you understand? None of it. We are not here to punish you. The Community is here to help in situations like yours. It is not your fault no one reached out to us for assistance. You cannot be held accountable for what you did not know, do you understand?" He crossed one long, lean leg over his other knee, revealing vampire rubber ducky printed socks underneath the cuffs of his formal suit, and I finally noticed his tie tac matched. No one with vampire rubber ducky socks could be that bad, right?

I sniffled, once—I hadn't realized I'd been on the verge of tears again—and nodded. I couldn't take my eyes off the vampire duckies.

"I like your socks," said Becca, before I could. She sounded genuinely delighted, which generated an actual smile from Iqbal.

"Thank you." He stretched out his ankle to better show off his footwear. "I received them from one of my students as a...winter holiday present." He winked at Becca and whispered, "My student has no idea."

Piff rolled their eyes. "That's over a thousand pairs of silly socks now, isn't it?" they asked. Piff did not seem like the novelty sock sort, despite sporting an equally dashing fitted suit.

"One thousand and thirty six pair, last time I counted. Ah ha ha."

My jaw dropped. I was not expecting the stern-looking man to make a *Sesame Street* joke. Becca snorted, and a small trickle of blood dripped down her upper lip from her nose. She absentmindedly licked it away before Esther could hand her a hankie from the pocket of her overcoat.

"You have students?"

"I am a highly selective tutor of mathematics for graduate scholars, mostly at the University of Chicago."

Well, that explained the Count Von Count impersonation.

"Now then," Iqbal continued, rubbing his hands together and nodding at Piff, "I think it is time to get to the bottom of everything that has happened in the last two months, so the Community can issue a fair and reasonable judgment in this matter once and for all." He pulled a small golden pendant from around his neck, and Piff did the same. Esther Red Willow pulled a similar pendant, in silver, from her coat pocket, and slipped it around her neck. The emblem was an owl, surrounded by a circle of moons, and some text in a language I couldn't make out. The design looked ancient, and I wondered how old the Community was.

Esther got up and indicated for Calliope to take a seat on the sofa next to Becca, where Esther had been sitting only moments before. It was hard to not feel like the four of us were on the firing line, even if Piff and Calliope seemed to have a history, and Iqbal clearly had a silly side.

"So Arailt Laing is not gone from us after all. Indeed, here he is mixed up in Calliope Jones's trouble once again. Although frankly I'm surprised to see it, after your infamous row at the Field Museum. How did you get involved, exactly? You haven't been around much in recent years. You used to be much more...social." Iqbal's reproving glare fixed on Harold, and neither man blinked.

"You accused me of killing my wife." I'd never imagined Harold's voice could sound so cold, and I gasped, squeezing my eyes shut, trying to block out as much sensory input as possible. Overwhelm tugged at my periphery and I rocked, but moving my body and fidgeting with the clasp of Mom's watch did little to make me feel secure. I felt the walls of the room closing in around me.

Iqbal seemed equally full of quiet rage, all of it directed at Harold. "You refused to cooperate with the inquest and immediately fled the country for the better part of a decade! Why should anyone believe in the innocence of a man who—"

My eyes flew open, reeling, just in time to see Harold fly to his feet, faster than I'd seen him move even in the Wisconsin house, when he'd first heard the car outside. I instantly stopped rocking, frozen in place. Iqbal was taller than Harold by several inches, but he still flinched and put both feet on the ground, though he did not stand up. The vampire rubber ducky socks disappeared under the hem of his trousers.

Esther stepped between the two men. "Stop it. Both of you. As I understand, the inquest was a formality—"

"Fuck your formalities—"

"He's the one who brought it up!"

"...and we had Calliope's word and blood to serve as witness to what happened," Piff finished for Esther.

"Do we have to go over that whole awful incident again?" Calliope begged.

"Irene Caldwell was one of us! She was Community!" Iqbal shouted over her.

"She was my *wife*!"

I felt sick, and the remnants of the blood in my stomach gurgled. No wonder Harold didn't want The Community involved in any part of his life. I didn't want to think of what might have happened without Calliope's intervention. I shrank down into the sofa cushions, as small as I could make myself; I wanted to disappear; evaporate into a puff of smoke and dissolve into the night.

Harold had said vampires couldn't do that.

The tension between the two men continued for several additional seconds that felt like hours. I decided I didn't like Iqbal anymore, either.

"Ta hell with this balderdash." Harold muttered, stalked away toward the main entrance to the suite, and slammed the door behind him. Becca recoiled and cowered against Calliope. Piff raised their eyebrows, but said nothing.

I scrambled up and followed after him. I wasn't sure what was going on, but I remembered what Calliope had said about him running off. I didn't want to get left behind.

Behind us, Iqbal angrily muttered something about a "...boorish recalcitrant Scottish *peasant*," while Piff and Calliope shushed him in tandem.

I thought I heard Esther mutter, "...and that is why I do not turn men."

<hr>

He made it all the way to the elevators before I caught up with him. I thrust my arm between the sliding doors as they closed. "Wait, please—"

He held my hand as I slipped into the elevator car beside him, but didn't say anything. His face was taut with anger, as bad as he'd been when his house burned down. I watched him draw in several deep breaths of air, and exhale, slowly. It wasn't the oxygen he needed, but the rhythm. Something to focus on.

"I. Hate. Dat illbistet, condescending son o' a bitch an' his *ugly* socks an' en'less accusations." Harold continued to shake as he ranted. I decided I preferred Harold's much-darned wool socks over Iqbal's fancy novelty versions, though I did not tell him so. "He's been takken ill wi' me fo' decades. Decades, Grace. Afore any o' de stuff w' Irene happened. I ne'er did a damn ting to dat man. Ne'er. So fuck him, an' de entire rotational council, if dey're goin' ta bring de damned ting up again. I've go' nothin' ta keep me in de city no more."

I grabbed his hand tighter and refused to let go. "So...you're leaving, then?"

"Come w' me. We'll drive all night, get anodder hotel before de sun rises, an' keep going e'ery night dereafta. Fuck bein' settled. Fuck de Community. I've go' money in de bank. We can keep goin' fore'er."

I shook my head. "I'm not leaving Becca."

"*Please*, kettlen..." He pulled my hand close to his chest and held it there, above the place where his heart should have been beating. There was a small loose thread tangling from the bottom hem of Harold's new sweater, and I wondered if it would all unravel if I pulled on that tiny string; the sweater that last night I'd imagined burying my face in whenever Harold held me close to him, until the sweater, and I, were both vintage. I took a step backwards, away from him, as the elevator car hit the ground floor, and the doors slid open.

"Dunna go." His voice cracked as he pulled me forward, out of the elevator, and into the lobby.

I shook my head. "I don't want to. Not anymore. I promise. But you can't just walk away from all that stuff in there." I thought about Esther Red Willow, and what she'd said. "What about Calliope? What will they do to her?"

"I dunna know." He stopped in his tracks, like he was thinking.

"I didn't know Irene was Community. Calliope left that part out."

"I dunna know all 'at she actually said ta you aboot—aboot her."

"That they were friends. That she was…hurting, a lot, and that she never learned how to hunt, that you always did that for her. And finally, one night, she killed someone, and it was…awful."

He seemed actually dumbfounded for a moment. "It admires me nae that Cal would be unhonest wi' you—Cal remembers what Cal chooses tae remember. But…it's a stretch tae imply that Irene could nae take care of herself." He sat down on a bench in an alcove, and looked around before he continued. "Irene could hunt. She knew how. She could, if she wanted tae. But dat in feth, she was nae the natural that you are, an' the first time we went out, things went…ill. I still dunna think the man died, after all this time. But Irene could nae let it go. She wasn't *normal*, the way she remembered things. And once I understood that, I tried tae protect her. I was her maker. It was my responsibility." He looked around again at the mostly empty hotel lobby. He'd kept his voice down, but there were a handful of patrons sitting at the bar on the far opposite end of the room. "We need tae go." He stood up and marched toward the exit.

I followed. "What was wrong with the way she remembered things? Was she delusional, or…?"

"Irene remembered everything," he said, as if that were the most obvious answer in the world. "Everything."

"Calliope said something about that, too. That she...never forgot a person's name or birthday or..." I paused as Harold had a word at the valet stand, and waited for the attendant to walk away before asking for any more information.

"It was so much more than that." Harold shook his head. "The smiles, the curiosity, remembering everything she could about anyone she ever met...all of it was just a distraction, from all the terrible things she could nae forget. Things that happened when she was mortal, with her brother. Everything that ever happened tae her, she remembered. It was something she couldn't turn off."

"So...probably the only person who ever lived who could beat you at cards?" I tried to lighten the mood; the air around me had turned to lead again.

"We were pretty evenly matched, aye...she was an absolute pain in the arse in a quarrel as well, if you can imagine..." a small smile teased his lips; I decided that I liked seeing him remember her. It was pointless, to be jealous of a dead woman.

It seemed to be taking a while for the BMW to be brought around. I noticed the attendant rounding the corner at the end of the block, communicating into a staticky walkie talkie. "Well, get security to check the camera footage, then."

Harold and I exchanged nervous glances.

"Problem?" asked Harold. His tone was light, but the tension returned to his shoulders.

The valet attendant stammered a series of profuse apologies; there'd been an incident; security was investigating. Of course, the hotel had limited liability for the damages, it was on the waiver we'd signed...

"Come on." Harold grabbed my hand and dragged me down the street in the opposite direction.

"You guys need warmer clothes! It's freezing out here!" The valet attendant shouted after us. Harold ignored him

"Harold, tires can be replaced. Listen to me. Listen! Marie DuChamps is in Chicago. She's the one who hit Becca."

Harold spun around and pulled me into the alley behind the hotel. "What did you say?"

I filled him in on what I knew, about the phone call from a woman named "Marie" that Becca had overheard when she was with Gavin the night of the first fire, and about the hit and run that killed Becca, how I'd been too panicked at the time to recognize the driver, but then Esther Red Willow had ordered me to come over to her room when she saw me out on the balcony, and she showed me some pictures and—I stopped. "She told me not to tell anyone about that," I whispered, suddenly terrified.

Harold leaned against the brick wall, all but disappearing into the shadows of the alleyway, deep in thought. I tried not to get overwhelmed by the stench rising off the dumpsters just behind him. "What do you know about Marie?" He finally asked.

"Only what you told me. That she's a psychopath. And I think she's the one who hit Becca now, and I don't think Gavin knew that part. And…last night, at the penthouse, Gavin thought she was supposed to be there, and she didn't show up."

Harold nodded, thoughtfully. "Marie DuChamps thrives on chaos. She likes tae disrupt things. Cause pain for the sake of making someone hurt. She'll throw a cog into a perfectly oiled machine just tae watch it all break down." He threw his head back and stared off into the distance as an empty plastic shopping bag rolled past us like a tumbleweed.

"You said you hadn't seen her since 1975…"

"Maybe I have." He shrugged. "That's the thing about DuChamps. She's a mimic like you would not believe. Fluent in at least a half dozen languages. She can imitate any accent. Disappear into any crowd. She's as much at ease in high society as she is squatting in abandoned warehouses with gutter punks and roaches. She's mutable. I could have run into her a million times on the street, and never known until she wanted to be seen. After the earthquake in San Francisco, she escaped the asylum, convinced some Red Cross social workers tae buy her a train ticket bound for Chicago stay with her family. She didn't have any family here. Cal's man picked her up at the train station when she arrived, thought she'd be an easy target. Within three months, she was bringing more girls into Calliope's brothel than you could imagine. Marie has a talent for making herself valuable wherever she goes."

"Wait, you mean she was a—?"

"Problem?" He asked sharply. I looked away, ashamed of myself.

"I was just remembering something Calliope said." *But I never would have allowed that kind of thing with one of my girls...* "I didn't mean to make it sound like I was judging anybody."

"Well, judge Marie as harshly as you want. She had a horrible talent for corrupting girls. The younger, the better. She'd find them at the train station, in work houses...she was always a monster. And Cal being Cal, decided tae turn the monster, instead of having her fun and feeding Marie's corpse tae the pigs like she should have. The bitch never should have been brought into the Community. Never should have been turned. Would have prevented a lot of problems."

"But then you never would have met Avie."

He raised a wry eyebrow at me. "Aye, and Avie deserved better. So did you. I'm sorry."

"It's not your fault..." I shuddered and flapped my hand against my thigh. Marie DuChamps sounded like the worst person ever, and I did not want to encounter her any closer than I already had. "We need to go back inside," I insisted. "Esther knows something that she doesn't seem to want you or Calliope or the rotational council to know. Marie DuChamps is still out there—according to you, she could be anywhere. I don't know what she wants, but she doesn't seem to be above targeting you. If she's the one who slashed the tires on your car, who knows what she'll do next."

"And she could be four hundred miles away already, up in her cuddy over all the trouble she caused last night. She doesn't stick around for long after she's caused whatever trouble she's set out to cause. I don't think she's that strategic, but I won't go back into that room. Marie might na be sloomit, but the rotational council is, and I want ta stay out of their crosshairs. Their problem this night is with Calliope, and I won't submit myself tae the judgment of a man who had more to do with Irene's death than I ever did."

"Becca. Is. In. That. Room," I hissed at him. "I'm not leaving her."

"Dammit, Grace..." his eyes scanned the alleyway, and I didn't think he was entirely convinced that Marie DuChamps had already moved on.

"Wait." *What was that about Iqbal?* "Calliope said Irene killed herself, that she went into the sun. She didn't say anything about the rotational council being involved. She said it was because Irene lost control and—"

"Killed the neighbor girl, and her baby...Something happened that night. Irene would never—it was so completely out of character. I don't know what came over her. I'll never know. Irene was catatonic when I came home; she wouldn't tell me anything." He sounded broken. "What I do know is that she'd been working together with Iqbal on some Community business, some ongoing project, and she never let me know the details. I didn't trust him. He already didn't like me. He was obsessed with Irene, though. With her memory. He claimed he could help her with her recall, some kind of mental visualization bullshit, in return for her assistance."

"He exploited her." Rage of my very own made my features grow taut.

"I don't know what he did. I don't even know if it was possible to help her; I've never known anyone else who could do what Irene did. She'd been a vampire for sixty years. Things were getting bad. She'd always had moods; she felt too much, cared too much. But I'd never seen her as withdrawn as she was that winter. It wasn't working. Whatever he was teaching her, whatever techniques he was making her practice, it made everything worse—it killed her. That's what I think. She would have been fine, if he hadn't gotten involved."

I wanted to believe him, but... "You think he blames you because he feels guilty?"

"I don't know. I don't know. Why shouldn't he blame himself? I never did any of the shit he hints at, alleges, without coming out and saying it straight—"

"He thinks you hurt her."

"Never! I yelled at her. Sometimes. It was an awful thing to come home to, what she...but I shouldn't have done it. Shouldn't have raised my voice. Not with you, either."

"I yell right back. It's an Italian thing. We're always yelling, in my family. It doesn't mean we don't love each other." And then I stopped, because talking about my family in the present tense still felt like the most natural thing in the world, but by now my dad had a death certificate with my name on it, and I didn't want to think about that. The sudden weight of that loss left me gasping, like a stiletto sliding between my ribs.

Grief, at least, was a language that Harold and I both understood.

"He's a stuck up ass, and I never did nothing tae him. I think he decided he didn't like me the night we met. He likes tae taunt me."

I leaned in close, and placed my head on his chest, feeling like I should be crying for both of us, but the tears wouldn't come. "So he's just a bully."

He nodded his head against me.

"Becca says fuck the haters." I remembered all the times she tried to convince me to ignore my own bullies. "Fuck them. If the rotational council's concern tonight is with Calliope, we should be there to make sure she ends up all right. We need to make sure that Becca is all right. And I don't want to see a bully bring you down. I know your blood, Harold. I know *you*. "I buried my face in his sweater, and missed the smell of engine grease and sawdust. He smelled like new wool and dried blood, like cold night air, and something more than just Harold, now. There was a part of him that smelled like me. Like us. There was a part of him that smelled like home.

I looked up at him, tracing my fingers along his strong jawline, the sideburns, my thumb softly grazing over the bones around his sea green eyes. How could I have ever seen him as anything but beautiful? "Come back inside with me. We'll replace your car's tires, and we'll leave town, and we'll never have to deal with Iqbal or the rest of the Community again, if you don't want to. But I need to make sure that Becca is all right. She'd do the same for me."

"Are you so certain?" Harold peered at me suspiciously. But he didn't know Becca like I did.

As if on cue, Becca's voice carried over the noise of the traffic and the wind whistling through the alley.

"Yeah. I'm certain," I said. And I shouted out to Becca where she could find us.

Becca rounded the corner at the sound of my voice and immediately started chatting away, as normal as anything. But nothing was normal. Her cheeks, which should have been flushed from the cold, were pale as the moon, and her green eyes seemed larger and more vibrant than ever before. I was struck by the image of a carnivorous orchid lurking in the sunless shadows. "Okay. So. I'm pretty sure that I just made Callie look bad in front of the rotational council people by running off after you both, and, like, there's some really heavy stuff I think you need to hear,

Grace. Hi, Harold. Are you all right? Callie says you like to run off. I'm Becca, by the way—I don't think we've been formally introduced. So, um, can we all go back inside, please? Callie's in a lot of trouble and I don't want to leave her alone, but you kind of freaked me out by running after him, Grace. And then I came downstairs and the front desk said you'd gone to valet and the valet said you'd walked off down the street—he was really concerned that you don't have the right kind of clothes for the weather, by the way. I think that's nice of him—" she ran out of air and abruptly stopped talking, and the startled expression on her face was priceless.

Harold chuckled as Becca drew a deep breath to refill her lungs, and I threw my arm around her waist.

"We were just about to head back," I insisted, leading her out of the alley and back toward the hotel entrance. As the three of us walked toward the elevators, I caught Harold's reflection in the mirrors lining the hallway, smiling at Becca and me, and I wondered if it was because Becca reminded him of Avie.

Jesus Mary and Joseph. Even the thought of the two of them in the same room spiked my anxiety.

The waiting elevator car wasn't empty. The doors dinged open to reveal Esther Red Willow, leaning dangerously against the handrail. She no longer wore the owl around her neck. "I wondered how far you thought you were going to get…" she mused, casually brushing her plush plum overcoat open just enough to show off her gun holster again as she thrust her hands into the pockets of her skirt. "I'd step inside if I were you."

Becca balked; she was apparently back to being nervous around guns again, and after the violence of the previous night, I didn't blame her. But there was something of a bully in Esther's demeanor, too, and I was just as done with bullies as I was with being afraid of dark parking lots and unlit stairwells. I straightened my shoulders and met Esther's humorless gaze with as much conviction as I could muster for someone who doesn't have the greatest track record with eye contact.

"Know something we don't?" I asked, crossing my arms in front of my chest.

"I know many things you don't know, child." But she blinked first and turned away.

"Bet you know something about how we couldn't get very far in Harold's car."

Her sharp smile was all teeth. "I have a job to do. That includes securing the perimeter, and making sure that no one gets away until I have all the information I want." She pressed the elevator button to the floor the suite was located on, and the car began to rise.

"I don't think we're going to be friends after all, Esther." Becca looked betrayed, and felt my own smile sharpen. *Good girl, Becca.*

Esther shrugged. "There are dangerous people out on the loose. Our strength in the Community is in our numbers. We should keep close. Calliope Jones has many fledglings."

"Oh, come on." Harold rolled his eyes. "Outside of Marie DuChamps, James Medlock is not a threat. Marcus Delafontaine is an asshole, but not a threat. Uriah Whitby is not a threat. And Gavin and Elvira are dead."

"Marcus, too."

"He's gone?"

"Someone burned down his house in Fort Wayne late last year. I found no evidence to suggest he escaped, and no one has seen him since. I'll let you draw your own conclusions."

"Does Calliope know?"

"She knows."

Becca chewed at her cuticles as one of her fingernails started to come loose, and she stared at it, preoccupied. Her face was an unreadable mask, but she didn't seem startled by what Esther said.

The elevator stopped. I grabbed Harold's hand again, feeling the hunger pull at his nerves through the tiny vibrations in his skin. "You need blood, too..." I reminded him with a whisper.

"Sometimes, the hunger makes things clear..." he strode a few steps ahead of me, then paused. "I have some questions of my own to ask tonight."

"So do I." A thought had been nagging at me for several nights. Something about burning... "What did Elvira Pearl look like?"

"Short. Brunette. Just another conventionally attractive white girl." Esther reached the room and opened the door with a magnetized key I didn't know she had.

Short. Petite. Pretty. I looked at Becca, still worrying over her fingernail, and the terrible theory began to take firmer shape.

Chapter Thirty-Nine

A Small Detail Like Death

"You're a smart woman, Cal. Always have been. You're very calculating." Harold strode toward the vampires gathered at the opposite end of the suite and didn't even wait to sit down before he began talking.

"I mean, I've always tried—" Calliope looked up from her quiet conversation with Piff, straightened her back, and squared her shoulders, reminding me of her body language when she'd visited Harold at his house, to take me away. It was a very different kind of posture than she'd had last night, in her element. Calliope only stiffened up when she didn't think she had the upper hand. It was a subtle tell, but unmistakable, once I'd noticed it.

Harold noticed, too. "You don't make mistakes often. Don't get caught off guard." He raised an eyebrow at his longtime friend, and his smile contained centuries of shared experience between then. When Becca smiled at me that way, I always knew exactly what she meant.

Calliope seemed unsettled by whatever unspoken subtext Harold's smile communicated. "As you've said, I—"

"But you do, of course, get caught off guard. From time to time." He stood directly in front of her, and waited.

Their eyes met for several inscrutable moments. No one else spoke.

"...from time to time," Calliope acknowledged, staring at him. Unblinking. Inhuman.

Harold nodded. "And I would know that, better than anyone here. When you get caught off guard, your instinct, as always, is to bargain. Cut a deal. Call in an old debt."

I thought about the visions I'd seen in Harold's blood, about the violent night that he and Calliope died, and were resurrected. I didn't think I was the only one remembering the flames and the fountain of blood, either.

"I'm sure I don't know where you're going with this. What happened with you was—"

"Not unlike what happened with Grace. You got caught off guard. Someone interrupted your plans, didn't they?" Harold sat back down on the sofa, but far more relaxed than he'd been before. He crossed one leg over his knee and leaned back, with his hands behind his head. He looked cocky.

I was unused to seeing Harold Laing look cocky.

"And what plans do you think I had?" Calliope seemed more defensive. Her eyes skirted the room, as though scanning for an escape route. The vampires from The Community, for their parts, seemed confused.

Becca looked confused. But I wasn't. The more Harold spoke, the more certain I became.

Harold continued. "I'm not sure I know the whole of it, but I started to put the pieces together after Grace showed me the pictures she found online. Of Becca, and you, and your late lamented fledgling—"

"Don't be crass. What pictures?"

"They're up on Facebook," I said.

"You're not as careful as you think you are, Cal."

"Wait, what pictures of me?" asked Becca.

"They're in your tagged photos, but you didn't approve them. I think Carlos was trying to take pictures of Miguel behind the bar, but you ended up in the frame, along with Calliope and Gavin, in the background. I wouldn't have known, if I hadn't been looking for them."

"How did you see my unapproved tagged photos?" Becca asked warily.

I sighed. "You haven't changed your passwords since college. And you weren't talking to me. And it was kind of a matter of life and death, really...though I guess that's a moot point now."

"You hacked my Facebook?" The look on her face told me this was a bigger deal than scavenging my trench coat.

"I didn't hack your Facebook, though Gavin hacked both of us, I'm sure of it now. I just logged into your account because I needed to find proof of—proof that—" I faltered, feeling guilty. "I wanted to find out if I could track where you and Gavin spent your time. Because I did want to break you up. He was right about that, at least. But then I found Calliope in the pictures, too, and that's when I realized—"

"Realized what?" Calliope asked. "I told Gavin Richardson to leave Becca alone. I told you I was keeping an eye out on her. I didn't want him to turn her any more than you did."

"Because you wanted to claim that privilege for yourself," Harold said the quiet part out loud, and everything started to fall together. "Not just Becca, but Grace too, I think. You wanted them both."

"You already knew my name. When you found me in your apartment," I reminded her. "And last night, when I played the piano, you seemed shocked that you didn't know that was something I could do. Almost as if...you'd been stalking me, and were surprised to discover a detail you'd missed."

"I mean, I prefer to call it vetting..."

"Why were you vetting me, Calliope Jones? Why Becca?"

"I knew it!" Harold crowed, triumphantly. "You are so predictable I could pick your types out of a crowd. I'm actually embarrassed it took me so long to put the pieces together. You wanted Grace for your own, and when you found out someone had gotten to her first, you were unprepared. You panicked. Called in an old debt. Someone to cover your tracks while you recalibrated your plan."

"You knew it was Gavin all along." I squinted at her. "You lied."

"Ah ha..." Iqbal leaned forward in his seat. "This is where the story gets meaty."

"You were only ever supposed to take her on temporarily. Once I'd dealt with Gavin, privately," Calliope hissed, ignoring both Iqbal and myself. "You weren't supposed to fall in love with her!"

"Last night, when you were fighting with Gavin, he said that he could never be...that other man, for you. James, you said? Your other fledgling. Harold told me they were similar."

"In appearances," Harold clarified.

"Right. Because he'd never hurt you, like Gavin did."

"I always did think that Gavin looked an awful lot like James…" Piff added with a smirk, appearing to enjoy the unexpected drama. "James was good people. I miss him. The local Community lost two good men when James and Mattie went off to Mexico."

"Tall brunette men, and petite brunette women…how many times have I watched you pursue the same features, over and over again…?" Harold shook his head and seemed almost exasperated.

"What do you think you're insinuating? That I wanted to turn both of them?" Calliope didn't seem very bothered. If anything, I thought she looked relieved.

"Two fledglings at once seems a little excessive, don't you think?" Unflappable assassin Esther Red Willow raised her eyebrows, which I thought was probably the closest thing to shocked she allowed herself to get.

"You know, some rich eccentrics get matching poodles, Calliope. Not people. Jesus." I wasn't trying to be funny—poodles are very smart dogs—but Becca, who could find humor in almost any situation, was a lost cause, her descent into giggles dragging Piff and Iqbal along with her. Even Harold and Calliope chuckled.

I suppose they needed the comic relief, but I always hated being the one everybody laughed at. Especially now, because I wanted to scream at Calliope Jones: How dare you? How dare you imagine that I would have ever wanted—

But I looked at her and Becca, laughing together and leaning into each other as comfortably as if they'd been partnered for years, and I wondered, if circumstances had been otherwise, and Becca had been turned first, if I might not have willingly allowed myself to be dragged into the night as surely as she dragged everyone else into laughter with her.

I'd always said I would die for Becca Moreno.

Becca cleared her throat, said "poodles," like it was the funniest thing she'd ever heard, and continued laughing for several more seconds. Calliope put her hand on Becca's back to calm her down.

"Gavin was the one following Becca around. Not you." I stared pointedly at Calliope, trying to understand.

"Are you so sure?"

"…No." I wasn't sure of anything.

"So what?" Calliope waved her hand dismissively. "But I wasn't planning on turning either of you, sweetheart. Not at first. I wanted to eat you." She shrugged, the tight smile around her words a small revelation of truth. She'd slipped off the facade of the polished and mature, self-assured businesswoman she'd been masquerading as like a snake sheds its skin. Something dangerous glinted underneath a surface that had been dulled by decades of careful pretension. Something deadly.

"That's hot. I would have let you." Becca's voice was still lighthearted from the giggles.

"Becca, that's not what she—"

"Darling, I wanted to fuck your brains out and bleed you dry."

"Oh." Becca paused to consider.

"I am not known to be cruel." Calliope sounded as defensive as she was defiant, and she ran her hands through her choppy, flaxen hair, practically striking a pose to go along with her confession. "I've lived a long time to practice my self control. But I have...appetites. And some nights the hunger gnaws at us worse than others. You caught my eye. The pair of you. It wasn't personal.

"So what if Harold's right and I have a predictable set of preferences? I was bored and hungry; when I saw you at the Drake I was momentarily entertained. You were adorable together. And it's been a while, since I killed anyone. I think I helped Gavin get the first one over with, when he was new. Just the first death. But I don't know any of us who last beyond our fledgling years who don't occasionally enjoy a good fuck and a kill. That's all I'm saying."

◆◇◆

Becca took me out for afternoon tea and after-tea cocktails at the Drake hotel for my birthday in September. She insisted on doing "something fancy" to celebrate, and the historic hotel bar at the corner of Michigan Avenue and Lakeshore Drive, where Carlos had just been promoted from bar back to full-time bartender, seemed the perfect spot to get dressed up, get elegantly wasted, and support our friend with lavish tips. Not that I could afford to be too lavish. Middle of the month bills were always due right around my birthday, but Dad and Nana each sent me a card and a check for $50, so I figured I could cover tips if Becca paid for cocktails. I never felt comfortable letting her pick up the whole tab when we went out, even though she swore it was okay. We both knew who made the payments on her credit card.

I wore my green wrap dress, and Mom's Cartier watch, and I'd pulled my hair up into the perfect French twist by following a new tutorial I'd just found online. Becca wore the infamously expensive Italian designer cocktail dress and a pair of five-inch heels she could barely walk in, but the added height and the cut of the dress made her look like a supermodel.

"Vivien Leigh and Olivia de Havilland!" Carlos cooed as we approached the bar. As if I looked anything like Olivia de Havilland. Becca was the one who looked like a movie star.

She wrinkled her nose. "Can we not? That's what Nonno's pervy poker buddy's been calling me since I was like, twelve."

"Ew." Carlos had the decency to look deeply uncomfortable.

Becca perused the cocktail menu but instructed Carlos to make me something called a "Boyfriend Forgetter." It had been just over two weeks since Dylan dumped me, and his plane was scheduled to depart for Portugal in the morning. I'd thought that, maybe, because it was my birthday, he'd want to see me one last time, just for fun, but he hadn't been returning my calls.

"Would that be a 'Panty Dropper' Boyfriend Forgetter, or a 'Deliverance From Heartache' Boyfriend Forgetter?" Carlos asked with a wink to Becca, as she handed over her Platinum card and ordered a martini for herself.

"That would be strictly the latter," I clarified. "Although we both know Becca wishes."

"Becca does wish!" She laughed. "But you're my best friend, Grace Kelly Cordero, and I'll take you in my life any way I can have you."

"Why do I always forget that your name is literally Grace Kelly? Ugh. It's too perfect." Carlos always said the nicest things.

"...Because I look nothing like her?"

"Psh! She was an icy blonde, you're an earthy brunette, you're cut from the same classy bolt of cloth."

I thought about telling Carlos that I was born on the anniversary of the day my namesake died, but that felt a little too morbid, given the occasion. The cocktail he set down in front of me had too much bourbon in it, but at least it was good bourbon.

"So you two are finally in between relationships at the same time, eh?"

"You sure this isn't the 'Panty Dropper?'" I lifted my glass and peered at the contents with exaggerated suspicion.

"Baby, any drink's a panty dropper if you have enough of them."

"Actually, I might technically kind of sort of be seeing someone..." Becca held up her hands and crossed her fingers. "We've had two dates so far, all PG-13, but..."

"Wait, really?" This was news...

"I didn't want to say anything when you were upset over Dild—"

"Staaahp!" I waved my hand in her face.

Carlos perked up from prepping his garnish station for when it got busy later with exaggerated urgency. "Girl, you can't just leave us hanging like that! I demand *todos los detalles*, I'm your bartender and you have to tell me. Those are the rules."

Becca waited for her martini before she said anything else. "You know Katja Hansen? Hangs out at Neo, helped organize some of the protests this summer?"

"Katja Hansen, she's the one dating the guy with the septum piercing?"

"No, Katja has the septum piercing, and no boyfriend. Do you think I should pierce my septum? I bet it'd look really cute. Nonno would kill me, though."

"Or worse, cut your allowance." I stuck my straw in Becca's drink to sample her martini and puckered my lips. *Too much olive juice...* why did she like her martinis so dirty?

"Don't even joke about that!" Becca crossed herself. "He was making all kinds of threats on Friday."

"Wait, what happened Friday?" I asked.

"...he got the credit card statement in the mail."

Carlos leaned in a bit closer. "Be careful around her, okay Bec? If you're talking about who I think you are...just have fun, and don't get your hopes up. There is only so much booze behind this bar, *claro*? One broken-hearted friend at a time."

"Speaking of broken hearts..."

"I don't have a broken heart." I took a swig of my own cocktail to erase the taste of olives, and immediately regretted my timing. Becca and Carlos both gave me very knowing, very sympathetic, side-eye.

Becca pouted. "You do, and it sucks, because he's not worth it. Carlos, I need you to help me help Grace catch a man. You like men more than I do, tell us what to do, oh wise and powerful tender of the bar."

"*Mira*, here is what you do." Carlos rubbed his palms together. "You find a lonely looking straight boy wearing cargo shorts and sandals when it's forty degrees outside..."

"I already don't like this..."

"And you say to him, 'Are you my appendix? Because I don't understand how you work, but this feeling in my stomach makes me want to take you out.' Straight boys love pickup lines. You'll be golden."

"The two of you are the worst wingmen ever," I muttered into my drink, while Becca laughed.

Bad wingman, good bartender. There were more drinks when the first round was over. The bar got busier as the evening wore on, and Carlos spent more time with other customers than he did with us, which was fine. The drunker Becca got, the more passionate she got about her recent hyperfixation. Currently, it was Ebola. She prattled on about disease reservoirs and herd immunity like the medical science nerd she'd always been, and I thought it was a shame her grades hadn't been better in college, because she could have made a hell of an epidemiologist. This month, at least.

That was the thing about Becca Moreno. She never stayed focused on anything long enough to get good at it.

"The really weird thing about Ebola is how long it can hang out in your body, and it's not just in your blood, it sticks around in saliva and semen and snot and even breast milk..." she said.

"Ew. Could you imagine? Lactation as a bio-weapon? Ready...aim...squirt!" I groped her boobs. In a friendly way.

Becca threw her head back and laughed until her eyes were squirting, attracting disapproving glances from a few other patrons at the bar. Whatever. Becca's dress cost more than twice my rent. My late mother's watch was worth more than my car. We were classy, well-dressed, very drunk millennials. Still, I tried to shush her, and eventually, we both stopped giggling.

"Still…" I said. "Of all the horrible viruses out there, I'd rather bleed out from Ebola than die of rabies."

"Well, yeah. You have a ten to sixty percent chance of surviving Ebola if you catch it. Rabies is a death sentence."

"No, I mean, if I had to choose. I'd rather bleed out than have a virus change the way my brain…change the things I…change who I am." I placed my hand over my heart for emphasis.

"Very maudlin, Celine Dion. Well, I can promise you, you're not going to get rabies."

"What if I'm bit by a bat?"

"They make prophylactic vaccines for that now."

"I don't want to change, Becca!"

Carlos came back before she could respond. "All right, ladies, I have some good news and some bad news."

"Give it to me straight, doc. What's the diagnosis?"

"Neither of us is straight, *mija*, but the two of you are cut off. I love you, but this is an upscale establishment, and you are getting Clark Street drunk. However, the good news is—" he handed Becca back her credit card. "You have a wealthy and powerful benefactor. Happy birthday, Grace Kelly. Your tab has been paid for."

"Who?" I looked around the bar to see if there was anyone I recognized, but the faces in the crowd were all strangers.

"I have been sworn to secrecy, but I can tell you this: The person who covered your tab is very rich, very famous, and very powerful." He teased a knowing smile and wiped down the bar top where our drinks had been sweating.

"Bill Gates!" Becca squealed.

"Off with you."

"Elon Musk!"

"Becca, come on…" I staggered as I grabbed her by the elbow and kissed her cheek.

"Warren Buffet!"

I swear, she'd listed off half the billionaires on the Fortune 500 list before I could get her back to her apartment and collapsed into bed beside her.

<hr>

"It was you. You paid the bar tab on my birthday." I narrowed my eyes at Calliope.

"You're welcome." She grinned at me, but the grin wasn't friendly. "Honestly, I was indecisive. I had business partners to pay attention to, but every time I glanced up at the bar, the chemistry between the two of you fascinated me. I wanted to know if you were going to kiss. I even made a bet with myself. Kiss, and I was going to find a way to get to know you both better, preferably in my bed. If you didn't, I could imagine any number of tastefully violent possibilities I would have found equally enjoyable, later that night." She shrugged.

"Jones, you are a deplorable stereotype sometimes." Piff didn't seem overly concerned about the fact that Calliope had just confessed to planning to murder Becca and me, but Harold had gotten more information than he'd bargained for; it showed.

The cockiness evaporated. "You asshole," he hissed at her.

Calliope rolled her eyes. "At least I'm forthcoming when pressed on an issue."

I thought Calliope Jones was more than forthcoming when pressed. There was something triumphant about her, just then—a gleam in her eye, a small twitch at the corner of her mouth. I don't know why, exactly, I was able to read her like an open book, how I knew she thought she was playing us. But at that moment, I understood. For every confession she made, she was hiding several larger sins. I couldn't even fathom the depths she was capable of.

The night that I was turned. She wasn't worried about the Community's reaction to finding out about me. She was worried about the Community finding out...

About Marie DuChamps's involvement.

I looked at Becca. How much did she know?

"So why didn't you do it?" Becca asked, shifting her body away from Calliope's. She seemed uncertain what to think, and so was I. It didn't seem fair that I had escaped Calliope's deranged attention, only to fall prey to the half-baked agenda of her fledgling. "Something stopped you."

"Not something," I whispered. "Someone. You stopped pursuing us when...you realized Gavin was talking with Marie DuChamps." I flinched as the words slid out of my mouth, and when I looked up, Esther glared at me with an expression that forced my silence.

"Oh, no..." Piff breathed. They seemed to deflate slightly into the tailored lines of their snappy green suit. Even Iqbal seemed taken aback.

"Well, as cathartic as this confessional has been, I think we've all got important things to do with the remainder of the night." Calliope stood up, and for the first time, I realized that she was wearing Irene's old blue wrap dress. It fit her perfectly, and I felt a pang of secondhand grief, knowing that she and Irene had been friends for so long. Calliope brushed her hands along the lines of the dress that belonged to her late best friend, and straightened the jeweled owl pinned to her perfectly squared-off shoulder, instantly transforming into the consummate businesswoman.

Iqbal, who hadn't risen from his seat at all over Harold's outburst, was looming above her before I could register the blur of movement. He wasn't quite as tall as Gavin had been, but he was imposing, suddenly, in a way that he hadn't been before, and I understood in an instant how the affable mathematics tutor with a fondness for puns and silly socks had survived for so many centuries. Harold's temper and Calliope's icy wrath had nothing on the volume of concentrated power that vibrated around his presence. "Calliope Jones, you will sit down," he commanded, and her body obeyed. I wondered if she'd even had the presence of mind to process his instructions.

Harold reached out and grabbed my hand.

"How long have you known that she was in the city, Jones?" Piff asked, pulling themselves into a stiff, formally seated position in the armchair. The indifference evaporated.

Calliope flattened against the upholstered back of the sofa. "Something happened at the end of September," she said, her mouth making words seemingly against her will. "I couldn't put my finger on it, at first. Gavin changed, it seemed, almost overnight. We hadn't always had the best relationship, I'll admit that. He moved on, into his own place two years ago. But we were close. We tried to stay cordial, at least. To make our mutual interests run smoothly. When he stopped returning my calls, I was concerned.

"He showed up unannounced one night, ranting and disturbed, full of accusations about my past—old investments, things I regret, things from years ago. Hundreds of years ago. What I did when I was still—before I was turned. He accused me of keeping secrets. As if any of that was his business. I made a joke about him having a midlife crisis—he was approaching forty, after all. I thought it was a funny bit of humor. He hit me. Threw me up against the wall, threatened me. It wasn't the first time he'd hit me. The bruises never last long on our kind, and I'm more than capable of defending myself. I figured he was just going through another one of his nasty patches, and he'd come around again...but he never did.

"I'm not certain, but I think she got to him sometime shortly after I discovered the girls. That's why I didn't act. I didn't suspect her at first—it's been decades since our last encounter. But I remembered her threats. And what happened with Heloise. I tried to lock down my security, and I hired bodyguards for my secretary."

"So the infamous Marie DuChamps has finally turned her sights on her equally infamous maker." Iqbal crossed his arms in front of his chest and looked down at Calliope.

"I don't know that for certain. God only knows what's going on in the mind of that woman. She's been a loose cannon for over a century. I never should have turned her—"

"Or Elvira Pearl, for that matter. But here we are." Iqbal raised an eyebrow.

"What did Elvira Pearl do, exactly...?" That was a name I hadn't heard before tonight, but now she'd been brought up twice.

"Remember what I told you about blood cults, Grace?" Harold said softly.

Calliope pulled herself up as straight as her vertebrae would allow her spine to stretch, regaining some of her bravado.

"I hadn't spoken to Elvira for decades before The Burning happened." Calliope sounded like she was reminding The Community of facts already well established. "She tried to kill me three times; after that, I kept my distance."

"And she took out dozens of other Community members when she decided to play her little game with the rising sun. Multiple rotational council members included. It will be decades, if not centuries, before our numbers are replenished."

"I had nothing to do with that, Iqbal. You know that. The blood cult business was her circus, her monkeys. I was just as shocked as all the rest of us when she—when it happened."

"Even so, don't you think it's alarming that this is the second time in two decades the Community has had to invest considerable resources to cover up incidents created by your brood?"

"I'll remind you of exactly how much of my money the Community has used to cover up incidents caused by other members—in this city and elsewhere." Calliope glared at Piff, and a complicated unspoken conversation passed between them. Piff blinked first, before Calliope continued. "I have always financially supported the Community's safety. I shouldered complete responsibility for the cover-up in Australia. I flew there myself, at considerable risk, mind you. I cooperated with the Community there. I saw the aftermath with my own two eyes. All those dark stains in the soil...I hadn't spoken to Elvira in decades, but I loved her once, long ago. I'll have you remember that, too."

"No one should have to see that, Cal..." the weight of the pain in Harold's whisper sent me reeling.

"You'll never hear me casting doubt on your commitment to Community service, Jones." Piff leaned forward in the armchair, their motions almost liquid as they shifted in their seat. "But we live in different times now. Grace and Becca were both declared dead, and both captured on surveillance cameras walking around after the fact. The situation in the morgue alone—all of this is going to cost more than money to cover up. There are mortal witnesses who will have to be eliminated, and that alone is always tricky. The internet is going to have a field day with conspiracy theories. There's no stopping that. This is bigger than The Burning."

"Yes, but none of that was my—"

"You have always been careful, Calliope Jones. Your fledglings, not so much." Iqbal cut her off. "And this time, there were two of them working in tandem against you. Against all of us. And the reemergence of Marie DuChamps anywhere is always...unsettling."

"She is dangerous." Esther nodded. "And she has many powerful allies within the Community, whether or not we want to admit that."

"Unfortunately, the one person who could provide clarity about her motivations this time around is, as someone so eloquently put it, 'shop vac filler'..." Iqbal grimaced, and turned to Piff. "It is too bad no one seems to know the whereabouts of Nadezhda Zimmerman these nights. DuChamps's fledgling might have insight we do not." He sat down again, the terrifying display of power he'd unleashed only moments before dissipating into nothing more than a vague sense of menace that surrounded him, more irritated than frightening.

Harold's reaction left little doubt about who Iqbal meant when he mentioned "Nadezhda."

"Leave her out of this bullshit," Harold growled. "The kid's got enough going on—"

"*Allah yakhthek*, Arailt Laing, if you know anything that could help us deal with a dangerous situation, you owe it to the Community."

"I don't owe the Community shit."

"A dog has more loyalty than you!"

"Drop it. Both of you," Piff commanded. I could not have disobeyed an order they issued in that tone of voice, even if my life had depended on it—I was certain. "I know next to knowing about DuChamps' fledgling, except that the two of them have been at their cat and mouse chase for decades. If she knew where Marie was and was in a position to take action, none of us would be here, I think.

"The bigger issue, Jones, is the safety of the Chicago Community," Piff continued. "I know I speak for the rest of the rotational council in the city when I say this. We don't want her anywhere near the city. If your fledgling is after you, you have to leave. I regret that. I want you to know. When the council discussed the matter earlier in the evening, I hoped that I'd be able to influence them to let you stay. But not if Marie DuChamps is involved."

"You can't be serious—I've spent most of my life in Chicago. I got here just a few years after the fire. Long before any of you." The sharp edge was back in Calliope's voice, but Iqbal waved her off.

"It's a unanimous council decision," he said. "Some of us have been awake for hours trying to deal with this mess."

Calliope wrinkled her nose. "What if I say I'm not going to leave? Don't forget what I am capable of. My resources and connections run deep. With a single phone call, I can—"

"You cannot," Iqbal said. "Calliope Jones died of smoke inhalation in an accidental kitchen fire in her penthouse last night. It's all over the news today. International news. To all your mortal contacts and connections, you are a dead woman."

"International news…" Calliope repeated. I wondered if she was going to start crying. I shouldn't have. Calliope Jones was incapable of showing defeat. "If you think I am so easily stripped of my ability to impact local politics—are you so certain that your homes are protected from eminent domain? You might wake up one night and find your finances frozen, your assets seized. I have resources you don't even know about. I'm owed favors by people who would never let a small detail like death get in the way of repayment. I could—"

"Your mortal secretary…Hannah Grisham, isn't it?" Esther Red Willow didn't even need to finish her threat.

"You wouldn't…"

"You know that I could. And I would, if I needed to. And more, if you needed additional persuading." Esther shrugged.

"Where do you want me to go?" Calliope's voice turned quiet. Not exactly defeated, though. Like she was already calculating. Trying to figure out what old debts to call in and from whom. I imagined she had a whole Rolodex of them, probably located inside one of the fancy suitcases Hannah Grisham had already dropped off, earlier in the evening.

"I've often heard it said that alligators are a friend to the Community," Iqbal suggested. He stood to go.

"You're trying to tell me I've been exiled to fucking Florida?"

"Consider yourself lucky. No other Communities in the States would have you, Jones." Piff shrugged. "Beggars can't be choosers."

Chapter Forty

A Settlement of Cinders

"IT'S NOT FAIR!" Calliope roared after the doors closed, after Piff, and Iqbal, and Esther took their leave. I felt the reverberation in my bones, and I wanted to feel sorry for her, still, even after her confession about...me and Becca. That's how likable Calliope Jones was. Even when she was incendiary with self-righteousness and rage, she radiated an otherworldly allure, and I was drawn in, a moth to her flame.

My mortal days had probably been numbered, one way or another, since the night she'd spotted Becca and me sitting at the bar at the Drake. It was only a matter of time.

I sighed and leaned into acceptance. The night and all its shadows stretched over the whole earth, as surely as the daytime did, and there was an entire moonlit world to explore now, and time to do it in. I turned to face Becca, who remained silent and still on the sofa, as Calliope raged and paced around the hotel suite, a brand-new cell phone plastered to her ear. Even Harold seemed to understand that she needed space, and he rose, moving away from the sofa, to stand by the windows that looked out over the balcony. He'd pulled the curtains aside, and seemed to be staring up at the moon, barely waxing gibbous in the sky above us, appearing exactly divided in half—just as the day was from the night. The symbolism felt almost Biblical.

"Becca?" I whispered her name to get her attention. She fingered another canister of blood between her hands, screwing and unscrewing the lid, her eyes unfocused, her body language almost broken, and I remembered what she'd looked like on that night after her disastrous date our junior year, when she'd almost kissed me in the showers, and I wished, more than anything, that I'd let her kiss me then.

It wasn't lost on me that I'd saved our lives with a kiss in September and hadn't even known it. "Where are we going to go, Bec?" I asked, leaning my head against her shoulder. I still wanted to kiss her, I realized—but not in front of Harold and Calliope. I wanted to grab Becca Moreno by the hands and drag her off with me into the night, but that didn't seem very wise.

"I don't...don't do that. There is no us, Grace." She shook her head and shrugged me off her shoulder. The physical rejection felt like getting shot in the chest again.

"Of course there's us. There's always us. There's always—"

"Please—just—stop. Please." She pushed me away. "All I want, all I've ever wanted, was for someone to want me. I wanted you to want me, for so long...but it was selfish of me to hope for that from you. I can see that now. Things are clearer."

"What if I told you that things...may have changed? That my feelings aren't...I don't understand everything, but I want to be with you."

"You ran away from the hotel suite tonight just because we almost kissed in the bedroom, Grace." Becca raised her eyebrows. She kept talking before I could try to explain what had really happened. "...and it's all right; you're straight, and you didn't suddenly have a queer awakening just because you became a vampire. That isn't how this works."

The problem with hallucinatory revelations is that they're entirely one-sided. How could I communicate to Becca the intensity of the love I felt for her? Last night, she'd saved both of us, just by existing. My light in the darkness. The idea of existing outside her illumination was terrifying. I felt my face fall, but I was outside my body, watching myself shake, rocking back and forth. My thoughts were a dial tone; I heard my voice ask, "What do you want?" But I had no awareness of the words leaving my lips.

"You want to be with Harold. And I don't know him. At all." She didn't answer my question.

"Why can't I love you both?" It seemed so simple in my head. An obvious solution.

She laughed at me. "Christ, you and Callie are so much alike...maybe that's part of what I like about her. Look. Maybe Calliope thought she wanted both of us at one point, but I know she wants me now. And I'll take that."

I stared at my best friend incredulously. "Becca, she wanted to kill us!" I wanted to put my hands on her shoulders and shake her. Calliope was in the washroom of the suite now, apparently trying to secure as much privacy as possible, but I still heard her voice echoing over the tiles. Something about a charter flight. I shook off the distraction and returned my attention to Becca.

"There's nothing Callie said tonight that changes how I feel about her. She needs me." Becca insisted. She'd followed my gaze to look for Calliope, and her eyes remained riveted in the direction of her unseen lover.

"She doesn't need you, Trash Panda. *She* doesn't even know you!"

"I know her blood, Grace. You wouldn't understand, the ways that she and I are connected." Becca wiped a tear from her cheek.

"Just because you drank her blood doesn't mean—" but I stopped myself. "...what did she show you, Bec?" My voice got very quiet.

Ay, Dios mio...My father is a drunkard, Blacksmith.

Hell is drinking yourself into a stupor every day and night like my alcoholic dad...

I tried to stand up too quickly, and I staggered, inelegantly, away from her.

No.

Becca was close to my family. She and my dad had been friends on Facebook for years. He'd called her his "other daughter" for longer than he'd known her in person. My whole family loved her, even if Becca's...complicated family didn't exactly love me. Her family couldn't even love Becca the way she wanted, the way she deserved to be loved.

I gasped. "Calliope's father was nothing like your dad—" but I remembered how fast Becca and I had bonded over our dead mothers.

"You have Harold, and...I have her." Becca looked at me, and for the first time since I met her, I felt invisible. Like I didn't belong in her world. Like she didn't see me, anymore. "I've loved you since the day I met you, Grace Cordero. And now I'll be your sister forever. Nothing will ever change the way I feel about you...but I don't want to be second fiddle or a third wheel, and I never want to be anyone's unicorn. Not even yours. And you know better. So if I have to choose, between that, or a love affair with an indeterminant expiration date, I'm going to chose the latter." She stood up and kissed me on the cheek. Her cool lips burned like a brand. I should have been ashes.

I want, and I want, and I want...

My shaking hands fiddled with the clasp on Mom's watch. The hotel room suite zoomed in and out of focus, red stars at my peripheral vision. I didn't know what to do.

"Becca?" Calliope walked out of the bedroom, over to the main entrance of the suite. I watched, helpless, as Becca crossed the room to go to the woman who, not even an hour ago, had confessed to wanting to murder us both.

"If she hurts you, I'll—" I swallowed hard.

"What? Get another trench coat and cut off her head, too?"

"I was thinking I'd use a sword, actually. I've got a supplier, now."

Becca shook her head. "You'll have to get through Harold and I both, I think..." a small smirk escaped her lips, and she stepped into Calliope Jones's orbit, and clasped hands with her. Calliope had changed clothes again; the old blue dress of Irene's was off, and she was almost unrecognizable in a boxy unisex sweater over a pair of well-cut jeans. A baseball cap and a pair of generic dark sunglasses obscured her face; she handed a pair of sunglasses and a cap to Becca, along with a medical face mask to cover her moth and nose, before quickly securing the small jeweled owl pin to Becca's blouse, and brushing Becca's dark hair away from her face. The dark enamel and pearls glinted softly, and Becca wordlessly touched the pin with an inscrutable smile. It might have been something akin to awe.

As they walked out the door together, lugging the black duffel bag and banker's box of documents and globetrotter luggage between them, Calliope spared a single glance over her shoulder.

Go ahead. Just try to take her from me. I could read Calliope Jones like a book. There was no animosity in that glance. Only calm, self-assured confidence. Calliope didn't have to resort to violence to kill me. Becca didn't even say goodbye.

I sank to the floor, wrapped my arms around my knees, and cried.

<hr>

"I'm sorry." The glass door to the balcony quietly opened, and Harold softly re-entered the room. I hadn't even realized he'd stepped out. "I didn't think they'd leave so soon…" I smelled the blood on his breath, and looked up at him through tear-stained eyes, unable to form words, still choking back sobs. *It wasn't fair…*

Silently, he wrapped his arms around my shoulders, and I let him. The flask in his hand was the one I'd bought for him back in January. The small discolored stain from the fire glinted, almost purple, like a bruise.

A scar to mark the damage.

I fixated on that purple discoloration on the surface of the metal until my sobs receded, and I was able to draw air into my lungs again. Maybe all the changes wrought on my body since becoming a vampire were their own kind of scar tissue. I remembered what I'd been told about what I had survived, how rare it was. To endure that. I straightened my shoulders and looked up at Harold. We'd both survived. That meant something, at least.

"Are you mad at me?" he whispered.

I shook my head violently. No. I felt many things, but I wasn't angry at Harold. "Should I be?"

He stroked my hair and knelt beside me on the floor, holding me close to his chest. "I shouldn't have shouted. I should not have raised my voice, let Iqbal get under my skin. I did not stop tae think of how I must have appeared tae your Becca."

"That's not why she left."

"She's only ever seen me angry—"

"She left because she doesn't think my feelings for her are real. That's why she left."

"I know. I heard that part, too."

"I love you. I love her. I can't expect anyone to understand what I barely comprehend myself. I don't know what's *wrong* with me. I don't know why you're still here. I could never expect Becca to it up with…any of this. But it hurts to love someone so much, and I don't know what I'm going to do without her!"

"I don't think there's anything wrong with loving more than one person," he soothed.

I wiped at my tears only half-heartedly as another, different thought overtook me. "What if Calliope hurts her? Gavin said Calliope always hit him first, and she hit me once, right in front of you!" I wanted to race to my feet and run out the door after them until I found Becca and pulled her bodily away from that scheming, manipulative, violent—

Harold held me back. "Calliope won't hurt Becca." His hand caressed my cheek, and his sea-colored eyes were very serious.

"You can't know that."

"I know Calliope. She's afraid of you."

"I'm no one to be afraid of." I scoffed.

I'm twenty-four years old. I'm from Ohio. I was a communications major.

"You decapitated her fledgling. She was seventy years a vampire before she had the chance tae kill the ones who turned us. Avie has been after Marie DuChamps for almost as long. You did it in...two months? Even Esther Red Willow respects that. Calliope is afraid of you, and she still wants you. Becca is her collateral. She won't hurt her. Besides, Calliope knows you're attracted tae her."

"I am not!" I protested, but Harold stopped me with another one of his looks, and I sighed.

"You didn't see your face when she said she wanted you in her bed."

No. I shook my head. I might have complicated feelings for Calliope Jones, but they were not—I did not want—

"It doesn't have tae mean anything, you know. Except that she wants you, she knows you're attracted tae her. She's also afraid of you. And by now, she knows how much you love Becca. And how much Becca loves you."

"She doesn't love me. Not the way I thought she did."

"Your hearts beat in unison, Grace. I don't know what exactly the two of you were doing in the bedroom earlier tonight, but we could hear your hearts beating from the other side of a closed door. I thought Cal was going tae lose it."

"You overhear too much. Nothing happened."

"Becca loves you. She'll come around. Let her be a spoiled pet for a while. Calliope is good to her fledglings, while they're young. And she's got a thing for Becca's type. In the meantime...you did say that you loved me?" His voice was so hopeful, I couldn't help but crack a small smile

"I do." I sniffled and laughed at myself because I felt ridiculous. But I also knew, absolutely, that I loved him. Wherever we ended up, I wanted us to be together. "It's different from the feelings I have for Becca, but it's just as real, I promise. I love you. I don't know how any of this works, but..." I sighed and felt defeated. I wanted to fuck Harold, marry Becca, and kill Calliope. Only one of those options seemed possible at the moment.

"Do you want tae go for a walk?" Harold suggested. "There's a rooftop deck that no one will be out using in these temperatures, and no security cameras, either, if what Calliope says is true..."

⚬

Our footsteps fell in tandem as we crunched over the snow and ice that coated the rooftop. It wasn't terribly late, and the city was far from asleep. Many stories below us, cars and busses navigated the winter streets; not far off in the distance, the L train started making its way toward the city center. You couldn't see the lake from our vantage point; the view was blocked by other, taller buildings, and we were facing the wrong direction anyway, but a cold wind rose up off the water, and I would have been freezing, if I were still alive.

Funny. I felt more alive than I ever had before.

"Why does Iqbal call you Arailt?" I asked, breaking the silence. The question had been bothering me for several hours.

"That's my name." He laughed. I peered up at him, confused.

"Your name is Harold."

"If you're English."

I pointed my finger at his chest, nowhere near angry, but irritated. "You told me your name was Harold."

He laughed as my fingertip made contact, grabbed my hand, and kissed it, nipping at the fleshy pad near my thumb. He barely broke the skin, and the injury healed over quickly, but the brief pain made me weak in the knees, and I staggered closer to him. He caught me in his strong arms and planted a kiss on my forehead. "No, *Calliope* introduced me as Harold. And after two hundred years, I'm tired of arguing with her and everyone else."

"So your name is Arailt."

"I told you. I'm Scottish. Well, half Scottish, at least. It's a Scottish name."

"And Iqbal…"

"I suppose if your name is Iqbal Mohammed Abi-Bakr and you live in America, you're going to take the time to learn how to pronounce people's names correctly." He paused to consider something, then shrugged. "It's his only redeeming quality."

"Arailt."

"Aye." He exaggerated an accent he worked hard pretend he didn't have, and I giggled.

"…is that what you'd like me to call you?"

He was quiet for a while. I thought he was probably remembering someone, and I let him mull over the memories in the easy silence that came so comfortably between us. I loved that about him. "That might be nice." He finally smiled. "It's been a long time since someone I loved called me that."

"Irene?"

"No, long before her." He shook his head, and I understood. Calliope had mentioned many things, back at the penthouse. Some things, I knew, were lies. But not everything.

"You'll have to tell me about him sometime." I leaned in close to him, even as I felt Arailt tense beside me for a moment, and then relax.

His smile was small, but satisfied. Content. "Maybe. One night…"

Arailt brushed the snow off of a low wooden bench, and we sat down, fingers entwined, foreheads pressed together, lips almost but not quite touching. "This…this is going to be nice." He smiled in the soft, boyish way I liked so much, the way he'd smiled at me when he was so excited to show off the lamps he'd repaired. I thought perhaps that's when I'd started to fall in love with him, weeks before the bloodlust—I just hadn't recognized it at the time.

"Nice?" I asked.

"Being with you," he said, "being with someone I don't have to hide part of myself from. Being loved by someone who can love all of me."

It was my turn to lift his hands to my lips, drawing his fingers in slowly, savoring the taste of his skin. I wanted to bite down, but I held back, flicking my tongue against the tips of his fingers. "Don't we all deserve that?" I exhaled softly against him, lost in thought, remembering Becca's face in the diner, the first night she told me about Gavin—the night she told me about Katja and her boyfriend. Curse Carlos for being right about her, all along. Becca deserved better than that. Arailt deserved better than love that only accepted part of him, too.

I wanted to be the one to give both of them the love they deserved.

"I wish I had your faith..." Arailt whispered.

I grinned. "Well, I don't know about *all* priests, but I'm sure we can find one who'd be willing to talk to you at night..."

"I'm not converting to the idolatry of the Roman papists." Arailt laughed, and so did I. It was hard to be offended by his disdain when he was so ridiculous about it.

"It was worth a shot..."

His lips and tongue met mine, then fangs drawing delicious sips of blood from uncountable tiny cuts and gashes. I gasped when Arailt's cool hands reached under my turtleneck to feel me up, and bit down hard on his lip when he pinched my nipples. I didn't know if I wanted to run my hands through his hair or stroke his erection, so I settled for one hand on each erogenous zone and made a half-assed, distracted use of either, but it was fun to try.

After a few minutes of making out like sloppy teenagers, Arailt pulled away. "I have a question, kettlen."

"You're going to have to tell me what the fuck a kettlen is, first. I've been meaning to ask, but..."

"You know what a kettlen is!" The look of shock on his face would have been funny, if I weren't so confused.

"I promise you, I absolutely do not."

"It's a—it's a *kettlen*, lass." He held out his hands to indicate something small, but that didn't exactly narrow down the possibilities.

I shook my head and shrugged. "Still no idea."

"A kettlen! Peerie fuzzy baby with razor claws! Meow meow!"

"A kitten?"

"Hat's what I said! Meow meow!" And he pawed at my hair with his fingertips til it tangled and we giggled.

"I was afraid you were saying I was a different kind of misbehaved sheep..." I kissed his cheek. "What was your question?"

"You and Becca."

"That's a statement."

"I mean, you're probably going tae end up together, at some point."

"Hmm..." I nuzzled my lips along his jawline and traced my fingers along the arteries of his neck; he shivered delightfully, and I laughed. "Probably. Someday...maybe..." I pulled away and gave him my most reproachful look. "I concede that your gaydar was, in fact, correct."

"Ha!"

"Still not a question." I continued my attempts to distract him with my hands and lips; he wasn't easily distracted.

He seemed very serious, in fact, mulling over his next words carefully before he spoke, kicking his feet in the pile of snow he'd knocked off the bench. "What if...what if I happened to find someone I wanted tae have a connection with...and they were a man?"

I stopped and looked at him carefully. "Is there anyone I should know about?"

"Not really. But I've enjoyed men before, and...it's not something I want tae just drop on you."

"...Irene *really* didn't like that part of you, did she?"

"It wasn't something that we talked about in those days. Until it was, mostly toward the end and...no, she didn't like that."

"She jealous, or just homophobic?"

He lifted his shoulders. An almost-uncomfortable silence settled between us. "She really was a wonderful person, you know."

"You don't need to defend her to me. I'm not the judgmental one."

"Mmmhmm...and the other night—"

"Overreaction on my part. But also, you should have told me before we had sex. Before we shared blood. I mean, just communicate with me, Arailt—" our fingers entwined, and I squeezed his, tightly.

"So I'm communicating now," he said. "I'm not the same man I was decades ago. I wouldn't want tae go back to the life I had before she died, with everything I know now. I want tae be with you. I never thought that I would feel this way again, about anyone...but I don't want tae give up a part of myself tae have you. And I wouldn't expect you tae change who you are, or who you loved, either."

"I mean...I'd want us to talk about it. If we were going to be seeing other people. I don't think their sex or gender has anything to do with it. But whoever you were with, or I was with...I'd want them to respect us. And I'd want to respect them. I think that's only fair, right?"

Arailt exhaled and smiled as though he'd been holding his breath for a very long time. He looked...almost giddy. I pecked his cheek.

"Let me guess...Irene wasn't exactly down for polyamory either?"

"It was—"

"If you say it was a long time ago, one more time, Arailt Laing, I am going to bite you."

"Yes, but I was rather hoping you'd do that anyway, kettlen. It was a lo—hey! Ow!"

...it's not like I didn't warn him.

The End.

Afterword

Relief is a Feeling

On December 27th, 2020, my husband and I were driving back from North Carolina, after visiting his father for what we knew would be the last Christmas. Pancreatic cancer is unyielding and brutal and awful. At the same time, we were hoping against hope to find a way to visit my own father in Arizona, whose decades-long fight with leukemia had taken a sudden turn for the terminal. To say that the car ride that night was bleak would be an understatement, and I was in a dark, overwhelming place. I've fought the demons of self-harm and suicidal ideation for longer than I can remember, and I found myself, on that night, wondering if there was a point to staying alive in a world filled with so much inescapable pain.

Life has an endless array of ways to humble us, to peel away the layers of our hubris and ego and show us who we really are. One moment I was listening to an audiobook with my husband, who was driving. The next moment he was slumped over the steering column, unconscious, as the car barreled down the interstate at 70 miles an hour. It was a hell of a way to find out that he needed a pacemaker at thirty-nine years old—but we wouldn't discover that until later, in the trauma bay. I'm telling you this now because I want you to know: he lived. We both lived.

You can't pull the emergency brake at those speeds when a car is on cruise control, and my options were slim. I had seconds to process what was happening, to formulate a plan. Time slowed like bullets in the "Matrix" movies. I grabbed the steering wheel from the passenger seat, got the hazzard lights on, navigated the car across three lanes of traffic without flipping over or hitting any other vehicles and finally, along the shoulder of the highway, found what I knew to be our only chance of survival: a small copse of young trees that would, hopefully, slow down the car enough for us to survive the crash.

…We plowed through the trees, skidded down an embankment, and careened to a stop into a cold swampy area off the side of the road, invisible to passing traffic; and I knew that my efforts were not yet over, if I wanted to live. My husband was moaning softly in the dark, and there was a lot of blood. I still did not know what had happened to him, but I knew that he needed help—fast. I could not wait and hope that our car would be discovered.

I was able to climb out of the busted passenger-side window, wade back across the swamp on that cold North Florida night, and crawl my way up the embankment we had skidded down. I counted my steps as I limped along the side of the road, trying to find help. I made it half a mile before a car stopped.

Later, at the hospital, the doctors and nurses discovered that my back was broken in three places. My sternum was broken. My dominant left hand was shattered. It was the height of the Covid surge and there weren't enough beds in the hospital; I waited on a gurney in the hallway of the ER for 24 hours before I got a room, and was assigned a nursing team, and finally recieved adequate pain management. In those hours, I learned that pain has depths to it I had not yet begun to plumb.

And I learned this, too, about pain, in the weeks that followed, during the hellish fog of my recovery and grief, as my husband underwent emergency heart surgery and we both lost our fathers within days of each other: the ebb and flow of pain is part of being alive. In the claustrophobic darkness, when pain and despair seemed to swell to contain the whole of my universe, I was reminded of a truth that's saved me, more than once. When we are in pain, when we want relief above all else:

Relief is a *feeling*. We have to be alive to feel it.

———◆O◆———

THIS CRIMSON DEBT is a novel that was viscerally informed by pain, and grief, and loss. Grace's struggle with suicidality, and Irene's tragic demise, come from a place of darkness I have long been familiar with. My own suicidal ideation in the car on that December night was swept away by an emergency situation that reminded me, in an instant, that I *absolutely wanted to live*. But so many people, fighting those same demons, don't get that moment of clarity.

If you, or someone you love, is stumbling though dark places, you are not alone. I was not alone on the side of the road after the crash, even though I thought I was: a passing driver, coming from the opposite direction of traffic, watched our car disappear into the undergrowth. He exited the interstate at the next offramp, got back on the road, and drove along the shoulder, looking until he found us. I never got that man's name. I don't know who he was. But he saved our lives. I was not alone in the shadows, although it felt that way, at the time.

You are not alone. There are others, out there in the night, looking for you.

———◆O◆———

If you're in the United States, you can access the National Suicide Hotline by simply dialing 988. I've called in to similar counseling hotlines before when I needed them. They can help you navigate past the acute stage of a crisis.

———◆O◆———

We are Community, those of us who fight this battle, and I am looking for you in the night. Your story isn't over. Neither is Grace and Becca's, or Calliope and Arailt's.

A BLOOM OF RUST, book 2 in The Community of Blood series, will arrive late 2023 or early 2024.

ACKNOWLEDGMENTS

A first novel is never completed without an extraordinary amount of support, and this book is no exception. I am beyond indebted to the following individuals:

Debra Warshaw, Kelly Kramer, Jeffrey Boydstun, Ashbet, Ally Mason, Amanda de Romanus, Kat Laine, Katie Shay, and Kim Gray for their unyielding love, jokes, late-night memes, and enduring faith in this project and these characters.

Natalie Sheppard-Baudean for saving the day with her insightful last-minute edits.

Peter Friesen, Jason Vincent, and Brad Hansen for answering my questions about weird details I knew nothing about.

Jessica Montecinos for fixing my attrocious Spanish misspellings (all remaining errors are mine and mine only).

Father Sebastiaan, Rachel Clinesmith, Karen Holton, and the rest of the Endless Night Krewe for believing in me and lifting me up.

Dorian Hatchett, Thomas Webb, and Sedna Hemlock for keeping a roof over my head when it all started to fall apart.

Scott Glab and the entire team at Sidney's Wine Cellar in the French Quarter for being my found family when I needed one.

And my husband, Adam Terrell—especially you.

ABOUT THE AUTHOR

Rose Sinister has been a vampire tour guide in New Orleans French Quarter, a podcaster, a milliner's assistant, a liquor store clerk, a jewelry designer, a goth and a punk and a nerd.

Many of those qualifiers still apply. And some don't. After a catastrophic car accident forced Rose to reevaluate her life and remaining options, she returned to her childhood ambitions of being a serious writer, and refuses to look back.

She divides her time between New Orleans and Florida's Emerald Coast, where she resides with her husband and three spoiled rotten fur babies.

THIS CRIMSON DEBT is Rose's first novel, but there will be many others that follow.